THE SHADOWED SUN

BOOK TWO OF DREAMBLOOD

N. K. JEMISIN

ORBIT

First published in Great Britain in 2012 by Orbit

Copyright © 2012 by N. K. Jemisin

Excerpt from *The Drowning City* by Amanda Downum
Copyright © 2009 by Amanda Downum

The moral right of the author has been asserted.

A CIP catalogue record for this book
is available from the British Library.

ISBN 978-0-356-50077-5

Printed and bound by CPI Group (UK) Ltd, Croydon, CR0 4YY

Papers used by Orbit are from well-managed forests
and other responsible sources.

MIX
Paper from
responsible sources
FSC® C104740

Orbit
An imprint of
Little, Brown Book Group
100 Victoria Embankment
London EC4Y 0DY

An Hachette UK Company
www.hachette.co.uk

www.orbitbooks.net

In the desert
I saw a creature, naked, bestial,
who, squatting upon the ground,
Held his heart in his hands,
And ate of it.
I said, "Is it good, friend?"
"It is bitter—bitter," he answered;
"But I like it
Because it is bitter,
And because it is my heart."

—Stephen Crane,
The Black Riders and Other Lines

1

The Sharer's Test

There were two hundred and fifty-six places where a man could hide within his own flesh. The soldier dying beneath Hanani's hands had fled to someplace deep. She had searched his heart and brain and gut, though the soul visited those organs less often than layfolk thought. She had examined his mouth and eyes, the latter with especial care. At last, behind a lobe of his liver, she found his soul's trail and followed it into a dream of shadowed ruins.

Piles of rubble loomed out of the twilit mists—crumbling structures so titanic that each single brick would dwarf a man, so foreign in design that she could not fathom their purpose. A palace? A temple? Camouflage, regardless. Beneath her feet the dust gleamed, something more than mica: each step displaced a million stars. She took care to put them all back in her wake.

To find the soldier, Hanani would have to first deal with the setting. It was simple enough to will the ruins into order, which she did by crouching to touch the ground. Threads of dreamichor, yellow-bright and gleaming, laced from her fingertips and etched the ground for a moment before vanishing into it. A breath later, the dust skittered up to seal cracked stone; the harbinger of change.

Then the earth split and the ground shook as great bricks righted themselves and flew through the air, clattering together to form columns and walls. All around her, had she chosen to watch, the outlines of a monstrous city took shape against the gradient sky. But when the city was whole, she rose and moved on without looking. There was far more important work to be done.

["This takes longer than it should."

"The injury is healing."

"That does no good if he dies."

"He won't. She has him. Watch."]

After first passing a stone archway, Hanani paused and turned back to examine it. The arch was man-height, the only thing of normal proportions in the dreamscape. Beyond the arch lay the same shadows that shrouded all—no. The shadows were thicker here.

Prowling carefully closer, Hanani attempted to step through the archway.

The shadows pressed back.

She imagined illumination.

The shadows grew thicker.

After a moment's consideration, she summoned pain and fear and rage instead, and wrapped these around herself. The shadows' resistance melted; the soldier's soul recognized kindred. Passing through the arch, Hanani found herself in an atrium garden, the kind that should have helped to cool the heart of any home—but this one was dead. She looked around, ducking splintered palms and wilted moontear vines, frowning at a suppurating mess of a flowerbed. Then she spied something beyond it: there at the garden's heart, curled in a nest of his own sorrow, lay the soldier.

Pausing here, Hanani shifted a fraction of her attention back to the waking realm.

["Dayu? I'll need more dreambile soon."

"Yes, Hanani— Um, I mean, Sharer-Apprentice."]

That done, Hanani returned to the dream of the hidden garden. The soldier lay with knees drawn up and arms wrapped about himself as if for comfort. In the curve of his body, a gaping wound spilled his intestines into a hole at the nest's heart. She could see nothing beyond the hole, only that perverse umbilical connecting him to it.

Death, said the air around him.

"Not here, petitioner," she replied. "These are the shadowlands. There are better places to die."

He did not move, hungering again for death. Again she demurred. *Memory*, she offered, to entice him.

Anguish flared up in cold, purple-white wisps, wreathing the area around the nest as a new form coalesced. Another man: older, bearded in the way of those who bore northern blood, also garbed as a soldier but clearly of some higher rank than Hanani's soldier. A relative? Mentor? Lover? Beloved, whoever he was.

"Gone," Hanani's soldier whispered. "Gone without me."

"May he dwell in Her peace forever," she said. Extending her hands to either side, she trailed her fingers through the ring of mist. Where she touched, delicate deep red threads blended and pulsed into the white.

["She uses *more* dreamblood? She'll run out at that rate."

"Then we'll give her more. The desert scum have nearly cut him in two, man, what do you expect?"]

Hanani's soldier moaned and curled into a tighter ball as red threads stretched forth from the walls, soaking into his skin. Abruptly the mists flickered, the bearded soldier's image growing insubstantial as shadows. New scenes formed instead, appearing and overlapping and fading with each breath. A lonely perch atop a wall. Sword practice. A barracks bed. A river barge.

Hanani coaxed the memories to continue, inserting gentle suggestions to guide them in a new direction. *Loved ones. Life.* The scenes changed to incorporate the bearded soldier and others—doubtless the petitioner's comrades or caste-kin. They laughed and talked and worked at daily tasks. As the images flowed, Hanani reached carefully around the man and into the hole that was devouring him. The first contact sent pain slamming up her arm like a blow—but cold, so terribly cold! She gasped and fought the urge to cry out as her fingers stiffened and froze and cracked apart—

No. She formed her soulname's syllables within her mind and clarity washed through her, a reminder that this was a dream and she was its master. *This pain is not my own.* When she drew her hand back, it was whole.

But the man was not; the pain was devouring him. She focused on the images again, noting one of a tavern. The petitioner was not there, although his dead beloved and other comrades were, laughing and singing a lusty song. There was danger in this, she realized abruptly. The petitioner had been injured in a raid, his beloved killed. She had no idea whether the rest of his companions had been cut down as well. If so, then what she meant to attempt might only increase his death-hunger.

There was no choice but to try.

["—As though you *want* her to fail, Yehamwy."

"Of course not. The Council simply wants to be certain of her competence."

"And if *the Council* knew the first thing about healing, that would be—"

"What is that noise?"

"I'm not certain. It came from the tithing alcoves. Dayu? Everything all right, boy?"]

Distractions could be dangerous, even deadly, in narcomancy. Focusing her mind on the task at hand, Hanani reshaped the tavern scene around her soldier. His comrades stopped singing and turned to him, offering greetings and reminiscences and sloshing cups. The beer shone a warm deep red in the dreamlight. Behind them, Hanani quietly faded the bearded soldier away.

"Look here," she said to the petitioner. "Your fellows are waiting. Will you not join them?"

The man groaned, uncurling from his nest and straining up toward his comrades. A great wind soughed through the dreamscape, blowing away the city and the shadows. Hanani exerted her will in concert with the man's and the garden swirled away, its shadows suddenly replaced by bright lanterns and tavern walls. The nest lingered, though, for the man was bound fast to his pain. So instead Hanani touched the edge of the nest and caused it to compress, shrinking rapidly into a tiny dark marble small enough to sit in his palm. He gazed mournfully at Hanani and clutched the marble tightly to his breast, but did not protest when Hanani caused the rope of intestine to fall free, severing his linkage. She pressed the dangling end against his belly and it vanished, as did the wound itself. Lastly she summoned clothing, which blurred for a moment before his mind shaped it into the gray-agate collar and loinskirt of a Gujaareen city guard.

The soldier nodded to her once, then turned to join his companions. They surrounded him, embraced him, and all at once he began to weep. But he was safe from danger now—and *she* had made him so, made him whole again, body and soul alike. *I'm a Sharer now!*

But no, that was presumption. Whether she'd passed the trial to become a full member of the Sharer path was a matter for her pathbrothers to decide, and the Council to confirm, no matter how well she'd done. And it was utter folly to let her emotions slip control while she remained in dreaming; she would not ruin herself by making a child's mistake. So with a deep sigh to focus her thoughts, Hanani released the soldier's dream and followed the faint red tendril that would lead her soul back to its own housing of flesh—

—But something jolted her awareness.

She paused, frowning. The dreamworld of Ina-Karekh lay behind her, inasmuch as such things had any direction at all. Hona-Karekh, the waking realm, was ahead. She opened the eyes of her dreamform to find that she stood in a gray-shadowed version of the waking realm, where the tension and busy movement that had filled the Hall of Blessings a few moments before were suddenly still. She stood on the dais at the feet of the great, looming nightstone statue of Hananja, but her petitioner was gone. Mni-inh and Teacher Yehamwy, who had come to oversee her trial, were gone. The Hall was silent and empty, but for her.

The realm between waking and dreams. Hanani frowned. She had not intended to stop here. Concentrating, she sought her soul's umblikeh again to complete the journey back to waking—and then stopped, hearing something. There. Over near the tithing alcoves, where Sharer-Apprentices and acolytes drew dreams from the minds of sleeping faithful. A slow, deep sound, like nothing she'd ever heard before. Grinding stone?

Or the breathing of some huge, heavy beast.

["Hanani."]

Nothing in the between realm was real. The space between dreams was emptiness, where the soul might drift with nothing to latch onto—no imagery, no sensation, no conceptualization. An easy place in which to go mad. With her soulname and training, Hanani was safer, for she had long ago learned to build a protective construct around herself—the shadow-Hall in this case—whenever she traveled here. Still, she avoided the space between if she could help it, for only Gatherers could navigate it with ease. It was troubling to say the least that she had manifested here unwittingly.

Squinting toward the alcoves, she wondered: had she forgotten some step in healing the soldier, done something wrong in the transit from Ina-Karekh? A man's life was involved; it was her duty to be thorough.

["Hanani. The healing is complete. Come forth."]

Something moved in the stillness near an alcove's opening. Emerged from it, behind one of the Hall's flower-draped columns, which occluded a clear view. She perceived intent and power, a slow gathering of malice that first unnerved, then actively frightened her—

["Hanani."]

The shadow-Hall shivered all over, then turned bright and busy with people and breezes and murmurs. Hanani caught her breath, blinking as her soul settled back into her own flesh. The waking realm. Her mentor stood beside her, a troubled look on his face.

"Mni-inh-brother. There was something…" She shook her head, confused. "I wasn't done."

"You've done enough, Apprentice," said a cold voice. Yehamwy, a heavyset, balding Teacher in his early elder years, stood glowering beside the healing area. Before her, on one of the wooden couches set up for Sharer audiences, Hanani's soldier lay in the deep sleep of the recently healed. Automatically Hanani pushed aside the bandages to check his belly. The flesh was whole and scarless, though still smeared with the blood and gore that had been spilled prior to healing.

"My petitioner is fine," she said, looking up at Yehamwy in confusion.

"Not him, Hanani." Mni-inh crouched beside the couch and laid two fingers on the soldier's eyelids to check Hanani's work. He closed his eyes for a moment; they flickered rapidly beneath their lids. Then he exhaled and returned. "Fine indeed. I'll have someone summon his caste-kin to carry him home."

Less disoriented now, Hanani looked around the Hall of Blessings and frowned. When she'd begun work on the soldier, the Hall had been full, humming with the voices of those come to offer their monthly tithes, or petition for the Hetawa's aid, or just sit on pallets amid the moontear blossoms and pray. The sun still slanted through the long prism windows, but now the Hall was empty of all save those on the dais with Hanani, and a cluster of Sharers and Sentinels near one of the tithing alcoves.

The same place she'd seen something, in the realm between. That was strange. And it was far too early for the Hall's public hours to have ended.

"Hanani had nothing to do with this," Mni-inh said. Hanani looked up in surprise at the sharp tone of her mentor's voice. He was glaring at Teacher Yehamwy.

"The boy was fetching tithes for her," Yehamwy said. "Clearly she is involved."

"How? She was too deep in dreaming even to notice."

"The boy was only thirteen. She had him ferrying humors like a full apprentice."

"And? You know as well as I that we allow the acolytes to ferry humors whenever they show an aptitude!"

The councilor shook his head. "And sometimes they aren't ready. This incident is the direct result of your apprentice's excessive use of humors—"

Mni-inh stiffened. "I do not recall *you* passing the Sharer-trial at any point, Yehamwy."

"And the boy's desire to please her? One need not be a Sharer to understand that. He followed her about like a tame hound, willing to do anything to serve his infatuation. Willing even to attempt a narcomantic procedure beyond his skill."

Hanani's knees had gone stiff during the healing, despite the cushion beneath them. She struggled clumsily to her feet. "Please—" Both men fell silent, looking at her; Mni-inh's expression was tinged with sudden pity. That frightened her, because there was only one boy they could be talking about. "Please, Mni-inh-brother, tell me what has happened to Dayu."

Mni-inh sighed and ran a hand over his hair. "There's been an incident in the tithing alcoves, Hanani. I don't know— There isn't—"

With an impatient gesture, Yehamwy cut him off. "She should know the harm she's caused. If you truly believe she's worthy of becoming a Sharer, don't coddle her." And his expression as he turned to her was both bitter and satisfied. "A tithebearer is dead, Sharer-Apprentice. So is the acolyte Dayuhotem, who assisted you."

Hanani caught her breath and looked at Mni-inh, who nodded in sober confirmation. "But…" She groped for words. Her ears rang, as if the words had been too loud, though no one would shout in Hananja's own hall, at the feet of Her statue. Hananja treasured peace. "H-how? It was a simple procedure. Dayu had done it before, many times; he knew what he was doing even if he was just a child…" A Moon-wild, joyful jester of a child, as exasperating as he was charming. She could not imagine him dead. As well imagine the Sun failing to shine.

"We don't know how it happened," Mni-inh said. He threw a quelling look at the councilor, who had started to speak. "We *don't*. We heard him cry out, and when we went into the alcove we found him and the tithebearer both. Something must have gone wrong during the donation."

"But Dayu—" Her throat closed after the name. Dead. Her vision blurred; she pressed her hand to her mouth as if that would push the horror from her mind. *Dead.*

"The bodies will be examined," Mni-inh said heavily. "There are narcomancies that can be performed even after the umblikeh is severed, which may provide some answers. Until then—"

"Until then," Yehamwy said, "on my authority as a member of the Council of Paths, Sharer-Apprentice Hanani is prohibited from further practice of any healing art or narcomancy, pending the results of the examination." He turned to one of the black-clad Sentinels who stood guard at the door leading into the inner Hetawa; the

Sentinel turned to regard them. "Please note this for your brethren, Sentinel Mekhi." The Sentinel, his face duty-blank, nodded once in response.

Dayu was dead. Hanani stared at Yehamwy, unable to think. Dayu was dead, and the world had bent into a new, unrecognizable shape. Hanani should have bowed over her hands to show her humility and acceptance of the Councilor's decree, and she knew that her failure to do so reflected badly on Mni-inh. But she kept staring at him, frozen, even as his scowl deepened.

"It is the Sharers' duty to discipline our own," Mni-inh said. He spoke very softly, but Hanani could hear the suppressed fury in her mentor's voice.

"Then do your duty," Yehamwy snapped. Throwing a last cold look at Hanani, he turned and walked away.

Hanani looked up at her mentor, who stood glaring after the councilor as if contemplating something most unpeaceful. Then his anger faded as he looked down at her. She read compassion in his eyes, but resignation as well.

"I'm sorry," he said. "Your work with the petitioner was flawless. I can't imagine our pathbrothers will discard your trial because of this, but..." His expression grew grim. He knew the Hetawa's politics better than Hanani.

This was not the future I imagined, some part of her reflected, while the rest of her soul fluttered in circles from grief to disbelief and back again. *This is not happening*. She forced herself to bow over one hand; the hand shook badly. "Yes, Brother."

He touched her hand again. "The boy was dear to you. Let me call a Gatherer."

The promise of a Gatherer's comfort was tempting, but then bitterness eclipsed that desire. She had lost her dearest friend in the Hetawa, and her hopes for the future seemed likely to follow him. She did not want comfort. *I want everything back the way it was.*

"No," she said. "Thank you, Brother, but...I would rather be alone now. M—" She forced out the words. "May I see Dayu?"

Mni-inh hesitated, just for an instant, before responding. That was when Hanani realized: something was wrong with Dayuhotem's body.

"It's a shell, Hanani." He said it gently, using his most persuasive tone. "He's gone from it. Don't torment yourself."

If Mni-inh did not want her to see the body, then Dayu had not died at peace. A soul that died in pain or fear or anger was drawn into the shadowlands, the dark recesses of Ina-Karekh, there to suffer for the rest of its existence amid endless nightmares. It was the fate dreaded by all who honored the Goddess Hananja.

Trembling, Hanani groped her way to a nearby bench and sat down, hard. She needed to curl up in the Water Garden to weep for a day and a night.

Mni-inh read her face. "Hanani," he began, but then faltered to bleak silence himself. Sharers were trained to offer comfort after a tragedy, but they were not Gatherers; their comfort was only words, ineffective as those were. Hanani had never felt the inadequacy of that training so powerfully as now.

And what if Teacher Yehamwy was right? whispered a little voice in the back of Hanani's mind. What if Dayu's death and damnation were somehow Hanani's fault?

The statue of Hananja, forty feet high and gleaming in white-flecked nightstone, loomed overhead. Would it help to pray? she wondered, distantly. Dayu and the dead tithebearer would need prayers where they had gone. But no words came to her mind, and after a long empty moment she stood up.

"I shall be in my cell," she said to Mni-inh.

And though she saw Mni-inh raise a hand as she turned away, his mouth opening as if to forestall her, in the end he said nothing. Hanani went away alone.

11

2

⊙

The Hunter's Test

Smoke rode far on arid breezes. The faint scent came to Wanahomen through his veil as he gazed across the green valley at a distant city. *His* city. The smoke-plume rose from within its walls.

"It was Wujjeg," said Ezack, at his side. He spoke in Chakti, the Banbarra tongue.

"I know," Wanahomen replied in the same language. Beneath him, his camel shifted restlessly and uttered a grumbling complaint. Wanahomen stroked her neck absently, his eyes never leaving the plume of smoke.

"I don't think Wujjeg meant to kill, not at first. But when the first Gujaareen went down, the second went mad and came at him wide open."

"He shouldn't have gutted the first one."

"What will you do?"

Wanahomen did not reply, turning his camel about and starting down the trail from the lookout point back to camp, traveling along a ledge path more safely traversed by four feet than two. Most of the horses and camels had been loosed to forage the steep trails below the shelf, though fodder had been piled nearby for the animals to eat as well. The younger men of the encampment had already lit the evening fire. The scent of brewing tea drove the scent of burning city from Wanahomen's nostrils, though not his mind.

Reaching the shelf, Wanahomen dismounted without removing his beast's tack or saddle, whistling the note that meant *stay*. The camel grunted in surly acknowledgement, and Wanahomen strode into the encampment, ignoring the eyes that followed and tried to read him, making no response to the few voices that murmured greetings. His gaze had fixed on a young man who squatted near one of the fires, laughing with a cluster of his companions. Someone nudged the young man—Wujjeg—as Wanahomen approached, and after a moment's hesitation Wujjeg stood and turned to face him. He had let his veil slip aside. With no women or strangers about, this was not an insult in itself, but all the camp saw the insolent look he gave to Wanahomen.

"I-Dari," he said, offering the respectful term in a tone that was anything but. "The raid was profitable, at least, you must admit."

"Indeed," Wanahomen said. "The tribe must be certain to thank you when praying to its ancestors." He laid a hand on the ivory hilt of his knife and waited.

Wujjeg's smile slipped for just a moment, along with some of his swagger. Automatically he put his hand on his own blade-hilt, though he did not draw it. "I-Dari," he began, but before he could say more Wanahomen's blade scythed from its sheath and drew a second mouth across Wujjeg's throat.

There was one gasp, from somewhere among Wujjeg's friends. No one else spoke or moved. Wujjeg made no sound either, putting his hands to the flood from his throat for a moment before toppling to the ground.

Wanahomen shook off his knife and turned to the youngest member of the troop. "Wrap Wujjeg for travel and stow him with the baggage. We must return him to his clan."

The youth swallowed hard and bobbed his head in silent acquiescence. Wanahomen sheathed his knife and stepped over the spreading pool of blood to walk to the next campfire. Just beyond the circle of stones he knelt, bowing his head. "Unte, may I enter?"

The man who sat beside the fire inclined his head. An elderly man with the rounded features of a westerner—a slave—hastened to move aside one of the stones, and Wanahomen stepped within the circle.

"Be welcome," Unte said, then signaled the slave. As the slave fetched a clamp to remove a metal cookbox from the flames, the man gave Wanahomen a long considering look. "I'm trying to decide whether I've claimed a fool or a genius as my hunt leader."

The slave handed Wanahomen a bowl. Roasted cercrus tubers, with flecks of spiced meat that might have been kinpan, a ground bird, or one of a half-dozen species of desert vole. Lifting his veil with one hand, Wanahomen ate quickly and neatly, not looking up at Unte. He said, "You came on this ride to see how I do things."

"Indeed. And now I see."

"I've done nothing that violates the customs of this tribe."

"True. You're always proper and careful, Wana."

Wanahomen set his plate down and rubbed his eyes. He was too tired for verbal games. "Will you cast me down?"

"I haven't yet decided."

No! I'm so close! But instead of voicing this protest, Wanahomen said, "If I may ask one boon, then, while I'm still your hunt leader?"

"Ask."

"Wait."

"Wait? For Wujjeg's clan to incite their kin in the Dzikeh-Banbarra to feud?"

"Every man in this troop is sworn to obey me, Unte. Wujjeg disobeyed my command. There can be only one punishment for that while we're on hunt-ride."

"He killed an enemy." Unte's voice was mild, but his eyes were cool and sharp over his veil.

Wanahomen tried not to sigh. "I have explained this to you, and to everyone else in the tribe. Only the Kisuati are our enemies, not all city folk."

"And I have explained to you that most Banbarra would neither agree with that statement, nor care about the distinction," Unte replied. The lines about his eyes relaxed in the firelight; he was amused behind his own veil. "Though I grant they may be more inclined to pay attention now."

Wanahomen relaxed as well, relieved. "So then. Fool or genius?"

"Not a genius, by any stretch."

"But not a complete fool?"

"Gods help us all, no, not a fool. My life would be easier if you were, because then I could be done with you."

Wanahomen set down his empty bowl, nodding thanks to the slave out of careless habit, and then rose to grip the older man's shoulder. "I promised to make you a king among kings, Unte. Is that not worth putting up with me?"

But Unte shook his head and said, "Only if you survive to succeed, Wana. Sleep lightly tonight."

Thus dismissed, Wanahomen rose and left. He kept his eyes forward as he passed through the encampment again, this time out of weariness rather than anger. Most of the hunt party consisted of his own supporters, few of whom begrudged him Wujjeg's death. Still, they would want to talk with him, to find out his plans or praise his forthrightness or reassure him of their loyalty. One or two would no doubt invite him to share their pallets for the night, though he usually refused such offerings to avoid accusations of favoritism. He wanted nothing more than his own pallet and the peace of dreams, but first he had to tend his mount; no respectable Banbarra would sleep before doing so. As he was not Banbarra, it was important that he keep within the bounds of respectability.

When he reached the trail below the shelf, however, he found Laye-ka already unsaddled, her cream-colored coat brushed clean. She chewed placidly on some bit of scrub and grunted at him by way of greeting, rattling the necklace of amulets he had woven for her. At her noise, Ezack leaned out from behind her rump and grinned at him. "Knew you'd come back. The lady here didn't want to wait. Started stomping about and grumbling once you were gone."

Wanahomen chuckled and went to the camel's head, reaching up to rub her hard forehead. She pushed against his hand, begging scratches. "Isn't that just like a woman?" he asked, obliging her.

"True enough! So..." Ezack darted a look around for listeners. "Is the old man angry?"

"No. He understood."

Ezack sighed in relief, his breath momentarily tenting the cloth of his own veil. "I thought he would, but still."

"He warned me to be wary. As if I needed that warning." As Wanahomen scratched Laye-ka's ears, his eyes drifted back toward the camp. Most of the knots of men had broken up, as if Wujjeg's death and Unte's approval had ended all debates. One remaining cluster—those who had been Wujjeg's friends—sat together whispering around one of the campfires. Wanahomen was not particularly disturbed by this, for Wujjeg had been the smartest and boldest of that bunch; without him they were little threat. Nevertheless, he would obey Unte, and be careful.

"Ha, you greedy thing; get on now." He slapped Laye-ka's shoulder, and with a last mournful look she turned and ambled off to join the other horses and camels. "Rest well, Ezack."

"In peace, Wana."

Wana paused, glancing back in surprise at the familiar, but quintessentially Gujaareen, parting phrase. Ezack shrugged at his look. "We Banbarra find a use for whatever comes our way. We've kept *you*, haven't we?"

With this, Ezack began stacking the saddlebags against the shelf wall, politely ignoring Wana when he murmured in Gujaareen, "Thank you." Too delicate a moment for Banbarra tastes; the sort of thing Wanahomen would never have allowed himself to do with anyone else, lest they think him as soft as most city-dwellers. But Ezack had learned to tolerate his commander's peculiar behavior years before, for which Wanahomen was grateful. He walked away quickly, before the urge to become sentimental got any worse.

His camp space was ready, the fire burning briskly and his pallet laid out by his own slave. There was no barrier circle here; a good hunt leader did not need to separate himself from his men. As he entered the area of firelight and sat down, shifting to lie on his side, Wanahomen nodded to the slave. "We'll be heading home tomorrow."

Charris—once a general of Gujaareh's army, though those days were long past—returned the nod from where he lay on his own pallet. "You handled things well." He spoke in Gujaareen, in part because his Chakti was poor, and in part for privacy. Only Unte and Ezack spoke anything of the tongue: Unte with marginal fluency, Ezack far less than that.

Wanahomen's cheeks warmed with the praise. "Father taught me to deal swiftly with defiance."

"If it's any consolation, the Gujaareen who was wounded will probably live. If his comrades kept him warm and took him to the Hetawa right away, the wound could've been healed."

Wanahomen nodded slowly, gazing into the fire. "I had forgotten about that. Healing. Amazing, isn't it? That I could forget such a thing." He fell silent as the capital's walls, golden at sunset, gleamed in his memory. For a moment he could almost smell moontear blossoms on the wind, and then the memory was gone. He mourned its passing; his memories were thin and rare these days. "No true Gujaareen would forget such a thing, Charris. Would they?"

Charris spoke gently. "We've been away a long time, my Prince, but we will always be Gujaareen."

Yes. And Gujaareh would be his again. Wanahomen repeated that thought to himself once, and thrice more under his breath; four repetitions made a prayer. *His*, by Hananja's grace.

"The appointment with the shunha," he said. "Is it set?"

Charris nodded. "Three days from now, at sunset. I told him in the message that it would be me." He threw an uneasy look at Wanahomen.

"I must see this man for myself, Charris. The shunha might give their first allegiance to Gujaareh, but they're still too close to their Kisuati roots for my comfort. I need to be sure we can trust this one." Wanahomen reached under his headcloth to rub the gritty back of his neck, missing with rueful fondness the scented baths of his people. "I'll be careful, never fear."

"And my other suggestion?"

Wanahomen scowled. "Never."

"The Hetawa is as much a power in Gujaareh as the nobility, my Prince. More."

"And I will never ask their aid for so much as healing a stubbed toe."

Charris sighed. "In peace, then, my Prince." He shifted to lie back on his roll.

"In peace, old friend." Wanahomen shifted to remove his boots, then lay down, securing his face-veil for rest. Watching shadows dance on the shelf's overhang, he shut his eyes—

—And opened them to a churning, storm-choked sky.

Where the stone of a sheltering ledge should have been, where Dreaming Moon and the million Lesser Suns should have filled the night sky beyond that, thick black clouds boiled and rippled. The lightning that flickered among these clouds was attenuated, thin and sickly, and it lingered, more like the thread of veins through flesh than light and fire. He had never seen such a sky, even in the worst of floodseason.

He sat up. Beneath this sky the world had turned gray and strange: leached of color, the shadows gone sharp and too deep to see into. As Wanahomen's outer robe fell away, he saw that all his dusty Banbarra clothing was gone—replaced by a loinskirt of fine tailored linen, a feathered waistcloak, and a collar of lapis teardrops. Clothing befitting a prince.

"As it should be," whispered his father's voice.

Wanahomen turned. The Banbarra encampment was gone; Charris was gone. Wanahomen's pallet and fire sat on the filthy bricks of a Gujaareen street, in a high-walled and shadowed alleyway. Near the back of this alley, where the shadows were thickest, a form at once familiar and hideous lurked. Its head listed to one side; he saw the gleam of teeth. And yet—

"Wanahomen," the specter whispered.

He got to his feet, filled with the certainty of dreaming. "Father."

"My son, my heir." The voice was soft, airy, yet Wanahomen would know its timbre anywhere. He bit his lip and took a step closer, wanting to close the distance. Knowing, despite ten years' absence from Gujaareh, that this desire was foolish. The land of dreams was incomprehensibly vast; it would take aeons for the souls of the dead to fill it. Most of the people seen in dreams were merely reflections of the dreamer's own thoughts and fears.

But...

"My reborn soul." The shadow of his father shook its head; dirty, limp braids swung back and forth. "Where is the Aureole, Wanahomen? Where is your kingdom?"

"In enemy hands, Father." He could hear the hate in his own voice, echoing from the alley's walls. "They've taken everything from me."

"Not everything. Not hope. Not Her favor."

Wanahomen shook his head, smiling bleakly. "Does She even know me, Father? I've made no offerings and enjoyed no blessings for many years."

"Blessings will come." Something in the voice, at once sly and amused, made this less a promise and more a warning. The figure lifted one crooked, palsied finger skyward. "They have come already, see? Such powerful blessings. They will shake all Gujaareh, waking and sleeping, and drown the weak in their own dark dreams. Her suffering knows no limits."

Wanahomen looked up at the grinding sky and shivered, though there was no wind. "Do you mean the Goddess? I don't understand, Father—"

"Don't you?" The shadows shifted as the shape lowered its arm to point at Wanahomen, stepping forward enough that the firelight illuminated its flesh at last. Wanahomen's gorge rose as he saw purpleblack sores mottling skin that had once been the pale gold of desert sand. The rot of death? No. These sores looked more like some sort of sickness.

The thing that had been his father uttered a thick, clotted chuckle. Following its finger, Wanahomen looked down at himself and gasped to see that his own torso bloomed with the same sores. Revolted, he swept his hands down himself to brush them off. But his skin was whole; the sickness was beneath it. *Inside him.*

"Hurry," his father whispered. "You see it has already begun."

Wanahomen opened his eyes again. The cavern and the Banbarra were back. The dream was gone.

No. Unlike most of his countrymen, Wanahomen had never been trained in the techniques of proper dreaming—his father had not permitted it. Yet it seemed some things were innate, training or no training. This much he could feel: some dreams were more than dreams.

He closed his eyes, but did not sleep again that night.

3

(⊙)

The Maiden's Test

Tiaanet, daughter of Insurret, maiden of the shunha caste, was legend in Gujaareh. Poets and songstresses had composed hymns in her honor; sculptors and painters used her likeness in their finest work. Those who spoke with her noted that her wit and grace matched her physical beauty, and no one could deny that the household had been run smoothly since her mother apportioned some of the management to her. So too were the family's investments profitable and well chosen. Some—lovestruck fools, mostly, but a few others besides—whispered that in her perfection, the shunha's godly ancestors were reborn.

So it was that as the season of third harvest began, in the tenth year of the Kisuati occupation, word spread throughout the higher castes of a momentous happening: Lady Tiaanet at last sought a husband. No one had expected such restraint from her powerful, influential family—for while women of the shunha rarely married as early as lowcastes or country folk, the river had flooded four times since Tiaanet's majority at age sixteen. Between her natural gifts and future wealth—for like the Kisuati, the shunha passed inheritance through the motherline—it was virtually guaranteed that every man of worth in the two lands would come calling on the next social occasion. This happened to be the funeral of Lord Khanwer, a cousin to Tiaanet's father.

Per tradition, Khanwer's funeral rites were held at the house of his nearest living relative, culminating in a Moonrise-to-Moonset celebration. In flagrant disregard for shunha tradition, however, it was not Tiaanet's mother but Tiaanet herself who served as hostess for the event—a great responsibility for so young a maiden, and a terrible scandal. Shunha did not disregard tradition. The elders of the caste would doubtless send her a letter of censure, and she would doubtless visit them to apologize, before continuing to do exactly as she pleased.

Tiaanet took care to maintain a sedate and graceful pace as she moved among the gathered guests, keeping cups full and conversation flowing. More importantly, she noted the eyes of the male guests, which strayed often to her throughout the evening. On her father's request she had worn her most alluring gown, linen woven so finely that it was all but sheer, and meticulously pleated so that it conformed to every curve of her body. The men's lips parted as her unbound breasts swayed beneath the translucent cloth; their gazes lingered on the soft curve of her belly, trying to pick out the dark triangle below. She had seen several of them approach her father throughout the evening, speaking in low, urgent voices and glancing toward her. But her father would only nod politely through these conversations, his smile growing wider with each new proposition as if it were he, and not Tiaanet, to whom they paid court.

"How tedious this must be for you," said a white-haired man as Tiaanet refilled his cup. She looked up to find him smiling at her, which surprised her—not for his smile, which was kindly, but for the fact that there was no lust in it.

"Not so very, my lord," she replied. A servant approached, offering her a fresh carafe of wine; she nodded thanks and exchanged it

N. K. Jemisin

for her nearly empty one. "It pleases me to honor the passing of such an esteemed man."

"Hmm, yes. The last of the true traditionalists was Khanwer. Gujaareh has lost a champion." The man sipped the wine and paused to savor its taste for a moment, his eyebrows rising in appreciation. "This is a southern spirit? It's exquisite."

Tiaanet inclined her head. "Daropalm wine, made in Sitiswaya. Rare and difficult to procure, but my father has many Kisuati merchant friends."

"How convenient. So many of the nobility are out of favor with our overlords, these days." He paused for another sip, closing his eyes in pleasure. "Yet I'm told your father was at odds with Khanwer before his death. Surely *he* was not out of favor?"

With a sidelong glance, Tiaanet examined the man again, wondering what he was about. Probing for information, certainly, but without knowing his status she could not guess why. Brown as nutwood, neither dark nor pale; he looked like some middling caste rather than nobility, and no lowcaste would have made the guest list. An artist, perhaps. And something about his attire—a plain robe of white hekeh—struck her as out of place amid the finery of all the other guests. Yet he would not have been present if he did not hold some importance in Gujaareen society. Tiaanet knew her father better than that.

She replied carefully, "Khanwer was kin, my lord."

"But of course. You would not speak ill of him to a stranger. Forgive me for prying." He paused and gave her another of those peculiar, kindly smiles. "You need not call me *lord*, by the way."

Abruptly her mind bridged the gap. "You are of the Hetawa."

He raised both eyebrows and chuckled. "Oh my, that is humbling! I've grown accustomed to being recognized these past few years."

Not just any templeman, then. Tiaanet bowed low over both flattened hands in apology. "The error is mine. I have often believed that living here in the greenlands, luxurious as our estate is, keeps our family isolated from the important events and personages of the city—"

The Superior of the Hetawa, leader of the Hananjan faith across every kingdom that honored Her, shook his head at once. "You've been a gracious hostess in every way, Lady Tiaanet, especially under the circumstances. How is your mother?"

"Resting, Superior."

"I'm told she's been ill for some time." He glanced about and then leaned close to her with such artlessness that every guest in the vicinity must have noticed. "I don't suppose your father would be amenable to a visit from a Sharer?" he asked in a low voice. "The chronic ailments are often easy to heal. It can be done discreetly."

Tiaanet favored him with a cool gaze, warning him off further pursuit of the matter. "We are shunha, Superior."

He sighed and straightened. "Well, please inform him of the offer, in any case. He wouldn't be the first shunha to quietly break tradition."

"I shall convey that." And her father had begun to watch them from across the room. She inclined her head to the man again and turned to leave. "Enjoy the rest of the evening, Superior—"

"Wait." He performed another of his too-obvious looks about; this time Tiaanet tensed inwardly, feeling her father's scrutiny as an almost palpable prickle along her spine. "Tell me, daughter of Insurret. Have you heard anything of *how* Lord Khanwer died?"

Ah. A Servant of Hananja might have little taste for women, but secrets? Not even dreamblood could erase that.

"He died in his sleep, Superior," she said. She smiled, which caused him to draw back, an uneasy frown flitting across his face. She did not smile often, for this reason. "As every good and faithful follower of Hananja should wish."

She walked away then, before he could ask any more awkward questions, and before he could get her into further trouble. Though as she poured wine for the next guest, she caught her father's cool expression and suspected it was already too late for that.

Some while later, the last colored sliver of the Dreaming Moon slipped below the horizon, leaving only tiny white Waking Moon and the winking Lesser Suns in the sky. With tradition satisfied, the guests one by one took their leave. Tiaanet saw to those who didn't feel like making the journey back to the city or their own estates, directing them to the house's guest chambers while her father exchanged farewells with the rest. Thus it was Tiaanet whom one of the servants approached, whispering that her mother required aid.

She glanced toward her father; he was engrossed in conversation with two other shunha lords. Nodding to the servant, she headed for the north chamber.

There were no sounds from within as she stopped at the heavy doorway curtain and nodded to the servants standing watch on either side. "Mother? May I enter?"

There was no answer, though she had expected none. Passing through the curtain, she found the chamber beyond in complete disarray—cushions and clothing strewn all over, a wooden chest overturned and spilled, one rug flung against the far wall. The oxbow seat near the window, where her mother usually sat, lay on its side. Amid the chaos her mother stood rigid, a small wooden statue of Hananja clenched tight in one fist, her eyes fixed on some distant point beyond the window. She did not turn as Tiaanet entered.

Tiaanet bent to pick up a cushion.

"Leave it," Insurret said. Tiaanet left the cushion where it lay.

Keeping her voice low, Tiaanet asked, "Shall I fetch you anything?"

In profile, her mother's smile was sharp as a winter-Moon sliver. "Your father, when you're done with him."

"He's with our guests, Mother."

Insurret glanced at Tiaanet over her shoulder. "And you came to see to my needs? Such a good daughter you are. Perhaps someday you'll have a daughter as fine."

Tiaanet said nothing in response to this, waiting. She usually tried not to leave before Insurret dismissed her. A good daughter stayed to do her mother's bidding.

"Does your father mean to let your sister out for the party?" Insurret's smile was venomous. "With so much light and noise, there could be no danger."

"Tantufi is in the field house, Mother." As Insurret well knew.

"Yes, yes. Another good daughter for me." Insurret's eyes abruptly grew vague; her smile faded. "Such good daughters."

There was no point to such conversations. Tiaanet sighed and turned to leave. "The servants will clean up in the morning, if you allow. Good night, Mother. In peace—"

The statue of Hananja struck the wall just past Tiaanet's head and broke in two. She stopped.

"Never wish me peace," Insurret snarled. "Serpent. Fawning whore. Never let the word *peace* cross your lips in my presence. Do you understand?"

Tiaanet crouched to collect the pieces of the statue; these she set on a nearby shelf, then crossed her forearms and bowed her head in manuflection as an apology to the Goddess. "Yes, Mother. Good night."

Her mother made no reply as she left.

Outside the room, her father was waiting. She stopped, searching for any signs of anger in his face, but he was watching the curtain of Insurret's room with a weary expression. "You did well," he said.

Tiaanet nodded. It was impossible to do well with Insurret, but there were degrees of success. "Have all the guests been settled?"

"Yes." He nodded to the guard servants and offered her his arm, which of course she did not refuse. He began walking her toward her room. "What did the Superior want?"

"To know how Khanwer died, Father."

"And what did you tell him?"

"That our noble cousin died in his sleep, Father."

He laughed, patting her hand. "Good girl. I received many compliments on you this evening."

Seeing his good mood, she dared a question. "And how many of those compliments came with offers of marriage?"

He grinned at her. "Four this evening alone. Auspicious, hmm? And more to come, once the men go home and tally their wealth to see if they're worthy of you. I'll keep a few of them dangling awhile, but never fear." He patted her hand again. "You won't be wasted on some paltry official or merchant. I have a finer suitor in mind for you."

Some Kisuati nobleman? Tiaanet wondered, though she knew better than to ask. That would make her appear interested, eager to leave. Which of course she could not possibly be.

They turned a corner and entered the corridor that led to her bedchamber.

"The Superior also offered to send a Sharer for Mother," she said. Perhaps it would distract him enough. "I reminded him that was not our way."

Her father snorted. "The man is a fool. His predecessor, now— that one got things done, which is probably why the Gatherers killed him. Ah, these days the Hetawa is too eager to appear harmless, too conciliatory to the Kisuati and everyone else..." They reached Tiaanet's door; he turned to her and cupped her cheek. "Enough politics. Are you tired?"

She made herself smile, wishing that her smiles disturbed him as they did so many others. "Very, Father, after so long an evening."

"I understand." He smiled, pulling aside the curtain for her to enter. "We'll be quick—and quiet, too, so that our guests don't wake. Yes?"

For a fleeting instant, the urge to scream rose in Tiaanet's mind. The house was full of guests; one cry would alert them all. Had the Superior stayed the night? If she accused her father of corruption in front of him, in front of the guests, the Hetawa would surely investigate. The Gatherers would come. She could show them poor, damaged little Tantufi as proof; perhaps even Insurret would be lucid enough to confirm her accusations. Perhaps the Gatherers would kill the whole family to rid Gujaareh of such a pestilence. Then Tiaanet and Tantufi could at last be free, one way or another.

But that urge, like a thousand others of its kind, faded as quickly as it had risen. She had not felt true hope in years. Most days—good days—she felt nothing at all.

So Tiaanet went into the room and over to the bed, keeping her eyes on the far wall. Behind her, he closed the curtain and came to join her.

"I love you, Tiaanet," he said. "You know that, don't you?"

"Yes, Father," she said.

"My good girl," he replied, and leaned down for a good-night kiss.

4

(•⊙•)

Sleeplessness

Sunandi Jeh Kalawe, Voice of the Kisuati Protectorate and governor of Gujaareh on the Protectors' behalf, was not a sound sleeper. Any movement woke her during the night. Even a breeze that stirred the bedhangings too often could keep her wide-eyed until dawn. In the years since her marriage she had adapted to this tendency, keeping a pot of watered honey beer on the nightstand, banishing her husband to the sitting room couches whenever he snored, or defecting to those couches herself to avoid disturbing him. She did sleep—just fleetingly, snatching rest in quick, insufficient rations. Sometimes she woke more tired than she had gone to bed.

Invariably there were nights when soothing drinks and counting by fours did no good. At such times she would go to her study to work so that at least the time would not be wasted. Or she went to the balcony of their apartment in Yanya-iyan to gaze up at the Dreaming Moon, drinking in her silvery, multihued light and thinking of nothing.

On this occasion, however, she stopped in shock, finding the balcony already inhabited.

"Don't scream," the Gatherer Nijiri said. He sat with one foot on the railing, the other dangling over an eight-story drop, watching her with amused eyes. "Your soldier husband would come charging out here, weapons drawn, and the whole palace's peace would be disturbed."

Letting out the breath that she had indeed drawn to scream, Sunandi walked out onto the balcony. "There would be little chance of that if you weren't perched out here like a skyrer watching for mice."

"I'm a Gatherer, Jeh Kalawe. Did you think I would come through the front gate with a full escort? Perhaps bringing a chantress to announce me and all my lineage? In any case, you should have been expecting me."

She rolled her eyes, coming to join him at the railing. "I expected you *at dusk*. I sent my summons right after the damned Banbarra finished terrorizing the city this morning." Her annoyance vanished as a more personal anxiety eclipsed it. "Have you been here long?" She had made love with Anzi just before midnight.

He smiled, the Moonlight momentarily making him seem younger—more like the boy she'd first met ten years before. He had grown taller in the years since, and his youthful beauty had refined into something elegant and hard-edged, but he was still quite young even by the standards of Kisua, where people did not live as long. It was his profession that made him seem older than his years.

"If I had come earlier," he said, "you would have had wistful daydreams of coming to this balcony then."

It took her a moment to understand his meaning, and when she did she wanted to kill him. "*Keb-na!* You know I don't like you tampering with my dreams."

He said nothing, only watching her, and after a moment she sighed. Of course he would tamper with her dreams as he saw fit. He was a Gatherer.

31

"You need to know," she said, changing the subject, "that these Banbarra raids must stop."

He continued to watch her in silence, possibly because he knew how much his damned Gujaareen calm irritated her, or because he simply had nothing to say in response. "They threaten the peace," she said, irrationally compelled to fill the silence. "If our control of Gujaareh slips, all manner of chaos could occur. Riots. Sabotage."

"Why are you telling me this?"

"The Hetawa has the people's ear. Someone somewhere has to have a Banbarra cousin or aunt. You people breed with anything."

Nijiri only sighed at the slur; he'd heard worse from her. They tolerated from each other what they would not from anyone else. "The Hetawa supports anyone who can give the city lasting peace. For the time being, that's Kisua. This has cost us greatly, in the people's trust."

"A Gujaareen was killed this time! A city guardsman. Another was badly wounded, though I'm told your healers managed to save him. They've killed twenty of my husband's men. Does that sound like peace to you?"

He frowned. "It sounds remarkable. Eight raids, twenty dead Kisuati, and only one Gujaareen death? What have they taken?"

She ticked off on her fingers. "The contents of three storehouses used by our troops, including one supposedly hidden cache of weapons. Horses. Barley sheaves bundled for shipment to Kisua, which I suppose they'll use as fodder for the horses; Merik knows what else they could do with it in the desert. Moontear wine. Leather and hekeh-cloth. Lapis and sea salt."

He said nothing for a moment, contemplating this. "Trade-goods," he said. "Would you say those are goods especially prized in Kisua?"

Sunandi frowned. "Most of it would fetch high prices in any

Kisuati market, yes. Such trade makes our conquest of Gujaareh less of a financial loss." She sighed. "Indeed, losing those goods has already done harm; there's a faction of merchants in Kisua right now calling for harsher measures in our control of the Gujaareen capital—"

"No people taken? They like slaves, those desert barbarians."

She ignored the jibe. Kisuati kept slaves too. "None. They've no qualms about drawing the blood of those who get in their way, but they take no prisoners. Luck, I suppose."

"I doubt that."

She frowned. Something in his manner had changed. She hesitated to call it excitement, for there was something wrong with any Gatherer who felt that. Still, there was no mistaking the new tension in his body. "Explain."

He nodded slowly as he gazed out at the city, his eyes roving back and forth, back and forth, over the rooftops and streets. Fleetingly, Sunandi wondered how well he slept.

"To the desert tribes," he said, "we city folk—Gujaareen and Kisuati alike—are soft, decadent, cowardly, and unworthy of the wealth we possess. Even the Shadoun, your own allies, treat with you only because they hate Gujaareh more. So for the Banbarra to take no slaves, and avoid killing Gujaareen while slaying fours of Kisuati…"

Sunandi gripped the balcony railing, groaning softly. How foolish of her not to have seen it. "They're courting Gujaareh as an ally!"

Nijiri did not reply, but there was no need; Sunandi knew at once that she was right. The tribes of the Empty Thousand had been at feud with one another for as long as anyone could remember. The wars between the Banbarra and the Shadoun—the two strongest tribes—were the stuff of legend, but there had been relative peace in the past few centuries as Gujaareh had grown in power. Neither tribe dared weaken itself fighting old rivals with a new threat lurking so near.

The raids were proof that the long stalemate had broken. The Shadoun were trading partners and sometime allies of Kisua—and now Kisua held Gujaareh. This trapped the Banbarra, whose territory stretched between the southwestern border of Gujaareh and the southern mountain fortresses of the Shadoun, between two allied threats. Small wonder they'd decided to do something about it.

"You believe the Banbarra are targeting trade-goods deliberately," Sunandi said, frowning as she mulled over Nijiri's words. "Why? To make our conquest of Gujaareh unprofitable? To trigger some sort of political shift in Kisua?"

"I didn't say that. But their tactics do show a certain forethought, don't you think?"

Too much. Sunandi scowled. "Ignorant camel-loving nomads did not think of this."

A flicker of annoyance crossed his face at last, fleeting and mild. "They aren't stupid, Jeh Kalawe. It demeans you to say such things."

"Even your people call them barbarians!"

"But trading with barbarians has made us rich, remember. Unlike Kisua, we have never allowed our prejudices to blind us to the potential *or* the threat of any barbarian race."

Sunandi waved off the scold, folding her arms across her breasts and beginning to pace. "The Banbarra were too proud to ask for help in their struggle against the Shadoun before; why seek it now? And from Gujaareh, when it's only a humbled captive of Kisua? The desert folk respect strength; Gujaareh has none."

"If you believe that, *you're* the stupid one," he snapped.

She clenched her fists and whirled on him. "The Gujaareen army—"

"Was only part of Gujaareh's power even before the Kisuati came. Have you forgotten our ties with the northlands and the east? As you say, half the zhinha are blood relatives to some barbarian king or another. And in this land there is the military caste, most of them *born* warriors, who have sat idle—and angry—since the army was disbanded. It was a mistake for you to do that; you have no idea how hard the Hetawa has worked to keep them quiescent. And the city guard; and the private forces the nobles employ to protect their lands...and the Hetawa itself. Have you any idea what my fellow Servants could do if roused? The Sentinels alone—"

He shook his head, swung both legs to her side of the balcony railing, and leaned forward. Sunandi fought the urge to take a step back from his sudden focus. Gatherers were not supposed to feel strong emotion, but Nijiri had always had a temper. "I know what Kisua thinks of us. You call us sleeping sheep, content to dream away all our troubles. But when Gujaareh's wrath is awakened it burns as hot as that of any other land—hotter, because we stifle it so often. If it ever bursts free, Kisua *will* lose control."

She stared back at him and tried to ignore her unease. "You said the Hetawa supported us."

"The Hetawa supports you *for now*. But if a better option comes along, Jeh Kalawe, if the swiftest and surest path to stability comes through slaughtering every Kisuati within our borders, then be assured the Hetawa will see it done." Then, to Sunandi's surprise, the anger in his eyes shifted, becoming something more sorrowful. "All these years and still we're strangers to you."

"Not strangers," she said, feeling oddly stung. "I know how important peace is to you."

"It's more than important, Jeh Kalawe. It is our god." He got to his feet and sighed. "This much I can tell you: your guess was correct. We have been approached by a representative of the Banbarra leader."

Sunandi caught her breath. "I didn't know they *had* a leader."

"The Banbarra are many tribes, true, with many leaders. But in times of war, they become one body with one head. The man we're dealing with is likely to become that head."

"When did they approach you?"

"After the first few raids on the city. What you've told me only confirms something we'd begun to suspect ourselves. And do not ask me when, or whether, the meeting will take place. Hetawa affairs are none of the Protectors' business."

And of course she could not promise to keep it secret, given her role as the Protectors' Voice, any more than he could promise a lasting cooperation with her. They each had their masters to serve.

So she kept her next question open-ended, to allow him room to maneuver between her loyalties and his own. "Is there anything you *can* tell me?"

He nodded with the faintest air of approval. "The Banbarra head's spokesman, when they came to us, was a Gujaareen military-casteman. High-ranking; he claimed to have been a general in the days before the conquest. Zhinha by birth." He watched her as he said it.

"Goddess protect us," Sunandi whispered, her skin goosebumping with more than the night air's chill. Shunha and zhinha, the two noble castes of Gujaareh, did not often join the military, being too proud to take orders from anyone of lesser birth than themselves. They would tolerate serving their peers, just. But there was one lineage that a zhinha-born general would serve gladly, even into exile.

Nijiri said nothing at her blasphemy—perhaps because he sensed, for the moment at least, that she was utterly sincere.

"Make of that what you will," he said. "Now go back to your husband before he misses you." He stood to leave, flicking one of his twin nape-braids back over his shoulder as he did so. The gesture, and the hairstyle, were so familiar that a soft pang stirred in Sunandi's heart.

"How are you, Nijiri?" she asked, placing the lightest of emphases on *you*.

He paused, but did not turn to face her. "I'm well, Jeh Kalawe."

"I . . ." She hesitated, then finally blurted, "I actually *miss* him. Can you believe that? We weren't friends. And yet . . ."

Nijiri took hold of the railing. "We will both meet him again someday. You may even find him before I do; you're a woman, you have more power than I to find your way within Ina-Karekh. And you can still dream."

She had forgotten that. He was a true Gatherer now, paying a Gatherer's price for power.

"I'm sorry," she said. She could not tell whether the note in his voice was sorrow or simply resignation; either way there was pain underneath it. Hesitantly she reached for his shoulder, for whatever good that would do. Her fingers barely brushed his skin before he turned and took hold of her hand.

"Don't be sorry," he said. He lifted the back of her hand to his cheek and leaned against it for a moment, closing his eyes and perhaps imagining someone else's hand in its place. It occurred to her in that moment just how lonely he must be, for no one touched Gatherers, not intentionally. They gave comfort to others, but bore their own pain alone.

But to Sunandi's surprise, Nijiri opened his eyes and frowned. "You'll never meet him at this rate. Why didn't you come to me? You know I would've helped you."

And before she could ask what he was talking about, he reached toward her face. She blinked in instinctive reaction and felt his fingertips brush her eyelids for an instant, and then he let her go. When she opened her eyes, he had vaulted up to crouch on the railing, nimble as a bird.

"Don't summon me again," he said over his shoulder. "Things are changing too quickly. I misspoke, Jeh Kalawe, when I said that you didn't understand us. As much as any foreigner can, and better than any other Kisuati, you do. That's why I'll forgive you, no matter what the Protectors make you do."

While Sunandi stared back at him, trying to puzzle this out, he stood up on the railing, balancing easily, heedless of the height. Taking hold of a ledge above, he levered his body upward in a single smooth motion. Then he was gone.

It was not until Sunandi returned to her bed that she understood what he had done. More precisely, she understood it in the morning, when she woke up wrapped in Anzi's arms, comfortable and more rested than she'd felt in years. Anzi had pulled her close during the night, surely jostling her in the process. Yet she had not woken up once.

5

The Tithebearer

"No," Mni-inh said.

Hanani kept her head bowed, arms folded before her with hands palm-down. Mni-inh, who sat on a cushioned bench massaging one knee, scowled when it became clear she had no intention of moving.

"I said no, Hanani." He straightened, flicking his red loindrapes back into place. "The Hetawa has already made its apology to the family of the tithebearer. He's to receive a full formal burial in the Hetawa's own crypt, an honor usually given only to Servants of Hananja. Let that suffice."

"The tithebearer's death was not *the Hetawa's* fault," Hanani replied, keeping her eyes on his chest. In the low morning light, the ruby collar of his office looked like droplets of blood scattered over his pale skin.

Mni-inh flinched and sat up. But the Sharers' Hall was mostly empty between dawn and the noon hour, as those who worked the night hours slept and the rest were kept busy with a Sharer's usual daytime duties in the Hall of Blessings or the herbs-and-simples chamber. Those few who lounged about the hall's benches and nooks were deep in study or conversation with others. No one looked at Hanani and Mni-inh, though Mni-inh darted his eyes about to make sure, and leaned close before he spoke again. "It isn't *your* fault either, little fool! Don't do Yehamwy's work for him, Hanani. How can you expect the Council to believe you're competent if you don't believe it yourself?"

She lifted her head and watched him draw back in surprise. "I don't believe I'm incompetent, Mni-inh-brother. How could I, after your training?"

"Then why visit the tithebearer's family?"

It was a question that Hanani had asked herself all night, during the hours that she'd spent weeping and praying and finally rocking herself to sleep. She had not dreamed; there had been no answer to her prayers for peace or understanding. And so she had awakened that morning with her thoughts full of a single impulse: to find out *why* Dayu had died.

"Because my heart is empty of peace right now," she said. Mni-inh drew back at this, frowning. "Doubt has come to fill the void instead. Did I truly press Dayu too far, too fast? Did that tithebearer die because I expected a child to do an adult's work? You know what doubt can do in narcomancy, Brother. Even if the councilor had not pronounced interdiction on me, I would refuse to perform healings now."

Mni-inh sighed, a tone of frustration. "That I understand. But how will apologizing to a grieving widow—who may blame you for her husband's death whether it's your fault or not—ease your doubts?" He sobered abruptly. "Wait. I know what this is about. This is the first time you've dealt with death."

"That isn't it," she said, though she had to look away from the compassion in his eyes. In the early months of her path training, Hanani had actually suspected Mni-inh of harboring a secret sadism in his soul, somehow concealing it from the Gatherers but gleefully inflicting it on his unwilling apprentice under the guise of mentorship. He had been twice as hard on her as the other Sharers with their—male—apprentices, noting when she complained that she would have to be twice as good to overcome petitioners' fears of her sex. And *his* hatred for same, she had been certain.

Yet as the months became years, and as Hanani matured, she had understood at last that Mni-inh's harshness was an act. Underneath it, his true personality was far softer. *Too* soft, Hanani now believed, sorely lacking the calm and stoicism that the faithful expected of Hananja's Servants. He took slights to her as a personal insult; he chafed constantly at the Hetawa's slow pace of change; he forgot tact and said things that damaged his standing among their pathbrothers. It was true that his unorthodoxy had probably made him the best teacher for her, but there were times when Hanani would have found the taskmaster of her youth easier to deal with than the brash and overprotective elder brother he had become since.

"Meeting her will make me feel better," she said finally, firmly. "And I just need to know more, Mni-inh-brother. I need to know the man who died with Dayu. I need to understand what happened, or at least begin to try. There can be no peace for me without that."

Mni-inh stared at her. Finally he sighed again, running a hand over his peculiar, wavy, oily-looking hair. "Fine. Go."

She sprang to her feet and had taken three steps before he spluttered, "You're going *now*? Oh, never mind, you probably should or I might change my mind. Just be careful."

"Thank you, Mni-inh-brother!"

He muttered something under his breath that she suspected was not a prayer.

So Hanani left the Sharer's Hall, crossing the enormous open courtyard of the inner Hetawa on her way to the Hall of Blessings. A pair of Teacher-Apprentices, their arms weighed down with scrolls, glanced at her as they crossed her path; they fell to whispering almost as soon as she was out of earshot. An elderly Sentinel sitting on a stoop watched her, eyes narrowed, as if taking her measure. She nodded to him; he gave her a nod in return.

It was not hard for Hanani to guess what underlay so many of the looks that had been thrown her way throughout the morning. She had joined a group prayer dance that dawn, and felt many eyes on her back. In the baths, some of the other apprentices had been more pointed than usual in averting their eyes from her nudity. Not all of her fellow Servants thought her responsible for the two deaths, she knew. But it was clear from the looks and whispers that many did.

If she had not already felt so low, the looks would have taken their toll. As it was, nothing could hurt worse than Dayu's loss.

The Hall of Blessings provided some relief, for the Sharers on duty were too busy to even glance in her direction. The line of petitioners was longer than usual, half again the length of the tithe-bearers' line. Nearly everyone in the petitioner line showed some visible injury—a slung arm, a bandaged foot or head. More injuries from the Banbarra raid, she realized, along with the usual accidents of harvest season and daily life in the city. The most injured, like the soldier Hanani had healed the day before, had been treated first. Now there was time and magic enough for the rest.

It would go faster if I were there, she thought as she passed the dais. But there was no peace or point in such thoughts, so she moved on.

The great bronze double doors stood open for public hours, and as she passed from the cool dim Hall to the noise and brilliance of outside, she paused on the steps to let her eyes adjust. The heat was so fierce that her skin tingled with it—pleasantly in this first instant, though soon she would begin to sweat. She put a hand up to shadow her eyes and gazed over the busy, crowded expanse of Hetawa Square. Nearby she saw a handful of devotees sitting on the steps to pray, and beyond them merchants moved about, selling water and cut fruit to passersby. Along the main thoroughfare at the other end of the square, dozens of folk milled and moved on their way to the market or the riverfront or dreams-knew-where else. Too many people, too much chaos, and too many who would stare at her flattened, wrapped breasts, or the red man's loindrapes strapped around a woman's broad hips. She had never liked venturing into the city. And yet—

Not one of those busy, brisk-moving people so much as glanced at her, as she gazed down at them from the Hetawa's steps. Even the ones who would stare, once she joined their bustling flow, wondered only that she was a woman in man's dress. They did not know what she had done, and moreover they did not care. It was strange, and somehow a relief, to contemplate this.

"You should have an escort, Sharer-Apprentice."

Hanani glanced up at the small balconies that overlooked the Hetawa steps. The two men who crouched there were each clad in black loindrapes and onyx collars and quiet, deadly stillness. Hanani recognized the one who had spoken to her as Anarim, a senior of the Sentinel path. The other was a Sentinel she did not know; while Anarim focused his attention on her, that one kept his gaze on the steps and streets beyond, alert for any threats to the Goddess's temple or worshippers.

She bowed to both of them regardless. "I've gone into the city to serve petitioners many times, Sentinel. I can find my way."

"Of that I have no doubt, Apprentice. But that was not why I suggested an escort." Anarim, like most of his path, was whipcord-lean; it was some effect of the training they did. He had taken this further by being a tall, narrow sort of man, with long fingers and an angular face, and lips as thin as a northerner's. Those thin lips twitched now in faint disapproval, though he kept his expression blank otherwise. She knew at once the disapproval was not for her. "The Kisuati seem unable to prevent raids and other disruptions within the city's walls these days. Things aren't as peaceful as they should be. I, or another of my path, can accompany you."

43

Hanani considered, but then shook her head. "I go to humble myself before a stranger, Sentinel Anarim. Bringing a guard might be taken amiss. Besides," and she gestured at her clothing. "These drapes afford me no small protection. That much hasn't changed, Kisuati or no."

"Very well, Apprentice. Go—and return—in Her peace." Then, to Hanani's great surprise, Anarim inclined his head to her. She stared, for she was only an apprentice and he was one of the most respected Servants in the Hetawa, a member of the Council of Paths. But when Anarim straightened, he resumed his guardian stance, eyes roving the square for potential threats, and it would have been disrespectful to distract him by speaking of such a small thing.

But the message was clear: he, at least, believed she was not at fault for the deaths. She walked away, unsure of how to feel—but feeling better, nevertheless.

The tithebearer's name had been Bahenamin, and he had been a wealthy member of the merchant caste. His family lived on the edge of the nobles' district, near Yafai Garden—the western half of the city, across the river. Although she could have shown a footcarriage-man her Hetawa moontear-token and been carried anywhere she wished, she hesitated to do this. The token was meant to be used only on Hetawa business. Did apologizing for a death that she might have caused qualify? She had no idea, but she had no desire to try justifying it to the Council. She walked.

As always, the crowds and traffic were a jarring contrast to the quiet order of the Hetawa complex. Hanani joined the flow on the thoroughfare, which immediately forced her to move at a pace that would have been unacceptable in the Hetawa except in emergencies. As she passed through a market the traffic slowed, thickening into a packed, jostling knot for no reason that she could discern other than the sheer peaceless nature of this human river: rivers inevitably had rapids. Here she was elbowed and pushed, her sandaled feet stepped on, and someone sloshed beer on her arm. When people saw her red drapes they moved aside, but in most cases they simply didn't see her. Not for the first time did Hanani wish that one of her foremothers had caught the eye of some handsome, *tall* highcasteman for a night or two.

Traffic thinned near the riverfront, thank the Dreamer, though this was largely because of the smell. The fishmongers were hard at work near the city's northernmost bridge, selling dried seaweeds and the morning's catch from their boats. Previous days' catches were here too, rotting in special sealed urns beneath the bridge. When ripe, the slurry enriched the soil for farms on the outskirts of the Blood river valley, which lay beyond the reach of the floodwaters that annually renewed Gujaareh's fertility. But though the slurry urns had been sealed with pitch and wax and hekeh-seed paste, enough of the noxious stench escaped that the very air made Hanani's eyes water. She held her breath and hurried across the bridge, pausing only when a group of stray caracals darted across her path, chasing one of their number who carried a fish head.

At last she reached the Yafai Garden district. Bahenamin's house was a tall Kisuati-style building with bluewood lintels, on a corner across from the garden itself. His lineage's pictorals had been carved into a staff set near the house's entrance. Leopard-spotted butterflies hovered over the bricks of the house's walkway, dancing on the heat haze; Hanani took care not to step on any of the lovely creatures. But to her surprise, the door opened before she could reach it, and a servant girl stepped out, a drape of deepest indigo—the mourning color—in her hands. The girl wore a short sheath dress of woven blue patterns, rather than going bare-breasted as most servants did on hot days; a family in mourning kept to formal clothes in case of callers.

Hanani waited while the servant finished wrapping the drape

around the lineage staff—then she spied Hanani and stopped as well, blinking in surprise. "Greetings, stranger. Have you business here?"

Hanani bowed, turning her hands palm-up in greeting. "I've come from the Hetawa. I wish to speak with the family of Merchant Bahenamin."

"This is his house, may he dwell in Her peace forever." The servant then stared at Hanani for a breath longer, looking her up and down with a familiar confused expression. "From the Hetawa, you said?"

"Yes," Hanani replied, waiting. The loindrapes were announcement enough, or they should have been, of her identity. As additional reassurance to those who might doubt, Hanani always took care to also wear the collar of small, polished carnelians that had been given to her upon her joining the Sharer path. Between that and the drapes, and whatever rumors ran in the city, most people knew her on sight: the lone woman permitted to pursue one of the four holy paths of Goddess-service.

It took a moment in the servant's case, but then Hanani at last saw recognition flow across her face. Only then did she add, "I'm Hanani, an apprentice of the Sharer path."

The servant finally remembered her manners and bobbed her head. "Please come inside, Sharer-Apprentice."

The house, when they entered its foyer, was far cooler and more comfortable than the late-afternoon swelter without. The foyer opened directly into the family's modest atrium, where small shrubs and plants surrounded a handsome, good-sized date palm. The tree's canopy kept the atrium in striped shade. Beneath this tree, a nest of cushions and blankets had been built. Here reclined a heavyset, graying woman in a deep indigo Kisuati wrap. Her face, Hanani saw when the servant girl went to speak to her, was lined and puffy, the whites of her eyes red from weeping. But they fixed keenly on

Hanani while the servant spoke, and after a moment the woman beckoned Hanani over.

Hanani came into the garden and bowed over both hands. "Thank you for the honor of your hospitality."

The servant girl hastened to set another cushion down. The woman nodded and said, "Please sit, Sharer-Apprentice, and be welcome. My name is Danneh. In waking I was Bahenamin's firstwife."

Hanani sat, and the servant girl withdrew on some unseen signal from Danneh.

"I've come to offer apology," Hanani said, once a peaceable amount of silence had passed. Inwardly Hanani held herself rigid, though she had already decided that she would accept whatever words the woman flung at her, endure whatever rage. "I feel I have some responsibility for your husband's death. It was my assistant who took his donation that day."

Danneh frowned. "The child who died with him?"

"Yes. He was an acolyte, contemplating the Sharer path. He had been trained, and the procedure was common, but..." She shook her head, groping for some explanation that made sense. Nothing did. "Something went wrong. The fault is mine."

But Danneh's frown deepened. "I was told it was an accident."

"My assistant was only thirteen, too young to bear a task of such importance—"

"No." Danneh shook her head. "The age of choice is twelve. Thirteen is old enough for a child to take some responsibility for his own deeds. You trusted him to do the task? You had no expectation that he would fail?"

"I..." Of all the reactions Hanani had prepared herself to endure, this was not one. "I trusted him, lady."

"Was that his first time?"

"No, lady. He'd done it before, many times. All acolytes learn to draw and give forth dream-humors, regardless of the path they ultimately choose."

Danneh sighed. "Then it was an accident. Or—" She gave Hanani a sudden shrewd look. "Has someone sent you here to make this apology?"

"N-no." That damnable stammer; it appeared whenever she was nervous. "No one sent me, but..."

"But they blame you. Of course they would." Danneh shook her head and smiled faintly. "The Hetawa's only woman. I thought you would be taller."

Hanani shifted a little on the cushion, unsure of how to respond to that statement. "I had hoped to know more of your husband," she said.

It was too sharp a verbal turn, a clumsy transition in the conversation. Danneh's smile faded at once, and Hanani silently berated herself for making such a graceless error. But then Danneh took a deep breath and nodded.

"Know more of him," she said. "Yes. That would please me. It would—"

To Hanani's alarm, the woman's eyes abruptly welled with tears. Danneh looked away and put her hand to her mouth for several breaths, fighting back a sob. Hanani reached out to touch her other hand and was even more unnerved when the woman caught hold and gripped her hand fiercely. But the contact seemed to help Danneh regain control.

"Forgive me," she said, after a few deep breaths. "I know I should go to the Hetawa, ask for peace. But it feels... *better*, somehow, to let the grief run unstanched."

"Yes," Hanani agreed, thinking of her own long nights since Dayu's death. Some of that must have made its way into her voice, because Danneh then mustered a watery smile.

"Tell me, then, what do you want to know of my Hena?"

Hanani considered. "Was Bahenamin a devout man?"

Danneh had never let go of Hanani's hand, though her grip had eased. Almost absently she petted Hanani's hand, perhaps seeking comfort in the physical because the intangible caused her such pain. "Not very. He gave his donations every month, made offerings on Hamyan Night, no more than that. Though he had gone to the Hetawa this time to pray."

"Why this time in particular?"

"Dreams." Danneh sighed and dabbed her eyes with a cloth. "He'd been having bad dreams."

Hanani's skin prickled as if a sudden cool breeze had blown through the atrium, though the fronds of the date palm were still.

"I don't understand," she said. "Every Gujaareen child learns to deal with troubling dreams."

"Hena tried, but the usual tricks didn't work. He said something was waiting for him. Stalking him, as a lioness does its prey. That was why he went to the Hetawa: he feared the gods might be angry with him for some reason."

Something was waiting for him. Movement in the dark. A lurking malevolence.

"Was he a strong dreamer?" Hanani asked. Her hand must have trembled in Danneh's, but Danneh did not seem to notice.

Danneh shook her head, smiling a little to herself in remembered fondness. "The Hetawa passed him over at four floods. They didn't even offer him lay training; he had no talent for dreaming whatsoever."

"And he had this dream only once?"

"Twice on two nights. The third night he didn't sleep; the fear kept him up. The next day I pressed him to go to the Hetawa, and finally he did." Danneh sighed. "I didn't think much of it, to be honest. I thought the Sharers would take his nightmares and give him a good night's sleep, and that would be the end of it. He'd been to a funeral a few days before—Khanwer, a shunha lord with whom he'd often had business dealings. Seeing a friend die can push any man near the shadowlands for a time..." She fell silent again, but Hanani saw the knowledge in her eyes. *He died of that dream.*

It was a truth Hanani felt too now, with instinctive certainty, though she said nothing aloud. What woman wanted to know that the small, seemingly unimportant thing she had noticed—noticed without concern—had made her a widow? What woman would not blame herself in such a case?

And more troublingly, what did it mean that Hanani had felt something waiting for her in the space between dreams that day, just as Bahenamin apparently had before his death?

"Thank you," Hanani said instead. "Perhaps that will help me and my brothers to determine how this happened." Then, greatly daring, she squeezed Danneh's hand in return. "May Hananja grant you peace in waking, until you can see him again in Ina-Karekh."

Danneh smiled before finally letting her go. "You're a good child," she said. "The Servants of Hananja chose well."

Sensing that the conversation had reached a graceful end, Hanani nodded shyly and got to her feet. "I would like to return," she ventured. "To hear more of Bahenamin. And if you prefer not to go to the Hetawa for your grief, then perhaps when next I receive a tithe from a Gatherer, I could return."

"I would like that too," Danneh said, "but not for the dreamblood."

The woman's smile warmed Hanani into a smile of her own, as Hanani bowed one last time in farewell. "Then I shall definitely return," she said. "In peace, Merchant Danneh."

"In peace, child."

Outside, Hanani descended the steps slowly, her thoughts churning like a floodseason sky. Because of this, she did not see the servant girl offer a full bow of respect to her back before closing the house door.

6

(⊙)

Occupation

So lost in memory was Wanahomen as he walked the heart of Hananja's City—again, at last, this time without the obscuration of Banbarra clothing if not as his true self—that he missed the Kisuati soldiers until it was almost too late. He had been ensnared by Yafai Garden's perfume, which was heavy with moontears and jasmine and reminded him of past evenings in Yanya-iyan playing dicing games with his father and Charris. By the time he glanced up to see two soldiers begin beating a Gujaareen man to death, he was almost on top of them.

Their victim was a fruit seller, who had spread a blanket near the garden gate and laid out small piles of figs and edaki melons and thick green dyar-a-whe to entice passers-by. The city's Law decreed that merchants could sell their wares only in designated market areas: that kept things orderly. But on days like this, when the street's bricks were hot enough to bake bread and a bite of cool refreshing fruit would be welcome to anyone, most city guardsmen would have looked the other way.

The Kisuati soldiers had not. The merchant groveled before them, his voice a high plea. "—A week's labor!" was all Wanahomen heard him say, as one of the men shoved him again with a foot. "My family will have no money—" And then his protest turned to a gasp as one of the soldiers stepped on the pile of figs.

"A week's labor? This?" The soldier spoke with a thick plainsland Kisuati accent. "I am a farm man. My week's labor would fill this garden! Ah, only in Gujaareh could lazy folk grow so rich." He glanced at his companion and grinned. "Shall we teach this *tingam* the value of hard work?" He stepped on another piece of fruit, which squelched ripely; his companion laughed.

A proper Gujaareen man would have gone stoic at that point, and endured whatever abuse the soldiers heaped on him in silence. It was the only sensible, peaceful thing to do; the soldiers were bored, and it was painfully obvious that resistance would only incite them to uglier behavior. But it seemed the merchant truly was concerned for his family's finances—or perhaps he simply wasn't feeling peaceful. Before the soldier could step on the edaki, the merchant moved to cover that pile with his body.

What followed was utterly predictable, yet still jarring to see— even for Wanahomen, who had witnessed far worse in the years since he'd left Gujaareh. The soldiers began to kick the man in earnest, first stomping on his back and shoulders in lieu of the fruit and then kicking him in the ribs and side when he did not move.

Wanahomen stopped on the corner opposite the ugly tableau. There were a few other folk on the street; Wanahomen could see them pointing and murmuring to one another. One of them might eventually muster the courage to intervene...or perhaps they would simply stand by and watch as the poor fool was kicked to death. Either way, Wanahomen dared not get involved himself. He had entered the city wearing a disguise: a clean but plain loinskirt and headcloth, worn sandals, and a cheap bronze collar. A common laborer's attire. Under the loinskirt was one of his Banbarra knives, however, strapped to his upper thigh, and there were Banbarra jewelry-pieces in his purse. If he confronted the soldiers they might arrest him, and almost surely find the knife and jewels. That would lead to dangerous questions.

Though it galled Wanahomen to turn away, however pragmatic a choice it might be—

"What are you *doing*?" demanded a voice, and Wanahomen's head whipped around in pure incredulous reflex.

A woman stood before the soldiers. The soldiers had stopped kicking the merchant to stare at her. Wanahomen could not help staring himself. The woman—girl, really, only a few years past the age of adulthood—wore men's clothing, from noticeably hemmed loindrapes to a collar that must have been made for broader shoulders than hers. Beneath the collar, her breasts had been bound tightly in white wrappings, like those used for bodies awaiting cremation. This did nothing to hide their fullness, but the whole getup looked too strange to be erotic. Her pouf of brown-gold hair had been pulled back in a severe northerners' knot that did nothing to adorn her face, and she wore no makeup, not even kohl to ease the sun's glare.

But it was the carnelian of her collar, and the deep, bloodlike red of her loindrapes, that puzzled Wanahomen the most. She looked like a Sharer of Hananja, but women did not become Sharers, or any other kind of Servant.

"Why are you hurting that man?" she asked, and now Wanahomen could hear the shock in her tone. She stood at the garden path's entrance; perhaps she had come through the garden, unable to see the beating through the fronds and flowers until she emerged right on top of it. "What kind of— How could you—" She trailed off, apparently too horrified to finish any thought.

The soldiers looked at each other.

Leave, Wanahomen thought at the woman. In spite of himself he had slowed his pace; at his sides his hands clenched. *Just turn away, and pray they don't follow.*

"Sharer—" This from the merchant, who coughed as he looked up; his breathing was labored, and blood spotted his face. "Sharer, you mustn't— Never mind these gentlemen. Yes?" He looked up at the soldiers, mustering a fawning smile. "They were just correcting me; I broke the Law. You should go on back to the Hetawa, it's all right."

"*This* is not within the Law," said the woman, and Wanahomen wondered if she was sun-addled or just a fool. The Kisuati claimed to respect Hananja's Law, but Wanahomen had made other clandestine trips into the city over the years, talked to traders and mercenaries who'd told him how things really were. Other beatings. Extortion. Disappearances. Nothing too blatant—they were not *openly* hypocrites—but enough that wise folk knew better than to cross the city's occupiers.

Perhaps that was why, though he'd meant to move on, Wanahomen found himself stopping.

"You should listen to this fellow," said the more talkative of the Kisuati soldiers, putting his foot on the merchant's back again. The merchant cringed, but the soldier did nothing worse for the moment. "We keep order, yes? Keep the peace. You like peace? Go away, and give thanks to Hananja that such good men are keeping your city safe." He grinned.

"I . . ." Some realization of the danger seemed to have penetrated the woman's shock at last. She swallowed and darted a look around. If she sought help, Wanahomen noted, none was forthcoming; none of the onlookers met her eyes. No—as Wanahomen glanced at the other watchers, one woman bent to her young son and whispered in his ear. The boy darted off down a side street, probably going to fetch help of some kind. It could not possibly arrive in time.

"I c-cannot go," the woman said. She swallowed and lifted her chin, though her stammering and trembling negated any courage that she meant to display. "I am a Servant . . . Let, let this merchant come with me. Keep his wares, his money if you wish, but let him go."

A look of annoyance crossed the face of the talkative soldier. Scowling, he raised a fist and stepped toward the woman—

—The woman tensed, bracing herself to take the blow—

—Wanahomen pivoted toward them and was halfway across the street before he even realized he had begun walking—

—People on the other side of the street shouted; the merchant cried out, "No!" and—

—The quieter soldier glanced around. Seeing that the watching crowd had grown to twenty or so, he reached out and caught the other man's arm. Wanahomen was near enough that he heard the soldier murmur in Sua: "*Wait. Too many people around. The general might hear.*"

That stopped the other soldier. He glared down at the girl, but after another breath's hesitation lowered his hand. Instead he leaned forward and whispered something in the girl's ear.

She stiffened, staring at him in fresh horror. The soldier grinned and stepped back, then with a final scathing glance at the merchant turned—and spotted Wanahomen. Wanahomen stood in the middle of the street, only a pace or two away. He had stopped when the soldier aborted his blow, but he was far too close to pretend he had been merely passing by. He froze, uncertain whether to fight or flee.

"*Nkua ke-a-te ananki, ebaa tingam?*" asked the other soldier, who apparently spoke only Sua. *What would you have done, sleeping sheep? Baa at us?*

Though Wanahomen knew common Sua well enough to understand the words, the contempt in the soldier's tone was plain enough to set his temper ablaze all on its own. He held himself rigid, however—or tried to. Too many years among the Banbarra. The urge to draw his knife and repay the soldier's insult with blood was so strong that his hands shook with it.

The talkative soldier snorted. "Look: he quakes where he stands!" He shook his head and clapped his comrade on the shoulder. "Come. Our shift is almost over. At least we've made the time pass quicker."

He walked away past Wanahomen, deliberately bumping Wanahomen's shoulder with his own. The soldier wore bronze epaulets and Wanahomen's shoulder was bare; the blow hurt like nightmares. That did not trouble Wanahomen half so much as the Sua-speaking soldier, who planted a hand on Wanahomen's chest to shove him in passing. Wanahomen stumbled back, though he managed to keep his feet with an effort.

The soldiers walked on, laughing between themselves. Before Wanahomen, the red-draped girl exhaled in relief, then crouched beside the merchant. Others came forward as well, so solicitous, so helpful, now that the danger was past. For an instant Wanahomen curled his lip in the same contempt that the soldiers must have felt—but his was compounded by shame that his people could be so weak.

But he had no right to get angry at them, he reminded himself. They had no weapons, no training for battle. They had spent their lives in the service of peace, and most had never even witnessed violence before the Kisuati's arrival. It had been the duty of the army and the Guard and the Hetawa to protect them—and the duty of Gujaareh's Prince as well. It was not their fault if they were helpless now.

Which only added to Wanahomen's bitterness as he turned away.

"Wait."

Frowning, Wanahomen turned. The red-draped girl. She stepped around the merchant to come to him. Up close, he saw that despite the masculine dress she was pretty, in a lowcaste sort of way: small but sturdy-built, her face broad and high-boned, with skin the ocher of ripe pears.

"You tried to help me," she said. "It wasn't the peaceful thing to do, I suppose, but... I thank you, nevertheless." She bowed over one hand; the other was already stained with the merchant's blood. "If you wait a moment, I can heal your arm. This man needs my help first, but it won't take long."

Wanahomen stared at her; it took him a breath or two to reconcile her words with her obvious femininity. "You really are a Sharer?"

She blinked and then ducked her eyes. "Sharer-Apprentice. Yes. My name is Hanani."

This was too much. The Kisuati had already inflicted their violent ways on his land, and now they were infecting the women of Gujaareh with their mad notions of a woman's proper place. Times had grown dire indeed if even the Hetawa had been forced to compromise its ancient traditions.

But if things are so dire in Gujaareh, who is to blame for that? whispered Wanahomen's heart, again.

He scowled, and if he spoke more sharply than he should have, it was because guilt and anger made uneasy allies.

"You're a fool," he said. The woman flinched back from the coldness in his voice, looking hurt; Wanahomen did not care. "If you truly are of the Hetawa, run back to it and never step outside its doors again. Servants of Hananja should be stronger than you."

He turned away, ignoring the mutter of his conscience and the feel of her gaze against his back, and walked off.

*　　*　　*

By the time Wanahomen entered the nobles' district, some of his temper had cooled. He reached his destination just as the sun began to set, painting the walls of the city in rich strokes of red-gold and amber. Before him stood a sprawling house, two floors high and the whole block wide. In style it was mostly Gujaareen, with walls of baked white clay and pathways paved with round river stones, but there were foreign touches here and there: a roofed side-area where the family greeted guests, lintels of dark southern wood. Kisuati touches, for this was a shunha house, and the shunha never forgot their origins.

A man of perhaps fifty floods sat fanning himself at a table under the guest-area roof, a flask and two cups waiting before him. After a moment's silent observation from the corner—making certain there were no soldiers or other undesirables watching—Wanahomen came to the house and stopped at the edge of the sitting area. He bowed over one hand, which was more than the man's rank merited relative to his, less than the common laborer he appeared to be should have offered. In formal Sua he said, "My greetings, sir."

"Welcome, stranger," said the man with equal formality, looking him up and down—and then his eyes narrowed. "Or perhaps not a stranger. Well, well. I was expecting your spokesman."

Wanahomen inclined his head. "My spokesman informed me you could be trusted, Lord Sanfi. I decided to come myself, given that."

"A great risk."

"Agreements between men are best made face-to-face. So my father taught me, in waking."

Lord Sanfi nodded, then gestured toward the table's other seat. "Then sit, stranger-who-is-not," he said, "and share welcome with me. Your throat must be dry after your long journey."

Wanahomen sat while Sanfi poured something into each of the two cups. "Forgive me," Sanfi said, shifting back to Gujaareen now that they were past the introductions. "I brought no servants from my greenlands estate, so you must make do with my poor efforts."

"I've been long among barbarians," Wanahomen replied. "Your courtesy alone is enough for me. And if they knew how I have been living, your servants would doubtless turn up their noses and declare me too corrupt to be worthy of their care."

"Corrupt acts, in moderation, are a necessity of power," Sanfi replied, pushing a cup toward him. "Even the Hetawa recognizes that, or did in the days before the taint invaded their own ranks. I'm no priest, but it seems to me your purpose is pure."

It was uncomfortable, engaging in such talk while sitting out in the open. The street in front of Sanfi's house was not busy, but neither was it deserted: passersby and neighbors appeared now and again, some of them nodding to Sanfi as they went about their business. But no respectable shunha would invite a stranger into his home without first sharing refreshment with him outside. To break tradition would invite suspicion.

"It pleases me to hear that," Wanahomen said. Then, as was traditional, he lifted the cup and took a sip. Beer, bitter-tart and as thick as honey, slid over his tongue. He closed his eyes and sighed in pleasure.

Sanfi chuckled. "You *have* been long without, to make that sound."

"Too long. My companions of these days scorn the small niceties that we of Gujaareh appreciate so much. We're soft in their eyes, and to win their respect I must scorn softness as well."

"The mark of a good leader."

"A necessity of survival, nothing more." Wanahomen took another sip of beer, savoring the fruity warmth of it. "My mother conveys her greetings."

"Ah—then she is well?"

"Well enough." Wanahomen gazed into his cup. It was not the shunha way to acknowledge sickness. Sanfi would hear the solemnity in Wanahomen's voice, and understand. "She misses my father."

Sanfi nodded. "As do we all. But I see his strength and wit in you, my young friend"—he did not say Wanahomen's name, mindful of passing ears—"and that should give your mother great comfort."

"I hope so. Is your own family well, and your estate in the greenlands?"

"Well enough." Wanahomen frowned and glanced up at the man, but Sanfi was gazing at a fig tree nearby. "My estate thrives: the date palms are fruiting, and our third harvest is already done. My daughter is here. You'll be able to meet her shortly."

So something was wrong with Sanfi's wife. Odd that he'd brought his daughter with him, though; Wanahomen would have expected a good shunha daughter to stay home and care for her mother. Unless there was more than one daughter? But no, he'd heard Sanfi had only the one child.

Best not to pry. "Trade is good, I hope?"

"Tolerable, given the circumstances. The Kisuati favor us shunha in their dealings. Things do not go as well for our fellow nobles of the zhinha, but that can't be helped. The Kisuati scorn them almost as much as they do northerners."

"Indeed." Wanahomen set down his cup, tracing a finger along its delicate edge. The cup was deceptively simple, lacking in any sort of design or tint other than its natural red coloring, but the fired clay was thin and the cup's shape had an elegant flare. The potter had been a superb craftsman, and Sanfi must have paid a great deal for a set that would make him seem at once humble and tasteful. "One might wonder, given such favor, why a shunha lord would then have any desire to meet with me."

Sanfi threw him an amused look, though he lowered his voice and leaned closer to speak. "Kisua aims to make itself, rather than Gujaareh, the crossroads for world trade. We now have unrestricted access to southern marketplaces and merchants, oh yes, a great boon. But the Protectors set higher taxes on goods from the north and east—especially if they come through our ports rather than those of Kisua. They restrict quantity and set higher demands for quality, which increases the cost to prohibitive levels. Some goods they forbid outright, on the spurious grounds that our land is already too corrupted by barbarian influences...but in reality, nearly all

Gujaareh's trade has been curtailed. So under Kisuati rule, I have more headaches and less money, and I'm tired of it." He shrugged and poured more beer for Wanahomen. "Forgive me if I seem purely self-serving."

Wanahomen shook his head, adopting the same low tone. "Self-interest too has its place in any peaceful society. But how many of the shunha feel as you?"

Sanfi snorted. "Any with brains and eyes. Think: the zhinha are already impoverished. The shunha, in truth, are not far behind. The merchants are getting into smuggling and other forms of illicit trade; half the military caste has turned mercenary, trading their flesh for money in the east. How long before all those families begin firing retainers and turning out servants? How long before even the Hetawa is too poor to feed those in need? Then we will see children starving on our streets, murder in our alleyways, despair on every corner...just like Kisua itself." Sanfi took a deep draught of his own cup, setting it down with a sigh. "No, Kisuati rule is not good for any of us."

Wanahomen thought of the Kisuati soldiers, and the woman in Sharer garb. "No," he agreed softly. "It is not."

Sanfi threw Wanahomen a half-smile then, and put a stopper in the flask. "Come inside now, where we may talk away from this damnable heat."

Wanahomen rose, taking the cups so that Sanfi could carry the flask. The house seemed dim inside after the fading sunlight without, especially once Sanfi closed the heavy wooden door behind them. Wanahomen's eyes adjusted as Sanfi led the way into the home's elegant greeting room, where ceiling apertures had been cranked open to allow in fresh air and more light.

And here Wanahomen stopped, as the light illuminated the most beautiful woman he had ever seen.

"My daughter, Tiaanet," Sanfi said. And though Wanahomen

could feel Sanfi's eyes drinking in his reaction, he could not help but stare. She gazed at him boldly, as was proper for a woman of her caste, but there was something intriguingly reserved about her manner. When she crossed the room to them, he could not look away, entranced by the sway of her body beneath the thick brocade Kisuati gown.

"I greet you, Prince of the Sunset, Avatar of our Goddess," she said. Her voice was low and rich like dark sweet wine, tightening everything from his throat to his belly and below as well. But then she knelt before him, startling him out of the spell. Gujaareen women did not kneel. They were goddesses; it was wrong. Wanahomen opened his mouth to protest but then stopped as Tiaanet raised her arms, crossing them before her face with her fists closed and turned outward. A manuflection, the highest display of respect that one could offer to mortals favored by the gods. The last time Wanahomen had seen a manuflection performed had been at Yanya-iyan a lifetime ago, as he watched supplicants approach his father.

But I am Prince now, not my father. And when was it appropriate for a goddess to kneel? Only when a higher god stood before her.

Sanfi put a hand on Wanahomen's shoulder, and he flinched out of staring at the woman. "Ten families of the shunha, and eighteen of the zhinha, have agreed to support our cause," he said. "For the Prince's son—for *you*, my Prince, they will commit their troops and resources. Between them and your Banbarra allies, the total will be small compared to the Kisuati army...but a small force can be effective under the right circumstances. The Sunset Throne could be yours again."

Then you could have a woman like this. The words were not spoken, but hung in the air between them, an implicit promise. And as Wanahomen gazed down at Tiaanet's bent head, he heard again her dark-wine voice naming him Prince, and saw himself seated on the oxbow throne with the Aureole of the Setting Sun behind his head. Tiaanet would sit beside him as his firstwife, and their children would cover the steps below, living ornaments to his glory and her perfection. It was the sweetest vision he'd ever experienced outside Ina-Karekh.

"There is an old, old tradition in guest-custom, my Prince," Sanfi said, his voice soft at Wanahomen's shoulder. "It has long fallen into disuse even in Kisua, but it seems fitting to revive it now. Once, long ago, a pact between men was sealed by more than hands."

Tiaanet lifted her eyes, gazing into what Wanahomen feared was his soul. She reached for his hand and took it—the softness of her skin was almost a painful shock—and got to her feet.

"We can discuss the details later," Sanfi said. He released Wanahomen's shoulder as Tiaanet stepped back, pulling Wanahomen with her. "In the morning. Rest well, my Prince."

What—? Wanahomen mustered enough wit to throw a look back at Sanfi, certain he had misunderstood. But Sanfi was smiling, and now Tiaanet's hand was on his cheek, pulling his face back to her. When she saw that his attention was once again hers, she nodded and resumed backing away, leading him along.

They reached her room and shut the hanging, and in her arms Wanahomen was Prince again, if only for a single night.

7

(⊙)

The Shadow

Hanani was still trembling when she reached the Hetawa. The sun had set by that time, for she had detoured through two markets rather than take the faster route through the artisans' district. Most artisans worked nights when it was cooler, which made the district relatively quiet—they would be just waking—but Kisuati soldiers would be on patrol there nevertheless: they were everywhere in the city. She was safer on the market streets, where there were more people around as the stalls began to shut down for the night.

She was glad that Anarim was no longer on duty as she trotted up the Hetawa's steps. His replacement barely gave her a glance. Had Anarim known that Kisuati soldiers were openly assaulting people in the city? No, if so he would have commanded, not suggested, the escort. She had heard rumors—they all had—but she'd thought that the Kisuati were at least trying to maintain a discreet semblance of respect for the Law and Wisdom that governed Gujaareen society. If the Sentinels did not know things had changed, then perhaps the Gatherers did not know either.

It was her duty to tell them.

She stopped in the shadow of one of the Hall's pillars, putting her hand to her breast as if that might slow her racing heart. She did not want to tell the Gatherers. Her reluctance was irrational, irresponsible—but just thinking of those moments brought back the sound of blows striking the merchant's flesh, the cruel eyes of the soldiers, the sour taste of her own fear. It had been her duty to intervene. Yet she understood, now, that if there had been fewer people on the street, the soldiers would have beaten her as well—or done worse. What should she have done, what could she have said, to stop them? Even now she could think of nothing, and somehow that was the worst of it. She was sworn to uphold the Law, yet she could think of no peaceful resolution to such an impasse. A Sharer should have known a way.

Perhaps Teacher Yehamwy is right about me. Perhaps that man was right—I'm not strong enough to serve Her.

But that thought filled her with anguish and shame, and such feelings were inappropriate in the sight of the Goddess. So with a deep breath she straightened, intending to return to her cell where she might pray and regain peace—

"Sister?" An acolyte came 'round the pillar and squinted at her in the dimness, then caught his breath as he got a good look. "Oh—forgive me, Sharer-Apprentice. I thought... well." He shifted from foot to foot in embarrassment. "They were looking for you earlier."

Hanani blinked in surprise. "They?"

"The Superior and his guests. He sent some of us around to find you, but no one knew where you'd gone."

Hanani's belly tightened in a new kind of unease. "How long ago?"

"Just after sunset, not long." The boy squinted harder at her face. "Are you all right?"

Hanani realized that she had wrapped her arms around herself, as if cold. She unfolded her arms and straightened. "Yes. Yes. I'll go now."

She hurried away, from the boy's curiosity as much as anything else.

The Superior's office was on the fourth level of the administrative wing that abutted the Hall of Blessings. She reached the office winded from the stairs and had only a moment to compose herself before one of the voices murmuring within came closer, and the heavy curtain opened. "Ah, here she is."

The Superior stood before her, smiling. He stepped aside and gestured for her to enter the office, which she did with some trepidation as she saw who else was present: two figures in cloaks and veils dyed a soft yellow, and a man in a sleeveless hooded robe. The first two were Sisters of Hananja, though because of the veils Hanani could distinguish little about them save that one was very tall. The hooded man Hanani recognized less by his face than by the blue lotus tattoo on his nearer shoulder: Nijiri, third-ranked of the Gatherers. Because they were in the Superior's private office, Nijiri lowered his hood as Hanani came in, revealing close-cropped hair and a face that was both lowcaste-pale and beautiful in a fey, untouchable sort of way. He stood against the wall with his arms folded, his expression closed.

"Please sit down, Sharer-Apprentice," the Superior said, gesturing toward the guest table. Hanani swallowed and took the open cushion, where she tried very hard to concentrate on the barley-sheaf inlays along the table's edge. Why had the Superior called her here? Why were a Gatherer and two Sisters present? She dared not speculate.

The Superior folded himself down on another cushion with a grunt. "Well. Hanani, these are Sisters Ni-imeh and Ahmanat; I believe you know Gatherer Nijiri."

Hanani swallowed and bobbed her head at the Sisters, giving the Gatherer a more careful bow over two hands. Nijiri returned the bow solemnly, as did Ni-imeh, but Ahmanat reached over and took

Hanani by the chin. This startled Hanani so much that she froze as the Sister turned her face gently from one side to the other.

"Pretty," the Sister said in a surprisingly deep voice. This then was one of the rare male Sisters; Hanani had never seen one in person. She could make out nothing of his face behind the veil, but she thought he smiled at her. "Though Sharer attire does not suit you at all. Farmcaste, were you? So was I, though you'd never guess it now."

Before Hanani could gather some response, the Superior tsked. "We in the Hetawa don't speak of the past, Sister Ahmanat."

"We of the Sisterhood do, Superior," Ni-imeh said. Her voice was female, with an elderly quaver, as cool as her companion's was friendly. She turned to examine Hanani as well. "But we shall preach the merits of our perspective at some other time. I must admit, I'm surprised to see how well she's done. I had expected her to be sent to us long ago."

Hanani resisted the urge to flinch at this. She turned her gaze back to the table edge, as it was clear the Sister was not speaking to her.

"Yes, doing well, apart from the recent unfortunate incident," the Superior said, "and even that is an indirect blemish on an otherwise spotless record. The consensus among her Sharer brethren is that she's a fine healer—and that is indeed a difficult admission for some of them." He chuckled.

"She's implicated, then." Ni-imeh seemed unsurprised by this. "To what degree?"

"That, the investigation will determine," the Superior replied. He reached for the water service and began pouring cups for everyone, serving the elder Sister first. "From the bodies, the Sharers ascertained that both the tithebearer and the acolyte died in a state of severe humoric imbalance, specifically an overabundance of dreambile. This is a symptom, of course; we do not know what in dreaming might have caused such an imbalance. But the physical result is that healthy function of the heart and brain ceased entirely." He sighed. "And there are certain other anomalies that still must be considered."

"Anomalies consistent with the reports we've given you?" There was a sharp note in Ahmanat's voice, much to Hanani's surprise. She had no idea of his rank within the Sisterhood, but surely if he had taken a woman's role it was inappropriate for him to address the Superior in such a tone. Women were supposed to create peace, not disturb it.

"Who can say?" The Superior offered a cup to the Gatherer, who quietly shook his head, as did Ahmanat. He set the cup in front of Hanani instead, not asking first. "You've brought us very little from which to draw conclusions. The people of Gujaareh have been under great strain for the past few years, and now with these desert bandit attacks..." He shrugged. "I would be surprised if there weren't a few more nightmares in the city these days."

"There is more to this than a few nightmares," Ahmanat said sternly. "There have been *deaths*, Superior."

"Deaths that even you admit have no clear connection to the dreams."

Hanani caught her breath as understanding dawned. There had been others like Bahenamin? But that meant—

"Sharer-Apprentice Hanani." Hanani looked up in reflex, and quailed inwardly as she met the Gatherer Nijiri's gaze. They were a strange color, his eyes: something of green, but mostly a pale brown that seemed reddish in the light from the office lanterns. The color reminded her of bricks, sharp-edged and unyielding.

"You look as though you have something to contribute," the Gatherer said.

The others had fallen silent when he spoke; now they all focused on Hanani. Hanani swallowed.

"Th-the tithebearer," she said. That damnable stammer! She

took a deep breath and tried again, praying silently for calm. "Bahenamin, of the merchant caste. I visited his widow today. She said—" Her mouth was dry; she swallowed again. "She said that her husband s-suffered from bad dreams as well. He came that day to give them to the Goddess in tithe."

And Dayu, sweet Dayu, had tried to collect that tithe. Her eyes stung again, but the Goddess must have heard her prayers. She clenched her fists beneath the table and the feeling passed.

The Sisters looked at each other. "Like the others," the Superior said. For the first time since the conversation had begun, he seemed nonplussed.

Gatherer Nijiri abruptly stepped forward, coming around the table and crouching at Hanani's side. Hanani resisted the urge to draw back from his bricks-and-jade gaze.

He lifted a hand before her face, forefinger and middle finger curved gracefully apart. His other hand slipped into his robe, and from somewhere within it they all heard the soft hum of his jungissa stone. "May I, Apprentice?"

Hanani nodded, too intimidated to question a Gatherer even though she had no clue of what he wanted. Almost before her nod had finished, his hand flashed forward, and she had only an instant to wonder if he frightened tithebearers this much before a great wave of drowsiness swept over her.

There was no gentleness to his magic. He found her soul right away and, in a fraction of the time that it ordinarily took Hanani to do the same, had her out of her body and in Ina-Karekh. Then he steered her through Ina-Karekh with such strength and speed that it blurred around her—before resolving into a city street bathed in golden afternoon sunlight. Butterflies danced in air laden with a garden's perfume.

A memory dream. In spite of herself Hanani observed in fascination as another Hanani, herself but not her self, appeared on the street. She shimmered and reappeared in front of a tall northern-style house. The servant appeared, they both vanished through the door, and then the dreamscape blurred into the atrium where the widow Danneh sat waiting beneath a palm tree.

But there was something wrong. In spite of the Gatherer's control, elements of the dream had begun to slip out of true. Danneh's ample body was curiously doubled, her possible-self overlapping and blurring with another form, like a shadow, though this shadow seemed somehow a part of her rather than a separate thing.

Abruptly the Gatherer's dreamform appeared beside Danneh. Here in Ina-Karekh where he was free to reveal his true self, Nijiri was clad in simple patterned loindrapes with no sandals or collar. Two thin locks, years in the growing, dangled from the nape of his neck over one shoulder; he swept these out of the way as he crouched to examine the shadow.

Freed for the moment from the Gatherer's control, Hanani cautiously manifested herself in the atrium as well. "What is it, Gatherer?"

"I have no idea," he said. "But it has a feel I don't like." He rose and gazed down at the memory, listening while Danneh told not-Hanani of her husband's dreams. When he spoke again, his tone was grave. "The taint of whatever killed Bahenamin is on this woman. You realize that it killed your assistant as well?"

Hanani nodded, forcing herself not to feel the grief; too dangerous in Ina-Karekh, where pain had shape and power. "Is it—" She hesitated out of respect, for she had heard the tales of his apprenticeship trial, but the question had to be asked. "Is it a Reaper?"

To Hanani's great relief, the Gatherer shook his head at once. "Thank the Goddess, no. This taint is subtle, and those monsters are anything but." He fell silent for a moment in thought while the dream blurred on around them. Now not-Hanani was leaving Danneh's house, and now self-Hanani's heart constricted as she realized what was coming. Already the not-Hanani was turning toward Yafai Garden, intending to cut through it as a faster route back to the Hetawa. And on the other side of the garden...

Away, she willed herself silently, hoping that the Gatherer was distracted enough not to notice her tampering. The not-Hanani would detour around the garden and miss the merchant's beating. Then the soldiers would not see her, and the angry young man in laborer's clothes would pass her by without a second glance—

The dream began to shift in response to her suggestion. And then it froze, a swirl of afternoon light and indistinct buildings. The Gatherer turned to look at her. "What are you doing?" His voice was very soft.

Caught, Hanani fell into helpless silence. She dared not lie; he was a Gatherer. And yet, the truth—

His eyes narrowed for a moment, and then he focused on the dream again. This time Hanani could do nothing. His will was as stony as his eyes, and when he commanded her mind to remember that afternoon, she was helpless.

Almost as helpless as when the soldier had raised his hand to strike her.

She shuddered and folded her arms over her breasts while the memory resumed. The Gatherer said nothing as the not-Hanani confronted the soldiers, though Hanani felt him grow very still beside her. Some of the stillness passed as the soldiers turned to leave, but when Hanani risked a glance at Nijiri, she almost gasped. She had never seen such open fury on a Gatherer's face.

Yet when he turned to her the fury vanished. "Forgive me," he said. His voice was just as soft as before, though more comforting now. "That was difficult for you, I see, and I have not helped you by forcing you to recall it. But you should not have hidden this."

"I'm sorry. It's only"—she had to swallow—"th-they did me no lasting harm."

"That's a lie, Apprentice. But hopefully one day the Goddess will make it true for you." He turned back to the dreamscape, which had frozen again, and walked over to the soldiers. After a long look at each man—committing their faces to memory, Hanani realized with a chill—the Gatherer nodded to himself. "What did he say to you?"

"I'm sorry, Gatherer?"

"The soldier. He whispered something in your ear before he left."

Hanani shivered. She had hoped he would not ask that. "H-he said that I was not as pretty as those other Hetawa women. If I was, he would have taken me back to the guard-station and..." He had spoken in a mixture of Gujaareen and Sua, of which Hanani had learned only enough to carry on simple conversations. She had not been able to translate the soldier's last words, but then, she hadn't needed to.

Nijiri frowned. "Other Hetawa women?" Abruptly he scowled. "I see. The Sisters. They should have told us— Ah, but they're proud." He sighed heavily. "If it helps, Apprentice, you should know that those soldiers will never harm you or any other Gujaareen again."

Hanani found that the idea gave her no comfort at all.

The Gatherer turned—and then paused, peering at the face of the young laborer who had come forward to help her. His eyes widened. "Well, well. So *he* is the one."

Hanani frowned. "Do you know him, Gatherer?"

"Yes, though I haven't seen him for ten years. I assumed he'd fled into a pampered exile somewhere in the north." He fell silent, studying the laborer's face; his mouth twitched in a wry quirk. "But I should've guessed better. He's his father's son—and his uncle's nephew."

Hanani came over to peer at the man herself, curious. Now that she had the chance to examine him closely, it was easy to see that he was no laborer. He was tall and lean, with the classic narrow eyes and angular features of a highcaste, and coloring only a shade shy of shunha-black. Handsome, if it had not been for the tight-jawed scowl on his face. "Who is he?"

"No one of importance. Though he did risk himself trying to help you..." Nijiri folded his arms, thoughtful. "Perhaps his lineage is worth salvaging after all."

"Gatherer, I don't understand."

"I know." To Hanani's shock, he threw her a wry, apologetic look. The expression, so startling after all his enigmatic solemnity, forced her perception of him to shift; abruptly she realized Nijiri had seen only a handful more floods than herself.

"You broke the interdiction," he said, sobering. "That merchant: you healed him."

Hanani caught her breath in realization. The interdiction had been the last thing on her mind in the wake of the soldiers, with the injured merchant groaning on the ground before her. Yet Nijiri was on the Council of Paths—neither of the senior Gatherers had the patience for it, rumor held—and so he would be well within his rights to judge her corrupt for violating Yehamwy's interdiction. "Y-yes. But after such a beating, he could have had bleeding in the vitals, broken bones—" Belatedly it occurred to her that she was making excuses; she sighed and looked away. "Yes, I broke the interdiction."

"You could have come to the Hetawa to fetch one of your path-brothers, and brought him back to do the healing. That did not occur to you?"

It should have. "...No."

"Of course not." He didn't seem displeased, to Hanani's great relief. Indeed, there was a warm, approving look in his eyes that Hanani had never expected to see. "That merchant was in pain, and terrified. If he'd died in that state while you went to fetch help, his soul would've been damned to the shadowlands for all eternity.

You did what was right, with no thought of propriety or punishment—as a Servant of Hananja should." He folded his arms and thought in silence for a long moment. Finally, coming to some decision, he nodded to himself and said, "Would you like to redeem yourself, Apprentice?"

Hanani frowned. "Pardon, Gatherer?"

Nijiri made a gesture and the city street melted away. A dreamscape of rolling dunes appeared in its place, spreading infinitely beneath a cloudless cobalt sky. She thought he intended it to calm her, but she had never been in the desert before. She found the dreamscape unnerving, and somehow lonely.

"You need a new apprenticeship trial," he said. "Though it's now obvious you had nothing to do with the deaths of Acolyte Dayuhotem or Merchant Bahenamin, there are those in the Hetawa who will never accept your innocence. They blame you because they fear you."

"Fear—" Hanani stared at him. "*Me?*"

"And the changes you represent for the future, yes." This made no more sense to her, but then, he was a Gatherer. They spoke in the language of dreams. "The only way to silence those voices is to undergo another trial—a trial so indisputably challenging that none of your detractors would ever willingly face it themselves. But if you succeed, no one will ever again question your right to wield magic in the Goddess's name."

He fell silent, watching her, and unbidden all the whispers she'd heard about him rose into Hanani's mind. They said Nijiri had defeated a Reaper; that he had helped bring to justice Gujaareh's last, mad Prince; that he had brokered the peaceful conquest of Gujaareh so that a minimum of lives were lost. And there were other rumors, less complimentary but more poignant. That he had been apprentice—and more—to the legendary Gatherer Ehiru; that he had Gathered Ehiru himself when the time came.

How does it feel to kill your lover? she wondered, staring at him across the desert his soul had conjured.

His eyes softened abruptly. "No one asked me," he said, as though he'd heard her thoughts. He might have; such things were possible in dreaming. "I faced my own trial with no choice but to succeed or fail, with my brother's soul in the balance. But you have a choice, Sharer-Apprentice Hanani. Will you accept the trial I have in mind?"

She swallowed. "What is the trial?"

"Free Gujaareh."

She stared at him. He smiled.

"A plan is in place. My brothers and I had thought to use your mentor. He has the flexibility we need, but frankly, I was worried about that temper of his. Now, though...I think you would do better for the role we have in mind."

"Wh—" She could not think. "What role?"

"That I can't tell you—not yet, or you might play it badly. Suffice it to say, it requires leaving the city, and some danger. Then again, if this plan fails, our entire way of life is doomed. We must act now, or lose everything." He sighed, gazing out over the rolling dunes. "You've proven yourself a healer, Hanani; this is not in question. But do you truly serve Her Law with all your flesh and soul? Will you risk yourself for peace, in waking as well as dreams? That is the test."

A low, soughing wind blew over the dunes, spinning dust devils in response to the turmoil in Hanani's mind. Had this been a healing dream she would have forced herself to calm, but with the dream securely in the Gatherer's control, she was free to feel all the terror she wished. It was not a boon.

And yet she could not deny the truth in his words. She might find enough supporters in the Hetawa to have her trial declared successful, but rumors would always dog her. The healer who had killed. The woman, whose magic could not be trusted. For a moment her fear vanished beneath resentment: it was not fair that she had to face this. No man would have to face this.

But if the world were fair, she would still be a half-literate farm girl with no future beyond crops and keeping house.

So she looked up at him and swallowed. "I will face this new trial, Gatherer."

He smiled, and for a fleeting moment she saw why Gatherer Ehiru had loved him. "Then come," he said, and returned them to the waking realm.

* * *

But two days passed uneventfully, during which Hanani wondered if her second trial would ever begin. Then one late evening, after another day of pointless routine, a Sentinel appeared at the door of her cell to hand her a small scroll tied with a complex sealing-knot of fine indigo cord. Hanani didn't recognize the knot—each high-caste family had its own distinct pattern, nothing she had ever learned—but the outer edge of the scroll bore the pictorals of Hanani's name. Begging a knife from the Sentinel, Hanani cut the knots, unrolled the scroll, and read:

Sharer,

The nightmare has come to me now.

Danneh, Merchant, Wife of Bahenamin-in-dreams

8

(◦⊙◦)

Poison

Tiaanet was still awake when Wanahomen groaned and began to shift fitfully in his sleep. She had not slept; she never did when another person was in her bed. When she sat up and struck the lantern, Wanahomen cried out and opened his eyes. She waved a hand before his face, but he did not react. When she laid a hand on his chest, his heart thudded hard and fast against her palm before he twisted away.

Men did not like to be awakened from bad dreams; this Tiaanet understood instinctively. Among Gujaareen, loss of control in dreaming was taken as weakness—even more so for warriors and men of godly lineage. But when Wanahomen cried out a second time, his body arching as if in pain, Tiaanet began to worry that her father would hear. So she shook him once, then harder. Still he did not wake.

So she did the only other thing she could, and touched his dreaming mind with her own.

It worked as well as it sometimes did with Tantufi. He caught his breath and started awake. "What—"

"A dream." Tiaanet stroked the beads of sweat from his chest. "Just a dream."

He frowned, sitting up and pushing one hand into the tumbled mass of his braids. "My father. I saw my father. He was on the steps of the Hetawa. Everything was gray, and the sky..." He swallowed; his free hand was trembling. "Something is wrong in this city."

She took his hand and pulled it to her lips. It took a moment, but then his eyes drifted to her. She was surprised at the wary look in them, though that vanished as soon as she nibbled at one of his fingertips. A hungry, almost pained look replaced the wariness, and a moment later he reached for her.

"Shall I make you one of my wives when I rule?" As he spoke, he pushed her down onto the bed.

She stroked his hair while he kissed her, resisting the urge to sigh when he lifted his head. "You are the Sunset Prince," she said. "Whatever you desire shall be yours."

His eyes searched her face, disturbing in their sharpness. "Have you another lover?"

"No one I want." Tiaanet reached up to stroke his face. "But you hardly know me, Prince."

Something even more startling appeared in his face then: loneliness. She had ceased to feel that or anything else years ago, but she saw it in Tantufi's eyes often enough that she could still recognize it. For that alone, she felt a flicker of sympathy for Wanahomen.

"My father hardly knew my mother when he married her," he said. "It took him fifteen years to win her love and bed; she was almost past childbearing by the time I was born." He gave her a half-joking smile. "I'm not as patient as he, but for you, I could try to be."

"It's too soon to discuss some things, Prince." She reached down between them then, which he had not expected; his eyes widened and turned smoky with desire while she stroked him. "But there are other things we might do in the meantime."

He nodded, mute to the force of his own need, and thankfully said nothing further about love.

*   *   *

The morning had grown late by the time Tiaanet rose and donned a robe. Wanahomen, who had slept more peacefully this time, opened his eyes the moment she moved. "Damnation," he said, and sat up. "I never meant to stay in the city this long."

She inclined her head. "May I at least prepare you a bath and a meal before you go?"

He smiled, bemused, and nodded. "Women of the Banbarra are nothing like you," he said. "They act like queens, expecting men to please them—or else they're like herders eying breeding stock. I had forgotten what Gujaareen women could be like."

"I'm not like most Gujaareen women, my Prince."

He looked abashed, ducking his eyes. "Of course, you are a lady of the shunha. Forgive me; I meant no offense."

That had not at all been what she'd meant, but she nodded nevertheless.

When the bath was drawn, Tiaanet brought him oils and other toiletries and once again apologized for their lack of servants. Wanahomen assured her that the bath alone was more luxury than he usually enjoyed, and proceeded into the bathroom on his own. She liked that he made no assumptions or crude suggestions that she attend him herself. She could not bring herself to like *him*, however—for in the end he had used her, the same as her father, and it meant little that he was more considerate about it.

And there could be nothing between them regardless, for someday he would know she was his enemy.

When Tiaanet went into the kitchen to prepare Wanahomen's meal, her father sat at the table, eating fish and crunchy dates. He lifted an eyebrow as she came in.

"I trust the night went well?" He spoke lightly, but Tiaanet was not fooled. There was a shadow of jealousy in his eyes. Even though the plan for Tiaanet to seduce Wanahomen had been his, he had never liked sharing.

"As well as can be expected," she said. Moving past him to check the stove, she added more wood and began to warm slices of cured meat for Wanahomen's meal. "He slept poorly. Bad dreams."

When she turned, her father had grown tense. "Bad dreams."

"Tantufi is not here," she reminded him. In the background she could hear sounds of water from the bathing chamber, which meant that Wanahomen would not overhear.

To her surprise, the reassurance did not calm her father. "I'm told," he said softly, "that four of the guests who attended Khanwer's funeral are now dead. The zhinha Zanem and her soldier husband; your mother's cousin Lord Tun; and a merchant, Bahenamin."

Tiaanet said nothing to this, frowning as she remembered the people he'd named. Tun had been elderly and married but not above a leering glance at Tiaanet. Zanem and her husband had been cool in their politeness, but that was to be expected from zhinha. Bahenamin, though...

"The last one, the merchant, died in the Hetawa itself," Sanfi said, "trying to rid himself of a bad dream. The Hetawa boy who tried to take it from him died as well." He folded his hands, watching her with cold eyes. "Have you any idea how this might have happened, Daughter?"

She thought as fast as she could. "Bahenamin," she said. "He was the one who wore no wig over his bald spot, wasn't he? He arrived earlier than all the others." Yes, now she remembered him. So many of the people who'd come to Khanwer's funeral had done so only to rub shoulders with their fellow elite. Bahenamin had wept, genuinely mourning a lost friend. "I had Tantufi moved to the field house at midday, but I showed Bahenamin to his quarters before that. He was distraught; he must have lain down to rest despite the hour."

"And the other three?"

"Bahenamin spent the night with us after the funeral. If Tantufi's dream was already in him, then anyone who slept in the rooms adjoining his would have been vulnerable." Never daring to allow accusation to enter her voice or eyes she added, "I was occupied that night, and could not walk the halls to stop any dreaming. And Mother was of course under guard in her room." Insurret too could chase away bad dreams, if she was so inclined.

Sanfi's lips twitched; after a moment he stood and began to pace in the tight confines of the kitchen. "Your mother. I never should have married her, beautiful or not. I saw the first signs of her madness even while I courted her, but I needed her wealth..." He stopped and sighed, his fists clenching. "And Tantufi. Every day I wonder why I did not strangle that creature at birth."

Tiaanet watched him, reading the signs and not liking what she saw. He would brood, she knew. It was what he did whenever his plans were thwarted. He would brood and seethe all the way back to their estate in the greenlands, and when they got there his anger would seek an outlet in Tantufi. She needed to distract him. But how?

"Father?" She pretended to concentrate on grating a shia nut as she spoke. "Does the Hetawa know of these deaths? Have they realized all four visited our house?"

"Not yet." He sounded even more displeased now. She struggled to think of something else to catch his interest. "Though if the dream spreads beyond those four—"

He paused suddenly, fell silent. Tiaanet poured sweetwine into a cup, set that and the plate on a tray, then lifted the tray. "I must see to our guest, Father."

"Yes," he said absently. His eyes were fixed on the table, thoughts racing behind them. She turned to leave, but paused as he called her name.

"Yes, Father?"

"Tantufi," he said. "If she were brought into the city, how fast would her dream spread?"

So that was the direction of his thoughts. She was not surprised at his cruelty, only at the method he'd chosen. He loathed Tantufi.

"I don't know, Father," she said honestly. "But among so many people, living so close to one another, it would probably go quickly."

He nodded, his eyes lighting as his thoughts progressed. "The Hetawa is a threat to our plans," he said. "They support the Kisuati these days. But Tantufi's dream should distract them, should it not?" He smiled at her. "Eventually they'll cure it, but until then..."

In her mind's eye, Tiaanet saw Tantufi's face. The child would weep to be the cause of such suffering. But she would do it, and spread her magic like a poison through the city's veins, because she could not help herself. And Father would be pleased to see Tantufi's curse at last put to good use.

"Yes, Father," Tiaanet said. "I'll send for her, if you wish."

"Such a good child you are," he said. "Do it as soon as our guest leaves."

9

Courtship

The journey from Gujaareh to the desert was lengthy and boring. To thwart possible pursuers, Wanahomen chose not to go west immediately, instead heading south to one of the upriver towns, where he treated himself to one last hot bath and Gujaareen meal before trading his horse and workman's guise for his camel and desert robes. Not the veil, of course, or any of the other tribal markers of a Banbarra; he'd even removed all of Laye-ka's telltale tack and ornaments before leaving for the journey, and stabling her in the town. While he was in the Gujaareen Territories, he was simply a desertman from one of the dozens of small tribes that made their living in Gujaareh's shadow. Only when Wanahomen reached the foothills, which marked the border between the Blood river valley and the desert, did he adopt the final layers of his Banbarra self: the veil, the looping headcloth, the indigo-and-tan robes.

He spent the journey through the hills in a kind of meditation, his thoughts pressed inward by the rhythm of Laye-ka's sure gait and the monotonous scenery of sun-seared rock. He had conceived a hundred plans along the journey in, but on this trip his thoughts were occupied by something altogether different.

Did you enjoy that, my Prince? Let me show you more.

Tiaanet. Gods, what a woman. He would marry her, of course. That had been Sanfi's intention, as obvious as the day was bright, and Wanahomen meant to oblige him. Despite the heat of the day he shivered at the memory of her lips, of her hands working magic on his flesh, of her patience in drawing out his release until he thought he might die of pleasure. How had she learned such skill? It didn't matter. He had to have her again, and if that meant making Sanfi grandsire to the next royal heir, then so be it.

By midday he had lost himself in fantasies, hardly bothering to direct Laye-ka as she plodded along the trail between two jagged outcroppings. When Kite-iyan was his again, he would install Tiaanet in his own suite, just as his father had honored his mother. And would not his mother be pleased by his choice of a shunha maiden as firstwife? Sanfi's lineage was a fine old one, eminently respectable—

Pebbles rattled on a ledge above.

Startled out of daydreaming, Wanahomen scrabbled for his knife and Laye-ka's reins at once, scanning the heights for movement or an out-of-place shadow.

Nothing.

Laye-ka grunted loudly as if chastising Wanahomen. He ignored her, continuing to scan the ledges as she plodded onward. There was no further movement, but Wanahomen's nerves were still a-jangle. The rock slopes on this part of the trail were too close and too littered with small caverns and boulders. He should never have allowed his attention to wander in a place so perfect for ambush.

Prompted by instinct, he dismounted and led Laye-ka off the main trail and up a narrow gulley carved by the springtime rains. It ran near the same slope from which he'd heard the pebbles, but there was more cover here than on the other side or the trail itself. He even spied a small cave as he moved behind a set of boulders twice Laye-ka's height—

—And then he spied a man, crouched in the cave.

Wanahomen whipped his knife up. "Who—" He cut the sentence off in surprise as the stranger put a finger to his lips, then pointed down Wanahomen's backtrail. In nearly the same breath, Wanahomen heard voices echoing over the hills, coming from the very direction in which the man had pointed.

What— But he tapped Laye-ka's shoulder in a quick Banbarra signal to be silent and still. She jerked her head once but obeyed, and Wanahomen peered between the boulders to try to see who was coming.

There, two hills back: the gleam of bronze and cloth dyed as green as rain forests. A four of Kisuati soldiers.

Wanahomen glanced back at the man in the cave, who nodded quietly. From this vantage, the man had probably seen them from even farther away. If Wanahomen had not heard and reacted to that pebble-rattle—something he now suspected the man had made to warn him—the soldiers would've seen him as they crested the last hill.

The man returned Wanahomen's gaze with an odd, somehow familiar calm. Something about that calm unnerved Wanahomen, though not as much as the nearness of the soldiers, so for the time being he focused on the greater threat.

That the soldiers were not searching for him was obvious almost at once. They kept their horses at a leisurely walk, the metal-shod hooves making far more noise on the rocky trail than a camel's toes. They talked loudly in some backcountry Sua dialect that Wanahomen could barely comprehend, but he gathered they were talking about a wager. One of them made some boastful-sounding statement, and their raucous laughter seemed to confirm this guess. Still laughing, they rode out of sight.

Wanahomen did not move for what felt like hours, listening until the last echoes of the horses' hooves had faded. Then, finally, he turned and climbed up to the cave's mouth so that he and the man could speak quietly. "Who in the gods' names are you?"

"Anarim," said the man, who rose smoothly as a dancer from his crouch. His loindrapes were unadorned black, and shorter than was currently fashionable. He wore no collar, though his skin was paler about the neck and shoulders; usually he did wear one, it was clear. Wanahomen's sense of familiarity increased—and turned ugly—as he saw black-dyed leather gauntlets about the man's forearms, shin-guards, and the hilt of a short sword peeking over one shoulder. As if sensing Wanahomen's sudden fury, the man nodded and said, "A Sentinel of Hananja."

Wanahomen hissed through his veil and tightened his grip on his knife, prepared to fight to the death. But logic seeped past the red hatred in his mind. The Sentinel could have let the Kisuati find Wanahomen. He could still do it now, simply by raising his voice; the soldiers would be on him before he could mount and get Laye-ka back up to speed.

Very slowly, Wanahomen lowered his knife.

The Sentinel shifted minutely, perhaps relaxing whatever defenses he'd readied. "I hadn't expected you for another day. You are Charris, once a general of Gujaareh?"

"Cha—" All at once Wanahomen understood; the fury returned. "So Charris has betrayed me."

The Sentinel's face registered surprise for an instant, and then went impassive again. "Ah. You are Wanahomen, whom Charris serves."

"I am Wanahomen who will kill Charris next I see him," he snapped. Charris, conspiring with the Hetawa against him! The only thing greater than Wanahomen's anger in that moment was the hurt that throbbed underneath it. *Charris, you damned old fool, I trusted you with my life!*

The Sentinel regarded him for a long moment. "So that is why he asked to meet in secret. You have no love for the Hetawa."

Wanahomen stared at the man, and only just remembered to keep his voice low when his rage found words. "The Hetawa *killed my father*. They opened the gates of the capital and let foreigners walk in to conquer us! As far as I'm concerned, all Gujaareh should rise up and throw your kind into the sea."

"As I recall, it was your father who set Kisua against Gujaareh." The Sentinel's tone, like his expression, was almost inhumanly neutral. There was no hint of censure in his manner, yet Wanahomen felt his words like a slap to the face.

"He never meant for Gujaareh to be conquered," he snapped, turning away and pacing in the tight confines of the cave. "Whatever mistakes my father made, he acted in Gujaareh's best interests. And I don't have to defend him to you!" Though he'd been doing precisely that. Furious with himself now, Wanahomen rounded on the Sentinel and pointed with his knife at that revoltingly calm face. "Tell me why you were meeting my man here."

The Sentinel regarded the knife for a moment before answering. "I bring a message from my superiors." Moving slowly, he pointed off toward a wall of the cavern, where a small shoulder-pouch lay atop a folded travel cloak. "For you."

Frowning to cover his surprise, Wanahomen went to the pouch, keeping the man in sight. When he flicked the pouch open, a scroll sealed with a knotted-cord binding—the generic pattern used by city officials—slipped out. Stamped along the scroll's edge were the pictorals of Wanahomen's recent lineage, ending with those comprising his given name.

"General Charris requested an audience on your behalf with the Superior," the Sentinel said when Wanahomen threw him a suspicious look. "The response is contained therein."

Wanahomen stared at the scroll, then burst out laughing. "An audience with the Superior? Gods, if I didn't know any better I'd accuse Charris of senility. Why would I possibly meet with *anyone* from the Hetawa?"

"You want your throne back. For that you will need our help."

Wanahomen nearly dropped his knife.

"An alliance," he said, after a long and stunned breath. "Charris actually believes he can forge an alliance between the Hetawa and the Banbarra?" He could hardly believe his own words.

"The alliance would be with *you*," the Sentinel replied, "though it may of course include others you deem appropriate." He paused, then added, "It is not so far-fetched a notion. The Hetawa created the monarchy, after all, and supported it for centuries."

"Yes." Wanahomen's hand tightened on the scroll. "Until your kind enslaved mine with dreamblood. An alliance requires trust, Servant of Hananja, and I'll never trust you or your murdering brethren. Charris should have known better."

He threw the scroll on the ground, and was irrationally annoyed that the Sentinel showed no sign of affront. Instead the man said, "Then you refuse the alliance?"

"I cannot refuse the impossible," Wanahomen snapped. He turned away and peered between the boulders again at the trail, which was now clear. He would have to find another way through the hills, since the easiest route was the way the Kisuati soldiers had gone. They must have begun patrolling the hills after the last Banbarra raid, perhaps hoping to forewarn the city or harry the raiders next time.

"I'll convey that to our council," the Sentinel said behind him. "Though they will doubtless send at least a representative to the designated place, in case you should change your mind." There was a pause. "You should know, if you expect trust of your allies, that the shunha lord Sanfi cannot be trusted, either."

Wanahomen threw a scowl at the Sentinel over his shoulder. "You've been watching me?"

"We've been watching Sanfi. He's been gathering his coalition of nobles for some time—long before your Banbarra began their attacks. You're useful to his plans, but only for now."

Two could play the stone-faced game. Wanahomen folded his arms and said, "Explain."

The Sentinel lifted an eyebrow minutely. "You will not trust this information."

"I'll decide whether to trust it later. For now I want to hear."

"You know that once—before the Sunset dynasty—we were like Kisua and the southern tribes, ruled by the most respected of our elders." The Sentinel shrugged. "Having the Kisuati Protectorate in control for the past ten years has reminded Gujaareh of that history. Sanfi leads the push to recreate a Gujaareen Protectorate."

Wanahomen narrowed his eyes. "The common folk of Gujaareh want a champion chosen by the Goddess to rule them, not a circle of doddering old rich people. They can see how much good—or how little—Kisua's Protectorate does its own land; orphan children prostitute themselves on street corners, and their slaves starve amid fields of grain."

The Sentinel lowered his eyes. "For the long-term preservation of peace, we've kept secret your father's true goals. No one in Gujaareh knows that King Eninket meant to slaughter thousands of soldiers to gain immortality. Yet the secrets that *have* come out—the murder of a Kisuati ambassador, the torture of three Gatherers, the conspiracy with northerners, the Reaper..." He shook his head. "The excesses of a Protectorate are distant and half-forgotten. The excesses of a Prince are a fresh wound. You cannot blame the people for thinking this way."

He could, Wanahomen mused grimly, but it would do him no good to do so. "I see."

"And even a Protectorate must have a leader. Sanfi is young for it yet, but he thinks long-term."

"I made contact with Sanfi a year ago. It was only sensible for him to make plans before that," Wanahomen said. The words sounded weak even to his own ears; he clenched his fists, scowling. Such plans, such plans! Not easily dismantled. And would any man who himself hungered to rule give up that idea simply because the true king had come along?

No. Such a man would not.

If I marry Tiaanet, Sanfi will gain influence through me. Then he could assassinate me and claim that he'd meant to put a Prince on the throne, but alas . . .

The Sentinel was watching him in silence, no doubt reading the turmoil in Wanahomen's body language; Wanahomen had heard they could do such things. To cover this, he turned to face the man. "The petty schemes of the nobility are nothing to me. You forget my father raised me to deal with such things."

The Sentinel inclined his head. "As you wish." He picked up his cloak and the pouch, tying the latter across his chest. "Please inform Charris that there's no longer any need for us to meet. In peace, Wanahomen, son of the King."

He left the scroll on the cavern floor where Wanahomen had thrown it. Wanahomen scowled at him, but the Sentinel walked out and began climbing a trail that led to higher ground. Perhaps he had a mount hidden somewhere.

And good riddance. "Son of the King"! He speaks of alliance and yet will not even give me my proper title! Ignoring the small voice within him, which pointed out that the title was currently meaningless and Servants of Hananja always told the truth, Wanahomen waited until the Sentinel's footsteps had faded. Then he went to pick up the scroll. He dared not leave it in the cavern where it might be found.

Damn them to shadows, anyway. I don't need them. I'll use Sanfi as he meant to use me, then kill him myself.

But Tiaanet would not make a particularly willing bride if he murdered her father.

Forcing silent the murmur of unease in his mind, Wanahomen shoved the scroll into a pocket. Then he went to Laye-ka, signaling for her to kneel so he could mount. After a moment's thought to determine a new route, he resumed the journey to the desert, his thoughts now convoluted and grim.

10

⟨ ⊙ ⟩

Sonta-i

They brought Merchant Danneh to the Hetawa on the morning of the Festival of New Beer. Hanani heard the revelry from the square outside when the Hall doors opened to admit four Sentinel-Apprentices, who carried Danneh's palanquin. The apprentices set the palanquin on the dais and removed its canopy to reveal Danneh.

The merchant was asleep but fitfully so, her face beaded with sweat as she shifted and made small fevered sounds. Beneath their lids her eyes moved with frenetic speed, as if the sights that tormented her in dreaming were too many and too swift for her to follow. Danneh's servant, who had come with them, put hands to her mouth, fighting tears.

"She will not wake?" Nhen-ne-verra, the Sharer on duty, knelt beside Danneh as the Sentinels stepped away.

Danneh's training showed as the girl composed herself. "No, Sharer," she said. "When I returned from delivering her message to the Hetawa last night, she had fallen asleep again. I thought perhaps she had finally found peace enough to rest, but when morning came and she did not rise, I went into her bedchamber to find her like this. I've tried to wake her many times."

Nhen-ne-verra nodded, pursing his lips as he pulled up Danneh's eyelids—Hanani caught a glimpse of the woman's eyes rolling wildly in their sockets—then opened Danneh's mouth to sniff her breath. "No recent drink or food. Has she any enemies?"

The servant looked horrified. "None who would poison her!"

"I'm simply eliminating possibilities, child." He tilted Danneh's head up and massaged her throat, checking her pulse and the glands in her neck that signaled disease. All part of the traditional ritual of examination, Hanani knew—and all wrong for this situation.

She mounted the first step of the dais. "Nhen-ne-verra-brother."

Nhen-ne-verra did not look up from his work. "You are under interdiction, Apprentice."

Hanani bit her lip against the sting of the reminder, though he'd spoken kindly. "This woman—" She swallowed. "I met her a four-day ago. She sent word to *me* about this. Brother—" She cut herself off, fists clenching. She would not beg. She would not.

Nhen-ne-verra finally glanced at her over his shoulder. He was half easternese, pale of skin with long limp hair that had gone shockingly white in his elderhood—but his eyes were as black and stern as those of any shunha. "Very well. But you may not enter healing sleep. Is that understood?"

"Yes, Brother." Quickly, before he could change his mind, Hanani crouched on the other side of Danneh's litter. Throwing a glance at the servant, she lowered her voice. "Brother, there's a dream—"

"Yes, the Superior has informed the Sharer path-elders, of whom I am one." Nhen-ne-verra threw a half-smile at her abashed look. "You must admit it is intriguing, Apprentice. I cannot help but feel some excitement at the prospect of being able to examine this mysterious dream at last."

Remembering the oily feel of the shadow in the dream she had shared with Gatherer Nijiri, Hanani shuddered. "Brother..." But she could not say what was in her mind. *Take care* would be an insult, implying that she thought him too old or incompetent to perform his duty. *Dayuhotem died of it* was even worse, for Nhenne-verra was a Sharer with over forty floods' experience; there could be no comparison between his skill and that of a child. So she bit her lip again and said nothing more.

He seemed to understand. "I'll be fine, Hanani. But perhaps you should go and fetch your mentor for me, if he's not on sleep shift right now. It would be sensible to have another Sharer here, just in case."

It was an acolyte's task to run errands and fetch, and humiliation coiled in Hanani's belly. But it was a way to help, and at the moment it was better than nothing. Nodding quickly to Nhen-ne-verra, she hurried off in search of Mni-inh.

Her mentor was just finishing a training session on woundbinding in the Sentinels' Hall. He spied her as he emerged from the naproom trailed by sleepy-eyed boys, who wandered off toward their next dream-implanted lesson. "Ah, Hanani. If you're—" He read her face. "What is it?"

When she explained, he sobered at once. "I'll go now. Find an acolyte and tell him to summon the Superior."

That threw her. "The Superior, Brother?"

"And Yehamwy, if he's not teaching right now." He read her stricken face and sighed. "Witnesses, Hanani. If the healing is difficult, I want them to see and realize Dayu wasn't incompetent, just confronted with something that could tax even an experienced Sharer's ability. I know you'd rather not use your friend to prove a point..."

Hanani shook her head, pushing aside an irrational sense of guilt. Gatherer Nijiri had said such tactics would be ineffective in clearing Hanani's reputation, but she understood Mni-inh's desire to try. She hoped it would work too. "It's what Dayu would want, Brother."

Mni-inh nodded, then let her go and hurried toward the Hall of Blessings. Hanani caught one of the acolytes emerging from Mni-inh's lesson and sent him in search of the Superior. Yehamwy's class was nearby in the Gatherers' Hall, so she hastened across the court-yard to the smallest of the Hetawa complex's buildings to deliver that message herself.

The walls of the Gatherers' Hall were gray marble, unlike the warm yellow-brown sandstone used in every other Hetawa building. The corridors here were cooler, dimmer, and quieter, with a feel that was somehow more meditative than that of the Hetawa's other halls. Hanani slowed her pace despite her anxiety, since the hurried slap of her sandals on stone was loud and unpeaceful. She had no fear of disturbing the Gatherers, whose cells were on the fourth level away from the noise and activity of the ground. It simply seemed irreverent while in the Gatherers' house not to move sedately, as they did, and speak softly, as they did, and behave in all the ways that pleased Hananja most.

But she could not remember the way to the correct classroom. Hearing voices some ways ahead, she followed them.

"...More dangerous than his father," one of the voices said. It reminded her of the marble along the walls, dark and cool and gray. "His life has been harder, and he has more cause to hate."

"We should assess him beforehand, true," said another voice—lighter, with a hint of laughter. "I'm not certain I like this plan, however. Desert folk are not given to peaceful behavior."

"If he permits harm to either of them, we'll know what sort of man he is." That one was a younger, less certain voice. Following it, Hanani turned a corner and saw light ahead: watery shafts of morning sunlight falling into the building's atrium. The Stone Garden, where the Gatherers danced their private prayers. The younger voice continued, "Though then the harm will already have been done."

"It cannot be helped," said a fourth voice, and Hanani stopped in horror because that voice was the Gatherer Nijiri's, and that meant Hanani should not be overhearing this conversation at all. "He would never trust one of us. But someone young, who couldn't possibly have participated in the judgment against his father; someone he is inclined to protect, not fear—"

"Be silent," said the cool gray voice abruptly, and the entrance to the atrium was shadowed as a tall, gaunt figure stepped into the light. "Sharer-Apprentice."

The figure wore a hooded eggshell robe; she swallowed and bowed deeply over both hands in apology. "I'm sorry, Gatherer. I, I was looking for Teacher Yehamwy. H-he has a class in this building."

"In that direction." The Gatherer inclined his head back the way she'd come. "Why are you looking for him?"

Hanani swallowed. "The wife of the tithebearer who died has been brought to the Hall of Blessings, Gatherer, suffering from the same dream that killed her husband." *And Dayu.* "Sharer Nhen-ne-verra is attempting to heal her. My mentor thought perhaps—witnesses—"

The Gatherer looked off to the side; abruptly three other figures appeared around him, all silhouetted in the light from the garden. One of them she recognized as Nijiri before he, like the rest of them, drew up their hoods.

"We will attend," the gaunt Gatherer said then. "I believe we will be more suitable as witnesses than Teacher Yehamwy, as we can observe in dreaming as well as waking. Lead the way, Apprentice."

There was nothing but command in his tone. Hanani could think of no proper way to protest. But the Gatherer was right that they would make eminently suitable witnesses; no one would dispute their observations. So hoping that her nervousness did not show, Hanani led them to the Hall of Blessings.

When they arrived at the dais, however, she stopped in surprise.

Nhen-ne-verra stood away from Danneh's litter, his shoulders hunched, body a-tremble as if some palsy had taken him. Mni-inh held him by the shoulders, nearly supporting him, his expression tight with worry.

The gaunt Gatherer flowed past Hanani like a serpent, all grace and focused intent. The tattoo on his near shoulder was the night-shade flower, done all in indigo: Sonta-i, eldest of the path. "What has happened?" he asked.

Nhen-ne-verra shook his head, wordless. Mni-inh said, "Nhen-ne-verra attempted to locate the petitioner's soul, the first stage of healing. Something disturbed him."

Nhen-ne-verra shuddered and shook his head again. "Not there. She was— I did not find her. But something else was. Goddess!" He pulled away from Mni-inh and looked up at the great statue of Hananja that loomed overhead, Her hands outstretched in welcome. He reached upward as if to grasp those hands, his own trembling.

"Nothing of You," he whispered. There was a fervent, unsteady note to his voice that Hanani had never heard before. When she glanced at Mni-inh, she saw alarm on his face as well. "Nothing of You has such a feel!"

Gatherer Sonta-i moved swiftly onto the dais and touched the old Sharer's shoulder. Nhen-ne-verra groaned softly and seemed to wilt; Mni-inh quickly put an arm under his shoulder and steered him over to one of the side-benches.

Sonta-i turned to gaze at the servant, who had drawn back from the tableau, her eyes wide. Then he focused on Danneh.

Another Gatherer stepped forward. He was taller than all the rest, though by the yellow safflower on his shoulder Hanani realized he was Inmu, youngest of the path. "Sonta-i-brother—are you certain—"

But Gatherer Rabbaneh put a hand on his shoulder. Inmu looked at him, then at Sonta-i, and subsided. Sonta-i knelt beside Danneh, laying fingertips on her closed eyelids.

It was in that moment that an irrational anxiety came over Hanani—irrational, for why should a Gatherer fear any dream? Nevertheless she stepped closer. "Gatherer."

Four hooded faces turned toward her, though she'd meant Sonta-i. To him she said, "It was in the realm between. Not in Ina-Karekh, not here in Hona-Karekh. *Between*."

His eyes narrowed. Gatherer Nijiri gave her a long, thoughtful look. Caught in their regard, Hanani cringed inwardly, wondering what in the names of the gods had compelled her to say such a thing. But before she could stammer out an apology, Nijiri turned to Sonta-i. Neither man spoke, but something passed between them nevertheless; anyone with even a whiff of dreaming gift could have sensed it. Sonta-i gave Nijiri a minute nod, and turned his focus to Danneh again. He closed his eyes, and a moment passed.

This will go wrong, whispered everything inside Hanani.

But before she could think of what to say, Sonta-i made a low, strained sound. Hanani caught her breath and ran up onto the dais, but Nijiri forestalled her with a hand like a vise on her shoulder. When she turned to stare at him, his face was bleak with mourning already, his eyes fixed on Sonta-i. She looked around at Rabbaneh, who was the same. What was wrong with them? They sensed the same danger that she did; why didn't they stop this? Only Inmu seemed troubled when Hanani met his eyes, and he looked away with his jaw set and tight.

Sonta-i gasped suddenly, his eyes and mouth opening wide. A dozen expressions flickered across his face, more than Hanani had ever seen on him, all too fleeting to identify. "So much rage," he whispered. "So much sorrow. I have never known feelings before now. What irony." He shuddered, his hand slipping off Danneh's face to brace against the floor. It was the first clumsy move she had ever seen a Gatherer make. He focused on that hand, seemingly with great effort. "The space between. Strength is not enough. A child, Nijiri. The Wild Dreamer is a child."

He pitched forward without warning, falling onto Danneh. Startled, Mni-inh moved forward and pulled Sonta-i up; Gatherer Rabbaneh crouched swiftly to assist. But Sonta-i's body hung limp between them, and the blow had done Danneh no harm either. Both were dead.

11

(⊙)

Betrayal

The sentries' birdcalls echoed from the walls of the canyon called Merik-ren-aferu, accurate enough in their mimicry that nesting skyrers along the sheer cliff faces called back in territorial challenge. The sentries had been watching Wanahomen for miles with longeyes, he knew, probably from the moment he and Laye-ka had appeared as a spot on the rolling desert horizon. Had he been an unexpected spot, or worse, multiple spots, the tribe would have been long gone from the canyon by the time he reached its threshold—gone but for the sentries, who would have stayed behind to welcome him with an arrow through the eye. Banbarra hospitality was infamous.

Because Wanahomen was known and expected, however, he saw signs of habitation as soon as he rode into the canyon. Through gaps in the high brush he glimpsed hidden orchards and patches of cultivated ground—tended by slaves from more agricultural tribes, of course, as no Banbarra would ever deign to work in the dirt. And the sentries appeared at last, lurking along ridges in rock-colored clothing and peering up at him from carefully disguised pits. The ones he could see nodded gravely as he passed; he knew there were others he had not seen. Then Laye-ka uttered a happy whistle as the corral came into view, where the tribe's camels and horses rested when not in use or loosed to forage.

Wanahomen dismounted here and tended Laye-ka before releasing her into the corral. "Thank you for bearing me back safe," he whispered as he removed her halter, and she grunted as if she understood the ritual words. Then she trotted into the corral and promptly shouldered aside three other camels to get to the feed trough. They gave way with a long-suffering air that made Wanahomen laugh.

The laugh brought forth another head, which poked up from behind a rock with headcloth askew and sleep-lines engraved in one side of its face. "Wana!" The boy brightened at once, hopping up and trotting over to him. "I didn't hear you come in."

"Yes, and if I'd been a thief our mounts would be long gone," Wanahomen said. He tossed his saddlebags over one shoulder, then put his hands on his hips and favored the boy with a stern glance. "What sort of guard are you if you sleep your duty away, Tassa?"

The boy ducked his eyes, abashed. "It was only for a little while. I stayed up waiting for you last night."

"I was delayed," Wanahomen replied with a grimace. He had taken a long detour down a lesser-used foothills trail in order to avoid the Kisuati soldiers. "Answer me this, though: has Charris claimed a horse today?"

"Your slave?" Tassa's tone held pure Banbarra scorn for a lesser being. "No, not yet. You let him ride off on his own?"

I would have, before he betrayed me. "Just be sure he doesn't claim one today—not before he sees me. And don't fall asleep this time." Tousling Tassa's hair, he answered the boy's sheepish grin with one of his own and headed away from the corral, finding one of the dangling rope ladders to climb up to the topmost ledge.

The Banbarra encampment, a forest of elaborately decorated

tents and fire circles, spread along several of the highest and broadest ledges of the canyon. All the tents could be packed to move in a matter of minutes, and would be in the event of danger. For now, however, the tribe was at rest, preparing for the next battle in its undeclared war on Kisua. Wanahomen nodded as he walked past men gossiping while fletching arrows or sharpening their swords; knots of women sat together sewing leather breastplates and boots. Though Wanahomen nodded to the women too—a Gujaareen habit he'd never been able to break—they did not return the gesture, and a few did not even deign to look in his direction. He felt their eyes on his back as he passed.

Eventually he reached a large, handsome tent of dark brown camel hide. The rods planted about its entrance had been carved with Gujaareen pictorals, and there was an emblem above its entry flap: the sun and rays of the Aureole of the Setting Sun, symbol of Wanahomen's lineage. The true Aureole, held somewhere in Kisuati-occupied Gujaareh, was a semicircle of beaten gold surrounded by red- and yellow-amber plates. This one was chiseled marble with rays of dark and light polished wood. Tasteful, and still valuable in the Banbarra estimate of things, but even after ten years Wanahomen could not help seeing the emblem as the paltry imitation it was.

"Are you going to come in?" his mother's voice called, from within the tent.

Wanahomen flinched at the sound of her voice, not only from surprise. Bracing himself, he lifted the tent-flap and went inside. "Sorry, Mother. Just thinking."

Hendet, wife of Gujaareh's King-in-dreaming, lay on a thick pallet of furs and woven sweet rushes with two tasseled pillows tucked behind her back. As he crossed the rug-layered floor, she set aside a thick scroll and opened her arms. "So much like your father," she said, as he knelt for her hug. "Always thinking, thinking, thinking. What is it this time?"

He had heard the weakness of her voice already. Normally she was deep-spoken for a woman, husky and strong, but now she spoke as if through a mouthful of dry wool. It was impossible not to notice her thinness as he hugged her, or the parchment-dryness of her skin as he sat back.

"Many things," he said, making himself smile. "You're as beautiful as ever."

"I've taught you to lie better than that," Hendet replied with mock sternness. That surprised an honest laugh out of him and eased some of his fear, for if she was feeling well enough to joke, there was still hope. "Unte said the raid went well."

He nodded, then sobered, reaching up to remove his face-veil and headcloth for her. "Tell me where Charris is, Mother."

She opened her mouth to speak, then gave him a second, shrewder look as she read his face.

"He's about to leave on an errand for me," she said finally.

"For—" He caught himself before his temper could explode, for she was Gujaareen and would never tolerate such a thing. He clenched his fists on his knees instead. "Mother, did you send him to negotiate an alliance with the Hetawa?"

Hendet gave him a cool look, which nevertheless had the power to sting. "I sent him to *finalize* an alliance with the Hetawa, yes. Unte has agreed to the Hetawa's terms, though one of them was that they meet you before the agreement was sealed."

"Unte! And you—" Getting to his feet, he paced back and forth in the small confines of the tent, taking deep breaths in an effort to slow the pounding in his temples. When he could finally bring himself to speak with a civil tongue, he stopped and faced her. "They *killed the man you loved*, Mother," he said. "They used and tormented him and corrupted the Goddess's magic for power..." But he trailed off, then, because Hendet was looking at him with a mixture of exasperation and sorrow, as if he had somehow disappointed her.

"You are so much your father's son," she said softly, startling him silent. "You've done well despite everything that's happened; so very well. I'm proud of you, and I believe in you. But in this one way"—her voice grew cold as ocean water—"you can be such a fool, Wanahomen."

He flinched. "What?"

"Gujaareh is built on a four of strengths." Hendet's eyes had gone hard as stone pillars. In a distant part of Wanahomen's mind, he reveled in the fact that there was no lessening of her ferocity despite her illness; she still had the soul of a queen, however much her flesh had failed her. But her words—"The river, the castes, the army, *and the Hetawa*. Those priests you hate so much educate our young, keep our people healthy and content, administer justice . . . And they have magic, Wanahomen. Power like nothing else in the waking realm. Without their cooperation, even if you regain the throne Gujaareh will *not* be yours."

"The military caste has promised to assist me in the final battle," Wanahomen said, stubbornly, "and now the nobles are behind me. I've sealed the pact with the shunha lord Sanfi. The common folk will welcome my return—"

"No! They won't! Not without the Hetawa's support! Wanahomen. You're too smart for this." She sighed and extended a hand to him. After a long, angry breath, he knelt at her side and took it. She stroked his hand and said, "Your father raised you to be wise; to ignore the Hetawa is not wise. You don't trust them—nor should you. I too remember their crimes." And now her hard look was more distant, her anger directed elsewhere. "But even I see that this is necessary."

He looked away in mute denial. She sighed.

"When you've regained the throne, you'll make agreements with Kisua, won't you? Much as you hate them. And to reward their efforts, you will give the Banbarra trading privileges that no other nation has had, which will anger the merchant caste—but you'll do it anyhow, because Gujaareh is too weak for another war. Is this not true?"

Wanahomen ground his teeth. "That's different."

"How? The Gatherer who slew your father collaborated with Kisua. And the nobles whose alliance you're so glad to earn—where was their support with your father dead and the three of us in desperate need? They left us to die!" She sighed then, reaching up to stroke his hair. "The plain fact is that you can trust *none* of your allies, my son. A king cannot afford trust. But neither can you allow hatred to overrule sense."

He resisted the truth of her words. Just the idea of cooperating with the Hetawa left the bitter taste of guilt, of betrayal, in his mouth. What would his father think, if he knew that Wanahomen had allied with his murderers?

That I'm doing what I must, came the reluctant answer, and at last he bowed his head before Hendet in acquiescence.

She stroked his braids approvingly. "Now. Tell me how you knew."

"I met a templeman, a Sentinel, in the hills. He gave me this." He pulled the scroll from a fold of his robe.

"And you didn't even open it? Well, at least you didn't throw it away. What does it say?"

He drew his knife, cut the seal-knots, and opened it to read the formal pictorals aloud.

To Wanahomen, chosen heir of Eninket King (may he dwell in Her peace forever), greetings.

Your request to meet is accepted. A representative shall make himself available at the location of this scroll's bestowing, on the fourth day of the eighth month of the harvest, at sunset.

It is requested that you and your allies make no further assault upon our mutual enemy until this meeting can occur.

There were no signature pictorals. Wanahomen scowled and threw the scroll on the floor, rising to pace again.

Hendet reached out to pick the scroll up. Some of Wanahomen's anger slipped as he saw how badly his mother's hand shook before she concealed it by laying the scroll on her lap to read closely.

"You must tell Unte at once," she said.

"I'd had no further raids planned, because of the coming solstice meeting," Wanahomen said, frowning to himself. "It's coincidence, but once they hear of this 'request,' the other tribe leaders will think me subservient to the Hetawa." He paused, considering. "I could ignore the request—"

"You will do no such thing," Hendet said, bristling. "You know as well as I that this is not a *request*, but a condition of the alliance. Unte will understand."

"Unte isn't the problem," he replied, and then told her of the slain Gujaareen soldier and his subsequent decision to kill Wujjeg. "It was defiance," he finished. "I ordered no Gujaareen deaths and he deliberately killed one."

"Then you were right to kill him," Hendet said. "Though it is unfortunate; Wujjeg's clan..." She faltered abruptly, visibly tired as she leaned back on the pillows to catch her breath. "They hold great influence with the Dzikeh-Banbarra. They will try... try to turn that tribe against you."

"I know," he replied grimly. Suddenly it was all too much to bear: the Banbarra, his mother's illness, the thrice-damned Hetawa. The priests were at the heart of all of it, he decided sullenly. If not for their Gatherers, his father would be alive and Kisua would be Gujaareh's newest territory, and Wanahomen would have nothing more important to concern him than how to woo Tiaanet.

But would she even want me if my father were still Prince? came the sudden, ugly thought.

Pointless to torment himself with such thoughts now.

"You need rest," he said to Hendet.

"I'm fine," she said, but she did not resist when he helped her to lie flat. Her very acquiescence was proof of how bad she felt: she obeyed him only when she was in pain. His stomach constricted at the thought of what would happen if she didn't improve soon. The Banbarra were nomads for part of each year, and they would not stay in Merik-ren-aferu much longer. After the solstice, the six tribe leaders would gather and decide whether to support Wanahomen's war. But then whether the war was fought or not, won or lost, the tribe would begin the long journey across the Empty Thousand to the continent's western coast, there to trade and grow wealthy from the goods they'd made or stolen during the year. Wanahomen had made the springtime desert crossing many times now in his years among the Banbarra, and he had seen the harsh reality of it: the old and infirm did not often survive the journey.

Then I must win Gujaareh before spring.

Tucking the blankets close around his mother's chin, Wanahomen leaned down and pressed his lips against her forehead. "Dream well, Mother," he whispered. "In Her peace."

"And you, my son," she said, and closed her eyes.

He had not told her of the images that had haunted his dreams for the past few weeks: his father consumed with rot, the rot threatening his own flesh, and the terrible flood of evil that threatened to swamp Gujaareh. His mother would see meaning in such dreams, and perhaps she would be right to do so.

But what good did that do, when all was said and done? Why should he worry about dream phantoms when he had fears enough for a thousand nightmares in the waking realm?

So he settled himself on the furs beside his mother's pallet and watched her until she fell asleep. Once she had passed into Ina-Karekh for the night, he got to his feet and left to plan the next stage of his war.

12

◖⊙◗

The Second Test

By Law and Wisdom, bodies were kept in state for a time after death. No one knew how long the final journey to Ina-Karekh took without the aid of a Gatherer; Gujaareh's most brilliant Teachers had debated the matter for centuries to no conclusion. Consensus held there was some possibility, however remote, that destroying the flesh too soon might upset the soul and send it hurtling toward the shadowlands. Women were safe from this, naturally, being goddesses who could steer themselves through Ina-Karekh: they were kept for one day, as a courtesy, though girls before menarche were given two since their womanly power was less developed. Men, however, were ordinary—therefore the Law dictated that male bodies be kept for a minimum of four days after death, and longer where embalming and sarcophagi allowed. The only exceptions to this Law were for male bodies that bore a Gatherer's mark, and any others whose souls were known to be safely beyond the waking realm.

They burned Gatherer Sonta-i two days after his death. He had given no Final Tithe; no one knew the disposition of his soul, or if it even still existed. Yet he was cremated as if his death had been proper and wholesome, because to do otherwise would invite questions that the Hetawa could not, dared not answer. *How did he die?* would be the least of them. The ones to follow would be far, far worse: *What is this terrible dream that killed him? What can the Hetawa do to stop it?* And the answer to that last one—*Nothing, we can do nothing*—would disrupt the entire city's peace.

For there were now five new victims.

Hanani stood at the entrance to the Hall of Respite, one of the buildings allotted to the Sharer path. It was in this building that the most difficult and disturbing healing magic was performed. While most displays of magic were believed to strengthen a worshipper's belief, some healings required that limbs be severed or broken, babies cut from their mothers, or worse. That did not apply in this case, but the sight of the five helpless dreamers was disturbing nevertheless because so little could be done for them.

Several senior Sharers moved among the Hall's beds, examining and tending the dreamers as best they could. Beyond them, Mniinh spoke quietly with a cluster of layfolk nearby—the families of the victims, Hanani assumed. She wondered what he could possibly have found to say to them.

Turning to face the central courtyard, she saw that Sonta-i's funeral pyre had fallen in on itself at last. The Dreaming Moon was high overhead; they'd lit the pyre at sunset. A handful of mourners had lingered throughout the burning, but now they drifted away in ones and twos as if the collapse of the pyre had been a signal. None of them spoke as they walked away, Hanani noticed. No one wept. Perhaps, with the state of the Gatherer's soul so in doubt, no one knew quite how to mourn.

"Sharer-Apprentice."

Teacher Yehamwy's voice. It was a sign of Hanani's own low spirits that she felt none of the usual dread as she turned to face him. But perhaps he felt the same; there was none of the usual distaste in his eyes.

"Teacher." She inclined her head to him, then glanced at the open curtain of the Hall of Respite. "I did not enter, Teacher."

He glanced at the entrance as if that was the last thing on his mind, and sighed. "Well. Given the circumstances, it seems clear the boy's death was unforeseeable. In the morning I shall inform the council that my interdiction is lifted. I'm sure they'll concur."

Just like that. Hanani stared at him, too numbed to speak. But then the breeze shifted, carrying a whiff of the funeral pyre—incense and fragrant wood-resin and the unmistakable odor of charred flesh—and whatever elation she might have felt vanished unborn. Soon she would be able to heal again. But what good did that do when even dreams had turned to poison? She could not bring herself to thank Yehamwy.

Yehamwy seemed to be ignoring her in any case, gazing across the courtyard at the pyre. He wore a Teacher's brown formal robes, which meant that he'd probably attended Sonta-i's funeral.

"There was a time when I thought you were the greatest threat to our way of life," Yehamwy said, not taking his eyes from the pyre.

Hanani started. "*Me*, Teacher?"

"You. Our walking, breathing capitulation to the Kisuati and their 'superior' ways." He sighed. "Their women are not goddesses, merely weak mortal creatures who do the same work as men—and can suffer the same torments. Their servants are bought and sold like meat, their elderly resented as a burden...I would not have this for Gujaareh." He shook his head slowly, his eyes reflecting the pyre's flickering light. "But in the end, you're just a foolish girl-child who will never know true womanhood. If you want to heal, why should I stop you? Compared to the real dangers in the world, you are nothing." He turned away from the pyre, and also from Hanani. "I suppose the Goddess has seen fit to remind us all of that."

He walked away then. Hanani stared after him until his brown robe blended into the darkness.

never know true womanhood

What did that mean?

"Hanani?"

You are nothing.

She felt bruised inside. The syllables of her name seemed to echo in her mind, but she turned to face Mni-inh, who had come to the door of the hall. He looked very tired.

"You should go," he said. "There's nothing you can do here."

For a moment, with some part of her mind expecting more pain, Hanani thought he had heard Yehamwy's last words and agreed with them. But then he gave a heavy sigh. "There's nothing anyone can do."

She dragged her scattered thoughts back to the present. "Sonta-i. That was why he did it, wasn't it?"

Mni-inh nodded. "Someone had to try. The Gatherers are the strongest narcomancers in the Hetawa. If this thing could be defeated by magic..." He sighed. "Well, now we know it can't be."

Perhaps she was dreaming, Hanani thought.

There had been a dreamlike quality to the past few days, an ever-present note of unreality that her daylight mind could not seem to grasp. In the waking world, bad dreams did not pass from soul to soul like a pestilence, and Gatherers did not die of them. Acolytes did not die at all, especially when they were bright and beautiful and well loved.

In waking, women were goddesses in and of themselves, not the Goddess's servants.

She forced herself to focus. Mni-inh looked as soul-weary as she felt; concern for him pushed away some of her unhappiness. "You should rest, Brother."

"I know. There's just... I've never been so useless before. It's not something I'm used to." He rubbed his eyes and sighed. "Oh— Damnation, I almost forgot. Gatherer Nijiri informed me earlier today that we'll be leaving tomorrow."

"Leaving?"

"Yes. For someplace in the desert, so wear your formal robe over your usual attire; it will protect you from the sun. Mounts and supplies are being packed for us. We leave at noon from the House of Children gate."

In waking, Sharers did not leave Gujaareh. Hanani frowned. "For what reason, Brother?"

"Nijiri said you knew." Some of Mni-inh's weariness faded, replaced by curiosity.

Nijiri's trial. Now? With Sonta-i dead and corrupt magic threatening the city?

"He spoke only of a task that he wanted me to complete," she said, "but he gave no details. He'd originally meant the task for you, but said he'd changed his mind."

Mni-inh frowned to himself. "What in endless dreamscapes could he be up to?" He sighed. "That boy's more meddlesome than any Gatherer I've ever known. I suppose Ehiru had no time to knock it out of him."

Mni-inh closed the door to the Hall of Respite and came to stand beside Hanani. In the distance the pyre settled farther in on itself. They both watched as a great shower of sparks rose to swirl and dance in the night air. Then Mni-inh touched Hanani's shoulder, and in silence they both returned to the Sharer's Hall.

*   *   *

There were more people present than Hanani had expected when she arrived at the House of Children's courtyard the next morning. The Superior stood on the steps nearby, watching the group prepare. Sentinel Anarim conferred with his equally solemn young apprentice and three other Sentinels whom Hanani did not know. Mni-inh looked on apprehensively as one of the Hetawa laymen tried to explain to him how to mount a horse. Gatherer Nijiri was already a-horseback, his hooded face gazing into the distance;

he did not look around as Hanani arrived. On impulse she went to him and touched his hand. He blinked and focused on her.

"Do you mourn for Sonta-i?" A fourday before, she would never have dared to ask such a personal question of a Gatherer. But that was before she had met his true self in the dreamscape, and watched him send a brother to die. In his face that day, she had seen the toll this took.

He gave her a rueful smile. "You should have become a Gatherer, I think."

She ducked her eyes, inordinately pleased, though given how Yehamwy and his ilk reacted to her as a Sharer, she couldn't begin to imagine the uproar—however peaceful—if she had chosen the Gatherer path instead. "I don't have your strength, Gatherer."

"I'm not strong." Before she could do more than frown at this, he sighed, reaching up to stroke his horse's neck. "Another journey into the desert. The last time..." He fell silent for a moment, then shrugged. "Well. Memories can be both sweet and painful."

She could not imagine why a Gatherer would ever need to go into the desert. But before she could think of a tactful way to ask him about this, Mni-inh spotted her and called her over.

"Let this fellow teach you how to climb these beasts," he said, jerking his head toward the layman as he tried, again unsuccessfully, to mount his horse. The horse grunted and sidestepped, and Mni-inh landed back on the ground. Irritated, he slapped the horse's saddle. "I don't want to ride you either!"

The layman, struggling not to smile, said, "Just keep trying, Sharer-lord." Turning to Hanani, he stared at her for a moment. Hanani waited again, patient; after a moment the layman recalled himself and gave a quick apologetic bow over one hand. "This way, Sharer-uh-lady."

"Lord," she corrected, and smiled. "Though in truth neither is appropriate. I'm only an apprentice."

"I see," he said, looking more perplexed than before, but he put on a smile anyhow. "Have you ever ridden a horse?"

"Yes," she said, earning a surprised look from Mni-inh. "But it has been many years since."

"Some things never change, l—Apprentice. You remember?"

She nodded, smiling as he led her to the horse that had been saddled for her. It was a beautiful tawny creature, smaller than average but with an intelligent eye. "What's this one's name?"

"Dakha," said the layman, obviously pleased. "She's part Banbarra, which you'll pardon once you see how she handles the foothills."

Hanani nodded, patting the horse as she moved around to its other side. The stirrups had been slung low to help the inexperienced riders mount, for which she was grateful given her height and lack of practice. Some things indeed did not change, however, for she pulled herself up as smoothly as if fourteen years had not passed since the last time she'd ridden. The layman whistled, impressed, as she settled into the saddle.

"In the desert, a good animal can mean the difference between life and death," he said, smiling up at her. "The Banbarra treat their mounts like family, you know. Give them the names of dead children, put jewelry on them, everything. So treat this lady right."

Hanani smiled, delighted, as she scratched along Dakha's mane and the horse's neck arched under her hand. "I'll be sure to, sir."

Out of the corner of her eye, she saw the Superior come over to Nijiri's mount.

"You're certain of this?" he asked the Gatherer. He spoke low; Hanani heard it only because she was nearby.

"No, I'm not." The sadness Hanani had heard in his voice earlier was gone, replaced by Gatherer calm. "But I'm certain that if we do nothing, we're doomed."

The Superior only sighed in response. Hanani dared not look at them. Instead she looked up as Sentinel Anarim raised his hand for attention.

"We'll leave the city through the east gate," he said. "It's little used, which suits our purposes for avoiding the notice of the Kisuati, though it will force us to circle the city before we proceed southwest. It should take us two days to reach the hills, another day to traverse them." He eyed Nijiri. "We'll be there in time."

Nijiri inclined his head, and Hanani wondered again what he and the other Gatherers had planned.

"We will ride by twos," Anarim continued. "We must be on guard even in Gujaareen lands, and the farther we get from the city, the more hazards there will be. I and Dwi will lead." He nodded to his apprentice, who nodded back with a briskness that belied his apparent calm. "Sentinel Kherkhan and Gatherer Nijiri shall take the rear; Sentinels Emije and Lemuneb shall flank. Sharers, stay between us if there's trouble."

Hanani threw a quick, worried look at Mni-inh, and saw that her mentor looked equally anxious. She had been born in the greenlands herself, but had not passed beyond the city gates since joining the Hetawa. She knew Mni-inh was city-born; for all she knew he had never left the city in his life.

Mni-inh let out an exasperated sigh. "Damnation, Nijiri. I've tried to be patient, but I've had enough. When are you going to tell us what this is about?"

Nijiri smiled as if he'd expected the question. "We're going to meet friends, Mni-inh. At least, I hope they're friends."

"You *hope*—"

"We'll know if they don't kill us. That's if they even show up in the first place."

Mni-inh stared at him. Still smiling, Nijiri nodded to Anarim, who wheeled his mount about and started for the courtyard gate, which four acolytes had cranked open for them. "After you," Nijiri said to Mni-inh. With a muttered curse Mni-inh carefully urged his horse forward, uttering a startled yelp when it actually moved.

Then it was Hanani's turn, and Dakha started out at a trot, as if eager to see them all meet whatever fate awaited.

13

◖⊙◗

Break

*In the garden of Kite-iyan there was a leopard. He could not see it, but
he knew that it was there. As the Prince's heir it was his duty to hunt and
kill it before it harmed his mothers or siblings.*

"Wana."

*Stalking through the garden as quietly as he could—his legs were
shorter, he had always been a quiet child—he hefted his spear and*

"Wana! Wake up, man! This is no time for daydreaming."

*Wanahomen looked up and saw that the leopard had a human face.
Unte. I must kill you, he thought.*

Then Unte was Unte again, and Wanahomen followed Unte's
arm to see what was the matter.

A party of eight riders on horseback approached along the rocky
trail that led through this part of the foothills. From the ledge high
above where he and the rest of the Banbarra waited a-horseback,
Wanahomen could make out only the voluminous hooded robes
that each rider wore: five black, two blood-red, and one the color of
sun-bleached bone. The last made him frown.

"Hetawa?" asked Unte.

Wanahomen nodded. "The black are Sentinels—the warrior-priests,

deadly without weapons, nightmares with. The pale is a Gatherer."
His lip curled; he could not help it. He had not expected the Hetawa to send a Gatherer. To judge him, perhaps? And execute him
on the spot, if they found him wanting? His hands tightened on the
reins; the horse grunted. "They can fight almost as well as the Sentinels, but their magic is the greater threat. Never let him touch
you. And they outrank the rest, so that one will be the leader. The
red—" He frowned. "Those are Sharers. Healers. But why they're
here, I haven't a clue."

"Hmm." Unte reached under his face-veil to scratch his beard.
"And how should we welcome these guests, hunt leader?"

Wanahomen heard the amusement in his voice, and smiled to
himself. His mother would disapprove, but—

"If they are to be allies," he said, "it would seem wise to show
them our strength, would it not?"

Unte chuckled and nodded, and Wanahomen raised his hand in
a signal. All around him he heard his riders shift, alert. He made a
circle and then a fist with his hand, and threw back his head to utter
the rising Banbarra battle cry of *"Bi-yu-eh!"*

Come, and break on us.

The warriors surged forward, riding down three different trails
toward the canyon floor. On the other side of the canyon, two more
lines of riders came too, their calls echoing from the rocky walls. As
the Hetawa party stopped and immediately turned back-to-back
with the two healers at the center of their formation, two circles of
Banbarra horsemen surrounded them, each riding in a different
direction to make their numbers difficult to count.

Wanahomen rode down with them, whooping and brandishing
his sword and laughing behind his veil. The templefolk would be
unnerved, he knew, not just by the number of armed Banbarra who
had come out to greet them, but also by the sheer noisy chaos of

them. Peace was the Gujaareen way, but there was no peace in the Banbarra—not these strong young warriors of Wana's, anyhow.

Yes, see us, he thought as he glared at the templefolk. *See what you ally yourselves to. If your sensibilities are too weak to bear us, then we don't need your help!*

But after the initial defensive movement, the Hetawa riders did not move, and at last Wanahomen began to tire of the game. So he signaled a halt, and the circling riders stilled their mounts and faced the party. They parted as Wanahomen moved through their ranks to stop before the pale-robed Gatherer.

"Show your face," he said. "I would know my enemy."

Most male Banbarra did not speak Gujaareen, but the few who did leaned over to whisper to the rest. They would all know that Wanahomen had demanded the Hetawa party's leader to bare his face to them—an act of submission in Banbarra eyes.

The Gatherer lifted his hands to his hood and paused for a breath, perhaps noting the whispers among the Banbarra party. But he completed the movement, and as soon as Wanahomen saw the man's face he flinched in shock.

"You!" Ten years unraveled themselves in an instant and he stood again on the deck of Kite-iyan, watching while his father faced the two Gatherers of Hananja who had come to kill him. One of the Gatherers had been his father's brother; the stamp of the Sunset was in his face. But the younger one—*"You."*

The Gatherer nodded, infuriatingly calm. He was taller and broader now, no longer a sweet-faced youth, but there was no doubt it was the same man. "I. I remember you as well, son of Eninket. Greetings."

I should kill you right here and now. The thought was beautifully tempting, though he knew it was foolish. But even as he sheathed his sword, he urged his horse Iho forward until she stood alongside the Gatherer's, so that he sat within reach of the man's deadly hands.

"Are you hungry, Gatherer?" He kept his voice low, and saw the man's eyes narrow. "I know your kind, remember. I watched my father break one of you. If you mean to punish me for that, then do it now. You'll get no other chance."

For a moment something glimmered in the Gatherer's eyes—not the mindless hunger Wanahomen had half expected, but a cold anger that was somehow more disturbing for its humanity.

"It was cruel of your father to make you watch while he destroyed Una-une," the Gatherer said, with a gentle viciousness Wanahomen had never seen in one of his kind. "How terribly it must have scarred you. I'm sorry we didn't kill him sooner, for your sake."

Wanahomen bared his teeth in a snarl and restrained himself from reaching for his knife only by a monumental effort of will. "I will never trust you, life-drinking demon!"

Wheeling Iho about, he rode away a few paces to calm himself before turning to face the Hetawa party again. "So. You propose alliance. I see how getting rid of the Kisuati will help *you*, but what do you offer *us*, Priest? Last I heard, the Hetawa had no armies."

The Gatherer nodded. "Fighting has never been our way, in any case. Except in defense of ourselves and others." He threw an apologetic smile at the nearest black-robed priest, who inclined his hooded head in return. "You know, however, that our support has been essential to the Princes of the past."

"Oh yes, I know it," Wanahomen replied. "But you have always charged a price for that support, which I refuse to pay. I will not be your slave as my forefathers were."

"And we will no longer demand such a thing of you." The Gatherer's voice went momentarily softer, and was there shame in it? "The Hetawa has been purged of that corruption. I and my brethren have seen to this with our own hands. We will deal with you fairly. On that you have my word, in Her name."

The Gatherer's candor surprised Wanahomen. He had heard about the purges, and privately marveled—but to hear the words aloud, openly, was another thing. A more satisfying thing.

Throwing a glance back at Unte, who had come down into the canyon but hung back silently observing, he said to the Gatherer, "So you offer your influence over our people, and to back my claim to the throne. This is all fine once I've taken the city, and once my men and I have spilled our blood in the effort. But allies share the risk, priest, as well as the reward. What can you do for us *now*?"

"You think we share no risk? If you fail, the Kisuati will destroy us."

"And yet you can withdraw from this alliance at any time before the final assault, and claim you had no part in it." Wanahomen gestured east, toward Gujaareh. "You've always operated that way, in the shadows, sneaking through windows in the night—but this is war. Commit yourself to the fight, or stay in your temple and pray. And wait for *me* to destroy you, when I win!"

The Gatherer inclined his head, as if Wanahomen had invited him to share wine. "We can offer supplies and funds—"

Wanahomen laughed. "We've stolen more than we need from the Kisuati already. Offer something *useful*, templeman. Perhaps you could Gather Sunandi Jeh Kalawe, and her general husband?"

The Gatherer's face hardened. "They have not been judged corrupt."

Wanahomen had not truly expected him to agree. "Then what?"

The Gatherer was silent for a long moment before finally sighing. "So be it." He sidestepped his horse a few paces and then stopped, turning back to gaze at the two red-clad priests who had been behind him. "These two are yours until your throne is regained."

The red priests stiffened. So did Wanahomen. Over the murmuring of his men, he scowled at the Gatherer. "Is this some trick?"

"The Hetawa's—and Gujaareh's—greatest asset is our magic," the Gatherer replied. "A Gatherer would be of little use to you, but

Sharers could save the lives of men who might otherwise die in the battles to come."

Two Sharers. Wanahomen stared at the red priests, torn between excitement and despair. The Gatherer was right: two Sharers could cut their losses greatly. And—his mind leaped to another possibility with shameful speed—*a Sharer could save Mother.*

And yet...

Two Sharers, thrown at his feet as prizes. Two Hetawa spies, right in the heart of his camp.

He turned to Unte, trying to school himself to nonchalance so that the disappointment would hurt less.

Unte walked his horse forward, gazing thoughtfully at the priests. Wanahomen had taught him a great deal of Gujaareen over the years; he'd probably been able to follow the whole conversation. Still, he spoke in Chakti to Wanahomen. "Am I hearing rightly? Have your people suddenly seen profit in the slave trade?"

Wanahomen, who had been watching the Gatherer, shook his head. The priest's eyes narrowed when Unte spoke; he apparently knew enough Chakti to recognize the word *slave* when he heard it. "Not slaves, but hostages to seal our alliance. To be freed when our goal is achieved."

Unte shifted in his saddle and sighed. "I've never been much for hostage-taking. Too much trouble for too little profit. Still, if they can do magic as he says, they would be valuable."

Wanahomen forced himself to say it. "They could also pass on our secrets to the Hetawa. We would have to take them to our encampment; they would later be able to reveal its location."

Unte smiled. "I've never yet known a city dweller who could find his own feet on the sand without a desertman's aid. And what reason would they have to spy on us? We have the same enemy."

It was true. But it had not escaped Wanahomen's notice that this was the only possible reason for the Gatherer to bring the two Sharers along: for all his dissembling, the Gatherer had intended to offer them as prizes from the beginning. "I simply don't trust them, Unte."

"You trust no one, my soul-son. Tell that pretty-faced fellow we'll take them."

Wanahomen started. "Are you—" He cut off his own question and bowed his head in submission when Unte threw him a mild look. "Yes, Unte."

He gestured for two of his men to ride forward and flank the Sharers. But one of the black-clads leaped off his horse and moved to block the Banbarra, radiating menace, and one of the red priests yanked back his hood and called sharply—"Nijiri!"

The Gatherer—Nijiri, Wanahomen committed to memory—sighed. "I'm sorry, Mni-inh. But I would not have your apprentice go with them alone, for all that she agreed to this."

"She *agreed*—" The Sharer looked at his companion incredulously. "Hanani, is this true?"

The other Sharer seemed too stricken to speak—as was Wanahomen, whose thoughts were suddenly afire with suspicion. *She?*

But it was unmistakably a woman's voice, trembling with fear, that finally answered. "I . . . Yes, Brother. But I did not realize . . ." The knuckles of her already-pale hands, on the pommel of her saddle, had gone whiter still. "I thought . . ."

"I told you there would be risk, Apprentice." The Gatherer's face was utterly without emotion. "The Prince thinks you're a spy. Perhaps he'll be less inclined to think so now that he sees you weren't prepared for this." And the Gatherer looked at Wanahomen.

Damnation. Wanahomen set his jaw, hating the Gatherer even more. The man knew full well what sending a Gujaareen woman into a Banbarra camp meant. Even sending the male Sharer along with her would do little good; Sharers did not fight. It would fall to Wanahomen to protect her. *We're in the middle of a war, shadows damn you! I haven't got time to bodyguard a useless city woman!*

But there was no other choice; Unte had commanded it, and the Hetawa's cooperation would no doubt hinge on how well the hostages were treated.

Sighing in irritation, Wanahomen rode forward, stopping when he faced the Sentinel—or Sentinel-Apprentice; the young man looked hardly old enough to have joined a path. He could barely see the youth's eyes within the hood, but he stared them down anyhow, and after a long moment the youth sighed and stepped aside.

Bringing Iho near the woman's horse, he reached up and tugged down her hood. It was her—the Sharer-girl he'd met in the city. She looked up at him fearfully; with his face-veil in place he probably looked like any other Banbarra to her.

"Go with them," he ordered her in Gujaareen, jerking his head toward his men. She started, animal panic in her eyes; for a moment he thought she might flee. But then she took a deep breath and assumed a mask of calm that would have been perfect if not for the brightness of her eyes. Nodding, she rode over to join the men. Her companion, a man of late middle years who had shiny, almost northerner-straight hair, scowled at Wanahomen but also rode over, staying protectively close to the girl.

"The alliance is sealed, then?" The Gatherer spoke to Unte, but his eyes flicked to Wanahomen.

"Between Gujaareen Hetawa and Banbarra of the Yusir tribe, it is," said Unte in thickly-accented Gujaareen. Wanahomen nodded as well, remembering the Sentinel's words from that day in the hills: *the alliance would be with you.*

The Gatherer inclined his head. "We await your attack, then. When the time comes, our fighters and magic will support you during the battle to follow. Will it be soon?"

"Yes," Wanahomen replied.

"Just after the solstice," added Unte, much to Wanahomen's chagrin.

"Walk in Her peace until then," the Gatherer said, and nodded to the Sentinels. They closed ranks about him obediently, and the six of them turned their horses back the way they'd come. Unte gave a quick signal and the Banbarra riders moved aside, letting the Hetawa party go.

Once they had vanished over the farthest hill, Unte turned to Wanahomen and sighed. "Well, that's done."

"There's still the vote, Unte."

Unte looked at Wanahomen in surprise, a hint of amusement in his expression. "So you don't blithely assume success there? I would never have thought your confidence so lacking."

"I'm as confident as always, Unte, but I would never presume to predict the actions of the leaders of the six tribes. If the vote doesn't go as I hope..." He looked after the diminishing figures of the Hetawa party, uneasy.

Unte smiled. "Well, we'll simply have to hope that it does. This alliance will help. Shall we go home?"

Nodding obedience, Wanahomen gave the signal for them to ride out for Merik-ren-aferu, with the Sharers as hostages at the center of their formation.

14

(⊙)

Merik-ren-aferu

She was among barbarians.

Gatherer Nijiri had *left* her among barbarians.

She was among barbarians and they would torture her, kill her, send her soul forth to flail through the horrors of the shadowlands...

This was the cycle of Hanani's thoughts for the four days that it took them to journey to the Banbarra encampment. The Banbarra set a hard pace, riding at a trot from before dawn until just before noon, pausing for several hours while the sun was hottest, and then riding from afternoon past sunset. Hanani's muscles, already sore from the days of riding that had brought them from the city, stopped protesting on the second day, and by the third day she was just numb. She healed her own sores, but they always came back.

Their hosts were anything but friendly. Each Banbarra warrior wore similar flowing tunics and robes in a variety of colors, elaborately wrapped headcloths, and cloth veils across the bottom halves of their faces, even in sleep. They rarely offered names, so Hanani had difficulty telling one from another. The one Nijiri had dubbed "the Prince" barely spoke to them except to bark orders; he seemed more annoyed by their presence than anything else. The other Banbarra followed his lead in their interactions with Hanani and Mni-inh, though Hanani caught a few of them throwing speculative glances at her from time to time. She had no idea—and did not want to know—what interested them so.

It was the tribe's leader, Unte, who spoke to them most often, coming over to pepper them with questions in fluent, though hard-to-understand, Gujaareen. Both he and the Prince wore outer robes and veils of shining indigo, and Unte was shorter, so they could at least see him coming and brace themselves before he began. How did they like the desert? Mni-inh, who was still seething over Nijiri's decision, answered that one with rather less diplomacy than he should have: "We don't." But his surliness only seemed to amuse the man. How long had they served the Hetawa? Was it true they could dream while wide awake, or put anyone to sleep in the middle of the day? How did they heal?

Mni-inh struggled to answer the questions as best he could, but Hanani had been unable to bring herself to react to the man's friendliness. Her mind and heart were frozen, as they had been since the Gatherer reminded her that she had agreed to face a trial. She had expected...Well, she'd had no idea what to expect. But not this.

Unte seemed comfortable with her silence, however, every now and again offering her what seemed to be a bow of respect. Mni-inh, Hanani noticed, did not get the same bow.

On the evening of the fourth day, just as the sun had begun to make Hanani's head beat fiercely, she saw that the scrubby land sloped gradually toward a great uneven crack in the earth. They continued forward, plainly angling to pass through this canyon rather than detour around. But just as they descended the trail that led them between the canyon's great jagged walls, Hanani smelled water. It was faint—nothing like the thick, earthy, river smell of

Gujaareh—but after so many days of sand and sun her nose seemed to wake up at the first whiff of moisture. Dakha, whom Hanani realized must have caught the scent some ways back, kept trying to urge the horses in front of her to go faster. Those horses, used to the journey, kept the same steady, ground-eating pace they'd employed all along.

Their surroundings began to change drastically. In place of the colorless desert scrub she began to see green grass, even trees as they moved farther into the canyon. The walls of the canyon were tall and sheer, as if carved by a great knife; their colors were deep, rich shades of red, a welcome change to the unrelenting tan of the scrublands. The green of the vegetation—though paler than that grown in Gujaareh's rich, flood-fed soil—was bright enough that it almost hurt Hanani's eyes.

Her spirits lifting, she looked at their companions and saw that the Banbarra too seemed in a better mood, some of them even laughing as they spoke to one another. One of them pointed up, and Hanani gasped when she followed his finger. There was someone up on one of the canyon's highest ledges!

Before she could cry a warning, however, Mni-inh elbowed her and pointed. Through the trees, she could glimpse a winding river. It was so small that the Goddess's Blood could have swallowed it without rising an inch—but it was unmistakably swift-flowing, fresh water. Where had it come from in the middle of the desert?

Unte, chuckling at her confusion, touched her arm and pointed. Far beyond the jagged walls of the canyon she could see, faint against the evening sky, a cluster of fat white-capped mountains.

"In winter, snow falls there," he said. "You know what snow is?"

"I've read of it," she said. "Rain and dew gone hard from cold?"

"Mmm. Snow there, in winter. Melts, solstice through spring— you call floodseason. Floods here, too. Little." He smiled and made a minimizing gesture with his hand, to indicate that their floodseason was nothing compared to Gujaareh's annual dunking. He pointed to the river, then back along the way they'd come, toward the desert. "Goes underground there, under the desert, but here all is green. Dries up fall and winter, 'til solstice again. Just starting now."

Hanani nodded, wonder overcoming her unease at speaking with a foreigner. Greatly daring, she pointed up toward the ledge where she'd seen what looked like a child running. "And there?"

She could not see his face through the veil, but his eyes crinkled in well-worn laugh lines. "You will see," he said.

They followed the river into the canyon, splashing through some of its branch streams, finally rounding a bend to stop before a broad grassy plain. A corral filled with horses and camels stood near the northern wall; the animals already in it trotted about, grunting greetings to the new arrivals and flicking tails in excitement. There, several unveiled Banbarra children waited, waving at the returning party. The men around Hanani began calling out to them in a babble of Chakti, and the answering voices seemed to come from all around—including above, Hanani realized, and she looked up and would have stopped in shock if Dakha hadn't been determined to follow the other horses.

Up on the ledges was an entire village. Most of what she saw were probably tents—round dome-shaped things festooned with furs and other decorations, in a variety of earth shades. But a few of the structures were made of sandy brick: permanent houses and storerooms and Goddess-knew-what else, built right onto the ledges! All of it hundreds of feet above the canyon floor.

The party halted at the corral. Tearing her eyes from the ledges, Hanani followed her hosts' lead, dismounting and trying to untie her saddlebags. Much to her surprise, Unte made a shooing sound and came over to untie them for her. When he'd gotten them loose, he threw them over his shoulder and bowed to her before walking off with them. He did not go far, however—only over to the Prince, to whom he handed the bags. Far from growing angry as Hanani had expected, the Prince frowned in puzzlement at Unte. Unte jerked his head back toward Hanani, indicating whose bags they were.

The Prince, even more astonishingly, looked chagrined. He took the bags with an apologetic murmur to Unte, and then came over to Hanani and Mni-inh.

"The children will tend your mounts, now that we're here in—" He said something in rapid Chakti, but Hanani caught the word *Merik*. It was the name of one of the gods, the craftsman who ground down mountains and filled up valleys. "This is the home of the Yusir tribe. Come with me."

It was the most he'd said to either of them the whole journey. They hastened to follow, both of them wincing and stiff after days a-horseback, as he headed toward the cliff with brisk long strides. When it became clear that his course would take him to one of several rope-and-wood ladders braced against the cliff face, Hanani's steps faltered.

The Prince stopped at the ladder. Mni-inh looked up it and sighed. "I suppose there's no other way?"

"None," the Prince replied, and for the first time Hanani heard a hint of amusement in his voice. "Though you could stay the night down here, if the climb truly troubles you. There are no animals more dangerous than scorpions, and a few varieties of snake..."

"We'll go up," Mni-inh said quickly.

The Prince beckoned to Hanani, indicating that she should go first. Uncomfortably she swallowed, came to the foot of the ladder, and looked up. It seemed so very high.

"Just climb," the Prince said. "And don't look down. Best to get it over with quickly, the first time."

Which reminded her, only somewhat reassuringly, that this had been new to him once. She looked at Mni-inh and saw that he looked equally nervous. He dredged up a smile, however.

"Go on," he said, shifting his saddlebags onto his shoulders as the Banbarra men had done. "I'll be right behind you. Mind you, only one of us can fall, because the other will have to do the healing."

Hanani smiled in spite of herself. "Yes, Brother." Feeling marginally less nervous, she took hold of the rungs and began to climb, going as quickly as she dared. Once she'd begun, it was less frightening; the ladder was solidly made and had been braced with pegs and hooks. Before she knew it, she had reached the ledge and was on solid ground again. She turned—

—And froze, her breath catching in her throat.

Before her spread the canyon in fiery light and sharp-edged shadow, beneath a sky as endless and blue as the Sea of Glory. The animals in the corral below were as small as children's toys, the crop-field nearby a neat series of greener rows amid the waves of windblown grass; the canyon's river was a mere thread, glimmering through the trees with the reflected light of sunset. She had been up high before, in the topmost levels of the Hetawa, but never like this.

Struck mute with awe at the canyon's beauty, she was still standing there when Mni-inh reached the ledge. He followed Hanani's gaze, then looked down the cliff face they had just climbed. He shuddered and took three quick steps back. "*Indethe a etun'a Hananja*—"

"*Enube an'nethe*," the Prince said, startling them both. He had come up behind them, still carrying Hanani's bags. When they looked at him, he too was gazing out at the view. "She turns Her gaze upon those who earn it, priest. Now come."

He led them through the Banbarra encampment. Despite the bizarre locale, it was much like a Gujaareen upriver village, just with tents instead of permanent houses. The tents seemed to be clustered together in outward-facing circles of three or four, each cluster separated by a space and sometimes a work area from others around it. The handful of permanent, brick-walled buildings seemed to have more practical purposes—she glimpsed a glowing kiln through one doorway, and from another building she could smell the acrid tang of molten metal: a smithy. And a water-cistern, and a grain house. Not so different from a Gujaareen village at all.

The people were different, of course. She had no idea of the Banbarra's origins—they had been in the desert for centuries when Gujaareh was founded—but they had clearly mixed themselves less widely than Hanani's folk. Though she caught the occasional glimpse of hazel eyes and paler or darker skin, for the most part they were brown as tawny marble, with sharp features that reminded Hanani of people born to the Gujaareen military caste. The men wore the same kinds of robes that the troop had worn in the desert, though here she glimpsed more elaborate variations on the style— softer cloth, beading, lace and brighter colors—and longer veils.

They all gazed at her suspiciously, she noted, and raised their veils higher as she and Mni-inh passed.

The women were another matter. She saw the first few gathered near a cookfire, watching her with open curiosity. Unlike the men they wore no veils or headcloths, though their jewelry and hairstyles were elaborate enough to impress even the most hedonistic Gujaareen highcaste. Hanani could not help staring at women with necklaces of gold hanging from nostril to ear, with braided hair dangling shell beads, with eyelids painted green and blue and shockingly white. Their clothes were closer-fitting and more brightly colored than the men's, girdled about the waist or hips, the voluminous sleeves wrapped at the wrists and festooned with still more ornaments.

When she stopped staring at their clothing and trappings, she noticed their faces: less suspicious than those of the men, but no more friendly.

When their host stopped at a large tent, Hanani stared for a moment at the sun-and-rays emblem above the door. Gatherer Nijiri had called this man *Prince*, but what did that mean? No Prince had ruled in Gujaareh since King Eninket had assumed the Throne of Dreams. Though of course he'd had many fours of children...

She looked at the man called the Prince, and found that he was watching her, wary sullenness in his eyes.

"This is my mother's—" He said something in Banbarra: it sounded like *an-sherrat*. "Her hearth, her territory. You will not disrespect her."

Hanani blinked, for that had been the last thing on her mind. She glanced at the emblem again, not wanting to believe her own suspicions. "Your mother is of the Sunset Lineage?"

"She is firstwife to the king who rules now in Ina-Karekh."

Mni-inh caught his breath and stared at the man as if they'd only just met him. "You're Wanahomen! The one everyone believed would become Prince after him."

Some of the sullenness went out of the Prince's eyes, though Hanani could not read the emotion that replaced it. Something bitter, whatever it was. "Did they? Clearly none of those people knew my father, then."

Mni-inh looked confused. Hanani ventured, "Then you were the heir he chose?"

"Princes of the Sunset designate heirs only nominally. The one who ultimately rules is the one with the strength to win and hold the throne. I mean to be that one."

"Is it—" She hesitated to ask him more questions; she had learned along the journey that he had little patience. But it had been drilled into her over and over in the Hetawa: the orderly castes and rankings of people within society contributed to Hananja's peace. "Is it proper to call you *Prince*, then?"

He let out an amused breath, briefly stirring the cloth of his veil. "You truly are one of them, aren't you, woman? As if propriety matters, given the circumstances..." He sighed. "Call me whatever you like."

He drummed his fingers on the taut surface of the tent. A hoarse voice within called, "Enter," in Gujaareen. Hanani saw their host tense slightly before he opened the entrance flap and stepped within. He held it for them to enter, and Hanani followed her mentor inside.

Almost at once the smell of sickness hit her. She stopped just within the tent, surprised by it. The tent was larger and more luxurious inside than she had expected, its floor lined with rugs, beautiful brass lanterns hanging from the poles and seams. A woman lay on a thick pallet of furs at the tent's center, peering at them curiously as they entered. The Prince tied the flaps shut behind them and then straightened, looking intently at them as he gestured toward the woman. "My mother Hendet, of Hinba's lineage and shunha caste, firstwife of Eninket King."

Mni-inh quickly bowed low over both his hands, as did Hanani, but Hendet said nothing as she stared at them—at Hanani in particular. Beside her sat a small boy of six or seven floods, holding a cup of water in his hands. The boy looked apprehensive at the sight of strangers, but brightened as soon as he saw the Prince. "Wana?"

"Tassa." Saying something in Chakti, the Prince held out a hand and the child went to him. Like the other Banbarra children Hanani had seen, this one wore no veil or headcloth. The Prince cupped the child's cheek in a brief affectionate gesture, and she saw the resemblance at once in the eyes—though the signs were also in the boy's more tightly curled hair and dark-for-Banbarra coloring. The boy was his son.

The Prince spoke to the child in Chakti, giving instructions of some sort.

"*Two* tents," Hendet said suddenly in Gujaareen, and the boy stopped and looked at her in surprise. The Prince did as well.

"Mother?"

"A respectable woman cannot be expected to share her tent,"

Hendet said. With what clearly took a great effort, she pushed herself up on one elbow; Wanahomen immediately went to her side to help. She panted a little and gave him a weak smile of thanks. "Order two tents, Wana. And tell Nefri that *I'm* buying them."

The Prince stiffened. "Mother, she is of the Hetawa, it doesn't matter—"

"She must be protected." Despite the sickness, it was obvious Hendet had been a king's wife: the note of command was in her voice. "Among the Banbarra, a person without wealth or kin is a slave. The Hetawa are our allies and these—" She faltered, visibly weakening. "They must both be protected…"

She fell silent, and the Prince caught his breath in alarm. "Mother!"

The urge to go to the woman was strong, but Hanani held herself back, deferring to Mni-inh as the senior Sharer. Mni-inh went over to them and crouched beside the woman, touching her forehead before the Prince could glare him away. "She's just fainted. The disease eats all her strength. Lay her back down and I'll examine her."

When the Prince didn't move, Mni-inh simply waited, gazing at him with the mild look that Hanani had always found worse than a reprimand during her training. Finally, with a soft curse, the Prince lay her down and got up, walking a few steps away and turning his back to them. His hands were fisted at his sides, but he said nothing. The boy, who had not left, went to him and touched one of his fists anxiously.

"Hanani." Mni-inh stood to pull off his formal robe, lest the loose sleeves get in his way. "I've seen something like this before, and I think we'll need a great deal of dreambile. How are your reserves?"

His brisk tone, the same he'd used in a hundred lessons and healings with her, was immensely reassuring. "Since the interdiction, Brother? I have little of anything *but* dreambile." This she had in plenty thanks to her own dreams, which had been ugly of late.

"Good." He raked her with a glance when she did not immediately move to assist him. "The interdiction was going to be lifted, Hanani, you know that. Your oath takes precedence over your doubts. This woman needs you."

The words washed through Hanani like a cleansing, so powerful that she let out a deep breath and hurried to join him. Pulling off her own formal robe, she knelt at the woman's side and set her hand on the woman's breastbone in secondary healing position. Mni-inh knelt at the woman's head and laid his fingertips on her eyes.

"It's a variation on the sickness-of-tumors," he said, closing his eyes while he began the search for her soul. "The disease is in the blood—or more specifically, in the bone, which makes blood. The feel is much the same as with other varieties of this sickness, so follow me in and we shall search for it."

"Yes, Brother." She closed her eyes as well and sank into healing trance with him, her dreaming-self seeking its partner in the woman's flesh. Mni-inh found the woman's soul before Hanani; it was hidden between two mid-ribs near the heart. He merged with it; Hanani did the same; and together they made the leap to Ina-Karekh.

After so long, performing an unrestricted, guiltless healing was a joy indescribable to Hanani—though the dream that Hendet suffered was anything but joyful. The woman's dreamscapes were full of chewing, flensing things: scarab beetles and many-legged mites and hot ash that burned everything it touched. Mni-inh assigned Hanani to cleanse this imagery and the sickness that it represented, while he dug beneath the dreamscape and used dreamseed to encourage her body to replace the diseased bone with healthy. It was slow work, but with two healers dreaming in tandem, it went easily.

"Oh—" Mni-inh stretched, grinning as they finally ended the

dream and returned to Hona-Karekh. "I've *missed* this, Hanani. It truly is Sharing when we work together."

Hanani smiled, shyly—and then paused as she spied the Prince, who sat on the far side of the tent watching them. Several hours must have passed since the healing had begun, for it was darker in the tent now. In the dimness she could just make out his face-veil and the glitter of his eyes above it.

"She should be well now," Hanani said, anxious to reassure him. "I've cleansed away the taint. My mentor has grown anew the diseased part of her, so that it will make healthy blood from now on."

Mni-inh nodded agreement as he completed his examination, sitting back on his heels. "Water, rest, and food—particularly red meat—will help her regain her strength most quickly."

The Prince's nod was a slow, barely visible movement in the darkness. "Congratulations," he said. "You've proven your lives worth preserving."

The absolute coldness of his voice was like a slap. Hanani drew back from it, looking instinctively to Mni-inh, but he too looked confused by the Prince's reaction. She had not expected the man to share their good spirits; happiness seemed beyond him. Gratitude, though—yes, she had hoped for that.

But before either of them could muster a response, the Prince got to his feet.

"My servant is outside," he said. He did not look at either of them, his eyes fixed on his mother. "He'll show you to your tents."

Hanani looked at Mni-inh again, but he only shook his head, getting to his feet. Hanani did the same, and moved to follow Mni-inh through the tent flap.

"This makes us even, templewoman," the Prince said, his voice forestalling her. "But no more than that."

"Even?"

He turned to her, reached up, and pulled down his face-veil. She caught her breath, recognizing at last the man who had tried to save her from the Kisuati soldiers. His expression held none of the contempt he had shown her that day, but neither was there friendliness. He might have favored an enemy or an insect with the same cold regard.

"Now get out," he said, and turned his back on her.

Shaken into silence, Hanani obeyed.

15

<(⊙)>

A Call to Arms

The eightday leading to the winter solstice was a time of great peace and contemplation in Gujaareh. In a month, perhaps more, the great river called the Goddess's Blood would overflow its banks and fill the entire valley. When the waters receded, they would leave behind thick black silt, whose richness made the garden that was Gujaareh blossom at the desert's heart. Once the storm clouds faded and the land's fertility was renewed, children born in the prior year could be named at last.

But until the floods began, Gujaareh existed in an arid limbo, waiting. The farmers sat idle, their fourth and last harvest done; craftsmen and artisans finished projects and closed accounts for the year; those with the means went on trips to estates outside the river valley, to avoid the floods' nuisance. It was at such times that families in Gujaareh came together to celebrate love, good fortune, death, and all the small, mundane joys in between.

The Sisters of Hananja were busiest of all during the days of the solstice. Hardly a street there was, from wealthy highcaste neighborhoods to fishmarket hovels, that did not know the sound of rhythmic bells and a soft stately drum, announcing the procession of a

Sister and her attendants. And the sight of a yellow Sisters' tent—within which these representatives of the Goddess would lay down their tithebearers and conjure for them dreams of purest ecstasy—was a common one during the winter's short days and long nights.

Likely it was because there were more Sisters about, and more people to watch for them, that two Kisuati soldiers were seen forcing a Sister into an old storehouse. A mob formed with astonishing speed, rescuing the Sister and her apprentice, who had been taken hostage to ensure her cooperation. The angry citizens then gathered around the soldiers with ominous intent. But as the soldiers shouted warnings and drew weapons to defend themselves, the crowd parted before a stocky, serene man with the tattoo of a red poppy on one shoulder.

"We've been watching you," he said to the soldiers, smiling. "Didn't think you'd be foolish enough to attempt another assault in the open like this, but— Well, here we are."

One of the soldiers, intuiting something of the man's intent, screamed and slashed at him with his sword. The watching crowd gasped. Quick as a striking snake, the man ducked the slash and caught the soldier's sword-wrist, jerking him off balance. The soldier stumbled forward, nearly losing his grip on the hilt, but before he could recover the tattooed man had put two fingers on his eyelids. He fell, asleep, and the man put something small, that hummed faintly, on his forehead.

The other soldier understood at last. Panicking, he fumbled for his own sword, but before he could get it out of its sheath, the man caught hold of his arm. "Peace," the man said—and that soldier too slumped to the ground.

The tattooed man then returned to the first soldier, laying fingers on his eyelids for several long silent breaths. When the soldier let out a long sigh and did not breathe in again, the crowd murmured its approval. The tattooed man then performed the same ritual on the second soldier, and when he too was dead, the crowd gave a great collective sigh. They fell silent, properly reverent, as the man arranged the soldiers' bodies into a dignified position, and then stamped a symbol on each forehead. The red poppy, same as the man's shoulder tattoo.

Just as he finished this, more Kisuati soldiers arrived in a rush, having word of the mob. The new soldiers' commander pushed through the crowd with his sword drawn and then stopped in disbelief, staring down at the corpses as the tattooed man turned to face him.

"These men have committed violence against citizens of Gujaareh," the man said. "Most heinously against those who serve our Goddess. They have been judged corrupt and granted peace in accordance with Hananja's Law."

"*We* don't obey your damned Law, you filthy—" the commander began, pointing his sword at the man. He fell silent as one of his men touched his shoulder; the crowd was murmuring again, its tone this time unmistakably angry. The commander hesitated, then lowered his sword.

"Hananja's City obeys Hananja's Law," the man said.

"*Hananja's City obeys Hananja's Law,*" echoed the crowd, soft and relentless. The soldiers started, looking around in alarm.

"Your people have been tolerable until now," said the man, "and we have welcomed you for that reason. You are our kin, after all. But if you can no longer accept our hospitality without abusing it, then perhaps it's time you left."

The commander caught his breath in fury and affront, but it did not escape his notice that the crowd, which was growing larger by the moment, signified its agreement with a few shouts and raised fists of encouragement. The shouts ended, however, as the tattooed man gave the crowd a mild look. This, far more than the crowd's agitation, turned the commander's fury into sharp, iron-cold fear.

He realized: if the tattooed man commanded it, the crowd would fall upon him and his men, and tear them apart.

"I would suggest you at least leave this street," the tattooed man said. His voice was gentle, his eyes genuinely kind; later the commander would recall this with great confusion. He had never been threatened so politely in his life. "Peace is a difficult creed to follow at the best of times, and certain provocations go beyond even a pious person's self-control. I'll summon some of my Sharer brethren to help distribute these soldiers' peace to the crowd, which should calm them. You should go and inform your superiors of what's happened here."

The commander's men looked anxiously at him, hoping for his agreement. The commander stared back at the tattooed man, suspicious. "You *want* us to tell what happened here?"

The man looked amused. "Of course. The Hetawa has nothing to hide."

And with that the commander understood: they had planned this.

"We must take our fallen comrades," the commander said. It was an effort to save face. He was too unnerved for true courage. To his surprise, however, the tattooed man nodded. Then, amazingly, the man folded his arms before his face and knelt, bowing his head. The people in the crowd—even the Sister who had been assaulted—did the same. Silence and stillness, save for the agitated Kisuati, filled the street.

They show respect to two rapists? the commander wondered at first. Then it occurred to him. *They show respect to two* dead *rapists. Because* they're dead.

And in Gujaareh, death was a thing to be celebrated, so long as it brought peace.

Quickly, the commander ordered his men to collect the two bodies and carry them back to the local barracks. Not a single Gujaareen head lifted while the soldiers left with their burden. When the tattooed man rose, so did the others in the crowd.

"Are you certain that was wise, Gatherer?" asked the Sister. She still looked shaken. The tattooed man regarded her for a moment and then touched her cheek. She shivered as the soldiers' peace passed between them, returning the calm that had been stolen from her.

"Wise or not, it's done," the Gatherer said. "A crisis is upon us. Gujaareh must be unified, now, if we're to survive."

"If the Kisuati punish the Hetawa for killing those bastards," snapped a man nearby, "we'll punish *them*." More than one murmur of agreement rippled through the crowd.

The Gatherer gazed at him for a moment, then sighed. "If Hananja wills it, then it must be so."

The man let out a cheer and the crowd joined him, some of its members hugging one another or laughing in an excess of good feeling. They had challenged the Kisuati—a small challenge, it was true, but a victory nevertheless. The Hetawa had at last come out of its complacent, complicit silence to champion Hananja's people before their conquerors. In the days to come, the tale of the Gathering would spread and grow in the retelling, stirring hope and the desire to act where before there had been only simmering frustration. In time—not very long at all—the city would be ready, eager, for a change. And more than willing to fight for it.

In the impromptu celebration that followed, Gatherer Rabbaneh slipped quietly away.

16

◖ ☉ ◗

A Sharer's Price

Hanani woke at dawn the next morning hungry, itchy, and in dire need of a toilet. Along the journey from Gujaareh she had grown used to functioning in the rough, but there was much to be said for the Hetawa's elegant chambers and jars, which made daily necessities comfortable. She had no idea of the Banbarra's customs in this regard, but it had now become necessary to ask.

Sitting up, she looked about the large, empty tent she had been given the night before. Charris, a Gujaareen man near Mni-inh's age who said he served the Prince, had given her a single thin pallet on which to rest and ordered her not to go wandering about the Banbarra camp alone. She had no plans to do so—but what was she to do if he wasn't about? Stiff from lying on the pallet, she rose, went to the tent entrance, and peeked out.

Only a few Banbarra were up and about so early. She spied, at the cluster of tents across the path from hers, a thin man with easternese features busy preparing a meal. The whiff of cooking food from nearer by caught her attention, and she slipped out of the tent to look around. In the fire circle created by her tent, Hendet's,

Mni-inh's, and a fourth tent that she assumed was the Prince's, Charris sat tending meat on a small spit.

Shivering with the early-morning chill, Hanani stepped into the circle and bowed to him. "Good morning, sir. Did you dream well last night?"

He started at her voice, then looked faintly amused. "I never remember my dreams, little Sharer," he said. He did not smile, but there was a quality to his manner that reminded her very much of Mni-inh; she found herself relaxing automatically. "The Hetawa dismissed me as hopeless before I'd even seen my third flood."

Hanani smiled and crouched near the fire, though this put uncomfortable pressure on her bladder. "I could help you with that if you like," she said. "But in the meantime, sir, I hope you could help me acquire some necessities."

He nodded as if he'd expected this. "Clothing, yes. You can't go around here dressed like that."

Thrown, Hanani glanced down at herself. She wore her everyday uniform—the collar of carnelian beads, the red loindrapes, her breast-wrappings. "What's wrong with my clothing?"

"Women wear more, here, than in Gujaareh. And they don't dress like men."

"My status as a Servant of Hananja—"

"*I* understand it," Charris said with a faint smile, "but the Banbarra will not. A woman who dresses as a man will be treated as a man, and here men who are strong may abuse or even kill weaker men with few consequences. These people don't believe in peace as we do. Respect that."

She sighed. "Very well. I'll put on my formal robe. First, though, is there somewhere I may relieve myself? And bathe? It has been... several days." She hunched in shame.

He looked surprised, then chuckled, though his laugh had a

wistful edge. "Ah, for the days when a few missed baths troubled me so! Well, for now I'll take you down to the ground level. Is your companion likely to wake anytime soon?"

"Yes," Mni-inh said, stepping around his tent. He looked as bleary and stiff as Hanani, though he nodded politely to them both. "I slept better on sand and gravel while we were traveling; at least that was softer than solid rock. These people's hospitality leaves much to be desired."

"They haven't killed you yet," Charris said with a shrug. Mni-inh smiled, but Hanani realized the man was completely serious. He set the spit farther back from the fire, pulled out several clay pots that had been warming, and got up. "Come with me."

He led them back to the ladder they'd climbed the day before. Here Hanani forgot all about her bladder, for it was much, much more frightening to climb down the ladder than it had been to climb up. She managed the trick by closing her eyes and hugging herself to the ladder as best she could, trying not to feel the chilly morning breeze that skated up her back as her feet searched for the next rung below. It helped a little that Mni-inh kept up a steady stream of curses all the way down, distracting her from her own fear.

At last they reached the ground level, none the worse except for their nerves, and Charris led them to a stand of trees a good ways from the river, where a neat latrine had been dug. This was what the tribe's slaves used, Charris explained; he did not say what more fortunate citizens did instead. Afterward he led them through the trees to a grassy riverbank, just around the canyon's curve from the encampment cliffs. The river had formed a small shallow pool here.

"There's another pool right over there," he said, pointing over a hill and looking at Hanani, "for you."

"I'll stay with my mentor," Hanani said. Mni-inh had already stripped and waded into the water; Hanani began to do the same. Charris looked startled, quickly turning his back as Hanani undressed. She puzzled over this reaction while she bathed, carrying her clothing into the water with her to wash as well. Charris was Gujaareen, after all; in Gujaareh it was not uncommon to see men and women naked in public, particularly on hot days. And this was for bathing, which was not remotely titillating. But when she got out and sat down on a rock to finger-comb her hair while her clothing dried, Charris made a sound very like one of irritation and walked off into the trees.

Mni-inh sat down beside her, glancing in the direction Charris had gone. Wet and freed of its usual braid, his hair had turned into a snarl of oily-looking ringlets threaded liberally with white. Having finished her own hair, Hanani moved behind him to help him pull out the tangles.

"I think," he said while she worked, "that you're going to have to be a woman again, Hanani."

She paused, her hands wrist-deep in his hair, and wondered whether he was joking. "My fertile cycle has already peaked for the month, Brother, but I'm quite certain I'm still a woman."

"Not truly," he said. "We discouraged that in you, making you dress like us and live as we do in the Hetawa. For you to become one of us—and for some of our members to accept you—that was necessary. But here, I think, you'll need to do the opposite."

Hanani resumed finger-combing his hair, troubled. She had always *felt* womanly, whatever that meant. Her life as a Servant of Hananja felt natural and right; did that not mean that it suited her—suited women? Still, she had never minded dressing as a man, or being called *sir* in formal situations, because those things made her a Servant of Hananja in the eyes of her brethren and the people. Without those male trappings—

never know true womanhood

—Could she even be a Servant anymore?

Her hands faltered in Mni-inh's hair.

Mni-inh sighed, misreading her stillness. "If only that damned Nijiri had let me know what he was planning. I can't believe he's put us into this kind of danger." He reached back and took one of Hanani's hands. "I'll do my best to protect you, Hanani. But I want you to understand—whatever happens, we're both going to have to do whatever it takes to survive and return to Gujaareh."

His talk of survival unnerved her. "Gatherer Nijiri wouldn't have left us among these people if he believed they would harm us, Brother."

Mni-inh's voice hardened. "Gatherer Nijiri would do exactly that, if it served his purposes. Death is just another kind of peace to a Gatherer, remember; they don't think as Sharers do. But listen to me." He squeezed her hand. "You aren't without defenses, Hanani, even now. You've guessed it, haven't you? Most apprentices figure it out at about your level. Those who heal can *harm* just as easily. The technique is the same, except for your intent. And the result."

She drew back from him, more unnerved than ever as she realized what he meant. He was her mentor, her elder brother, her father in all but blood. He had always taught her right from wrong. But this— It went against everything she had ever learned. It felt so wrong she had no words to describe it.

"But o-our oath, Brother," she said. "We are n-never to do harm."

"If someone tries to harm you, you'd damn well *better* harm them, Hanani." He turned to face her; when she tried to look away he squeezed her hand again. "There can be no peace without safety. That's why Gujaareh keeps an army, after all—and that's why I'm telling you, *ordering* you, to protect yourself if it comes to that. Your duty is to heal those in need, and you won't be able to fulfill that duty if you've been killed by some savage, or by the corrupt among our own people." He scowled up at the cliff face, and belatedly Hanani realized he meant the Prince. "Promise me you'll do what you must to survive."

She was saved from the necessity of a response when a rustling in the trees behind them announced Charris's return. They both got up, Mni-inh quickly tying off his hair and Hanani reaching for her clothes. They were still damp, but would dry soon now that the sun had risen.

Charris kept his eyes averted while they dressed. "Lady Hendet is awake, and asks to see you."

Hanani paused while winding her breast-wrappings over one shoulder. Mni-inh reached for his drapes and said, "Is there some problem?"

"No. She just wants to see you. *You*," he added, risking a look up and meeting Hanani's eye. "Not both of you."

Hanani blinked in surprise, but when she glanced at Mni-inh he only nodded. They finished dressing in silence, and then followed Charris back up to camp.

At Hendet's tent, Charris drummed his fingers on the taut hide, then thrust his head inside when a voice murmured within. After a few exchanged words, he stepped back from the tent entrance and gestured for Hanani to go in.

Inside the tent, the scent of sickness was already fading. Hendet sat propped up by pillows, her lap and the rug beside her covered in scrolls. She didn't look up as Hanani entered, her eyes busy scanning a column of numeratics. Inexplicably nervous, Hanani stopped on the rug at the center of the tent and waited, unsure whether it would be more respectful to remain standing or to sit.

"Sit down," Hendet said, to Hanani's relief. She sat on her knees, as she had done during so many lessons in the Sharers' Hall.

Closing the scroll she had been reading, Hendet at last turned a deep, thoughtful gaze on Hanani. It was obvious now that she had been beautiful in her younger days, for she was handsome still, long-necked and graceful of feature, if too gaunt after her illness. And it was equally obvious that the Prince had inherited her temper, for the same coldness was on her face as she gazed at Hanani.

"So the Hetawa inducted a woman," she said. "To appease the Kisuati, I gather?"

Hanani ducked her eyes. "Yes, lady."

"To see them so weakened...It should please me. A fitting revenge for what they did to my husband." Hendet sighed, then eyed Hanani, who had not been quick enough to keep anger from her face. But to her surprise, Hendet grew thoughtful. "Forgive me; they're family to you. From now on I won't speak ill of them in front of you."

Hanani hesitated, frowned more, then finally said the thought that had come to her mind. "I would rather hear the words aloud than hear nothing, and know there are ill thoughts behind your eyes."

Hendet gazed at her in silence for a long moment before she finally said, "Very well. We'll speak frankly with one another." She set aside the scroll and beckoned Hanani closer. Hesitating for only a breath, Hanani moved to kneel beside the older woman's pallet.

Hendet reached out and touched Hanani's collar, examining the stones. "You're an apprentice. A shame; if you were a full Sharer, these would be rubies, not carnelians."

"Why does that matter, lady?"

"Because you require wealth. Among the Banbarra a woman is as valuable as the inheritance her mother gives her, and *that* is dependent on what wealth she can build through a lifetime of clever trading. A man may luck his way to wealth through the spoils of raids or battle, or by coaxing a wealthy woman to marry him and bring him into her clan—but for women it's nothing but wits." She let go of Hanani's collar and took hold of her chin, turning her face from side to side.

Hanani endured this examination with some consternation, remembering that the Sister Ahmanat had done the same. What was it these people sought in her face? It would be nice if one of them ever bothered to tell her.

"I'm not a Banbarra woman," Hanani said, struggling to keep her tone properly neutral. "I'm a servant of the Goddess; I own nothing but the talent She has granted me and the skills that my brothers have trained."

"Yes, there is that. Be certain you demand proper payment when you heal, girl. Altruism will win you no respect in this tribe."

Hanani pulled back from Hendet's fingers, no longer able to contain her affront. "I don't ask *payment* for my skills."

Hendet looked amused. "Who buys those pretty red drapes you wear?"

Hanani started, reflexively looking down at herself. The drapes in question belled around her knees, bunching a little across her lap. They had always been too long for her.

"The dye is expensive," Hendet continued, "especially in that rich dark shade, which is imported from the east. I know because my husband, Eninket, bought me such finery when he was alive, and few other nobles of Gujaareh could've afforded it. Yet the Hetawa adorns all its dozens of healers in cloth worth a small fortune. How, I wonder?"

Hanani touched the soft cloth of her foredrape, troubled on a level that she had never been before. "D-donations," she said. "I've seen people at the tithing halls. They ask if the Hetawa needs any labor done, or they bring offerings of money, food, and goods—"

"Enough to pay for the dye in those drapes, and the stones in your collar? And the food that fed you all these years, and the pallets you've slept on, and the craftsmen who built the cisterns and ducts for your daily baths?" Hendet shook her head. "The nobles pay—"

"That has ended!" Hanani gripped the cloth of her drape

between her hands. "The Gatherers purged the Hetawa of all who sold dreamblood for profit or gain."

Hendet sighed, long and wearily, and pinched the bridge of her nose between two fingers. She was newly recovered from a life-threatening illness; Hanani knew she should've urged Hendet to stop talking and rest. But she could not bring herself to speak, and Hendet eventually focused on her again.

"The Banbarra worship no gods," she said after a moment. "Did you know that? Or rather, they call on all gods with equal fervor—but no one in particular. I've heard them pray to Hananja; swear by Shirloa, Lord of Death; dance to call the night-spirits of the Vatswane. I have seen them burn sacrifices to their ancestors and be possessed by animal gods, and now and again they paint themselves in stripes, like the Dreamer. Do you think them faithless to all those gods?"

Hanani stared at her, trembling inside. Hendet glanced at her and laughed softly. It did not feel malicious. Just pitying, which was worse.

"The Banbarra worship that which made the world, in any and all forms it takes," Hendet continued. "But they do not worship *people*. Or rather, they trust people to be people—even the ones who claim themselves holy. Sometimes I cannot help but wonder if they have the right of it, these 'barbarians.' They at least never dupe *themselves*."

"I have not been duped," Hanani said, tightly.

"You never had to be. You *believe*, unquestioning; that is enough." Her pity had become exasperation; she shook her head at Hanani's rigid stance. "Think, Sharer-Apprentice. What of all the nobles who had already grown dependent on dreamblood? They can't stop, or they go mad and die. And what of those who come asking for it willingly, knowing the risks? Dreamblood gives sweeter pleasure than timbalin paste; it's more powerful than any wine or smoke. If those who can afford it want it, why should your Hetawa turn them away?"

Hanani stared back at her, unable to speak, unable to think past the dawning horror in her mind. Yet beneath the horror lay shame at her own naïveté. It was so obvious. She should have known.

"The Hetawa does great good in Gujaareh," Hendet said, more gently. "Without it, the orphaned and the ill would be left to fend for themselves, and most of our people would be as ignorant as the folk of other lands—illiterate, superstitious, and worse. Our very lives are made longer and healthier through priests' magic. This is why Gujaareh does not begrudge the Hetawa its little schemes and airs, provided your superiors don't overstep the bounds of propriety. And this, foolish girl, is why you should ask payment from the Banbarra. You've always been paid for your work, whether you realized it or not." She shrugged. "But do as you please; I've given you my advice."

"Thank you," Hanani said, more out of polite habit than anything else. It was very hard not to hate Hendet in that moment.

Hendet inclined her head, though she smiled thinly, as if guessing Hanani's hatred. "And if you would hear more advice, sell that collar of yours."

Hanani started, putting a hand to her collar. "*Sell* it?"

"You need belongings. Proper clothing. A chamber pot, a decent bed. You're hungry, aren't you? No one eats free here. Give your collar to Charris, and have him take it to a tribesman named Nefri. He'll keep an accounting for you, and give you fair value for it. Tell your mentor to do the same. I've given you each a tent out of my own wealth; in the eyes of the tribe this means I've claimed you as kin. That will force them to treat you with some respect, provided you do nothing to offend them."

Do what you must to survive. Hanani fingered the stones of her collar and bowed her head, hating herself now for even thinking of following Hendet's advice. But Hendet knew these people, and Hanani did not.

"Why?" she asked. "Why help us, if you hate the Hetawa so?"

Hendet smiled. "Because you're my son's allies. And because I too have made hard choices in order to survive and ensure my son's future." She looked Hanani up and down, then added, "And because in spite of everything, it pleases me to see a woman in the Hetawa. Now go; I have much to do."

Obediently Hanani got to her feet. After another moment's hesitation she bowed to Hendet; Hendet inclined her head in regal acceptance of this. With her mind full of questions, Hanani left.

17

(⊙)

The Negotiation of Steel

Wanahomen found three of his men crouched at the northeastern lookout, passing a long-eye between them and sniggering like virgin boys. "I-Dari," one of them called, spying him. "Come and see."

"What foolishness are you up to now?" he asked, coming over to join them. Ezack grinned and handed the long-eye to him, pointing down toward one of the pools at ground level. Wana put the viewer to his eye, focused it on the spot, and started. The men read his expression and laughed.

"She could birth an army with those hips," Ezack said.

"And feed them all with those breasts!" laughed another man.

It was true, Wanahomen judged, permitting himself a small smile as the female Sharer, nude after bathing, stood to fetch her clothing and afforded him a particularly good view of her virtues. She was nothing special in her features, coloring, or bearing, but there really was something to be said for certain qualities of lowcaste breeding in Gujaareh.

"I'd heard Gujaareen women had no shame," Ezack said, taking the long-eye for another look, "but I had no idea it was like this.

Look at her, bathing with that man of hers without any modesty at all. Are they lovers?"

Wanahomen shook his head. "Men of the Hetawa use magic to stifle the natural impulses; they're hardly even men. I imagine the girl is the same."

"She looks woman enough to me!"

"I can't wait to get my hands on her," said one of the men, and Wanahomen's amusement vanished.

"Unte's made it clear they aren't to be harmed," he said, keeping his tone nonchalant.

"I don't want to *harm* her," the man replied, and even Ezack joined in on laughing at that—though, as he noted Wanahomen's face, Ezack's laughter faded quickly.

"My mother has claimed her as a member of our clan," Wanahomen said, and then smiled when all three men stared at him in surprise. "She always said she wanted a daughter. I suppose I've been a trial."

He turned to leave before they could question him, because he had no answers in any case. He had no idea why Hendet had chosen to give tents to the two Sharers. Rather, he understood the reason—it would afford them a greater degree of status, and therefore safety, in the tribe—but the fact that she had done it still angered him. He would never forgive the Hetawa. Let their priests fend for themselves, as he and his mother had been forced to do.

"That was neatly done," said a voice as he hopped down from the lookout's ledge. He stiffened, then turned to face the Banbarra woman who had spoken to him.

"Yanassa," he said, with careful formality. "The morning pales to your brightness."

She smiled, gesturing to indicate that he was to walk beside her. Sighing inwardly, he did so.

"Tassa informs me," she said, "that the two strangers worked some sort of magic last night on your mother. Is this true?"

The question eased his mood somewhat. Hendet had awoken that morning feeling better than she had in years. Wanahomen had helped her wash and dress, reveling in her returning strength, her fierce appetite, the brightness of her eyes. "The Hetawa's magic is a gift from our Goddess," he said. "If nothing else about them is reliable, that much is."

"I'm glad to hear it," Yanassa said. "I've heard all sorts of odd rumors about the strangers, particularly the woman. They say she walks about wearing nearly nothing, and doing whatever her male companion—or any male—says." She shook her head, sighing. "I suppose one of us women will have to take her in hand before the men get the wrong idea."

Wanahomen stopped walking, frowning at her in suspicion. It would indeed ease much of the burden on him if Yanassa looked after the Hetawa girl. But that would put him in debt for the favor, and he had learned years ago that Yanassa did nothing that did not benefit Yanassa.

"What do you want?" he asked, abandoning politeness.

She gave him a disapproving pout. "Will you never learn proper manners? Ten years among us and still you behave like a city man."

"I won't come to your bed again, Yanassa. I told you that two years ago: it was the last time."

"And I don't want you in my bed again. I have another lover now, if you hadn't noticed." But for a moment she grew serious, and he saw a shadow of sorrow in her eyes. "Tassa asks, sometimes, why you never visit."

"He'll understand when he's older and learns the ways of your sex. Tell me what you want in exchange for looking after the woman."

She sighed and shook her head. "Nothing, Wana. The girl interests me, that's all. It could be valuable to have a magician in my circle of friends." She smiled at him sidelong.

"You would do better to befriend a jackal. No one raised by the Hetawa can be trusted."

Yanassa raised her gracefully arched brows at this. "So there's something you hate more than me? I'm almost pleased to hear it."

He didn't hate her, and she knew it. He stopped and sighed.

"Take the woman in hand," he said. "The man too. I haven't the time to nursemaid them. The hunt parties of the other tribes will be arriving soon, and I want my men to practice shooting—"

She threw him an exasperated look. "It's the solstice, Wanahomen. Tonight is the start of the festival, or have you forgotten?"

Damnation. He had. "I see no reason why we can't prepare and celebrate too. We *are* contemplating war."

"Even warriors must refresh their spirits." She eyed him meaningfully and stopped, reaching up to brush her fingers along his cheekbone above the face-veil. "Even you, O great king."

Perhaps the stresses of the past few days had worn him down, or perhaps Tiaanet had made him crave more of a woman's softness for a change. He sighed and permitted Yanassa's touch, even when her fingers teased the veil down enough to reveal his lips, which she stroked with a fingertip. He smiled, just a little, and saw an answering smile on her face. He had always admired her audacity.

Then the moment passed, and Wanahomen took her hand and kissed it before gently pushing it away. Wordlessly—for there was so little they could safely say to one another these days, and these small peaceful exchanges were too fragile to jeopardize—he raised his veil, inclined his head to her, and walked away.

He went first down to the ground level, where like the templefolk he reveled in the chance to bathe after their long journey. When the tribe was in Merik-ren-aferu, he could not help reverting to his old Gujaareen habit of bathing at waking and sleep. He had even spent some of his precious tradable currency to buy fine soaps and scented oils in Gujaareh, which he preferred over the plain ash-and-fat stuff the Banbarra used. The Banbarra shook their heads at his foolish city habits, for they bathed more frugally and, having an aversion to wasting water, had been known to "wash" by scrubbing off old skin and sweat with dry sand. He did as they did in the desert or the foothills, but when plentiful water was available, he saw no reason not to take advantage of it.

Perhaps that was why, immersed in the pleasure of his daily ritual, he did not hear the attacker's approach.

He had just climbed out of the pool, glancing warily up at the cliffs to be sure he saw no telltale gleam of a long-eye, when a blur of motion at the edge of the nearby trees warned him. He turned just in time and locked his hands around the wrist of an older man with hate-filled eyes over his veil. The knife he held was inches from Wanahomen's belly, quivering as he strained to drive it home.

Wanahomen tried to think through the shock of his own thoughts. The man's eyes were familiar, but— The man snarled and threw his weight behind his knife-arm, forcing it close enough to score a shallow slice across Wanahomen's abdomen. Wanahomen hissed at the pain and then twisted, shoving the man's knife-arm off to the side and shifting his weight, pulling where before he had pushed. The man stumbled and went sprawling. Wanahomen kept hold of the man's wrist, swiftly throwing a leg around the arm and dropping to the ground in a wrestling move he had once learned from the Kite-iyan palace guards. Now the man was pinned, one of Wanahomen's legs across his chest, the other bracing his arm, which Wanahomen now twisted sharply. The man cried out, dropping the knife, but Wanahomen did not release him.

"Who are you?" he demanded. The man cursed and struggled to get up, but could gain no leverage. Wanahomen pressed his arm down sharply in warning, and the man cried out as he realized Wanahomen was ready to break the arm at the elbow. "Who are you, coward?"

"Wutir," the man finally gasped. "Wujjeg's uncle!"

So that was it. In disgust, Wanahomen sighed and threw the man's arm away from him, scooping up the knife as he got to his feet. He was filthy now from scrabbling in the dirt, and bleeding at the middle, but that did not trouble him half so much as the fact that he was naked. Banbarra did not reveal themselves to others lightly, and to be naked before an enemy was the greatest humiliation. Doubtless Wutir had counted on that to make Wanahomen clumsier in defending himself.

But he was Gujaareen, not Banbarra. And as Wutir rolled to his feet, Wanahomen stepped closer and laid the confiscated knife against his throat. Wutir froze, eyes widening over his veil. "Hands up," Wanahomen said, and reluctantly Wutir raised his hands.

Wanahomen felt about his waist for more weapons, then crouched to feel for a leg- or ankle-sheath, finding neither. Satisfied, he straightened again and wrapped his arm around Wutir's waist in a gesture that might have seemed intimate, if not for the knife he pressed to the man's throat, and if not for his belly-wound smearing blood on Wutir's clothing. "Now," he said, "I think you fail to understand, sir, that Wujjeg was in the wrong. He disobeyed my orders, and I am hunt leader. His death was his own fault."

"You—" Wutir's face darkened with fury and disgust as he tried to pull away. "You're a foreign demon who should've been gelded and sold at auction—"

Wanahomen let out a venomous laugh and released Wutir's waist to reach down between them with one hand. It was an easy matter to yank aside Wutir's robes and find the drawstring of his pants; even easier to break the string and tear his pants open at the front. Wutir gasped and tried harder to jerk back, but Wanahomen pressed the knife to his throat enough to draw blood. Wutir subsided, gritting his teeth. To take the man's life, Wanahomen only had to slash.

"But you didn't geld me," he said with a fierce grin. To his great amusement, Wutir was not flaccid. The excitement of battle, perhaps, or—"It seems you coveted me instead! Me, a city-born demon. You came upon me naked from the bath and attacked me, meaning to take my flesh in revenge for your nephew. But alas, I have no taste for ugly men, and so—"

He took a thorough grip of Wutir's penis and wrenched it to one side with all his strength.

Wutir's scream was most gratifying. Wanahomen swiftly tripped him to the ground, keeping the knife at his throat although he graciously allowed the man to curl into a howling, sobbing knot. As an added insult, he ripped the veil from Wutir's face and tossed it into the river.

"I owe Yanassa an entertainment." Wanahomen smiled down at Wutir, waiting to speak until the man had gone hoarse from screaming. "Perhaps I can drop word to her of what you tried to do, and what I did in return. And tonight at the festival, when woman after woman invites you to her tent and you have to refuse every single one of them, the whole tribe will enjoy laughing at your humiliation."

Wutir managed to glare at him, though his face was shiny with sweat and it was weak as glares went. Wanahomen laughed, stepping away from him at last. Backing away, he crouched near the river and rinsed himself, taking care to sand-scrub the hand that had injured Wutir. No telling what filth the man had down there. Then, laying the knife on a nearby boulder, he reached for his drying clothes and quickly dressed, keeping an eye on Wutir the whole while.

"N-no," Wutir blurted at last. He was still curled in a ball, his hands clamped between his thighs. "D-don't tell ... the women."

Wanahomen slipped on his sandals and picked up the knife

again, sitting down on the boulder to examine it. Surprisingly, it was a good-quality blade—Huhoja steel, no less, from a southern tribe famous for the stuff. Only a handspan long, but nicely balanced. He could see no smearing of the blade's sheen that might indicate poison, for which he thanked all the Dreamer's children. A smarter or more cautious man would've hedged his bets by using it; Wutir clearly had no such gifts.

"What other guarantee do I have that there won't be more of you after me?" he asked. "Every weakling, cowardly member of your clan, hunting me down to take revenge for your ass-stupid nephew? Did your mother send you?"

Wutir shook his head fervently. "D-didn't know."

"Ah, good. She's always struck me as a sensible woman, Shatyrria, in spite of her prejudice toward my mother and me. How do you think she'll like it when your foolishness makes her the laughingstock of all her powerful friends?" He reached into his purse and pulled out a handful of dates, part of a small supply he'd brought back from Gujaareh. Chewing on one, he wrapped the knife in a scrap of leather from his purse, then regarded Wutir thoughtfully. "Will she disown you, I wonder?"

Wutir only groaned in response. Wanahomen chuckled and got to his feet, putting the knife and the rest of the dates away. Crossing the space between them, he crouched at Wutir's head. Wutir looked up at him—and cringed, for Wanahomen was no longer smiling. He wanted to kill Wutir so badly that his hands itched for the knife and the slick covering of blood. The fool had come closer to killing Wanahomen than any enemy in years. Now, when Wanahomen's plans were so near fruition!

And yet—

Never be quick to kill, Wanahomen. His father's voice came to him through the bloodlust. *It offends Hananja—and in any case there are other, better ways to destroy an enemy.*

"Understand this," Wanahomen said. He kept his voice soft, so that Wutir would cease his whimpering and pay attention. "Everyone will see you stumble back to camp later today, barely able to walk. They may wonder what happened; think up whatever excuse you like while you lie here. No one will believe it, of course. They'll see the blood on your robes, and the blood on mine, and they'll know *who* did this to you, if not what or why. But I can choose to say nothing ... for now."

He leaned closer, taking a great risk. If Wutir had another weapon on him in some hidden place ... But some messages were best delivered like this, eye to eye.

"Your mother hopes to convince the other Banbarra tribes not to support my cause," he said. "And with her uncle leading the Dzikeh tribe, she may succeed. I need every tribe's warriors under my command if we're to have a chance against the Kisuati in Gujaareh. So you will tell me all Shatyrria's plans."

Wutir's eyes widened. "B-betray my clan? Are you mad?"

"I've told you what will happen if you don't. Would your clan keep you, after that?"

Wutir moaned and began to weep. Among the Banbarra, a man was nothing without the ability to sire children. Fertility was wealth to them, bodies sacrosanct; things that meant nothing in Gujaareh were life and death here. No woman would acknowledge him as her lover. No hunt leader would take him into his troop. He would be useless, a pet at best and a slave at worst, doomed to obscurity and a life of squalor.

"Show me that you understand," Wanahomen said.

Wutir nodded, turning his face away as the tears spilled down his face. Wanahomen rose and returned to the boulder, feeling a stir of pity beneath his contempt.

"Satisfy me," he said, "and perhaps in a few days I'll let the Gujaareen healers see to you. The man, not the woman, for the sake of your dignity. They can make even your sorry stick straight again, however bad the damage is."

Wutir nodded again, his body slumping in defeat.

"Speak, then," Wanahomen said, and Wutir spoke. When at last Wanahomen knew everything, he headed back toward the camp ledges, raising his veil to conceal his troubled thoughts. Shatyrria had moved faster than anticipated, he understood now, and that meant the Dzikeh-Banbarra would be a serious problem whenever they arrived. He would have to devise some means of dealing with them quickly.

He spared no further thought for Wutir, left shivering on the ground behind him.

18

(◦)

The Negotiation of Silence

Amid all the bizarre configurations of Gujaareen society—birth-castes and chosen-castes, lineages and by-blows, servants who were not slaves and pleasure-givers who were not whores—the shunha were the one group that made sense to Sunandi Jeh Kalawe. Gujaareh was awash in foreign influences, from northern architecture to western music and eastern textiles. Its language was a stew so tainted with the flavors of other tongues that it now bore only the faintest resemblance to the Sua its people had once spoken. Half the time Sunandi couldn't tell a Gujaareen from a member of any other race; they had mingled even themselves so thoroughly with foreign peoples that only they could make sense of the aesthetic mess.

The shunha were the stones around which this churning social river flowed. While their fellow nobles, the zhinha, led the drive to spread Gujaareen trade and power ever farther, it was the shunha who kept that drive from forging too far or too fast and overtaxing the land's resources. And if they were sometimes derided as old-fashioned or stagnant, that did not change the fact that Gujaareh could never have become as great as it was without their steadfast, sensible restraint.

But Sunandi never allowed herself to forget that for all their adherence to Kisuati tradition, the shunha were still incontrovertibly, *insanely* Gujaareen.

Lord Sanfi and his daughter Tiaanet had come to the palace Yanya-iyan at Sunandi's invitation, as she had continued the habit from her years as an ambassador of dining with all the notables of the city. The meal had gone well and both her guests had behaved with perfect decorum—yet there had been something off about the pair from the very beginning. It was a subtle thing, but persistent, and by the end of the meal Sunandi was sure of only one thing: that she did not like Sanfi. Not at all.

"It would be easier for you," Sanfi said, "if you had kept one of the old Prince's children alive."

Sunandi, sipping fresh-made palm wine and relaxing on cushions after their meal, said nothing. She had learned, throughout the evening's conversation, that Sanfi responded better to Anzi than herself in discussions of controversial topics. He got more defensive when Sunandi questioned his stances, and showed more temper when she pointed out flaws in his reasoning. Most likely he had some prejudice against women: it was a common failing in Gujaareen men. Perhaps, she mused, that was why Sanfi's daughter Tiaanet had been largely silent 'til now.

Her Anzi, who had no such problem, had taken the lead in the conversation: he had grown used to playing off her most subtle cues over the years. "There are still a few children of the Sunset here in the capital," Anzi said. He took a deep draw from his pipe, which Sunandi permitted him to smoke in their apartments only after meals like this. Evening had fallen, humid but cooling, and in the palace courtyard below, a hired chantress offered a lilting paean to the dusk. "If they swore off all claim to the Gujaareen throne and pledged allegiance to us, we let them live."

"Not those," Sanfi said, his tone laden with scorn. "The ones in the city are mostly daughters, and sons too young or foolish to have any clout. No one would follow them."

"There have been female Princes in Gujaareh's past," Sunandi said, turning her cup in her fingers.

"True. But they all had to work harder to earn respect and power than a man would have." Sanfi leaned forward to pour more wine for Sunandi, the picture of solicitousness. "A son of the lineage could be more easily made into a figurehead. Dress him in fine robes, put the Aureole behind him, and the people will be so happy to have their Avatar back that much of the unrest you've seen lately would ease. Even if, in fact, Kisua remained in control."

Did the man think them such fools, Sunandi wondered as she nodded thanks and sipped more wine, that they had not thought of such a possibility long ago? Sunandi herself had suggested using one of the Prince's sons to the Kisuati Protectors' Council. Unfortunately, after the Hetawa's purges and the necessary power consolidation were done, those of the Prince's older offspring with sense had fled north or west into exile, or protected themselves through marriages and alliances with Kisua's elite. The few who remained were all but useless—children, wastrels, or worse.

And the one who might have served best, who had a respectable lineage, his father's favor and, by all accounts, the wit and bearing of a true Prince... no one had seen or heard from that son since the day of the old Prince's death. Though after her conversation with Nijiri, Sunandi now had an inkling of what the boy had been up to.

Just as well. If he had stayed in the city, most likely I would've had to kill him.

"And have you a candidate in mind for this figurehead?" asked Anzi, amused.

"No, no, not at all." Sanfi laughed, though there was an insincere edge to the sound. Beside Sanfi, his daughter did not smile. "And frankly, it's too late these days for Kisua to put forward a figurehead who wouldn't be a laughingstock. Your people, I'm afraid, have lost much credibility in Gujaareh these last few years. That tax on exports to the north, for example—"

"A necessity," Sunandi said, smiling although she would have preferred not to. Firstly because it was impertinent of Sanfi to bring it up, but also because the Protectorate had insisted on the tax over Sunandi's protests that it would further alienate the wealthier families of the land. The occupation of Gujaareh had grown increasingly unpopular back in Kisua, and the Protectorate now sought to increase profit from that occupation so as to appease its angry citizens. But even with the tax, Gujaareh had not yielded up the riches that the Protectors had expected. Deprived of imported northern luxuries, Gujaareen did not accept the southern goods that Kisua offered in replacement; they did without. Forced to buy Kisuati timber for construction, they stopped building. Pressured to bind their servant caste into contracts that more closely resembled Kisuati slavery—a highly profitable enterprise in Kisua—the damned Gujaareen had started shipping their servants to relatives overseas. Now labor costs in the city and larger towns had tripled, and it was only a matter of time before there were shortages of food, cloth, and everything else.

Sunandi herself had been surprised by all of it, because there had been no warning. Her spies would've known if there had been any sort of collusion—a concerted effort on the part of the merchants or farmers, perhaps, or a revolt among the servants. But as far as she could tell, the whole kingdom had suddenly, spontaneously, decided to turn contrary in every possible way. They did not fight back. They did not protest. But neither did they *obey*.

The longer Sunandi remained in Gujaareh, the more she was beginning to realize that something critical, some delicate balance that kept Gujaareh stable—and *safe*—had been disrupted. But Sunandi had no intention of explaining this to Sanfi.

Instead she said, "We've seen already what happens when the northfolk are permitted to acquire superior weaponry and goods. Why, Anzi tells me that after the war, when the northern troops were rounded up, they had more Gujaareen bows than those of their own design! They brought those bows to our shores, to draw Kisuati blood."

"Gujaareen bows are famous the world over," Sanfi said with a shrug. "Our merchants are just as happy to sell them to Kisua as the north. Come, now, Speaker—we all know that isn't the reason for the tax."

"It may not be," said Sunandi, still smiling although she allowed an edge to creep into her voice. She was tired of this man, who seemed to believe his charm was sufficient to excuse his insolence. "But it is the only reason that should matter to *you*."

Sanfi's smile faded. For an instant anger flickered in his eyes, along with a high gleam that would have unnerved Sunandi deeply had they been alone. She had seen that look in other men's eyes during her lifetime, and knew it for what it was: hatred.

But before Sanfi could voice that hatred—or act on it—Tiaanet surprisingly broke the silence. "It should matter to all of us, Speaker," she said. Her voice was deep for a woman's, husky; Sunandi imagined she broke hearts with her words alone. "I've heard the Protectors are less than pleased with the revenue losses in Gujaareh, especially since the Banbarra raids began. Does that not bode ill for Gujaareh's governance—and governess?"

Silence fell over the chamber. Anzi stared at Tiaanet, stunned at her audacity, while Sanfi whirled to glare at her. Sunandi, after a moment's astonishment, realized the evening had suddenly become much more interesting.

Clever little leopardess! Your father is a fool to keep you leashed.

In a silent acknowledgement of the verbal parry, Sunandi inclined her head to Tiaanet. Tiaanet returned the nod, solemn as ever.

"Your daughter is well informed, Lord Sanfi," Sunandi said. She could not help smiling. Sanfi threw her a look of consternation, but when he realized that she was far from offended, he relaxed.

"As the heir to her mother's esteemed lineage should be," he said, though he shot Tiaanet an expressionless glance. And—again a great strangeness—Tiaanet lowered her eyes as if in shame.

She may have just saved her father from political suicide. He should be proud of her; she should be smug. That is the Kisuati, and shunha, way. What in the gods' names is wrong with these two?

Setting down her own cup, Sunandi politely waved away Anzi's offer to refill it. "And she's right, in essence. But rest assured, Lord Sanfi; if the Protectors grow too displeased, the security of my position will be the least of Gujaareh's worries."

"What would likely happen?" Sanfi took a sip from his cup, perhaps to appear casual. But he was too tense; Sunandi could see that he was listening intently.

"I am here as a courtesy, Lord Sanfi," she said. "I'm known in Gujaareh, and—more or less—respected. I respect your people in turn. Because of that, this occupation has gone more gently than it could have." She swirled the liquid in her cup, from the corner of her eye watching him watch her. "But if the Protectors remove me, it will mean they've lost interest in gentleness. They will take direct control of the capital and the larger towns. They would then institute harsher measures to maintain control. Even higher taxes. Summary executions and mandatory slavery. Conscriptions to the Kisuati army. Rationing."

Sanfi frowned. "And what of the Hetawa?"

Sunandi raised an eyebrow, wondering what had made him think of that. "I've made it clear to the Protectors that the Hetawa has cooperated with us thus far. In token of that cooperation, and the favor your Gatherer Ehiru did us in dealing with Eninket, I believe the Protectors would allow the Hetawa to continue operating as usual—for the time being, at least."

Sanfi sniffed. "You would do well to watch them more closely, Speaker. They once ruled Gujaareh, after all, and bent every other power in this land to their will. Your people are unfamiliar with magic. It can be a formidable weapon in certain hands."

"A weapon." Anzi looked skeptical, though Sunandi knew that was a front. They had both been on the plateau at Soijaro ten years ago, and seen the horror of Eninket's Reaper. "Sleep-spells and healing? What will they do, attack my men and leave them healthy and well-rested?"

Sanfi smiled, but shrugged. "Magic comes in many forms, not all of which are benign. Who is to say what the Hetawa could do, if they wished?"

Anzi glanced at Sunandi; he was as puzzled as she. Why had the man brought this up? Sunandi frowned and turned back to Sanfi. "I shall keep that in mind," she said, with absolute sincerity.

The rest of the evening passed quickly. There was no more talk of politics; after delivering his warning about the Hetawa, Sanfi seemed inclined to move to less sensitive subjects, like gossip about his fellow nobles. Sunandi was happy to let him. After the last flask of wine was served, Sanfi offered all the usual praises and thanks to his hosts, made a closing libation to their ancestors, and finally took his leave along with his daughter. In the wake of their absence, Sunandi found herself staring at the cushions they'd sat upon, turning and turning the evening's conversation over in her mind.

Anzi, relaxing now that he could toss aside his general's mantle—he hated being formal any longer than strictly necessary—came over to rest his head on her thigh. "Are you done being the Protectors' Voice?"

She smiled and stroked his forehead, amused. He had never had much interest in politics; she often marveled that he'd made it to such a high rank. Perhaps it was only that he played the game well when he had to. It was solely for her sake, however, that he put up with evenings like this. "I am always their Voice, my love. But for you, I can be a little less so for a while."

He frowned, his broad forehead crinkling beneath her fingertips. "A strange pair, those two. Never seen a shunha daughter so...I don't know. Cowed."

Sunandi nodded in hearty agreement. And why did it seem that Sanfi's whole purpose that evening had been to raise her suspicions about the Hetawa?

But Anzi chose that moment to sit up and kiss her. He would want attention now: for a flinty-faced warrior, he could be as demanding as the most pampered pet when the mood took him. And so, as Sunandi had promised, she put aside her responsibilities and worries to become, for the rest of the night, just his wife.

19

Barbarian

In the mirror-surface of a thin sheet of metal stood a woman: not tall, with hair of honey and almond skin, and lips as lush as the Blood river valley's fields. Kohl lined her eyes, brown tint her mouth. The top half of her hair had been pulled into its usual bun, though bound with strands of white shells from the distant Western Ocean. The bottom half had been separated into a dozen or more locks, each captured at the tip by a heavy, teardrop-shaped gold ornament. They made a subtle rattle, drawing the eye, whenever she turned her head.

"This will do," said the Banbarra woman beside Hanani, in accented Gujaareen. She drew a finger along one of the crisscrossing belts that held Hanani's new many-layered skirts about her hips. Hanani started at the touch, her eyes darting away from the mirror—but after only a moment her gaze drifted back. She could not stop staring at the stranger there.

Yanassa made a pleased sound at her reaction. "You might grow vain at this rate!"

Hanani turned to the woman, moving gingerly in the unfamiliar skirts. How did one avoid tripping in them? She would have to learn. "Yanassa, I...I have never..." She looked down at herself. "I cannot even think how to react to this. This woman is not me." She lifted her arms, which were draped in bracelets and tasseled cloth. How was it that these were hers? *Her* arms should have been bare, her hands unencumbered so that they could be quick and clever and save lives. Yet they were the same arms, the same hands.

Yanassa smiled. The Banbarra woman had come to Hanani that morning, after Charris carried away her collar and Mni-inh's to the tribe's "accounting master," whatever that was. With Yanassa had come a small horde of chattering Banbarra women, who invaded Hanani's tent en masse and attacked her with clothing, makeup, and jewelry. When Hanani weakly questioned the sudden attention, Yanassa had been succinct: "You have offered value to the tribe," she said, gesturing around her throat to indicate Hanani's collar. "Your priest-man has instructed that his wealth and yours are to be shared equally. And Hendet has adopted you as her own. You're now a rich woman of a good clan, and among my people that changes everything."

Clearly it did. Throughout the operation Banbarra men and children had continued to arrive at Hanani's tent, bringing additional pallets, cushions, lanterns, rugs, containers of food—a toilet jar. All the necessities and comforts her tent had previously lacked. On Yanassa's order the women had left and returned with more clothing of the type that Hanani now wore, including undergarments and sandals and a greater profusion of jewelry than she'd ever seen in her life. "Value for value," Yanassa said in her brisk, choppy accent. She had inspected each parcel as it arrived—sending a few back with loud complaints—while Hanani stood dumbstruck. "We're not much for guests, but it will never be said that the Banbarra cheat in trade."

It was through such acerbic statements, delivered like Hetawa pronouncements, that Hanani at last began to understand some of the peculiar traits of Banbarra behavior. The men's practice of veiling, for example; it was not simply unfriendliness. Yanassa explained that a man might bring in spoils from hunting and raiding forays, but it was the duty of his female relatives—who were less likely to be recognized, arrested, or killed—to parlay those raw goods into usable wealth by trading in cities. Thus men cultivated a habit of concealment around strangers, while women learned the skills that would help them bargain for the tribe's needs. "I was taught Gujaareen and four other tongues by my mother, along with writing, figuring, and investing," Yanassa had told Hanani proudly. "She did not bother with my brothers. But me she doted on, for she knew I would one day bring great wealth to our clan."

It seemed she had, for all of the Banbarra Hanani had seen so far, even the other women, deferred to Yanassa by the rules of some incomprehensible hierarchy.

"Now, little mouse," Yanassa said. (Hanani was not fond of this term, but it at least seemed affectionate.) "At tonight's festival, you must take care not to flaunt yourself. That is what women of the cities do, and our men have no respect for it. Your worth advertises itself; there is no need to try harder."

Hanani frowned in confusion. "I would never 'flaunt myself,'" she said, speaking slowly in case something had gotten tangled in translation. "I don't even know what you mean."

"Then this should be easy for you. The men won't approach you—not now, when they can all see that you are a proper woman. If they *do* press you, let me know." She scowled. "Some of them are fools. The sensible ones will let you know of their interest in subtle ways. You will know: a touch, a look, an unexpected kindness. If you desire him in return, all you need do is drop some trinket or a sash near him."

"*Desire* him?"

Yanassa was hanging brightly-colored satchels, containing Hanani's new wardrobe, along the tent frame. She did not see

Hanani's look of shock. "That's the custom. If there are many men around, look the one you want in the eye before you drop the item. Then simply return to your tent, and wait. If he desires you in return, he should come to your tent to bring you what you 'lost.' Often he'll bring some other gift on top of it." She threw a smile over her shoulder at Hanani. "Then you let him in. But he must leave in the morning, mind you." She paused, frowning to herself. "And you'd better not bother with Wana, if he's to your taste. I've seen him throw women's tokens back at their feet, if he's in the wrong mood: he's picky and has no manners. But it means most women leave him alone, which I suppose is what he wants."

"I—" Hanani groped for the words, too stunned to speak for a moment. In Gujaareh, people simply *knew* that Servants of Hananja vowed celibacy. She had never had to explain before. "Yanassa, I can't."

"Eh?" Yanassa paused in her tidying, frowning at Hanani.

"I cannot be with a man. Not in that manner. It's forbidden."

Yanassa stared at her for a long breath, mouth open. "Not *ever*?"

"No," Hanani replied. "Those of my path—we healers, I mean— we take Her magic into ourselves and share it with others. We must often share something of our own souls in the process. This is all great Hananja permits; the rest of us belongs to Her."

"How old are you?"

"I've seen twenty floods of the river."

"Gods of clouds and cool wind." Yanassa looked horrified. "Do you never feel hungry for a man? Are you permitted at least to pleasure yourself?"

Hanani felt her cheeks heat. No one in Gujaareh asked such pointed questions, either. "I...have...felt hunger, yes. But it is a measure of our strength and discipline that we work past it," she said, quoting Mni-inh. "And, and— If the desire becomes too great to bear, I can ask one of my brothers or a Gatherer to share dreamblood with me. That quiets all passions. But I've never needed that—at least, not yet." She considered. "Perhaps it's because I'm a woman, and passions run cooler in me."

Yanassa said something in Chakti. Hanani did not understand it, but it sounded very rude.

"Is that the foolishness they teach in Gujaareh?" Yanassa shook her head. "No wonder city women have no pride! And you—no men? Women, at least; they must allow you pleasure with women."

"Th-there are no other women in the Hetawa."

"Then you don't even have friends with whom to share your troubles? How cruel!"

Hanani shifted from foot to foot, wishing wholeheartedly that the conversation would end. "I have my mentor, and— I have never, ah, regretted my choice—"

"*Unu-vi*. How can you, if you don't know what you're missing?" Yanassa sighed and came over to fuss with Hanani's hair. "Such a shame. But if those are your ways, then so be it." She paused and frowned, thoughtfully. "Shall I tell everyone of this vow of yours? Otherwise the men will be curious about you. Also, those who want him may be offended by your priest-man's refusal."

"Yes, please," Hanani said, relieved. "I mean no insult to anyone— that is, everyone has been, well." Better by far to have Yanassa act as an intermediary than for Hanani to endure this conversation ever again.

Yanassa smiled and patted her shoulder. "It's all right. Poor thing; this must be hard for you. We are a passionate people, we Banbarra, and passion is what your kind seems to fear most. A shame more of you are not like Wanahomen—but then, he warned me long ago that he was atypical of city folk."

A chance to change the subject. Hanani seized on it as smoothly as she could. She had already learned that pausing to speak just meant getting talked over. "Do you know him well, the Prince?"

"As well as any Banbarra can know that one." There was a combination of ruefulness and affection in the woman's voice as she turned to Hanani's mirror and checked her own hair, in its elaborately braided upswept coif. "We were close once, but then I misjudged him on what seemed to me a small matter, and he's never forgiven me for it. That man positively cherishes a grudge."

Abruptly Hanani intuited something. "The child who was tending his mother last night." What had the Prince called him? "Tassa."

"Mine," Yanassa said fondly. "He was tending Hendet? Soft-hearted child—so different from his father. I don't know yet whether I should be thankful for that."

If the son had not inherited the seething, sharp-edged moods of his father, Hanani could see it as nothing but the Goddess's blessing. "The alliance that Gatherer Nijiri spoke of." She had almost forgotten it in the shock of the past few days. "The Hetawa supports him, then—the Prince. But the Kisuati would never leave peacefully."

Yanassa looked at her oddly. "Of course not. Your 'Prince' has asked all the tribes of the Banbarra to join with him in one great battle to drive the Kisuati back to their own land. They vote on war at the end of the solstice."

Hanani caught her breath; her skin goosebumped. *War*—it was anathema to Hananja. War turned the waking realm into the darkest of nightmares, and sentenced its victims to shadows in the afterlife as well. Could the Hetawa truly support such a thing?

"I do not believe that," she whispered.

"What?" Yanassa asked. But before Hanani could respond, Yanassa blinked and frowned, looking away at the sound of shouts and commotion outside. "Now what?"

She went outside, and Hanani followed, to see that the tribe had begun to gather at the northern edge of the main shelf. Over the milling heads of the tribesfolk, on the lookout shelf, she saw a man standing rigid, holding a strange long conical object. At first Hanani thought this was a horn, but the man held it to his eye.

"Hanani." She turned—and stared, shocked, at Mni-inh. Her mentor grinned back at her sheepishly, swathed from tip to toe in Banbarra robes and a headcloth. They had even given him a veil, though it hung loose around his chin. Then she saw that he was staring at her, a slow smile crossing his features.

"I knew that had to be you," he said. "No one else here has such hair. But this... Well, well." He put his hands on his hips, grinning, and she ducked her eyes so that he would not see her face heat. Yanassa, at her side, made an amused sound.

Then the murmurs of the tribesfolk softened as the Prince appeared from the crowd, along with Unte. Hanani barely noticed the tribe leader, for the smoldering anger in the Prince's manner made her heart clench with apprehension. There was blood on his clothes, and death in his eyes.

The Prince stopped then, and Hanani realized he had seen her. His eyes drifted down, then back up. She had never in her life wanted to be noticed less.

But he said nothing, inclining his head first to Yanassa, then after a moment's pause to Hanani. Then he turned and strode over to the lookout. Unte lingered longer, his eyes crinkling in what was unmistakably a smile behind his veil. Then he headed to the lookout as well.

"I seriously begin to question the Gatherers' judgment," Mni-inh muttered, gazing after the Prince. "If *he* is the one they've chosen..."

Hanani recalled her earlier thought—*the Hetawa supports a war*—and kept her silence, too troubled to do otherwise.

Yanassa called out to some fellow tribesman in Chakti. The man answered quickly, and the people around him murmured in surprise and alarm in response. Yanassa looked surprised herself. "A caravan has appeared," she told them in Gujaareen. "They've sent the correct greeting-signals. But none of the other tribes' delegations were supposed to be here for at least a fourday."

Unte held up a hand signal atop the lookout, and the tribesfolk who saw it cheered.

"What?" Mni-inh asked. "Delegations?"

"There are six tribes of the Banbarra people," Yanassa replied. "Usually the tribes gather only at the Spring Conclave in the west, but Unte has called for the hunt-troops from all six to come here and decide whether to join Wana's war. The first of those parties seems to have arrived early."

Mni-inh started, as Hanani had done before, at the word *war*. He frowned, squinting across the landscape. Only then did she notice the tension in the air around her; the tribe was waiting for something. What?

The man with the strange contraption said something to Unte, who smiled and turned to face the crowd. "Dzikeh!" he cried, and another cheer went up. But Yanassa, Hanani noticed, was no longer smiling.

"Dzikeh-Banbarra are opposed to the union," she said softly. "For them to arrive early . . . They mean to fight it."

"What will that mean for the Prince?" Mni-inh asked.

Yanassa shook her head. "No way to say for sure. But he cannot win back his city without more warriors and aid than he has now."

As Unte shooed his tribesfolk away to begin preparing for their new guests' arrival, Hanani saw the Prince turn in her direction. It was impossible to be certain from a distance, and with his veil in place, but where her eyes failed, intuition supplied: he was smiling to himself. She did not know how she knew it, but she was certain.

And when his eyes found hers across the crowd, she was equally certain that his smile grew wider still, and that there was nothing good in it.

20

⟨⊙⟩

Bait

It would have to be the templewoman, Wanahomen decided.

There was no better option. Not now, with the Dzikeh on the horizon, over a fourday early thanks to Shatyrria's scheming. Not even with the bribe he had assembled over the past year—his share of the spoils from raids on Gujaareh and other Kisuati outposts. Unte had guaranteed him at least two votes: his own and that of the leader of the Issayir-Banbarra, who was Unte's brother. The other tribes varied in their likely willingness to join, especially under the command of a city-born foreigner. Wanahomen had reminded them of their power thanks to the successful raids on Gujaareh, and they were eager for more of the wealth to be had from the campaign—but one strong objection could stir them to refuse out of pride and solidarity. The Dzikeh's tribe leader, Tajedd, represented that objection.

But with Hanani, Wanahomen could perhaps have him too.

"Put fresh clothing on," Unte said, turning to clamber down from the lookout point. He grimaced as the movement aggravated his knees. "Tajedd will be looking for any sign of weakness in you. He doesn't need to see your blood so easily."

"Yes, Unte." As surreptitiously as he could, he took hold of Unte's elbow. "The same goes for you. Shall I fetch one of the Sharers to banish your aches?"

"They can do that? Amazing." Unte chuckled. "It's tempting, Wana, but they shouldn't waste their magic. Nothing can cure old."

Dreamblood could. But that thought stirred too many dark memories, and Wanahomen pushed it from his mind as he left.

His mother was waiting for him as he returned to their *ansherrat*, and he filled his eyes for a moment with the sight of her standing—standing!—at the entrance of her tent, watching the goings-on. He went to her, took her hands, and kissed her on the forehead. She chuckled, though he noted that she did not pull away.

"You'll make the other women think I indulge you too much," she said, then frowned, pulling back as she noticed the streak of blood at his midriff. "What has happened?"

"Too much to tell right now." He squeezed her hands. "But don't worry. You should rest; the priests said you would need time to recover—"

"Yes, yes, fine." She sighed, only mildly annoyed at his fussing. "I'll want a full report later, of course."

"Of course." He bowed to her, then headed quickly to his own tent to change. He made sure to don the finest of his indigo robes—the color of nobility among the Banbarra, which Unte had granted him permission to wear some years before. He also tied on the beautiful bronze sword that had traditionally been given to the Sunset Throne's heir, called Mwet-zu-anyan, the Morning Sun. He did not carry it often, because it was so plainly not a Banbarra weapon—they favored curved blades—and because he feared losing it. But now it was important to show the Banbarra that there was strength to be gained from foreign allies. Even his city-born hands could spill blood.

By the time Wanahomen found Unte again, the Dzikeh party

had entered the canyon. It was difficult to tell from so far, but Wana-homen thought he glimpsed Tassa's slight form among the corral attendants greeting their guests. The boy loved being in the thick of things. For just a moment he worried that the Dzikeh would scorn Tassa when they saw him; most Yusir gave him no trouble for it, but the Banbarra as a rule were not overly fond of half-breeds. Yanassa had warned him off trying to protect the boy, years ago. *He must find his own way, and you hovering will do him no favors*, she had said, and she had been right. So he'd clenched his fists but done nothing when Tassa came home bloody-nosed and bruised-knuckled, though he'd taught the boy how to fight using all the tricks his own father had shown him, long ago. And he would do nothing now, so long as Tassa could bear it. But if they crossed that line—

Well. Best not to summon Gatherers too early, as they said in Gujaareh. He had enough trouble to deal with already.

There was a stir at the ladders, and a moment later the Dzikeh party began to climb up. First came the tribe's leader Tajedd, Wana-homen guessed, for this man was into his elder years, though not so far as Unte. That would give Unte the advantage of seniority, which was good. Tajedd was tall and lean and mournful-looking, with shoulders beginning to round into a stoop. He stopped in front of Unte, who stood waiting, and the two leaders exchanged greetings.

The man who came up next set Wanahomen's hackles all a-rise even though Wutir had forewarned him: *Tajedd brings a special weapon for you.* This new man was not as tall as Tajedd, but what he lacked in stature he made up for in bulk, with yoke-broad shoulders and arms—bared to the elbow, a rarity among concealment-obsessed Banbarra men—that looked muscled enough to hurl boul-ders. Not one but two swords hung at his side, their scabbards festooned with charms and amulets, and by the ready way he stood, Wanahomen had little doubt the man knew how to use them.

This was the Dzikeh-Banbarra's hunt leader, no doubt about it.

And by the sharpening of his eyes above their veil, Wanahomen knew the Dzikeh man had marked him for the same.

He will find a reason to challenge you, and then he will kill you. And though Wanahomen had scoffed at those words when Wutir said them, he saw now the truth of it. Wanahomen was a capable warrior himself, trained by Charris and Kite-iyan's formidable palace guard—but this Dzikeh was something else altogether. A weapon indeed.

But weapons could always be turned against their masters.

"So this is the cause of our gathering," Tajedd said, giving Wanahomen a long look. "I've heard much about you, Wanahomen of Gujaareh."

With Shatyrria's clan doubtless sending him letters every turn of the Waking Moon, Wanahomen was not surprised. "And I you, Cousin," he said. He saw Tajedd's eyebrows rise at the word *Cousin*. The Dzikeh hunt leader scowled.

"Wanahomen's mother consented to become my fourth wife shortly after they first joined our tribe," Unte said, his voice deceptively mild as always. "Wanahomen is a son of my clan now."

"I see." Tajedd regarded Unte as if he would've liked to say something about that, but in the end he opted for diplomacy. "I hope that our hunt party may be welcome among the Yusir tribe for the next several days, Unte. We rode hard in hopes of arriving in time for your solstice festival."

Unte put a hand to his heart in mock astonishment. "So this is why you arrived early? To court our women and eat our food? I might've known." The watching tribesfolk rippled laughter, and after a moment Tajedd joined in. Much of the tension of the gathering dissipated. Wanahomen had always admired Unte's skill at that.

"Come, then," Unte said, gesturing broadly for the Dzikeh pair to follow. The rest of the Dzikeh party—Wanahomen guessed they numbered a good eighty warriors—had completed the climb and were being welcomed by the tribe, offered drink and food and cloths to wash their faces and hands. Wanahomen checked to make certain that his own men were in their places: a few were down among the tribesfolk greeting their guests, but most stood quietly about the perimeters of the encampment, alert for trouble. Ezack remained on the watch-heights; when Wana met his eyes, Ezack nodded. All was well. Satisfied, Wanahomen turned to follow Unte.

Unte's tent was larger than most, since he often hosted gatherings. Inside, his three slaves must've worked like demons to prepare so quickly for the arrival of guests. Unte's usual mess—half-written scrolls of poetry, half-smoked pipes—was gone, leaving the tent neat and welcoming. A low table had been set out, laden heavily with refreshments and teas. An ornately engraved censer in the corner burned a relaxing blend of herbs.

Tajedd settled on the cushions at one side of the table with a contented groan, reaching immediately for a flask of cactus-fruit wine—a traditional drink for travelers who had been in the high desert. The hunt leader settled beside him, waiting for his tribe leader to refresh himself first, as was proper.

Wanahomen settled across from the Dzikeh hunt leader. "You have the advantage of knowing my name," he said politely.

"I do," the hunt leader replied, and said nothing more. Wanahomen had the impression that he smiled behind his veil.

Unte lifted an eyebrow at this. "Are we at war, then, that names aren't given freely? Are we wary of one another, to keep our faces veiled in-tent?" He pulled down his own veil and looked boldly at the two Dzikeh. "I was unaware of this, if so."

Tajedd quickly pulled down his veil, revealing a face as thin and mournful as the rest of him, though he gave them a broad smile. He had several missing teeth. "Not at war, Cousin, of course not. And neither of us has come in fear. Yes, Azima?"

The Dzikeh hunt leader scowled as his name was given, but then he reached up to pull away his veil. Wanahomen did the same so that they might reveal their faces to one another in the same moment. In Azima's case, this meant a face of hard planes and piti- less angles, though he had the large eyes of a westerner. This raised him, and Tajedd by proxy, a notch in Wanahomen's esteem: the man was a half-breed too.

"I see nothing to fear here," Azima said to Wanahomen, and smiled.

Wanahomen returned the smile, thinking behind his eyes, *I would so enjoy killing you.* But he could not do that. Azima would be infinitely more useful to him alive.

While Tajedd tasted the wine and, as was polite, recited a poem in praise of it and his hosts, Wanahomen signaled one of Unte's slaves, who crouched nearby. When the man came over, Wanaho- men murmured in his ear: "Fetch the healer-woman. Tell her some- one in Unte's tent needs a minor wound healed." The slave nodded and slipped out.

When Tajedd was done, Wanahomen inclined his head to show his approval. "Is it a long journey from your tribe's *an-sherrat* to here?" he asked. Unte poured wine for himself. Wanahomen inclined his head to Azima graciously, indicating that Azima, as guest, should drink next. Azima's lips twitched; he did not reach for the wine-flask. He would not drink, and that meant Wanahomen couldn't either. Wanahomen was honestly surprised: did the man really believe such simple pettiness would infuriate him?

Then again, Banbarra weren't given to the kinds of intrigues that Wanahomen kept expecting, even after ten years among them. He had grown up watching Gujaareen noblemen offer ten layers of insult with a shift in tone and an out-of-place bow. Banbarra were so direct that he found them refreshing, even when they meant to be rude.

"A full month, give or take an eightday," Tajedd said. He seemed oblivious to Azima's behavior, but Wanahomen knew otherwise. "That's with trained warriors, moving at hunt-pace."

"A difficult journey," Unte agreed.

Wanahomen chuckled. "Well, our women will no doubt help your men forget the hardships of the journey." He poured himself a cup of tea, preempting Azima's stupid game with the wine. "They like new faces. Though you may have some competition; there are novelties aplenty around camp these days."

Unte was watching Wanahomen thoughtfully, no doubt sensing he was up to something. He had grown to trust Wanahomen over the years, granting him wide latitude in the politics of the tribe, but Wanahomen knew he would tolerate no open insult to the Dzikeh. The Banbarra might be unfriendly toward strangers, but among their own they took guest-custom very seriously. Wanahomen was counting on this.

"You refer to yourself?" Tajedd asked, and then perhaps to reduce the implication of insult he added, "Though if you are of Unte's clan..."

"No, not myself," Wanahomen replied. He gave them a self-deprecating smile. "My novelty wore out long ago. No, I mean that we have two Gujaareen priests among us, given as a gift by their Hetawa to seal our alliance. You'll see them about—pale, soft people, typical city-dwellers. We had to put them in Banbarra clothing, since their own was indecent."

Tajedd's eyes widened. The Banbarra tribes kept in contact with one another by messenger and messenger-bird, but the Dzikeh had probably left their tribe's encampment before word of the alliance could reach them.

Azima seemed less impressed. "A gift. Priests?" He laughed. "Do we need extra prayers to support us in battle, then?"

"Oh, they have many talents," Wanahomen said. He smiled at Azima, who looked annoyed. He sipped tea and then heard, with near-perfect timing, the slave return with the female Sharer in tow. The tent-flap opened as the slave led her inside.

Unte frowned at the slave in puzzlement. "What is this?"

The templewoman spoke quickly. Slavery went against Hananja's Law; no doubt she feared the slave would be punished. "I apologize for interrupting," she said in her own tongue. "I, I was told someone here had a wound that needed healing."

Wanahomen could not have planned it better. Both Tajedd and Azima stared at her, astonished by her soft voice and deferential manner. She was dressed properly, for Yanassa had done an astonishing job on her; Wanahomen himself had been impressed. Yet no woman who knew her value to the tribe would stand there stammering like a child.

"Here," Wanahomen said, curtly beckoning her over. She came at once—another thing a Banbarra woman would not have done, given the rudeness of his gesture—and knelt on a cushion at his side.

"Where is the wound?" she asked. Already she was wholly focused on her duty, oblivious to the stares of the two Dzikeh men. Over her shoulder, Wanahomen could see Unte frowning at him, though the tribe leader had obviously decided to let him play out this game.

Wanahomen lay back on the cushions, getting comfortable, and then lifted his robes to reveal the slash Wutir had made across his belly. This too caught the Dzikeh's attention, for Banbarra men bared the vulnerable parts of their bodies only to relatives, other men, and women with whom they had been—or intended to be—intimate. "Here," he said. He pulled off the strip of cloth he had bound over the wound to keep it from bleeding through his robes.

The Hetawa woman leaned forward to examine the wound with her fingers, touching its edges gingerly. "Shallow," she said briskly, almost spoiling the effect he wanted to create. With a task before her she was confident, cool. He would have to do something about that. "But because of its location it will reopen again and again. Infection is likely."

"Yes, that was my thought," Wanahomen said. Then, making the gesture seem casual, he lifted a hand and brushed the girl's ornamented hair back over her shoulder. She started just a little, throwing a confused look at him, but, as he'd hoped, she did not protest or pull away. In fact— Ah, she was blushing! Her lowcaste-pale skin warmed like a lantern.

In other circumstances he would have laughed. But it was crucial now that he appear soft-spoken with her, intimate, affectionate. The Dzikeh probably had only the vaguest idea of what they were saying to each other, if they knew any Gujaareen at all, but they would be paying attention to postures and tones of voice. He wanted them to see a lustful man and a reluctant woman—reluctant, yet unable or unwilling to refuse his attentions.

Speaking too quickly she said, "Yes, of course. The healing won't take long. Do you remember how this is done?"

He had seen one of his brothers healed once, after a boyish adventure in Kite-iyan had gone badly. In answer he leaned his head back, closing his eyes. A moment later, her fingertips landed on his eyelids, light as feathers. Then—

He opened his eyes with a start, the dream fading before he could even recall it. His belly itched; lifting his head he saw that the wound had healed, the already-shed blood beginning to dry. He wiped it away with the cloth that had covered the wound, and only then noticed that the templewoman sat pale and still beside him, something in her expression that might have been fright. But since her back was to the Dzikeh, Wanahomen dismissed it.

He sat up so Tajedd and Azima could see his healed belly. "You see?" Tajedd caught his breath; Azima scowled.

"Magic," Tajedd said, awed. "I'd heard the priests of Gujaareh had such power."

"They kill, too," Azima snapped. "Like demons, creeping in on night-breezes and breathing poison into your sleep."

"That's a different kind of priest," Wanahomen said, in a dismissive tone that said, *and I don't fear them.* He closed his robes and nodded toward Hanani. "*This* kind can do nothing but heal. They'll heal our men after battle, leaving us strong and ready to fight while our enemies are still treating their wounded. Now do you see the value of the Hetawa's friendship?"

Tajedd looked thoughtful. Azima leaned over quickly to whisper in his ear. Unte was no longer frowning; his face had gone as expressionless as a statue's, though he too was watching the Dzikeh. The Sharer had managed to compose herself, though she still looked troubled about something as she bobbed her head in absent farewell and made as if to rise. He reached over and took her by the chin, startling her into wild-animal stillness.

"Thank you," he said, and leaned over to kiss her.

If she'd been standing, he thought her knees might've buckled. He kept the kiss light, a lover's tease, even though she didn't fight him and he could easily have made a show of devouring her in front of all of them. As it was, it took her two tries to get to her feet when he let her go, and even then she was unsteady, visibly shaken. He could not help smiling as she went to the door and nodded farewell again—to the *slave* of all people, dearest gods, even in Gujaareh no one did that—and finally exited.

There was little more than small talk after that. By Banbarra custom, one did not discuss important business immediately after a journey; it was considered unfair to the more tired party. Then too the sun was setting, and already Wanahomen could hear the tribe's musicians warming up their lutes and hand-drums. The eightday of the solstice always began and ended with a grand party, and with guests to share the revelry, tonight's was certain to be legendary even by Banbarra standards.

Unte had one of his slaves take Tajedd and Azima to a guest-tent. When they were gone, he let out a long sigh before turning to Wanahomen.

"If you fail to win Gujaareh," he said, "you must leave this tribe."

Wanahomen stiffened in shock and unexpected hurt. "Unte?"

"Not because you are incapable, Wana." There was a softness in Unte's face that soothed some of Wanahomen's shock. "In fact, I know that if you were to become leader after me, the tribe would prosper."

"Then why must I leave?"

"Because I love you as if you were the son of my blood—more—but you frighten me, Wana. I know you'll use anyone, destroy anything, to assuage the anger that burns like Sun's fire in your heart. This entire tribe included. You love some of us, but not enough. Not enough to keep us safe if you ever began to hate us."

"I—" He stared at Unte, unable to think. He groped for some response within himself. Any would do.

"Do you deny it?"

His heart constricting, Wanahomen looked away and said nothing.

Unte nodded as if he'd expected nothing else, and sighed. "Have your slave keep a close eye on the Gujaareen girl from here forth. You planted a dangerous seed today."

It was a dismissal. Wanahomen got to his feet, as shaky as the templewoman had been, and made for the door. When he touched the door-flap, something shifted in him and he saw—

—His father, extending a dead arm to him, skin mottled with foulness—

—That same taint creeping over his own flesh—

—And then the vision, daydream, or whatever it was, vanished.

"Wana?" Unte's voice behind him. There was concern in that voice, and sorrow, and love. The love drove the pain of Unte's words deeper into his heart, because it meant that Unte truly believed them.

What a lucky man he was to have two fathers, both kings, who cared for him so deeply, and who would never willingly allow him to rule their kingdoms.

"Good night, Unte," Wanahomen murmured. Pulling up his veil, he returned to his own tent.

21

Set, Trap

Hanani found Mni-inh in his tent, sitting on a stack of new pallets the Banbarra had brought, his eyes closed and head slumped. He might have been truly sleeping, but more likely he was praying. It was a reminder to Hanani that she herself had not prayed for many days. But as she crouched on the rug to gaze into her mentor's face, she found that she had no desire to try it now. To find peace in Ina-Karekh, it was necessary to have peace within oneself. She could not remember the last time she had been at peace.

Still, it was a comfort to be near Mni-inh's body, even if his soul was elsewhere. She curled up on the pallets beside him, resting her head on his thigh as she had not done since she was an acolyte. He had begun gently pushing away her hugs and other childish gestures of affection around the time that her fertile cycles had begun. Not because he did not welcome them, he had assured her, but because as the only female past childhood in the Hetawa she needed to keep not only the substance but the appearance of propriety at all times. "You're a daughter to me," he had told her, "but in the upriver towns it's not uncommon for a man my age to take a wife your age. Others will remember that, even if you and I never think it."

She had never thought of him this way before or since. She had never had such thoughts about any of her Hetawa brethren, not once in all the years she had lived among them.

But now the taste of the Prince was on her lips.

Hanani shuddered, hating the memory of the kiss, yet seeing it in her mind, feeling it, again and again. The Prince was using her. That was obvious even to her untutored eyes. He hated her and everything she valued. And yet she still felt his fingers tucking her hair behind one ear.

She closed her eyes and wished with all her heart that she had said no to Nijiri's test. She wished that she could go back in her small cell in the Hetawa, where she had been safe from the world's chaos.

A hand fell on her hair and stroked it lightly, making the gold ornaments clack together. "We'll be able to go home soon," Mni-inh said. He had always been good at intuiting her moods. She closed her eyes and fought not to cry, because that was not something Servants of Hananja did.

He sighed, still stroking her hair. "Would it help you to know I have been talking with Nijiri?"

"What?"

"In dreams," he said. "It's a simple technique. We agree upon a meeting place in Ina-Karekh—some singularly powerful image, important to both for similar reasons—and then specify a time when we will both travel to it. In this case, the Hall of Blessings. Dreamer-rise, on the eve of a new Waking Moon."

Hanani frowned. "Gatherer Nijiri told you ahead of time to meet him?"

"Yes." Mni-inh's smile turned sour. "He didn't tell me *why* we needed to arrange a meeting, just that it would be necessary. I gave him a piece of my mind when he got there, that I can tell you."

Hanani sat up, though not so quickly as to dislodge his hand.

"Why did he do this to us, Mni-inh-brother? These people could kill us. They have no peace in them at all—"

"I know," he said. "But we're doing all right thus far, aren't we? Honestly, from what Nijiri's told me, we might even be safer here than back in Gujaareh."

Hanani frowned. "Has the nightmare affected more people?"

"Yes, there are thirty sick with it now, the Hall of Respite is filled with them, but that isn't what I meant. Yesterday, the Gatherers themselves commissioned, and collected, the tithes of the two Kisuati soldiers who threatened you."

Hanani caught her breath, her mind filling with images of the Hetawa in flames. "Th-the Kisuati," she whispered. "They warned in the conquest that any harm to their soldiers would be returned fourfold. If they attack the Hetawa—"

"No, Hanani. They aren't foolish enough to jeopardize their occupation of Gujaareh over such corrupt men. The soldiers accosted a Sister before the Gatherer judged them: tensions are high in the city as a result. Nijiri thinks the Kisuati will wait until people have calmed a little before they act." He sighed, rubbing his eyes with one hand. "And when they do act, who can say what might happen? So I hope to the gods our young princely friend is ready to retake the city soon, and that he succeeds when he finally begins."

The mention of the Prince reminded Hanani of the afternoon's healing, and what had followed. She lowered her eyes and pushed the memory aside, concentrating on the more important matter. "Brother, there's something you should know. I healed the Prince this afternoon. He had a shallow wound to his belly; I think it was done with a knife. But that was not what troubled me." She shook her head. "Mni-inh-brother, he has the dreaming gift."

"He wh—" Abruptly Mni-inh frowned, thoughtful. "It does run in that lineage. Gatherer Ehiru was his uncle. How strong is he, would you say?"

Hanani swallowed, remembering the healing dream. She had tried to impose a simple construct on his dreamscape—a Banbarra tent with a tear in one camelhide wall. But before she could coax his mind to repair the tear, he had wrenched control of the dream from her, hurtling her into a shadow-Gujaareh over which a monstrous cloud, like a devouring mouth, churned in the sky.

"I couldn't direct his dreaming," she said. "He took me where he pleased within Ina-Karekh. He has no control; I don't believe he meant to do it. But if he had been trained—if he had *tried*—I think he could have held me there for as long as he wished."

But she had felt it the moment the dark Gujaareh manifested: the Prince hadn't wanted to be there either. Something about that dreamscape frightened him—*him*, a man so full of anger that she marveled there was room for fear in him at all. Yet because of that fear he had allowed her to pull him back to her gentler, simpler dream of the desert and a quiet morning sky, and the torn tent. He had repaired it almost as an afterthought.

"I've never felt such strength except with Gatherer Nijiri," she said finally. And in truth, she was not certain Gatherer Nijiri was as strong.

"A gift like that. Holiest Goddess. But we've always been careful with the Sunset Lineage. Too many damned madmen among them as it is. I can't believe we missed this one." He sobered abruptly. "Then again, the Prince—er, King, I mean, Wanahomen's father— schemed against the Hetawa for decades. If Wanahomen *was* tested, doubtless the Prince found some way to bribe or otherwise subvert the examiners."

Hanani only shook her head, too hollowed out by the day's events to think any longer. Night had fallen: Mni-inh's tent was almost dark inside, illuminated by the single lantern he must have lit before his prayer. Outside somewhere, a musician played a lively tune on some sort of lute. She could hear people clapping and singing in time with it. The Banbarra's solstice festival had begun.

"He's not mad," she said.

"No, I don't imagine these barbarians would harbor him if he were. Though if his gift is that powerful, it may only be a matter of time."

Hanani shook her head and got to her feet, struggling a little within the unfamiliar constriction of the skirts. "I need to rest, Brother." The Banbarra's strangeness, the unchecked chaos of their customs and ways of thinking, had exhausted her. She would not tell Mni-inh about the kiss; she didn't understand it herself. The Prince had probably done it just to torment her in any case.

Mni-inh watched her rise, a faint worry-line visible between his brows. "All right. But just remember, this will be over soon. It won't be long before you're regaling the House of Children with tales of your exploits, and convincing them to come join the Sharers in droves."

Hanani nodded, mustering a smile at his attempt to cheer her. "Rest well, Brother."

"Go in Her peace, Hanani."

She braced herself before stepping out of his tent, yet she was still unprepared for the riot of sensation that greeted her. Nearby, a crowd of people stood around a blazing fire, cheering as dancers stomped and leaped near the flames. A cluster of children ran past, three of them carrying some sort of toy festooned with long ribbons; she had to stop or be run down. The air was thick with good smells: wood smoke, charred meat, incense, tea. Farther away, a smaller crowd had gathered around another fire, where two musicians sang something ululating and discordant. By the rapt attention of their Banbarra audience Hanani could see that they loved the music, but to her Gujaareen ears it was just noise.

She turned toward her tent and stopped as someone resolved out of the crowd in front of her. Charris.

"Where have you been?" he asked, with a hint of command in his voice. She'd heard he was the Prince's slave—though the notion of a Gujaareen keeping a slave was abhorrent in and of itself—but this was not the first time she'd seen hints that Charris had held higher status in his pre-Banbarra life. He might even be zhinha, which meant that she should accord him more respect... but she was too tired to care.

Hanani wordlessly pointed toward her mentor's tent. His eyes widened. He took her by the arm and steered her sharply away.

"In this tribe, unrelated men and women do *not* mingle," he said into her ear, "except for one purpose. If you want the tribe to treat you like a whore who is willing to receive any man who wants you, then by all means continue to spend time in private with your priest friend!"

It was too much. She jerked her arm out of his grip. "Do these people think of nothing else? Can women have no other purpose? Is the whole world beyond Gujaareh nothing but violence and pleasure and money and—" She shook her head. "No wonder King Eninket wanted to conquer all of it. I almost wish he'd succeeded!"

She walked away from him, and to her great relief he did not come after her.

Her tent, thankfully, was on the opposite side of Mni-inh's, facing away from the loudest music and dancing. Inside it was dark. She stumbled on the unfamiliar rugs and cushions, finally falling onto the pile of pallets and blankets that was somehow hers. Bought and paid for with the apprentice-collar she had spent her life earning. She laughed bitterly at the thought, and wrapped her arms around a pillow for what paltry comfort it could offer.

When the flap of her tent opened, spilling firelight across her face, she raised the pillow to block the light. "Please leave me alone."

"*Elin aanta?*" The voice was deep, and not Charris's. She lifted her head, frowning, as the man said something else, a long string of Chakti. Amid the jumble of words she thought she caught the name *Wanahomen.*

"I don't understand you," she said. "Do you have some message from the Prince?" It felt wrong to use Wanahomen's given name. While the Prince of Gujaareh inhabited the waking realm he had no name; only after death did he become more than his office. Still, it was the name these barbarians knew—"From Wanahomen?"

She could see a large man's frame silhouetted against the light. He watched her for a moment and then nodded to himself, though if he spoke no Gujaareen he couldn't have understood her. But why—

The man stepped into her tent, letting the flap fall shut behind him. Hanani sat up, alarmed. "What are you doing?" She could hear him approaching in the dark, though the tent's shadows were too deep for her to see. "Charris said men here don't—"

He snapped something then, so close by that she gasped: he was right in front of her. Her heart pounding, she tried to scramble away, but a callused hand caught hold of her ankle. It jerked her toward him, throwing her onto her back. She cried out and another hand was clapped over her mouth, the fingers fumbling a moment in the dark before securing their grip. The man's weight fell on her then, so heavy that she could barely breathe.

She was back in Gujaareh, standing before the Kisuati soldiers. One of them leaned close, radiating menace. "If you were prettier, do you know what I would do to you?"

The man was yanking at her clothing. She heard cloth tear and suddenly one of her legs was free. She kicked with it, blind, panicked, but it was like kicking stone. He only grunted and shifted his weight in some way, and suddenly he was between her legs—

You aren't without defenses, Hanani, even now, Mni-inh's voice whispered in her mind.

She caught hold of arms as solid as the pillars of the Hall of Blessings, clawing. He hissed and sat up, and suddenly the tent went bright as a blow stunned her—for how long she could not say. But as she recovered her senses she could feel that her breechcloth was gone and the man was busy removing his own pants and underclothes. It seemed to take a great effort, but she tried to wriggle free of him. He simply pulled her back into place.

She whimpered as she realized she lacked the strength to stop him—

Those who heal can harm just as easily.

In her mind, tents tore. Insects chewed. Pillars shattered.

Twisting, Hanani planted one hand on the man's chest. All the fear and horror and pain and anger that she'd felt—yes, *anger*, every terrible thing she had ever felt in all her life, all of it gathered into a knot within her and then

shattered

And the man flew backward off her as if the hand of the goddess Herself had struck him a blow.

An interminable time later, the flap of Hanani's tent was flung open again and another man entered, this one with a lantern. He spoke, but the words were meaningless, a jumble that her mind would not interpret. Her eyes had fixed on the motionless shape in the dark, which resolved into an unknown Banbarra man as the light came near. His headcloth and veil had fallen away; his robes were clumsily hitched up and pants down; his eyes and tongue bulged from his face.

The man who had entered—Charris, was his name Charris?—stared at her, then down at the corpse for a long moment. Without a word he reached into his robes, drew a knife from a hidden fold, and knelt to plunge it into the dead man's chest.

Hanani screamed.

22

◖⊙◗

Recoil

Wanahomen was laughing, watching Tassa try to out-jest the other children by standing on his head, when Charris came and touched his elbow. "Azima has disappeared," Charris murmured in his ear. "I last saw him lurking near your mother's *an-sherrat*."

So the trap had drawn prey already. Wanahomen kept smiling, though he rose and winked at Tassa in lieu of farewell. Tassa tumbled to the ground, righted himself, and waved dizzily at Wanahomen before another boy tackled him in good-natured wrestling.

"I thought he would send a proxy," Wanahomen said as they strolled away. Another child, this one older, approached with a tray of spiced meat-and-vegetable skewers. Wanahomen accepted one with polite thanks and the child moved on. He lifted his veil to eat it. "Keep his own hands clean."

"Then it would be one of his men who earns your challenge, and possibly the privilege of killing you." Charris glanced toward the *an-sherrat* of Wanahomen's mother, where the Sharers' tents were pitched. "I should check on her—"

"Yes, yes. Go."

Charris slipped away, and Wanahomen continued his stroll

through the camp, nodding as friends or warriors greeted him in passing. As he'd expected, Unte's Yusir-Banbarra were in high spirits, taking the early arrival of the Dzikeh as a good omen for the coming year. He spotted Unte amid a knot of Dzikeh warriors, gesturing broadly as he regaled them with some tale of his youthful exploits. It was no great surprise to Wanahomen that a full four of Yusir women lingered near this gathering, one of them pretending to tune an instrument but the rest blatantly looking over the new arrivals with speculative, greedy eyes. He stifled a snort of amusement at the predictability of women, then paused as an even better sight greeted his eyes.

Hendet sat in a small group near one of the fires, listening while another woman sang a song. She looked up and smiled when Wanahomen went to touch her shoulder.

"Don't scold me," she said in Chakti. The women around her smiled.

"I would never dream of such a thing," he said. She even smelled healthier. He had to fight the impulse to hug her in front of the others. "As long as you feel all right."

She opened her mouth to reassure him and started as they both heard the templewoman's scream.

Even though he was ready for it, the scream caught Wanahomen off guard, for it went on and on, longer than any woman should have had the breath to manage. And there was no fear in her voice, or outrage, as he had expected. There was no sanity in her voice at all.

The singer faltered to a halt, along with the dancers near the largest fire, and Unte in the middle of his tale.

Damnation! Drawing his knife, Wanahomen sprinted toward the sound, from the corner of his eyes noticing several other warriors reacting in kind. Three of them reached the tent just as the scream finally ended, and Charris threw open the tent flap from within. All of them stopped, even Wanahomen drawing his breath in shock.

The woman sat amid the scattered cushions of her bed, clutching her head with her hands, her eyes wide and wild. One of her eyes, in any case; the other was already swollen nearly shut, that whole side of her face purpled and ugly. Her overskirts were torn, her underskirt slit and ruined, leaving her legs indecently bare from the thighs down. At her feet, sprawled and exposed and most definitely dead, lay the Dzikeh tribe's hunt leader Azima. A Banbarra knife-hilt stood up from his chest.

"What—" In all his plans, Wanahomen had never expected this outcome. He faltered, tried again. "What in the names of the gods..."

Charris dropped to one knee before him. It was not the usual posture that a slave gave his master among the Banbarra, but Charris had always made it clear that he considered himself a slave only to Wanahomen. "My Prince, I entered the tent because I saw this man come in first," he said in Gujaareen, "and I thought I heard a struggle when I came near. The woman is of the Hetawa; she would not have invited him."

More feet pounded up behind them, and more voices rose in query, horror, anger. Abruptly they quieted as Unte arrived, pushing through the crowd. He stopped and stared at Azima, throwing Wanahomen a hard look.

Wanahomen shook his head minutely, praying Unte would see the shock in his own face. *I never intended this.* He'd expected to find the girl shaken but furious, and Azima defensive, caught in the act. To touch a woman against her will, any woman except a slave or an enemy of the tribe, was one of the highest dishonors a man could bring upon himself. To do it in the *an-sherrat* of an ally, violating guest-custom...It would have settled the contest between them more firmly than any challenge.

He heard Yanassa's voice coming through the crowd, snapping at men until they moved out of her way. Reaching the front, she took in the scene at a glance, then sighed and went to Hanani. The templewoman had never taken her eyes from Azima's corpse. Even as Yanassa crouched beside her and touched her shoulder, Hanani jerked violently but did not look away.

"Shh, shh." Yanassa pulled a blanket from the tangled pile behind the girl and draped it 'round her shoulders, then threw another over her legs. Turning to the watching men, she glared. "What's wrong with you? Isn't it obvious what's happened here? Someone take that corpse from her sight before she goes mad."

Unte took a deep breath. "Where is Tajedd?"

"Here—" Wrapped in a blanket and accompanied by one of the older Yusir women, the Dzikeh leader pushed through the crowd and stopped, gasping. "Azima! Oh gods, Azima…" He went to the corpse's side, touching the slack face with a shaking hand. "Who? How?"

"I killed him," said the templewoman. If the murmurs around the tent had not ceased when Tajedd arrived, no one would have heard her: her voice was barely above a whisper and toneless. "I killed him."

"Hanani!" The other priest now. Wanahomen moved aside as Mni-inh shoved his way through the crowd with no attempt at politeness, then swore a string of the filthiest gutter Gujaareen. He went to the templewoman's side, but Yanassa swatted his hands away.

"What's wrong with you?" She switched to Gujaareen so he could understand her, though her protective body language and outraged tone were clear enough. "The last thing she needs right now is a man's touch!"

Sharer Mni-inh had never looked so furious in all the time Wanahomen had known him. His voice actually trembled with rage. "She's in shock, you barbarian cow, and she wouldn't be if your people hadn't hurt her—*now get out of my way!*"

Wanahomen might have laughed, under other and better circumstances, at the way Yanassa started and drew back in inadvertent obedience. The priest dropped to one knee and took the girl's hands, then drew a deep breath and looked hard into her eyes. He had to move into her line of sight, blocking Azima's corpse with his body, to do it. She looked up at him, her movements jerky and quick.

"I killed him, Brother. I *killed* him." She began to shake all over, so violently that Yanassa grew alarmed and the priest could barely hold her hands. "I killed him!"

"Shh," the priest said, and then closed his eyes. Abruptly the girl's tremors ceased. She sagged backward, asleep. The priest lifted her legs to move them onto the pallet, and adjusted the blanket.

Yanassa sighed and got to her feet. "That's a blessing." She turned to Tajedd, her face hardening. "In this tribe, a man who violates a woman deserves death. I'm pleased our Gujaareen cousin saw fit to deliver the sentence herself."

Tajedd started. "Are you mad? That slave killed my hunt leader!" He pointed at Hanani. "I want her life!"

Yanassa put her hands on her hips. "She was no slave! What slave has her own tent, and such wealth?" She gestured around at their surroundings. The tent was still sparsely decorated by Banbarra standards, but even to Wanahomen's foreign eye it was obvious the tribe had accorded high value to her Hetawa jewelry.

"No slave?" Tajedd blinked in confusion.

"No slave," said Hendet's voice, and Wanahomen turned to see his mother behind him. She nodded to him as she moved past. "I gifted her with this tent myself. My son and I have claimed her as family in accordance with the guest-custom of our homeland." She inclined her head to Tajedd—a small gesture of respect from one high-ranking person to another, tacitly reminding everyone present that she was his equal in status.

"She's a priestess among her people," Yanassa said. "I'll grant that she has no knowledge of proper behavior, but I'm absolutely certain she had no intention of inviting this man into her tent." She threw Azima's corpse a scathing look. "She told me she'd never had any man, and was forbidden from doing so by the Goddess of Dreams. She'll be a virgin all her life."

"A virgin?" Tajedd stiffened, understanding and fury lighting his face. He turned and threw a look of purest hatred at Wanahomen.

Wanahomen set his jaw. Virginity meant nothing in Gujaareh—an inconvenience that most rid themselves of the moment they reached the age of choice—but it was a status that the Banbarra accorded great value. Raping a virgin broke half their laws in one blow: clans had gone to feud and tribes to war over less. Tajedd would never believe that Wanahomen had not planned Azima's death now. He had no choice but to play this to the hilt.

"Customs differ indeed, Cousin," he said to Tajedd, meeting Tajedd's fury with coolness. "Perhaps Azima mistook the girl's strange ways as a sign of her availability, or an invitation. Mistakes happen. Still…" He stepped into the tent and went over to peer down at the girl. The male Sharer had his fingers on her eyelids, including the blackened one; as Wanahomen watched, the swelling diminished. "It is odd that Azima struck her, isn't it? A wonder she was still able to stab him, after a blow like that. She might've died of it." He turned to Tajedd, whose anger was gone now, eclipsed by sick realization. "A slave wouldn't have fought at all, yes? They know better. Indeed, a slave would not have been in a tent by herself, unless she had been commanded to wait there by its owner. Did Azima think this was someone else's tent, perhaps?"

Unease tightened Tajedd's jaw as Unte turned to look at him with narrow eyes. There were few things the Banbarra took more seriously than privacy. Each clan's *an-sherrat* was its own small kingdom within the greater body of the tribe, ruled by its highest-status female member. Within an *an-sherrat's* borders, men could feel safe in lowering their veils if its mistress approved; women could disrobe or indulge in any pleasure with dignity intact. No one could enter another clan's *an-sherrat* uninvited, save in the event of an emergency.

"It must've been a mistake," Tajedd murmured.

"Which?" Unte asked. He kept his voice mild, but only a fool would have mistaken his calm for a lack of anger. Wanahomen was grateful for his support—but then, the Yusir tribe was implicated in the death of a Dzikeh hunt leader. Unte too had to see this through. "Invading the tent of a proper woman, beating her, attempting to steal that which is hers and hers alone to bestow? Or invading the *an-sherrat* of Hendet Hinba'ii with the intent of damaging her clan's property? Which was Azima's mistake?"

Tajedd went silent for several damning breaths. Finally he lowered his eyes, accepting the dishonor. There had been no way out of it for him, really; it was simply a matter of which wrong did less damage to his tribe's reputation.

"My hunt leader is dead, Unte," he said at last, in a heavy voice. "He was my sister's child, beloved to me. Let us discuss his error in private, so that I might make amends."

Unte nodded. "Yes. This is a matter between tribe leaders." He looked up at the entrance of the tent, where Yusir and Dzikeh-Banbarra crowded the opening for a glimpse of the goings-on. "This will be settled properly by dawn," he said to them. "One man's folly need not cast a shadow over the whole night. All of you return to your revelry, save those of you who would help us move Azima's body."

Several of the Dzikeh pushed through the crowd, but the rest of the gathered folk began to mill about and murmur at once, only a few of them drifting away as Unte had commanded. One woman stepped forward. "Unte, will there be a feud between us and the Dzikeh?"

A few people looked at Tajedd, who did not raise his eyes. "No,"

Unte said in a firm voice. "A wrong has been committed and Tajedd means to see justice done. The ties between Dzikeh and Yusir are too strong to be damaged by this."

Wanahomen noted more than one relieved face among the onlookers as more of them began to leave the area of Hanani's tent. He did not blame them; he too had heard tales of the Banbarra's brutal, generations-long intertribal wars. There had once been half again as many Banbarra tribes as the six that remained now.

The Dzikeh men came in and gathered up the body of their hunt leader, wrapping one of the templewoman's floor-rugs around it to keep more blood from spilling. There was less blood than he would have expected given that the knife had struck the heart. Even so, Wanahomen did not think the woman would mind the rug's loss.

Unte left with Tajedd, though he threw one unreadable glance at Wanahomen beforehand that tied Wanahomen's stomach in knots. But the scheme had worked, however wrong it had gone. The Yusir-Banbarra might even gain status thanks to this, though Wanahomen could not be sure of that; even after ten years there were things about the Banbarra he would never understand. Unte's likely reaction was one of them.

Finally there were only five of them in the tent: Wanahomen, Charris, Yanassa, and the two Sharers. Yanassa hovered near Hanani, though she seemed to have finally yielded the contest to the male Sharer, who had finished healing the girl and now sat quietly beside her.

"My Prince." Wanahomen focused on Charris with a guilty flicker; he had left the man kneeling all the while.

"Rise, Charris. What is it?"

Charris got to his feet and switched to Chakti, throwing a quick glance at the male Sharer as he did so. "The Dzikeh was already dead when I arrived. There was no mark on him. It was I who put the knife in his chest."

Wanahomen stiffened. Yanassa frowned, uncomprehending. "How can that be?" she asked. "A man that age and healthy does not simply fall down dead." Abruptly her eyes narrowed in thought. "But it's true that she had no knife before, and I did not buy her one. I thought she'd only hurt herself with it, to be honest."

Magic. There was no other explanation. Wanahomen turned to stare at the male Sharer's back. "Yanassa, please leave me with our clan's guests. Charris, go with her."

Charris snapped a bow, turned on his heel, and exited the tent. Yanassa scowled and looked as though she wanted to protest, but to his everlasting relief she sighed and left as well. In the silence that fell, Wanahomen pulled off his headcloth, rubbed a hand over his braids, and sighed.

"You want to know how he died." The male Sharer.

Wanahomen blinked in surprise: did this one know Chakti? Or was it just a guess? "Yes," he replied. "Considering the Law and Wisdom say nothing about Sharer-maidens who can strike down barbarians with a scream."

"She screamed because of what she'd done," the Sharer said, getting to his feet. When he turned, his face was the coldest Wanahomen had ever seen it. All along the journey from the foothills, this one had seemed the more good-natured of the pair, annoyed at their situation but still determined to make the best of it. There was nothing good-natured in him now.

"To heal a man, we touch his soul and teach it to crave wholeness. To hurt a man, one must teach the soul to crave its own torment." The Sharer stepped closer and reached out to lay a hand on Wanahomen's chest. Wanahomen started and drew back, abruptly uneasy, but the Sharer moved with him, keeping contact. "And to *kill* a man—"

Pain snapped jaws shut around Wanahomen's chest with such sudden savagery that he could not draw breath enough to cry out. He staggered back, scrabbling at his chest, at the Sharer's hand that was now a claw hooked into his tunic and the flesh beneath. But even as his heart screamed in his chest, even as he struggled to escape this new Hetawa-spawned monster, the strength seemed to vanish from Wanahomen's limbs. He sagged to his knees, gasping for breath.

"I saw what happened in her dreams," said the Sharer. Wanahomen squinted up at him through tears of pain and suddenly knew: this man had no compunction whatsoever about killing him. Whatever oaths he had sworn, however ingrained his healer's beliefs, they had been completely subsumed by his fury. "I saw you bring her into that tent to heal your wound. She didn't understand what your kiss meant, but I do. You marked her as a target. *You used her as bait.*"

His heart. The pain had wrapped around his heart like the coils of a serpent—or a dozen ropes, their raw fibers abrading him even as they pulled tighter. He moaned, wishing the ropes would loosen just for an instant so the pain would ease. Or better yet snap—

Through the haze of his vision, he thought he heard the pop-hiss of fibers parting. An instant later he could breathe again, and the Sharer had let him go.

"I see," Wanahomen heard the Sharer murmur, almost to himself. "She was right about your strength. If you were trained you'd have me—but you aren't trained, young Prince, and I can tear your body apart faster than you can break through my constructs." Footsteps moving toward him. Wanahomen scrambled backward, though ineffectually; the pain had left him weak.

The Sharer crouched before him. He did not scowl; his expression was as calm as any Hananjan priest's should be. All the fury was in his black eyes. "Tell me why, Prince."

"Wh-why...?"

"Why you put my apprentice in harm's way! If you had any idea—" The Sharer's face constricted in sudden anguish. "I hadn't warned her she could kill this way. She's so young, she tries so hard.

This night will taint her soul forever and I want to know why you did it, Prince of Gujaareh, Avatar of Hananja. I want to know if you're as much of a monster as your father, because if you are—" He clenched a fist, trembling with suppressed rage, and for a moment the fading pain in Wanahomen's heart was eclipsed by fear the mad priest would attack him again.

He tried to think. "I needed—"

"Don't lie to me."

"I'm not lying, damn you! I n-needed Tajedd's vote." His heart was a raw ache, but he took more deep breaths, reveling in the taste of the air, the feel of it in his lungs. "In a few days there will be...a gathering of the tribes. Yusir, Dzikeh...f-four others. They vote on...whether to join in war against the Kisuati. Free Gujaareh."

The Sharer's eyes narrowed. Why, Wanahomen wondered, did all Hetawa priests look so alike when they meant to kill? Though if he had known even the healers were deadly, he would have told that Gatherer where he could throw them both.

"And the vote wasn't likely to go in your favor?"

"S-six tribes. Because enemies see no difference between one Banbarra and another...four of the six must vote in my favor. Even a tie loses. Dzikeh would not have supported me. They could have turned others. I had to win them *now*."

Was there some hint of understanding in the Sharer's eyes? Wanahomen didn't dare hope for it. "And how did hurting Hanani win these—" He stumbled over the unfamiliar syllables. "Dzikeh?"

He started to protest that the girl hadn't been hurt much; it was obvious that Azima hadn't managed to penetrate or loose seed into her. Just in time he realized the utter stupidity of saying so.

"I made them think Hanani was mine," he said. "My slave, my woman. Azima—the dead man—wanted an excuse to fight me. To damage another man's property is an insult that must be avenged. He attacked her to provoke me."

With that, Wanahomen glared up at the Sharer. Some of the feeling was coming back into his limbs. Could he defend himself now? He wouldn't have cared to lay a wager on it. "But I need the Hetawa too, though I wish to all the gods I didn't. So I had Charris watch the girl, ready to intervene before... well, before. You may not believe me, but I did *not* intend Azima's death. And I didn't intend for the girl to be... damaged. Alarmed, perhaps. Offended. Nothing more."

The Sharer said nothing for a long while, considering. Then, before Wanahomen could flinch away, he lifted his hand to Wanahomen's face. Wanahomen blinked instinctively, and then there was another of those curious disjuncts of time. The Sharer took his hand away, and Wanahomen's eyelids tingled. He sat up, aware that more time had passed than his mind could immediately grasp.

Then he realized the pain in his chest—even the twinge of the bruises where the priest had gripped him—was gone.

"The Gatherers see some value in you," the Sharer said softly, his lip curling. "They think you're better than your father. I can't say I agree, but they are closer to Hananja than I." He got to his feet. "Do what you must to free Gujaareh and return peace to our land, but don't ever use my apprentice in your schemes again."

The Sharer turned then, and went back to kneel at the girl's side. Plainly he meant to keep vigil for the rest of the night. And plainly Wanahomen had been dismissed.

After several tries—the strength was returning to his limbs, but slowly—Wanahomen managed to get to his feet. It was even more difficult to leave the tent at a pace that did not seem like fleeing, so that some morsel of his dignity could remain intact. The Sharer never turned back to him; the man didn't care. But it mattered to Wanahomen.

Though later that night, when he reached his own tent and collapsed into the pallets, he did not stop trembling for a long while.

23

◖☉◗

The Negotiation of Magic

The child sat up and looked around. After a moment she got to her feet, then spun in a circle. Her mother gasped, then threw her arms around the girl in a tight embrace, earning a muffled protest from her.

"She's been weak for several months," Yanassa said for Hanani's benefit. "But with this fever, her mother had begun to fear she would die. The clan has only the one girl-child to inherit the *an-sherrat*."

Hanani got to her feet and brushed her skirts straight, nodding to the teary-eyed mother who babbled thanks at her. "All thanks to the Goddess," she said. "I've cured the fever, but the underlying problem remains. Please tell them that the child must take care to eat certain foods or she may weaken again, especially now that her fertile cycles have begun. Meat would be best, but..." She glanced around the tent. It was one of the poorest she had seen among the Banbarra camp, patched and old and containing few of the trinkets and decorations most Banbarra women seemed to collect. "If the family cannot afford meat, then there are other foods that should serve as well. If I tell you the Gujaareen names, will you know them?"

"If I don't, I'll find out," Yanassa replied. She got to her feet as well, then followed Hanani out of the tent. "Too many children die needlessly in this tribe. Will it help if all the tribe eats these foods?"

"It would help anyone, but especially the young and women of childbearing age, yes."

"Then I must tell Unte, and in the spring trading we'll make certain to collect stores of those foods." Glancing sidelong at Hanani, she smiled. "Once again you have given value to the tribe. If you stay with us much longer, we'll have to send you home with a horse or two!"

Hanani said nothing. Two days had passed since the first solstice celebration; one since Azima's quiet, unlamented burial. Even the Dzikeh had not attended the interment—by Tajedd's order, since Azima had shamed their tribe. The slaves had seen to the matter, and besides them, only Hanani had stood at graveside to whisper prayers in a language Azima would not have understood, offered to a goddess he probably scorned.

Since then she had devoted herself to duty to distract her thoughts from that terrible night. Yanassa had helped her find those members of the tribe who suffered from illness or injury, and with the Banbarra woman's help she had coaxed most of them to accept her magic. With Hendet's advice in mind, she had accepted the gifts and services they offered in return, but she knew the truth. She had not performed the healings for their sake.

"Are you still troubled by it, little mouse?" Hanani felt Yanassa's gaze on her face. When Hanani did not reply, Yanassa sighed. "I may never understand the gentle hearts of you city folk. To mourn a man who did you such an insult . . ." She shook her head. "Do you mourn the enemies you kill in war too?"

"Yes."

Yanassa stared. "I was joking."

"I was not. Murder, violence, causes corruption unless done with the purest of intentions. That's why my people kill only for mercy, and never in anger. It's why we consider war anathema...or we did once." But the world had changed in so many ways.

Mni-inh came toward them from the far end of the encampment, nodding to Yanassa with cool courtesy before falling in to walk with them. He gave Hanani a measuring look, then brushed his hand against hers. "Your reserves are low."

"I have enough left for minor injuries and illnesses."

"We're here for a war, Hanani. You must be ready for more than that. Come; I'm going to see Unte right now. We might as well both ask."

Yanassa gave them a curious look. "Ask?"

"For dream-humors," Hanani said. She had half hoped to do without them, working what small magic she could out of her remaining reserves and her own dream-generated energy. Then she would have no further ability to perform higher narcomancy. Then she would no longer be able to kill.

Mni-inh nodded, throwing Hanani a disapproving scowl. "My apprentice seems to have forgotten that the Goddess Hananja— She Whose dreams encompass the afterlife—gives us the gift of magic to serve others. Our own dreams are not enough, however; we must ask your people for donations."

"Donations...of dreams?" Yanassa considered this and sighed. "We like Gujaareh's gods as well as any other land's, but yours in particular seem uncommonly pushy. Does it hurt, this donation?"

"No," said Mni-inh, "and it does no harm except when one takes dreamblood; only Gatherers are sanctioned to collect that. Though I suppose if we find volunteers, we could siphon off a tiny amount from each. That should be safe enough."

Azima would have had more dreamblood than we needed if he had died in peace, Hanani could not help thinking, but she did not voice the thought.

"Dreamseed will be a problem too," Mni-inh went on, musing to himself. "Given these people's feelings about sexuality, I'm not certain of the appropriate way to ask for donations of that. And I'm no Sister; I haven't a clue how to actually—well." His face flushed red. "But we'll definitely need that humor too."

Yanassa shook her head, uncomprehending. "Well, whatever you need, Unte will provide. I understand now why your people offered you in trade: this magic of yours is a great treasure." She slowed as they reached Unte's tent. To Hanani, pointedly, she said, "I'll come to check on you later tonight." Then she bowed and headed away.

Mni-inh gazed after Yanassa for a moment. "You've won a friend, it seems."

"Yes." The Banbarra admired swift, efficient killers.

The interior of Unte's tent was cooler than the heat outside, but smoky thanks to the long wooden pipe smoldering on a plinth near Unte. Unte, his face-veil and headcloth laid aside—he was bald as an egg, she saw for the first time—smiled as they came in and beckoned them over to the low table that Hanani had seen before. And as before, Wanahomen was there, though this time he sat upright and solemn on a cushion near the table. His veil was off as well; he did not look at them as they came in. Hanani had no great urge to look at him either.

"Everywhere I go, my people exclaim of your magic," Unte said, gesturing them toward empty cushions on either side of the table. Hanani waited for Mni-inh to choose a seat, but he beckoned for her to sit down first, and she recalled that this was Banbarra custom. Awkwardly, fighting the feeling of wrongness, she sat down beside Unte. Mni-inh took the remaining seat next to Wanahomen.

"That is why we're here, Lord Unte," said Mni-inh.

"Lord! These city folk have pretty manners, don't they?" Unte looked at Wanahomen and smiled. "I haven't been called that since *you* first arrived."

Wanahomen managed a faint smile, but it went nowhere near his eyes. "In my land, it's considered politeness."

"Hmph. The day my people need a fancy title to know their leader is the day I ride off into the desert to meet Father Sun." Unte laid out small cups and poured tea for each of them, not bothering to ask whether they wanted it. Hanani, following Mni-inh's lead, picked up her cup and sipped it carefully. To her surprise the liquid was cool rather than hot, spicy and richly sweet.

Mni-inh raised his eyebrows in appreciation as he also sipped the tea, though he set it down. "May that day not come for many years," he said. "If you like, one of us can check your health, and perhaps stave it off a little longer. But for that and any other healing, we require your assistance."

"Oh?"

Mni-inh glanced at Hanani. They had discussed this; among the Banbarra it was improper for a woman to stay silent, even if that woman was a lowly apprentice trying to show respect for her master. Even if that woman had no particular desire to speak in the first place. So Hanani took a deep breath and set her tea aside.

"Our power comes from dreams, L—" She winced. "Unte. In the city, in the Hetawa, we take dreams from others who come to offer them to our Goddess in tithe. But here we have no tithebearers, and soon we will run out of magic."

Unte sat back, surprised. "I didn't know you *could* run out. Is it dangerous to, er, offer these dreams?"

Hanani started to shake her head no, then remembered Dayuhotem. "Not ordinarily. It's painless, taking no more than a few breaths."

Unte glanced at Wanahomen. "You've heard of this?"

Wanahomen nodded and looked at each of them for the first time since they had come in. Hanani could not read his eyes; he kept his expression carefully neutral as he faced her. "In Gujaareh's capital, all citizens are expected to make regular tithes, though I have never done it myself." To Unte, he added, "Charris and I are more familiar with this than anyone else in the tribe. With your permission, I'll arrange volunteers before we leave."

"Leave?" Mni-inh asked.

Wanahomen threw him a guarded look. "With so many visitors expected in the next few days, it would be easy for spies of the Shadoun, or some other of our enemies, to breach our borders and perhaps even launch a sneak attack on the canyon. I and part of my hunt-troop are going to patrol the heights for the remainder of the solstice." He gestured vaguely toward the walls of the canyon.

"Ah." To Hanani's surprise, Mni-inh's face assumed a coldness that she had rarely seen in him. "This is punishment for your role in that man's death."

A painful silence fell for several breaths. Wanahomen's eyes turned even colder and his lips pressed tightly together, but he said nothing. It was Unte, after taking a long sip of tea, who finally answered.

"Wanahomen has done no wrong in the eyes of my people," he said. "Azima was unfit to be the Dzikeh hunt leader, as he proved when he attacked your daughter-of-the-soul. That's no fault of Wana's." He set the cup down and looked at Hanani. "Still, I'm aware that you have been harmed in the process, maiden of Gujaareh. It is the duty of the Yusir-Banbarra to console you in the wake of your injury. Thus I've decided to send Wanahomen away for a time so that his presence will cease to offend you."

"His presence doesn't offend me," Hanani said.

They all looked at her in surprise—even Wanahomen.

"Hanani." Mni-inh reached over to take her hand, concerned. "You don't realize what he did."

She looked at his hand, then his face, wondering if he realized just how much his words—and their implication that she was too stupid to know any better—hurt. He did not realize, she saw at once; that caused the hurt to recede a little. But not completely.

"I know exactly what he did, Mni-inh-brother," she said, earning another look of incredulity from him. "I know he manipulated that man into attacking me, though I don't know or care why. But to gain and keep power has always required a degree of corruption, which the Hetawa permits so long as our leaders keep the greater good of our people in mind." She looked at Wanahomen. "Was Gujaareh's good in your mind, Prince?"

He did not answer for a long moment, and when he did there was an odd intensity to his words. She could not tell if he was angry, frightened, or overwhelmed with some other great emotion, but his voice wavered as he said, "In my mind and heart and soul, Sharer-Apprentice. Every part of my life serves that purpose."

Hanani inclined her head. "Then I must accept that what you did was Hananja's will."

Which was the only reason she had not yet offered her own dreamblood to Mni-inh.

Unte seemed truly taken aback, but then he shook his head and sighed. "Nevertheless, the patrol should be done. It's Wanahomen's duty to guard the tribe."

Wanahomen made a curt bow at the waist. "My duty and pleasure, Unte." When he straightened, however, he continued to frown at Hanani.

"So, so, and so." Unte picked up his teacup and drained it. "Wanahomen, you may leave to make whatever preparations you require. And you, my Gujaareen friends—was that your only request of me?"

"Yes," Mni-inh replied. Then he hesitated and added, "For now."

Unte laughed. "You learn at last, city man." He gave them a flourishing gesture that seemed part salute and part farewell, and picked up the still-smoldering pipe. "Return whenever you like. Or feel free to stay and enjoy the sun-hour rest with me."

As in Gujaareh, the Banbarra dealt with the hottest part of the afternoon by sleeping through it. "Thank you, but no," Mni-inh said, getting to his feet. "Our best time to work is when others sleep."

"Ah, yes. So then, rest—and work—well."

They filed out of the tent, Wanahomen coming last to make sure the flap was closed properly. When he straightened from that he faced them. "You may take whatever dream-humors you need from myself and Charris," he said. "I can also ask my mother if she is willing to tithe. Will that suffice?"

"Your mother cannot," Mni-inh said. "Her body is still healing. And Charris must volunteer himself, for Hananja will not accept unwilling offerings."

"I think he'll say yes; he has always been devout. But I'll summon him so you can ask."

Mni-inh nodded. "As for you— Well, you understand the dangers. Are you willing in spite of that?"

Wanahomen gave them a blank look. "Dangers?"

Mni-inh's eyes widened. He looked over at Hanani and she stared back, needing no narcomancy to share his shock. How could Wanahomen not know the dangers? Unless he had never been warned of the problem in the first place.

"Explain these dangers," Wanahomen said. He had caught their exchanged glance; his eyes narrowed in suspicion. "You mentioned no dangers with regard to Charris."

Mni-inh only shook his head, muttering to himself in wonder. It was left to Hanani to explain as Wanahomen looked at her. "You should never tithe," she said.

His frown deepened. "*Explain*, woman."

"It would be dangerous. Your dreaming gift is powerful. Even the slightest imbalance in your humors could send it spiraling out of control. Without dreamblood to keep you tethered to yourself, you would go mad."

The Prince flinched, his face working from horror through confusion to rage as he stared at her. After a long moment he said, "Dreaming gift." It was a question.

"Your father must have known," Mni-inh said. He was smiling, but there was a cold, angry edge to it that Hanani found quite alarming. "You said you'd never tithed. All the Prince's other dozens of children gave tithes whenever they were in the city, yet somehow there was no time to bring you?" He uttered a contemptuous sigh. "Ah, but the Hetawa was corrupt in those days. It would only have taken a bribe to the right person to keep his precious heir's secret."

Wanahomen's fists had clenched at his sides, his body rigid. "What in nightmares are you talking about?"

Hanani interjected quickly, before Mni-inh could say anything else.

"In some people, the ability to dream is too strong to stay within their minds, or to come only during sleep," she said to Wanahomen. "Their dreams are more vivid, their minds able to navigate between Ina-Karekh and Hona-Karekh as if dreaming and waking were one. We consider that level of strength to be a gift from the Goddess. Those who possess it are usually claimed by the Hetawa."

His eyes filled with such horror that Hanani inadvertently drew back. Why was he so upset? Unnerved, she ventured, "It's a great honor to possess a gift as powerful as yours. If you had been found and trained young enough, you could have become a Sharer too, or a Gatherer. Perhaps you could even have served alongside the Gatherer Ehiru, your uncle . . ."

Though she trailed off as she realized what that would have meant. Wanahomen was of the same age as Gatherer Nijiri, or close. Had he been claimed by the Hetawa as he should have been, *he* rather than Nijiri might've been the one to help slay his father.

She put her hand to her mouth, at last understanding the terrible realization in his face. But before she could think of some way to rectify her error, he pressed his lips together and walked away.

"Prince—" Hanani moved after him, but stopped as Mni-inh caught her arm.

"Let him go."

"Brother!"

"Let him go, I said." Mni-inh watched as the Prince's indigo-clad form disappeared amid the tents. "He's just learned he belongs among the very people he's hated his whole life. That won't be easy for him."

"You've made it no easier!"

"No, I haven't," said Mni-inh. There was no apology or guilt in his expression. "And neither should you, after what he did to you. You're too gentle, Hanani."

It was the second time he had spoken to her as if she were a fool. And though it was improper and unpeaceful of her to feel anger at his words—or to show it if she felt it—she felt it so fiercely in that moment that she jerked her arm roughly out of his grip.

"I had better be gentle, hadn't I, Brother?" He stared at her, taken aback by her vehemence; she took a step closer and had enough presence of mind to drop her voice to a heated whisper. "Does anger give you comfort? I assure you, it's not so easy for me. Someone else might die the next time I lose my temper. Better I should pray for *more* gentleness, don't you think?"

"Hanani—" he blurted, and then faltered silent. Before he could say anything else, Hanani did as the Prince had done, and walked away.

24

⊂⊙⊃

Legacy

"Yes," said Hendet. "Your father knew, and so did I."

Wanahomen closed his eyes. *You could have become a Gatherer,* the Sharer had said. Like Ehiru, who had slain his father. Like Una-une, the mindless soul-eating Reaper.

He'd woken Hendet out of a sun-hour nap to demand this truth from her. "Why?" He whispered the word. "Why didn't you tell me?"

"The gift runs in the male lineage," she said. Her voice was flat and cool, but he knew her. She was afraid. "You've heard the tale of Mahanasset the First Prince many times, Wanahomen; have you never understood its message? He was the first to know the marvel of dreamblood, because without it he couldn't tell reality from the visions that plagued him—"

"And that is what I can expect for myself? Madness?" Wanahomen leaped to his feet. "Demons and shadows, is that what you're saying to me?"

"Sit down!" Her voice snapped like a whip. He opened his mouth to protest and she glared him silent. "*Sit*, fool boy, and listen to me."

Seething quietly, he obeyed, kneeling on the cushion farthest from her. Seeing this, Hendet sighed and rubbed her eyes.

"I don't blame you for your anger," she said finally. She looked at him and some of the anger in his belly unknotted at the pain in her face. "The priest who tested you told us that with the strength of your gift, there was an equal chance that you would grow up a madman, or suffer no ill effects at all. It seemed worth the risk."

"An equal chance." He clenched his fists in his lap. "I could become a raging lunatic at any shadows-damned moment, and you thought it *worth the risk?*"

"Your father thought so, yes," Hendet said quietly.

He stared back at her and finally asked aloud the question that he had wondered—and resisted—for ten years. "And was *he* mad?"

It jarred him badly that she did not immediately say no.

"I don't know," she said after a long silence. She looked away, rubbing her palms on her lap. She had been trained never to show nervousness. "Certainly he knew dream from daylight. With me he was always kind, always so clever. But the things he did toward the end— Those things—" Her jaw flexed; she fell silent.

Then perhaps the Gatherers were right to claim him, came the thought to Wanahomen's mind before he could habitually reject it.

No. The Hetawa had abused his father, abused all his forefathers. Any crimes Eninket had committed were done only in response to that.

"You must understand," said Hendet, her voice softer than usual. "If the priests had tried to claim any other of his children he might have yielded, but *not you*. So your father took the chance, and bribed the priest to say that you lacked the gift."

"That was all well and fine," Wanahomen said tightly, "but you could have told *me*."

Silence fell, Wanahomen's taut and Hendet's heavy with guilt.

"I'm sorry," she whispered at last. "You're right, of course. I just...

You had so many other troubles to deal with. And the longer I kept the truth from you, the harder it became to tell."

In the wake of that, there was nothing else Wanahomen could think to say. He shook his head, sighed, and finally got to his feet. Hendet sat forward, anxious. "Where are you going?"

"To prepare for our patrol. And to find the Sharers."

"Wana—"

He held up a hand to silence her, unwilling to hear any more of her half-truths. "We can speak again when I return."

"I'm sorry," she said again as he stepped through the tent-flap. He looked back at her and could not muster a farewell as the flap fell shut.

It did not take long to find the templewoman. "She looks for you," said one of the tribe's elders when he asked. "That way." Thus he found her near the *an-sherrat* of Shatyrria, mother of Wutir and grandmother of Wujjeg, looking about. By the unease in Hanani's face, he knew she had noticed the hostile looks from Wutir's relatives. The looks they gave Wanahomen were worse; he ignored them.

"Prince." There was a note of relief in her voice when she saw him. On another day he might have found irony in that. "Please forgive my mentor. He's still angry—"

"I know," Wanahomen said. "Come with me."

He got three steps before he realized she was not following. When he looked back, she studied his face, and he realized she had taken that time to consider whether it was safe to go with him. That the Azima incident had made her more cautious was good; that she felt the need to be cautious with *him* was sobering.

But do I not deserve it? whispered his conscience as she finally moved to follow.

Yes. He did. Which was why, in the end, he would forgive his mother. He could not fault her when he too had committed shameful acts.

Hanani threw glances at him as they walked through the camp, but she said nothing to break the silence, for which Wanahomen was grateful. Only when they reached Yanassa's *an-sherrat* did she make a sound, understanding. "Your son."

He stopped and turned to face her. He did not hate her anymore, not after seeing her face on the night she'd killed Azima. Did she hate him? He prayed she would be true enough to her vows to help him, even if she did.

"I need to know," he said. "*Tassa* needs to know."

She nodded slowly. "I can administer the fourth-year test. But the gift passes most often and most powerfully through the father-line, from male to male. If he has the gift—"

"It doesn't guarantee he'll go mad."

"No. But what will happen if he does? How do the Banbarra care for their mad ones?"

"They take them into the desert and leave them to die."

She stiffened. When she finally spoke, there was a level of contempt in her voice that he had never heard before. "'A people shall be judged civilized by how the least among them are succored.'"

It startled him to hear one of Mahanasset's proverbs in her mouth—but then, the Hetawa stinted nothing on its adoptees' education. "There's some truth in that," he said. "But even in Gujaareh, no one is expected to slice the throats of his own ailing parents, or drown his own malformed children. There are no Gatherers here to do such things."

"The mad are neither dying nor malformed! These barbarians—" She trailed off, probably struggling to remain polite. He almost smiled at the pure Gujaareen arrogance in her tone. He hadn't known she had it in her.

"Life in the desert is difficult, Sharer-Apprentice. The Banbarra are not wealthy like Gujaareh; they have few resources to spare on 'the least among them.' And remember: the mad can be dangerous."

She made a dismissive gesture, quick and angry. "Then tell them to bring their mad to Gujaareh! We can help them have good long lives. Or if they're brought young, they can help others as Sharers or Gatherers. Tassa's age, or younger."

Wanahomen stiffened, but reminded himself that the woman had not specifically mentioned claiming Tassa.

"When I return to Gujaareh, I will lose my son," he said. He kept his voice soft and neutral, but some hint of anguish must have filtered through his efforts. She fell silent, some of the righteous anger fading from her face. "He is my firstborn, but he'll never sit on the Sunset Throne. In blood, Tassa is only half Banbarra—but in spirit he's wholly so. Taking him from the life and clan he loves, forcing him to live under a permanent roof, chaining him to people he holds in contempt... These things would destroy him. Do you understand?"

She spoke gently too, perhaps meaning to be kind. "Madness would destroy him too, Prince. There's only one certain way to ensure it won't, if his soul ever begins to wander in earnest."

"I won't have him enslaved with dreamblood, either."

She allowed a moment's silence, to cushion her next words, and so that he could brace for them. "Then if he goes mad, will you take him to the Gatherers?"

"They won't have another of my line."

"Then..."

"If he goes mad, I'll kill him myself."

It did not hurt to say the words, only to think about them. And because she was Gujaareen, her face filled with compassion, rather than horror.

"That choice should be his," she said.

He nodded curtly. "Yes. And should the need come, I'll ask him. But if he is already gone into visions and gibbering, if the choice has been taken from him by this curse you call a gift—" He shook his head. "I won't let him suffer."

227

She sighed, but did not protest his words. "I'll check him now."

Tassa was inside, playing with the toy sword Wanahomen had given him after one of his trips into Gujaareh. The boy opened the flap to invite them in with an eagerness that spoke of long boredom. "Mama told me to stay inside today," he said. "Dasheuri found a scorpion and dared me to pick it up, and I did. Mama saw and got mad."

"As she should have," Wanahomen said, scowling. "Those creatures can kill a child your size."

"I knew what I was doing," Tassa replied, with not a little arrogance of his own. Then he turned his bright, curious gaze on the woman. "She's the one Mama's been helping."

"She's a healer," Wanahomen said. The woman looked at both of them, obviously sensing that they were talking about her. "From the land where I was born. She wants to read your dreams to check your health."

Tassa beckoned them over to the cushions set up for guests around a small square rug. "She can look into my dreams?" His voice held fascination rather than the unease that an adult might have felt. "How?"

"Lie down, and she'll show you," Wanahomen said. When Tassa eagerly flopped down on two cushions, Wanahomen nodded to the woman, who knelt beside the boy.

"Dream—remember I?" Tassa asked her in halting, awful Gujaareen. Wanahomen blinked in surprise, then suddenly understood: Yanassa. She must have decided to teach Tassa Gujaareen, even though traditionally Banbarra boys were not taught women's skills. For a moment he felt tears sting his eyes before he quickly blinked them away. He would have to thank Yanassa later.

The templewoman looked surprised as well, but smiled. "I can make you remember, if you wish," she said. When Tassa frowned in incomprehension, she simplified. "Yes. You will remember."

Tassa looked pleased. "I don't remember most of my dreams," he said, switching back to Chakti. "I wish I could remember more."

"She can teach you how, if you like."

The boy's eyes narrowed in suspicion. "I don't want to learn magic. That's a foreign thing."

It's half your heritage, he almost said, but held his tongue.

"That would be up to your mother," he said, "but lie back and be silent for a while, or *this* magic will take all afternoon."

Tassa got comfortable. "What now?"

"Close your eyes. She'll lay her fingers on them, and make you sleep."

A hint of worry flickered across the boy's face. "Have you done this?"

"Yes. So has Hendet. You've seen that she's better now?"

"Yes. All right, then." He closed his eyes, eager now.

The woman laid her fingertips on his eyelids and uttered a soft, monotone hum. After a moment Tassa's body relaxed into sleep, and Wanahomen sat back on his heels to wait.

It took less time than he'd expected. Barely five minutes later she exhaled and opened her eyes. "Such gentle dreams," she whispered. "I did not expect that of your son."

Unsure how to take that statement, Wanahomen decided to ignore it. "Does he have the gift or not?"

"No. His dreams will never leave Ina-Karekh."

The wave of relief that passed through Wanahomen was both painful and sweet. On a completely irrational level, he had hoped to see yet another sign of his blood in the boy. That foolishness passed quickly, however, and Wanahomen closed his eyes to whisper a prayer of thanks for his son's good fortune. When he opened his eyes, the woman was looking at him.

"I didn't think you prayed," she said.

At this he scowled. "It's the Hetawa I hate, not the Goddess," he said, moving over to Tassa. On impulse he gathered the boy into his arms, as Yanassa had so rarely let him do when Tassa was a baby. "If She sees fit to grant me some small blessing, I am Hers enough to be thankful for it."

"And yet you don't obey Her Law."

Tassa sighed contentedly in his sleep, snuggling into Wanahomen's chest; Wanahomen could not help smiling. He would be sure to tease the boy about it later.

"No, I don't," he said. "In my heart I do, but in plain fact . . . I'm a harder man now than I was when I left Gujaareh, and I admit: sometimes that troubles me. But it's for Gujaareh that I do such unpeaceful things. I try to make certain they're the *right* things, but . . ." He threw her a look. The bruises had been healed and Azima was dead, but the shadow of what had happened still lurked in her solemn face. He sighed, and made his next words as much of an apology as his pride could bear. "I don't always succeed."

She frowned a little—not in disapproval, he guessed, but in thought. And in particular, she watched him hold Tassa. He sensed she was considering something, or perhaps withholding something.

"He lacks the gift," she said, "but he's still your son. His own children could possess it. Such things sometimes skip generations." When Wanahomen said nothing—because he could think of nothing to say to that—she added, "You will need to tell him of this, Prince. Knowledge is a weapon; do not leave your descendants unarmed." She paused again. "As you were."

He looked sharply up at her, angry—but that was pointless, because *she* was not the one who had withheld the truth from him. She did not flinch from his anger, either, perhaps because she knew she had the right of it. This thought made him sigh, and relent.

"I'll explain it all to Tassa," he said. "Tomorrow. I'll tell Yanassa, too, and convince—and *try* to convince her to let Tassa visit

Gujaareh, at some point in the future. He'll need to know how to take his children to the Hetawa to be tested, if he can."

Hanani frowned. "Ah, mothers control such things here. I see." She considered for a moment. "I'll discuss the matter with Yanassa and the women I know. I'm no mother, but perhaps if it comes from a woman, that will help."

"Thank you," Wanahomen said, surprised. "Yes, that would help." *But why are you helping?* he did not ask. It was an unnecessary question, really; she obviously felt that helping him served the Goddess Hananja in some way. And, too, perhaps she saw it as helping Tassa, and Wanahomen was merely a means to that end.

But abruptly the woman sighed, and Wanahomen realized that while he'd been pondering her, she'd come to some decision.

"There's another way for you to prevent the madness," she said. "Dreamblood is the surest way, but since you won't have that..." She hesitated, then sighed. "You could learn to restore the balance of your own humors when they slip out of true. It's a skill that those of us who manipulate humors must learn. If you could master it, your sanity would be safe."

He frowned at her for a moment, then shifted to lay Tassa back down so that the boy could sleep away the rest of the sun-hour. "Would it be difficult, to learn this skill?"

"It was easy for me, but I was well practiced in narcomancy at that point of my training. Much would depend on how quick to learn you are, and how patient my mentor is likely to be—"

"No." Let that torturing, hateful bastard into his dreams? Was *she* mad? "You will teach me."

She started. "Prince, I'm only an apprentice."

"I don't care. Are you capable of teaching me?"

She hesitated. Not from doubt, he guessed from her face, but from a sense of propriety. "Yes, but Mni-inh has many more years of experience—"

"Then it shall be you. But tell me why."

Now it was her turn to stare at him as if he'd gone mad. "Because you won't let my mentor—"

"No. Tell me why you offered this in the first place. I've given you insult, Sharer-Apprentice Hanani. I'd do it again if it would win me the Banbarra vote, and I cannot apologize for it. Yet you've forgiven me. Why?"

She drew back, and abruptly all expression vanished from her face, making her as cold as a statue. He was, fleetingly, reminded of Tiaanet.

"I never said I had forgiven you," she snapped.

"Then why help me?"

"Because, I now believe, this is why the Gatherers sent me. I was commanded to free Gujaareh. Helping you will accomplish that goal."

"You were commanded to—" He stared at her, not knowing whether to laugh. Who in their right mind could have commanded a shy, shrinking little thing like her to free her people from their conquerors? And who in all the desert would have expected her to actually try?

And yet she was not shy or shrinking now. He would never have believed it from his first impressions of her, but there was stone in her eyes. Had the incident with Azima brought it out, or had it always been there, hidden beneath her demure Gujaareen manner? He did not know—but he knew to respect it.

"Teach me this magic," he said at last, speaking softly because that was the only humility he would permit himself to show a priest of the Hetawa. "I'll teach it to Tassa, so he can teach his own children. When I win back our land, I'll teach it to all of my heirs. Gujaareh need never fear a madman on its throne again."

She inclined her head. "We should begin at once, then. Tomorrow. I need to discuss the method with Mni-inh first." She rose to leave.

Wanahomen stared at her back. "I leave for the heights in the morning!"

She had opened the tent-flap; here she paused and turned back. A light breeze, fragrant with the scent of late-season wildflowers, blew through the aperture, wafting her sashes and skirts around her in an earth-toned cloud. She looked cool and dreamlike and so quintessentially Gujaareen, even in Banbarra clothing, that Wanahomen felt homesick.

"You'll camp up there?" She pointed beyond the tent, toward the nearby cliffs.

"At night, yes. By day I'll be riding the rim with my men—"

"Then I'll come to you at night." She inclined her head to him and left, the tent-flap *thwap*ing shut behind her with a soft retort, like a hollow laugh.

25

(⊙)

The Negotiation of Pain

Tiaanet realized the danger as soon as she entered the room where her father and three other nobles sat plotting the Kisuati overthrow.

The woman speaking was tall, pale, haughty, and barely older than Tiaanet, though she wore a diadem on her braided hair that marked her as head of her family. Iezanem, zhinha and daughter of the Lady Zanem, recently orphaned by her parents' mysterious deaths in sleep. Her tone was scathing as she said to Sanfi, "What good does that do us now? With one stroke the Hetawa has won the people's hearts back as if the last ten years never happened."

The danger was hidden behind her father's calm mask, Tiaanet noted, but it was there. He could not afford to antagonize Iezanem, who spoke for the handful of zhinha families that had managed to retain any real power under Kisuati rule. Still, he had never liked being spoken to in such a tone by any woman, and as Iezanem did it now, Tiaanet felt her belly clench in apprehension.

"The people's hearts are fickle," he replied, nodding thanks to Tiaanet as she refilled his cup with sweetwine. "They'll hate the Hetawa again the moment the Kisuati start killing them in retaliation for the soldiers' deaths."

"You can't guarantee that," said another of Sanfi's guests. This one was Deti-arah of the shunha and military castes, once poised to become Gujaareh's next general. The fact that he had not already achieved the rank was the only thing that had saved him from a Kisuati execution after the conquest. "Neither that the Kisuati will retaliate, nor that the people will turn against the Hetawa. I've met Sunandi Jeh Kalawe and her husband Anzi Seh Ainunu. Anzi is a soldier, granted; he may want blood for the deaths of his men. But Sunandi will understand the danger in doing so. Those soldiers robbed, beat, and raped Gujaareen citizens. To retaliate against the Hetawa for killing such filth would infuriate the whole city."

"Anzi controls the city's military power," Sanfi said, taking a sip of wine. "How likely is a man to listen to his wife, no matter how sensible her advice might be, when he's angry and has the power to act on his rage?"

"Sunandi speaks for the Protectorate," said Ghefir, another shunha who owed Sanfi for a substantial business loan. He picked at his lower lip as he spoke, his brow furrowed with unease, not looking up at Tiaanet even when she poured him more wine. "They put her in place precisely to prevent him from making such mistakes. If he ignores her and things go wrong, he must later answer to the Protectors."

"But the damage would be done," said Sanfi.

"That is beside the point," snapped Iezanem in an unpeaceful tone that made Tiaanet wince. "We're moving too slowly. Our troops have gathered at the edge of the desert; why are we waiting to attack? The longer we delay, the more power the Hetawa gains. At this rate, even if we win, the people will cheer us as their liberators, then still turn to the priests for guidance."

"Or to whomever the Hetawa endorses," said Deti-arah. He sighed and steepled his fingers. "Word is spreading in the city that the Banbarra are on our side now, and they're led by a man of the Sunset Lineage. Is that your doing, Sanfi?"

Tiaanet went to a serving table at the edge of the room to refill her flask. In the long silence before Sanfi's answer, the sound of the pouring wine seemed very loud.

"No," Sanfi said at last, and there was thunder in his voice now, dark and gathering. "That was information we had agreed to withhold until the time of the final assault. Someone among us has been talking."

Deti-arah was shaking his head when Tiaanet turned back to face the room. "I heard this from the Hetawa," he said. "I went with my son to tithe some dreams two days ago. The priest who took my donation told me that the Goddess would soon answer my prayers for peace, because Her Avatar would be returning to restore the city's freedom. The fellow seemed almost gleeful about it; most unlike a templeman."

Silence fell. Tiaanet saw Sanfi's hand tighten on his cup.

"But... they would only know that, and be happy about it, if the Prince's return served their purposes," said Ghefir, picking even harder at his lip now. "Wouldn't they?"

"Yes," Sanfi said quietly. "It would seem the Hetawa and the Prince have forged an alliance of their own. That is... unfortunate."

"Unfortunate?" Iezanem stood; she was shaking with rage. "*That's* what you call it? Who in the city will want a Gujaareen Protectorate now, when the Hetawa is making Wanahomen's return sound like some sort of much-heralded prophecy? This is what comes of your delays, Sanfi. We have no choice but to act—"

"*No.*" Sanfi glared at her, no longer bothering to be polite. "The Kisuati in the city are on alert, fearful of an uprising at any moment. We must wait until they're off guard."

"That could take months!"

"It will not. It will take only days."

Ghefir rolled his eyes in exasperation. "Sanfi, old friend, what are you talking about?"

236

Deti-arah was more direct as he leaned forward. "What are you hiding?"

Sanfi sighed, pinching the bridge of his nose between his fingers as if weary. Tiaanet knew better. He was furious, but he needed to sound calm, look confident.

"A four of Protectors is coming to Gujaareh," he said at last. The others in the room reacted with murmured alarm; he waited until they subsided. "One of my merchant contacts there sent word, though they travel in secrecy for the sake of security; he handles barge traffic on that part of the river, and was contracted to bring them here. They should be here by the end of the solstice eightday. And they are coming, at the very least, to evaluate Sunandi Jeh Kalawe and determine whether she should remain in control of the city. Their arrival can work to our advantage. Any transition of power is a time of confusion.

"And there is a plague loose in the city." He paused and inclined his head gravely to Iezanem, who tightened her jaw. She did not wear mourning colors because zhinha did not bother with tradition, but her grief was still plain. "Again a contact of mine has told me a secret: the Hetawa has some two or three dozen layfolk sequestered in the inner Hetawa, sleeping their lives away. The priests say they're studying the sickness, seeking some cure for it. But what if there is no cure?"

Iezanem went very still. Deti-arah frowned. "I don't understand."

"A Gatherer died several days ago. Sonta-i."

"Yes," said Deti-arah with an air of impatience. "What do you imply? Sonta-i was old as Gatherers go. There's nothing untoward about his giving the Final Tithe now."

"What if he didn't give the Final Tithe?" asked Sanfi. "What if he too died of this sickness? What if word spread that the Hetawa, with all its magic, can neither control nor stop the spread of this sickness? What would happen then?"

Deti-arah's eyes widened. Iezanem shook her head in confusion, setting her dangling lapis-and-gold earrings a-rattle. "The city would be rife with fear and unrest," she said, "and the Protectors would likely turn on the Hetawa once they can no longer perform their basic function of keeping the city healthy and content. But none of those things has happened, Sanfi."

Sanfi shrugged, though Tiaanet could see the tension in his shoulders. "What if they could?"

"You," Deti-arah said, his voice shaking and horrified. "*You* have caused this sickness?"

Iezanem whirled on Sanfi, her body going rigid.

"No," Sanfi said firmly, looking at Iezanem as he spoke. "The sickness is magic. Who controls magic in Gujaareh? The Hetawa. Perhaps they even caused the sickness themselves, somehow. I merely suggest that we find some way to remind the people, and the Protectors, of this."

Iezanem caught her breath; beneath her scowl, her eyes were bright with unshed tears. Ghefir stopped picking at his lip. Only Deti-arah continued to gaze at Sanfi with something close to suspicion, but he did not voice his concerns aloud, whatever they were.

There was little more to be said after that. Iezanem and Ghefir agreed to spread the rumor via their connections. Sanfi, as one of the most prominent nobles in the city, offered to arrange a meeting with the visiting Protectors, once they arrived, in order to express his concerns regarding the Hetawa. Then Tiaanet offered their guests a tray of small edibles to refresh them, and they made their farewells for the evening, leaving Tiaanet alone with her father.

Sanfi remained in the greeting-room where he'd sat throughout the meeting, gazing at his folded hands while Tiaanet cleaned up. He was silent for so long that it startled her when he said, "Has Tantufi been settled?"

Tiaanet had almost knocked over a vase at his sudden words. She

238

righted it quickly, concentrating on it so that she would not frown. He was too used to seeing empty serenity on her face; the change would've been too noticeable. "Yes, Father. I have her in the storage cellar."

"Take me to her." His voice was very soft.

Tiaanet turned to face him with the vase in her hands, tense. He glanced at her; a muscle in his jaw tightened.

"Don't defy me, Tiaanet," he said. "Not tonight."

Setting the vase down, Tiaanet stayed where she was a moment longer to fuss with the arrangement of flowers in it. All the while her mind was racing, trying to find some way to appease the wrath that she could feel radiating from him like a fire's warmth. But the longer she delayed, the hotter that wrath would grow. Finally she turned to him, bowed, and walked toward the cellar room.

She could hear him walking behind her, his pace as measured and sedate as her own, though his breathing was uneven and harsh. The corridor leading to the cellar was dim; the short stairwell leading under the house was even dimmer. In the dark he could not see her hands shake, but she knew he would sense her fear nevertheless. This was the one thing that *could* still make her afraid, and they both knew it.

Inside the small cellar, a single lantern burned steadily on a shelf stacked with sealed jars. The lantern's oil was scented of hyssop, but this was not quite enough to mask the scent of mildew wafting from the earthen floor and walls. The cellar never quite dried out from floodseason to floodseason; they used the space only to store those items that were proof against the smell. And those items that were otherwise deemed unimportant, like the little girl chained against the far wall.

Sanfi came into the cellar behind Tiaanet and stopped, his eyes narrowing. The girl leaned against the wall, her head lolling, but in the silence her soft mutters were audible, as was the sound of her ankle-chain, rattling as she methodically rubbed her leg against the stone wall.

"Why isn't she asleep?" he asked.

Tiaanet swallowed. But before she could formulate an answer, Tantufi's head lifted. She focused on their voices with an effort, blinking huge rheumy eyes.

"No sleep," the girl muttered. "No sleep sleep sleep so many nearby, so many."

Sanfi set his jaw, his fists clenching. He stepped toward the girl, his whole posture warning of his intent. Tiaanet quickly stepped in front of him.

"It's habit, Father," she said. "She's just used to being kept awake by the guards. She doesn't understand that you *want* her to sleep now."

"Get out of my way," he said.

"She won't be able to help it, Father, she'll have to sleep eventually—"

He reached up to caress Tiaanet's cheek, and she fell silent, frozen.

"I want her asleep now," he said softly. "Her magic works just as well if she's unconscious."

No. Tiaanet closed her eyes, hearing her heart pound in her ears. So few things could hurt her now, but this she had no defense against. *Goddess, please, no. I can't stand to watch again while he beats her, she almost died the last time, no. Hananja, please help me.*

Then, as if in answer to her prayer, the solution came to her.

"You promised, Father," she said. In the closed stillness of the cellar, her voice sounded unnaturally loud, dangerously harsh—much like that of the zhinha Iezanem. She saw him frown in response to it, saw his anger begin to focus on a new target.

Yes. Me, not her.

"You promised that you wouldn't hurt her again, after the last time." She squared her shoulders and lifted her chin. She was taller than him by a fingerwidth or so, and normally kept her head tilted down so as to avoid looking down on him. Now she did it deliberately, belligerently. "And did I not please you that night, Father? Did I not buy her safety well enough for you?"

His eyes widened, his whole body going taut with fury. "How dare you," he whispered.

"If you want her to sleep, I can give her an herb-draft," she said. Deliberately Tiaanet stepped closer to him, crowding him, glaring into his eyes. "Then you can have your plague. But you don't want her *asleep*, do you? You want her dead. You're too angry to think right now, Father, because Wanahomen stole the march on you, but why does that anger you so? He'll be a good son-in-law. He uses others and lies as you do. As you *will*, if you hurt Tantufi when you promised not to, or do none of your promises in bed have any value? That wouldn't surprise me, nothing else you do in bed has any—"

It was almost a relief when the storm broke. She'd been running out of ways to taunt him. He roared in fury and backhanded her so hard that she spun around and fell among several piled sacks of decorative white sand, meant to be used in the atrium garden. The sacks were soft enough that she broke nothing falling on them, but the breath was knocked from her lungs, and between that and his blow her vision went gray for a time.

Through the gray Tiaanet heard Sanfi shouting, something about how she was just as much a poison as her mother, a curse on his lineage, a curse he didn't deserve. He took hold of her hips and she waited for him to drag her off the sacks, onto the floor where he could finish venting his rage. But he left her where she was. Instead she felt the back of her dress torn open, her legs shoved apart. There was more fumbling and cloth ripping and then a stunning new pain came into her, four times worse than the blow he'd struck her, forty times worse than the first night he'd ever come into her room, so many years ago that she barely remembered any of it but the shame that she had once felt. There was the potential for shame here too, and perhaps a bit of disgust as he snarled and grunted and ground himself against her backside, but she felt none in spite of the pain. The time when she had been ashamed of him, and of herself for being his daughter, had passed years ago. Now all that mattered was that it was *she* who bore the pain, and not Tantufi. Not Tantufi.

Thankfully, he was too angry to try to please her, as he so often did to assuage his guilt. That made it go quickly.

When it was done, she waited, listening to him gulp air and compose himself, knowing that the apologies would not come now. For a time he would still blame her for provoking him. For making him hurt her. At most he might worry that she would leave him, and then she would have to endure being shadowed by his guards everywhere she went. He had warned her since childhood that he would have her hunted down by assassins if she ever tried to flee. They would not use weapons, though; he would authorize their slowest and most brutal methods as a parting gift for his only beloved child.

(She did not fear this for herself. What was more pain? But he would do it to Tantufi too, and that she could not endure.)

Only later would guilt replace her father's anger, and then he would offer apologies that meant nothing, and gifts she did not want, and yet more promises never to be kept.

After a while he got up and left the cellar. Tiaanet lay where she was, feeling moisture cooling on her body, waiting for the last of the ache to fade from her head and ribs and elsewhere. For a time she drifted, thinking that she imagined the touch of gentle fingers along her lips, and the soft patter of tears on her cheek. But they could not have been her own tears, since she no longer cried.

"Sleep," whispered a voice in her ear. "Sleep now, sleep. I will stay awake for you. Safe safe safe. Sleep."

Tiaanet slept.

26

Teacher

"I am wondering," said Mni-inh, speaking slowly so as to make his anger very clear, "whether you have lost your mind."

Hanani, sitting beside the bathing pool with her hands folded in her lap, sighed. A day had passed since their last argument; it seemed the time had done little to smooth the ground between them. "This is the only way, Brother."

Mni-inh sat on a rock opposite her, where he had been braiding his hair until Hanani told him of her plan. Now he sat half naked, hair a mess, glaring at her in his fury. "That, my apprentice, is not true at all. You don't have to help the Prince in any way, much less follow through on this ridiculous plan to teach him narcomancy."

"He could go mad—"

"*Let* him."

Hanani stared at Mni-inh, shocked. After a moment Mni-inh sighed, rubbed his face, and stood to begin pacing.

"Hanani—" He shook his head in frustration. "You say anger gives you no comfort; fine. You're a better Servant of Hananja than I, because I want him to hurt as deeply as he hurt you."

Hanani frowned. "The desire for vengeance is natural, Brother, but there's no peace in it."

"I know that! But I cannot bear what that arrogant jackal's machinations have done to you. You never smile anymore. You won't even speak to me of—of what happened. There's a space between us now where once we were closer than blood."

Hanani sighed and closed her eyes, reaching for calm. She didn't want to talk about Azima; didn't even want to think about him. Yet Mni-inh kept bringing the subject up, over and over, worrying at it like a child with a half-healed scab. Never mind that *she* had borne the wound.

"All of that is irrelevant, Brother," she said, when she felt herself able to speak in a neutral tone. "Whatever the Prince has become, the Hetawa had a hand in creating—"

Mni-inh made a sound of annoyance. "*Wanahomen* is irrelevant, Hanani. Nijiri is mad to rely on him, and I couldn't care less what happens to him!"

The anger was returning. Hanani clenched her fists on her thighs and prayed for the Goddess to make her strong against it. "*He is why we're here*, Brother. Or would you rather all of this be for nothing? The pain I suffered—" Now the anger was eclipsed by revulsion and the ugly memory of Azima's hands, and the uglier memory of her own hands shredding his soul. She focused on her words. Words could not hurt her. "The life I took. Anger doesn't comfort me, Brother. But knowing that what I endure, what I do, may help Gujaareh—*that* comforts me, yes. Helping the Prince helps Gujaareh."

Mni-inh had stopped pacing to stare at her, and as she watched, his face flickered through sorrow to anger to comprehension, then back to sorrow.

"I should have protected you," he said softly.

And just like that, Hanani understood why he was so angry.

"What happened to me was not your fault," she said, as gently as she could.

"I was two tents away! I should've heard. I should've *known*—" He faltered silent, his fists tight at his sides.

Hanani rose, went over to him, and took his hands, looking into his eyes so that he would see she did not blame him. "I am some years past childhood, Brother. You can't protect me from all the world."

He looked at her with his eyes full of regret, lifting a hand to her cheek in a way that he had not in years. He had stopped that at the same time he had stopped hugging her, and she had missed both terribly in the years since. So she leaned against his hand, letting him know without words how grateful she was for the gesture, and he let out a long pained sigh.

"You're the daughter I never knew I needed," he said softly. "No one can love another person so powerfully and still keep perfect peace in his heart. I shouldn't love you as I do. But I don't care, Hanani. I do not care."

Nor do I, Brother, she thought to herself. *I could never regret loving you as much as I do.*

Yet Mni-inh had spoken truly. As Sharers, they had pledged devotion only to their petitioners and tithebearers and fellow Servants, in service of the Goddess. Individual love—the selfish, powerful stuff of families and lovers—interfered with that.

So Hanani said nothing, but she lifted her hand to cover his. Mni-inh smiled, his face wry and somber. "And here I've been adding to your burdens," he said. "Even as you struggle with this yourself, you must take the time to comfort me." He sighed. "Forgive me."

She shook her head, not wanting to speak. But something within her relaxed, just a little, as he put words to the frustration she'd been nursing for days. So she felt better when Mni-inh let out a long, slow breath, and let her go.

"Train your Prince," he said. "If you can. He's old for it, and probably too barbarian-minded. But if you're determined to do this, I'll help you."

She managed a smile, for him. "Thank you, Brother."

He nodded, sighing. "Now. If you're going to try and bludgeon magic into that fool's head, you'll need all your strength. Let's go see whether these savages can manage a decent meal, hmm?"

* * *

So it was that later that evening, after an absolutely delicious meal at the communal hearth for those who lacked slaves, Hanani followed young Tassa up a long trail that was little more than a series of vaguely connected ledges along Merik-ren-aferu's eastern wall. Tassa, born and raised to canyon life, scrambled over rock piles and up steep slopes like a lizard, snickering at Hanani whenever she balked or had to stop and rest. But he did not leave her, for which she was grateful.

During one rest, as she sat on a flat slab of rock and prayed the snakes and spiders under it would stay put, he came to sit beside her, his eyes bright and curious. "Why?" he asked. "Go, Wana. You." He pointed up toward the top of the cliff, which Hanani could not see; the lantern she carried cast a bright circle, but beyond it was darkness. She could only hope they were close.

"To teach him," she said, keeping the words simple. "Dreams." She pantomimed sleeping, resting her cheek on her folded hands.

He frowned at that, considering. "Because…" He groped for words for a moment. "Go, Wana. To, to Gujaareh. You teach dreams, because?"

It was too difficult to explain. Even if Tassa had spoken Gujaareen fluently, he was still just a child. But she had seen how it pained the Prince to withhold his Gujaareen heritage from the boy. So she lifted her fingers in front of Tassa's eyes, though she did not reach for his face. "May I?"

He frowned—looking much like his sire in that moment—but finally curiosity won out: he nodded and shut his eyes. Hanani laid her fingers on his eyelids and wove him a quick, delicate teaching dream. She had been to the palace Yanya-iyan a few times in her life, usually as part of the Hetawa's annual Hamyan processional. She showed Tassa this, walking in her dream through the shining palace gates into the vast courtyard, and stopping before the dais where, traditionally, the Prince of Gujaareh oversaw the annual celebration. There had been no prince on the dais for ten years, but Hanani had glimpsed the old Prince, Wanahomen's father, once in her childhood. So she drew upon that memory to create him, lean and proud and statue-still on the white oxbow seat that was his throne, with the gold-and-amber Aureole of the Setting Sun behind and above him.

Then, slowly, she replaced that Prince with another: Wanahomen. He sat on the same throne, his face full of hauteur and power, wearing a red silk skirt and a collar of gold plates, a red headcloth making a portrait of his face beneath the domelike ivory crown.

When she ended this dream, Tassa stared at her in wonder. "*Wana?*"

Hanani smiled and nodded. "Gujaareh is the City of Dreams. Wana, he must have good dreams, healthy dreams, to rule us. To be our Prince. Do you understand?"

Tassa frowned, but not in incomprehension, she thought. He drew up his knees on the rock, and Hanani saw melancholy in his eyes. "Prince here," he said sullenly. "Hunt leader before, under Unte, is tribe leader *after* Unte. But..."

He could never be satisfied with this, Hanani knew. She saw that new understanding in Tassa's eyes, and then regretted showing the boy the truth. The Prince had been raised amid a magnificence that not even the richest Banbarra tribe could match. Tassa could have that glory too, as a son of the Sunset—but only at a terrible cost.

Yanassa had explained: Banbarra children belonged to their mother's clan, with aunts and grandmothers to help rear them and uncles to teach boys the ways of men. Banbarra men had no claim on the children they sired, only the ones born to their own female relatives. To give Tassa his Gujaareen birthright, the Prince would have to steal from him his Banbarra birthright, and all the family he'd known and loved.

When I return to Gujaareh, I will lose my son. Recalling the Prince's words, Hanani understood two things at once: that Yanassa was both generous and brave to allow Tassa so much contact with his father, and that the Prince was less selfish and arrogant than he seemed.

Hanani sighed and touched Tassa's hand. "My parents sold me away when I was younger than you," she said. "You're very fortunate to have parents who love you as much as yours."

He didn't understand; she saw that in his puzzled look. But then his eyes flew wide, and he leaped to his feet and drew a chunk of chipped rock—a homemade knife, Hanani realized as she rose as well—from a fold of his robes. He turned to face a dark part of the trail beyond the lantern's light, tense and trembling.

But it was only the Prince who stepped quietly out of the shadows. Tassa caught his breath and slumped in visible relief.

The Prince came over to them, his eyes amused as he looked at Tassa's paltry knife. He said something in Chakti, and Tassa squirmed with embarrassment and tried to put the knife away. Before he could, the Prince took his hand and crouched, taking the knife from him to examine. He shook his head, but then his eyes went soft as he gazed at Tassa. He lifted a hand to the boy's cheek, and in spite of herself Hanani could not help remembering the warmth of Mni-inh's hand.

Then the Prince stood and untied one of the knives around his waist. The hilt was polished bone, the sheath beautifully worked leather; he drew the blade for a moment and its steel sheen caught the light. Then he sheathed it again, wrapped the tasseled cords around its hilt, and handed this to Tassa.

Tassa inhaled sharply, taking the knife with both hands. In a reverent tone he asked a question; the Prince nodded. Tassa, eyes shining, babbled an excited, barely coherent thanks and then ran off into the shadows, clutching the knife to his chest and grinning like a fool.

The Prince watched the boy leave, sighing hard enough to lift his veil. "Wujjeg's folly comes in handy. Though Yanassa will have words for me."

"A knife is a dangerous gift for a child."

"Yes. But among the Banbarra, boys who aspire to be warriors usually get one at about his age." He examined the small stone knife—little better than a sharp rock—and then tossed it into the shadows. "And if he's so determined to have one, he should have one that won't fail when he needs it."

He seemed oddly somber; Hanani could detect none of the usual brooding or scorn in his manner. She ventured, "If it is traditional, then Yanassa—"

"Yanassa wants him to become an account-master or a talekeeper or a smith. Anything but a warrior." He shrugged. "Yet he is my son, for all she might regret that now."

He had overheard her conversation with Tassa, she realized. The rocks echoed sound; on such a quiet night every word must have been clear.

"Well, children rarely grow as their parents wish," he continued, moving to sit across from her, getting as comfortable as he could against a sloping rock face. "Yours must be astounded by you."

Hanani folded her hands in her lap. "Mine likely do not think of me often, if at all."

He hesitated. "You said they sold you."

249

"Yes. We were farmcaste; our crops failed one year. It's a girl-child's duty to see to the well-being of her family in times of trouble. So I asked them to sell me."

He frowned. "I'd heard such things happened among lowcastes, but...How old were you?"

"I had seen six floods of the river."

"Six!" He shook his head. "You couldn't have known what you were asking."

She shrugged. She had not, but it no longer mattered.

"Why the Hetawa?" he asked. "They have little use for females—or at least, that was the case before you. Surely your parents could have gotten more selling you to another farmcaste family that had no daughters, or a timbalin house, or elsewhere."

Hanani watched the lantern's flame dance in a chilly breeze. The movement was nearly as entrancing as a sleep-spell. "It was my choice," she said. "The Hetawa always seemed so magnificent to me. All the fine, wise priests, and the magic, and the chance to learn as much as I wished...Even if only for a few years, I wanted it."

"And your parents did what would make you happiest, even though it made you less valuable for their needs." His eyes, above the veil, watched her steadily.

It was something that had never occurred to Hanani. For children adopted by the Hetawa, the Goddess Hananja became mother, the Servants fathers, fellow adoptees an army of siblings. It had helped to believe that—and to forget the family that had birthed her—during those first lonely, homesick nights. Eventually it had become true. But perhaps she too had been fortunate to have parents who loved her so well that her happiness mattered more than their desires.

She inclined her head to the Prince, grateful for his insight. He looked briefly flustered, then sat up straighter. "Shall we begin this lesson?"

"Oh. Yes." It was a blunt, jarring transition in the conversation.

She had never known a Gujaareen to be so inelegant. Even the Kisuati had more delicacy. "Well. May I examine you?"

He nodded, and she rose and went to him. It was difficult to position herself properly in the encumbering skirts, but she managed to do it by resting a hand on his shoulder. This caused him to glance down at her hand, an oddly thoughtful look in his eyes.

"It didn't bruise," he said.

"What?"

"Where the Kisuati soldier struck me. You offered to heal me that day, as I recall."

Hanani had forgotten. It jarred her, especially given that he had tried to save her then from the same sort of treatment Azima had inflicted later.

She could not, would not, dwell on that thought. "Close your eyes," she said. The words, and the tone, were just as clumsy as his own attempt to change the subject had been, and her voice sounded cold even to her own ears. His eyes went equally cold in response. But without another word, he leaned his head back against the rock and closed his eyes.

There's too much anger in my heart for this, Hanani realized. But the words were said now, and the lesson begun; she had no choice but to proceed.

So she laid her fingers on his eyelids and sought his soul. There were layers and layers of him to search, not just flesh but constrictions of will and emotion. It would have gone more easily if she could've put him to sleep, but it was important that she know him in waking as well as dreaming—more, Mni-inh had advised her, because it was his waking self that she would teach, regardless of the realm they entered. So she delved down through the fierceness and loneliness and pride and protectiveness of him, and when she entered the rush of the great artery above his heart she found his soul and then—

What?

Something shifted.

Instead of the darkness behind her eyelids, she found herself adrift in a far deeper black. For a moment she was disoriented, and then she realized: she was not inside the Prince anymore. The connection remained, she saw: a bright, blood-red line crossed the space. His tether, the umblikeh, which bound his soul to flesh. Hanani's own was visible too, in this formless place.

She did not like the formlessness. But just as she thought this, the space around her brightened, becoming the Hall of Blessings again. All in gray.

The realms between. Alarmed, Hanani whirled toward the Hall's alcoves, where before she had glimpsed—she now knew—the force that had killed Dayuhotem. But nothing was there. Relieved, she turned back to Hananja's statue and the dais, and saw *herself*, another her, clad in voluminous robes that billowed in an unfelt wind.

Kneeling at the Goddess's feet, and using a knife—the knife the Prince had just given his son—to hack repeatedly at a tiny figure before her, which was already an unrecognizable red desecration.

Hanani screamed. The other Hanani paused and looked up at her, and smiled through tears and splattered blood.

No! I would never! Wildly, Hanani grabbed for her own tether and—

—Fell back into herself, so swiftly and powerfully that she jerked back from Wanahomen with a gasp.

His eyes snapped open, surprised and puzzled. "What is it?"

"I—I don't—" She was disoriented, sluggish; she could not muster her thoughts. Had he not seen that vision of horror? Did he have no recollection of his own dreams at all? "I don't know. I was..."

"Gods, you're swaying like a drunkard." The Prince reached out to steady her, one hand on her waist and the other on her thigh.

On her thigh, like Azima's hands—

The panic struck before Hanani could think. *"Don't touch me!"* Her voice was barely intelligible, a scream with words, and she kicked and flailed to get away from him. Tripping on her skirts, she fell amid the rocks and dust, panting and gasping and trembling so hard she could barely breathe. She kept scrabbling on hands and knees, stopping only when she reached a big slab of rock that blocked the trail.

There was a long silence behind her, and in it Hanani's terror began to fade.

"I won't touch you," the Prince said. He spoke softly, his voice subdued. "What shall I do, to help you? I could go fetch your mentor, but that means leaving you here alone."

She had begun to regain control of herself. The tremors eased as she pushed herself up slowly, groping for dignity as she turned to face him. "N-no," she said. "I'm sorry. I, I don't know why..." Oh, but she knew why. They both did. "I'm sorry."

"Of all people, *you* should not apologize to *me*," he said. She would not think about his words, or recognize the regret in them, until later. "It's safe here, Sharer-Apprentice. I will allow no one else to harm you, ever again."

Amazingly, impossibly, the words actually comforted her. They shouldn't have. She had no reason to trust him. Still, the fact that he was the only man there, and had made no move to touch her again, had its own wordless power, and she calmed further. He fell silent then, which helped more: she could pretend he wasn't there and seek peace within herself. So at last, she took a deep breath and shifted to sit on her knees.

"I think," she said, enunciating carefully, "that we should end the lesson here for the night."

The Prince had come to a crouch near the dwindling lantern; he nodded. To her relief, he didn't ask again about the strangeness she had found in his dreams, or whether she was all right. "Let me escort you back."

She nodded, getting to her feet. The Prince picked up the lantern and came to stand near enough that she could see by its light, but not near enough to touch her. She did not look at him. In silence, he led her back to camp.

27

⟨⊙⟩

Dreaming Awake

There was a strange feel to the night air. Gatherer Inmu noticed it while leaping from one rooftop to another on his way back to the Hetawa. If the rooftop had been one of the sloped, tiled monstrosities favored by zhinha and others with exotic foreign tastes, Inmu would have ended up counting his bones in the alley below. Fortunately the roof was flat. Inmu landed badly, rolling once to dissipate the force of the impact, but unharmed aside from pride.

His pride took another blow as he looked up and spied Gatherer Nijiri's still form in the shadows of the roof's cistern.

Embarrassed, he got to his feet. But to his relief, Nijiri did not chide him for his clumsiness. In fact, though they had agreed to meet here at the end of their rounds, Nijiri had not seemed to notice Inmu at all. As Inmu stepped closer, he saw that Nijiri was utterly still, one hand braced against the cistern, his gaze turned inward and a look that was part anger, part fear, frozen on his face.

Nijiri may never know true peace, Inmu's mentor Rabbaneh had told him once. *He has enough for his petitioners, but I think he may never find what he needs for happiness. Not here in the Hetawa, anyhow.*

It troubled Inmu, sometimes, to think that one of his brothers suffered so. They all knew why: Ehiru. Yet Nijiri was a perfect Gatherer in every other way—swift and silent on the hunt, deadly in combat, tender in the taking of tithes. Was it his lingering grief that made him so competent? Inmu had no idea, but he had resolved to study this brother until he found a way to help him.

So he stepped closer still, into the shadows with him. "Nijiri-brother?"

Nijiri's head whipped up, and for an instant Inmu feared his brother would strike him. Then the wild, defensive look faded from his eyes. "Inmu. Do you feel it?"

That strange sense of pressure, filling the night around them; it was what Inmu had noticed during the leap. It seemed to dim even the Dreaming Moon's colored light. "Yes," Inmu replied, frowning. "But I don't know what it is."

"I thought—" Nijiri faltered, swallowed. As Inmu's eyes adjusted, he saw that Nijiri's face was beaded with sweat. "For a moment—Sonta-i *is* dead, isn't he? We burned him…" He closed his eyes and shuddered.

Alarmed, Inmu touched Nijiri's shoulder, delicately. "Brother, are you all right?" He tried to remember the last time Nijiri had undergone the pranje, the ritual of cleansing and reaffirmation required yearly of all Gatherers. Wait, yes: Nijiri had put himself into seclusion around midsummer, only a few months before. Too soon for him to need it again. But what else could be causing his agitation?

Abruptly, Nijiri looked up. "No, I'm a fool, blinded by memories. This is something different." He pulled away from Inmu's hand and stepped over to the edge of the roof, his eyes narrowing. "Inmu. Come look."

Even more confused, Inmu came over to stand with Nijiri, following his brother's pointing hand. Another building, abutting the one they stood on. Through the window they could see a couple in bed, both asleep. The wife was whimpering in her sleep, her voice faint but audible in the night's stillness. The husband tossed and thrashed as if fighting some invisible enemy. As they watched, he groaned and flailed out with one arm, striking his sleeping wife. She did not wake; just kept making those pathetic, broken sounds.

Inmu frowned. Nijiri scowled, his earlier distress gone; now the cool, deadly Nijiri had returned. "Something is wrong in this," he said.

Perhaps they're just heavy sleepers, Inmu considered saying. But he did not, because the ominous note in Nijiri's words had frightened him—and because he worried Nijiri might be right. He could not say how, but he felt the same imprecise wrongness about the sleeping couple.

Then he recalled the woman whose dream had killed Sonta-i. Years of training kept him from gasping aloud, but when he looked at Nijiri, Nijiri nodded.

"We must help them," Inmu whispered. Even as he said it, despair clenched his belly. Sonta-i had already proven there was nothing they could do. And Nijiri shook his head, though Inmu saw the same frustration in his brother's eyes.

"There's more to this," Nijiri said. "This strange feel, the light, the taste of the air. I've almost forgotten it in the years since I became a Gatherer, but I know it now—I feel as if *I'm* dreaming."

And Inmu realized Nijiri was right. Inmu had been a full Gatherer for eight years now, riding the edges of Ina-Karekh only with the aid of his tithebearers, but he had not yet forgotten how it felt to dream on his own. There were times when the land of dreams seemed so like waking that the only way to tell the difference was instinct. That was what he felt now—the subtle whisper of senses beyond the physical, warning him of unreality.

"*Are* we dreaming?" Inmu asked.

"I hope not," Nijiri said, nodding toward the couple. "Or it's only a matter of time before whatever killed Sonta-i takes us."

Rabbaneh-brother would be most annoyed if we left him as the only Gatherer, Inmu thought, then had to stifle the inane urge to laugh. Another sound at the edge of his hearing wiped away the momentary levity.

He rose and crossed the rooftop to its opposite edge. The Moonlight was stronger here, so he could see the source of trouble clearly: a young man not much older than himself, curled up on a doorstep sleeping. By his attire and the threadbare blanket that covered him, Inmu suspected that the man was a servant, being punished for some error by having to sleep outdoors for the night. Though the steps of his home couldn't have been comfortable, he had fallen asleep—and he too stirred restlessly, groaning in the depths of a nightmare.

"I do *not* like this," Nijiri said. Inmu jumped; Nijiri had come to his side so silently that Inmu hadn't noticed.

"The dream passes by proximity," Inmu said, troubled. "We've seen that. Merchant Bahenamin had it, then his wife, then their servant girl. And others among the victims have lived in the same household, or in houses adjacent. Anyone who sleeps while a carrier sleeps nearby."

Nijiri nodded. "It would seem we're witnessing another outbreak." He sounded grim as he said it. The Sharers had collected all the victims of the plague they could find, isolating them together in the Hall of Respite. They could do nothing to help the victims, but they had consoled themselves with the knowledge that when those poor souls passed on, there would be no others. Now it seemed the Sharers were about to be robbed of even that small comfort.

But something else about what they had seen troubled Inmu. "Brother," he said, "we *found* all the victims before. The Sentinels brought everyone who suffered the dream, and everyone who had contact with them, and everyone who *might* have had contact with them. They brought some even against their will." Inmu and some of the Sharers had gone with the Sentinels on those trips. It seemed wrong to use sleep-spells as a weapon, especially given the chance that some of the ones they put to sleep would never wake, but the maintenance of peace often required painful actions. "Our Sentinel brethren were so thorough that I can't see how they missed anyone."

"They must have. And there's a greater problem: where's the source of this evil dream, Inmu? No one has ever found that."

As Inmu pondered this, yet another odd sound caught his and Nijiri's ears. A woman's voice? And something else, this louder than the rest, and familiar: carriage wheels, clattering on stone.

"Late for traveling," Nijiri said.

"Some fellow heading home from a visit to his lover, or an alehouse." Inmu shrugged.

Nijiri pivoted where he crouched, following the sound. "Did you hear which direction it came from?"

"There—" Inmu pointed, and was surprised to find that he pointed toward the Hetawa itself. The street that ran alongside the Hetawa, specifically, near the east complex wall.

But why did that make Nijiri's frown deepen?

"It came *from* there," Nijiri murmured, almost to himself. "Not from the streets around, where the houses are. There was silence, and then we heard it move..."

Abruptly he stiffened, his eyes widening with horror. "*Indethe*—" And before Inmu could ask what was the matter, Nijiri took off. He was over the rooftop's low wall and halfway to the ground before Inmu could collect his startled thoughts. By the time Inmu reached the ground too, Nijiri had vanished around the corner.

Wondering again whether his elder brother was entirely sane, Inmu ran after him. But Nijiri had already vanished amid the narrow streets; even the sounds of his footfalls had faded.

But the sound of the carriage was not far at all. Inmu hesitated, then turned in the direction of that sound and trotted on a course that would intersect it. As he jogged, drawing nearer to the rattle of wheels on bricks, he heard the woman's voice again. Singing.

Just up ahead now. He had reached a cross street; the carriage would pass on the avenue before him in another moment.

"*Goddess, sweetest Goddess, no*—" Nijiri's voice, raised to a most unpeaceful volume, echoed along the empty streets. Startled, Inmu skidded to a halt. *What*—?

The carriage—a simple two-wheeled affair, drawn by a brawny servant-casteman who wore enough weapons that he was clearly a guard as well—passed on the street ahead of Inmu. The cab was open, though a mosquito-cloth hanging obscured any clear look at the carriage's occupants. In a stray flicker of Moonlight and a breeze that stirred the light cloth aside, he caught a glimpse of movement and then spied a woman's face, turning as she noticed him. They were the most beautiful eyes he had ever seen: black as the Dreamer's dark side, captivating as a jungissa stone.

And sad. So terribly, achingly sad that Inmu wanted to go to her, offer any comfort she desired in order to take that look from her face. He would Gather her, if she wished, or just hold her, because he had never seen anyone bear such a stoneweight of bitterness and despair alone. Not bear it and still live, at least.

Then something stirred in the woman's arms. A child, he realized, though he caught only the most fleeting glimpse. Five or six floods in age, boneless with sleep. The look in the woman's eyes changed. Now Inmu saw warmth in her, and a tenderness so profound that tears sprang to his eyes. She drew back into the shadows behind the hangings, holding the child to her breast. As the carriage traveled on past, rounding a corner to head toward one of the bridges, he heard her voice rise again, singing that same soft song he'd half-caught before. A lullaby.

Longing for what he had never before missed, Inmu stared in the direction the carriage had gone for a full five breaths before he remembered Nijiri.

Turning back toward the Hetawa, Inmu ran until he reached the street along the eastern complex wall. He found his fellow Gatherer leaning against the wall, his head bowed and shoulders heaving and fists pressed against the old stone as if they could somehow force it aside by will alone.

"Brother!" He rushed to Nijiri's side. "Nijiri-brother, what in shadows—"

"Here!" Nijiri rounded on Inmu and gripped his shoulders; his eyes were wild. "It was here. It has to be the source, people are catching it right now, the source! It was *parked* here, *waiting* here, do you know what this means?" He stabbed a finger toward the wall. "*Look!*"

Inmu looked, uncomprehending, and saw the wall. "It's just the eastern wall, Brother. I don't—"

And then, suddenly, terribly, he understood.

Each group within the Hetawa had its section of the complex. North belonged to the Sentinels, and the Hall of Children. West was the Gatherers' Hall, where classes in narcomancy were taught. South was the Hall of Blessings and the complex of offices, libraries, and classrooms used by lay servants of the Hetawa, the Teachers, and the Superior.

East held the cluster of buildings that housed those of the Sharer path.

The source, Nijiri had said. The source of the nightmare plague. *Had been parked near the Sharers' Hall at night while they slept.*

"No," he whispered. He could not think. He could hardly breathe. "No."

Then Inmu remembered the carriage, and the woman. Singing her lullaby.

He tore away from Nijiri and sprinted down the street, running as fast as he could with no regard for the noise he made or the peacelessness of his movements. What did it matter that his sandals slapped against the bricks, that he was sobbing as he ran? No one in the houses around him would ever wake.

He reached the street where he'd last seen the carriage and stopped, trying desperately to still his panting so he could hear and track the wheels of the carriage.

But all around him, there was only silence.

28

(☉)

Mercy

Just after dawn, Hanani went into Mni-inh's tent and sat down. He, newly awake and bleary-eyed, took one look at her face and came fully alert. "What happened?"

Hanani told him of the Prince's first lesson, though she omitted her moment of panic afterward. When she spoke of being hurtled into the realm between, and the vision of herself committing violence, Mni-inh's eyes widened.

"It was a child," she said, her hands knots in her lap. "A toddler, or a very small older child. I would *never* harm a child, Brother. I know the things in Ina-Karekh are reflections of ourselves, but what I saw was *not in Ina-Karekh*. We were in the realm between dreaming and waking. Have you ever heard of this before?"

"Not precisely." He scratched at his chin, where a scattering of stiff hairs had grown overnight; the sound was very loud. "What you experienced sounds like a true-seeing—a vision of something that will actually happen"—Hanani's belly tightened further at this, but Mni-inh quickly shook his head—"but I've never heard of that happening in the realm between. Only the Goddess can create worlds, whether in waking or dreaming. The realm between is eerie, but should be *empty*." He sighed. "But this fits something else I've suspected."

"Which is?"

"Well..." He sat back on his cushions, a half-rueful look on his face. "I've heard, in roundabout fashion, that there is a reason the Hetawa supported the Sunset Lineage these many years. King Eninket was not the first to disgrace the line, after all; they're men, with the same weaknesses and failings as any other. But it has something to do with *them*, that lineage, in particular."

"Why?"

"I don't know." He gave her a wry smile. "There are some secrets that only the Council and the Gatherers are privy to, and— Well, you know what the other seniors think of me." He sighed. "But I'm told that, years ago, no one was surprised to find that Ehiru—who was given to the Hetawa by his mother, to save him from Eninket— turned out to be one of the most powerful narcomancers in recent memory. And I do find it interesting that Nijiri, who has been one of the chief voices counseling appeasement of the Kisuati all these years, changed his tune when Wanahomen began his campaign."

And Gatherer Nijiri had been particularly interested to see that Wanahomen had tried to save her, Hanani recalled. *Perhaps his lineage is worth salvaging after all.*

"I also find it interesting," Mni-inh said, "that every Prince we have ever had—*every one*, so far as I can tell—has had the dreaming gift in some measure."

Hanani blinked. "Even King Eninket?"

"Oh, yes. His gift was weak, but there. And a handful, including First King Mahanasset, were quite powerful, and mad as rabbits before the Hetawa aided them. We took some of those, like Ehiru, for ourselves—but not all. You watch that Wanahomen." He waggled a finger at her. "He hides it well; may not even be aware of hiding it. But with a gift like his, his soul must wander between waking and dreaming all the time. He can't help it."

Hanani smoothed out invisible wrinkles in her skirts, contemplating. She felt calmer, at least. "I don't believe what I saw was a true-seeing," she said. "Only Gatherers have those."

"He *is* a Gatherer, Hanani, in essence. However much he might hate it." As Hanani blinked, Mni-inh sat up and stretched, working out the kinks from the night's rest. "And by touching his dreams, you can be dragged along by his power, so be careful. This is why each path trains its own, frankly." *And why I tried to warn you off training him*, he did not say, but that argument was done. For the sake of peace he would not bring it up again, for which Hanani was grateful. "Keep your soulname and wits about you, and be prepared for anything."

While Hanani considered that, Mni-inh got to his feet. "How I miss the Hetawa baths! The gods put hot water and fragrant oil in this world for a reason, I tell you."

Hanani could not help smiling at that—which surprised her, for she had not felt like smiling for days. The omnipresent guilt remained and might always, for she had taken a life without bestowing peace and there was no higher sin in all the Hananjan faith. Yet the lingering, irrational fear seemed to have faded at last.

I have the Prince to thank for that, I suppose. The gods are not without a sense of irony—

"I've bathed already, Brother, forgive me for not joining you," she said, also rising. "I need rest, since it seems teaching the Prince will be even more challenging than I first believed. But may I come and share the eveningdance with you, later?"

Mni-inh paused and stared at her, then a slow smile spread across his face. "I would be delighted," he said. "We haven't prayed together in ages. At sunset, then."

Hanani touched his hand as she passed him to leave. He caught her hand and squeezed it, encouraging, before letting go. It felt good to smile again, so she did it all the way back to her tent.

*　　*　　*

A change in the ambient noise of the camp woke Hanani. Drawn from a pleasant dream of a steaming, sandalwood-scented Hetawa bath, she returned to the waking realm and through the walls of her tent heard—

Angry shouts. Calls—for Unte, for Tajedd, for other important folk within the tribe. Jeers and laughter, edged with hatred. And corruption.

Someone drummed on the flap of her tent. Rising to open it— she always kept the laces tied tight now—she blinked as Yanassa poked her head in.

"You're still here? Good. Stay in here 'til tomorrow." The Banbarra woman's expression was uncharacteristically hard and cold. "Wana has caught us a spy."

Hanani started. "I thought— I thought his patrol was a punishment, just for show."

"That may have been what was meant. But no one expected a Shadoun to be so bold as to walk right into our territory." She shook her head, then threw the flap of Hanani's tent closed with such force that it slapped loudly, much to Hanani's surprise. "They'll pay for such disrespect!"

Gingerly, Hanani eased the flap open and peered out. Beyond Yanassa, she could see a great gathering of folk near the center of the camp—a shouting, gesticulating mass. Children ran past, giggling and excited. Two of them carried sticks.

Hanani felt a sudden, terrible chill. "Yanassa. What will happen to this Shadoun?"

"Nothing good." Abruptly Yanassa sobered, looking hard at her.

"But it's no business of yours. Just stay in the tent 'til morning, and pay no mind to what you hear." She reached to close the flap again.

Hanani caught her hand. "What are you saying? Will there be violence?" That was a stupid question; violence hovered like a heat-haze in the very air. "Yanassa—"

In the background the crowd parted for a moment, and Hanani got a glimpse of the Shadoun spy.

The *female* Shadoun spy.

It was hard to tell, at first. Hanani was used to seeing women adorned in face paints and jewelry; this woman wore neither. Like Banbarra men, she wore loose desert robes and a headcloth, which obscured many of the details of her face and body. The headcloth had been yanked half off, revealing straight black hair chopped short, and a face that was not so very different from that of a typical Banbarra. Her features were more rounded, her eyes a lighter hue—pale green in this case—and her skin a deeper shade of brown, closer to that of western folk. But she had the same fierce hauteur.

And she was smiling, even as she was dragged along by two warriors of Wanahomen's hunt.

But that was not half so troubling as the grim anticipation in Yanassa's manner. "Tell me what you plan to do with her!" Hanani demanded.

Yanassa scowled and finally stepped into the tent, pulling the flap closed behind her. "It isn't up to me—or at least, not me alone. The hunt will give her to Unte. Unte will probably give her to the tribe. Specifically, the tribe's women. It is for us to decide another woman's fate." She folded her arms. "Some of us are angry enough to tear her apart ourselves, or throw her from the cliffs, but most likely, we'll make a gift of her to the tribe's men. They'll see that she suffers long enough to satisfy all."

Hanani stared at her, too revolted for words.

Yanassa sighed and looked away for a moment, a whiff of shame in her eyes—but she was angry too, and it was the anger that made her turn back to glare defiantly at Hanani. "It's what they do to our women, when they can!"

"And that makes it right?"

Yanassa shook her head, not in response to Hanani's question, but out of some great inner turmoil. "The last woman survived, if you can call it that. The Shadoun sent her back to us. Broken, gibbering—" She clenched her fists. "We actually took her to your people for help, though it near choked us to do so. And they tried, out of simple kindness. But she was damaged beyond the ability of magic to repair...They could heal her body, but not her mind. So they killed her for us, as a mercy. And we were glad for it." Yanassa's eyes welled with tears; sorrow and hatred competed in her face with an ugly mixed result. "That was twenty years ago, my great-aunt. I remember the look in her eyes, little mouse, and if you had seen her too—" She drew in a deep breath. "So no, it's not right. But *I do not care*."

Hanani shivered, though the tent was not cool inside. She had seen people so wounded by tragedy or other misfortune, a handful of times in her Hetawa life. When madness was not inborn or the result of some humoric imbalance, when the problem was memories and not the flesh that housed them— No, even magic could only do so much. That was why Gatherers existed.

Yet, as she looked at Yanassa's trembling lips, her clenched jaw, it occurred to Hanani that sometimes the real damage was not to the souls released, but the ones left to mourn. Corruption was the most virulent of diseases, after all, and it needed only the smallest wound in which to fester.

"So stay in here," Yanassa said. Her face had softened a little. "Unte and Tajedd plan to question the woman first. They may yet kill her outright—if only because anything worse would taint the solstice celebrations."

She exited the tent, and Hanani stared at the swinging tent flaps for a long moment after she'd gone.

Then she pushed through them herself, and headed straight for Unte's tent.

29

(⊙)

The Protectors

The messenger-bird had come and gone, a harbinger of change.
Now that change was at the palace gates, and Sunandi Jeh Kalawe
was afraid.

Anzi put a hand on her shoulder as they stood waiting in the
courtyard. The courtyard was still, though on their way through the
palace Sunandi and Anzi had seen courtiers and guards hurrying
about the marble halls to prepare for their unexpected guests. Only
the servants—most of them Gujaareen and unimpressed by the
arrival of yet more Kisuati—had been calm as they went about their
duties. A few of the Kisuati had paused to bow to Sunandi and Anzi
in passing, but most had paid the couple no attention. No doubt
they considered Sunandi useless to whatever political ambitions
they held, now that a quartet of Protectors was arriving to take control of Gujaareh.

"You don't know what they'll do," Anzi murmured. She looked up
at him, more grateful than words that they had settled their differ-
ences in the wake of the incident six days before. The two Gathered
soldiers had been his men. But he had listened when she'd cautioned
him against going at once to arrest the Gatherer involved. Instead

he'd waited, calming himself and his restive officers, and waiting too while the tensions in the city eased somewhat. And when the message had come from Kisua that Sunandi should prepare for the four members of the Protectorate who were already on their way downriver to Gujaareh, he had returned the favor by calming her, and reminding her that she had done a good job of governing the kingdom given limited resources and difficult orders from the homeland. Whatever shift the political winds had undergone in Kisua, no one could deny that.

But Sunandi, who knew exactly how fickle those winds could be, was not so certain.

She had chosen to meet the Protectors in the great courtyard of Yanya-iyan, before the glass-topped pavilion that had once served as the outdoor throne dais of Gujaareh's Prince. Now the dais was merely a natural focal point for attention as visitors entered through the palace's gates and crossed the swept sand. Soldiers came first, fanning out to flank the courtyard's walls. Then came household retainers and baggage carriers, and lastly four fours of strong young men, each quartet carrying the poles of a mid-sized palanquin on its shoulders. The palanquins were green-draped, bedecked with tassels and polished shells; she could see only faint figures within. The groups stopped and set the palanquins down before the throne dais, and Sunandi and Anzi knelt to show their respect as the Protectors emerged.

And the moment she looked up to greet their visitors, Sunandi knew the winds in Kisua must be ill indeed.

Two of the Protectors Sunandi knew personally: Sasannante, a great scholar and poet whom Sunandi had studied in her apprenticeship; and Yao, called Mama Yao because she'd had thirteen children and used them to become matriarch of one of Kisua's most powerful shipping families. The other two she knew only by face and reputation. One was Moib, a former general who had lost an eye against Gujaareh-backed troops at the Battle of Soijaro ten years before. The other—a man so tall that he had probably been miserable the whole way in that palanquin—had to be Aksata, another merchant, whose family had made its fortune selling swords and armor to Kisua's standing army. Moib the Warmonger, he was called, and Aksata the Profiteer.

So things have gotten that bad. Lovely. There can be only one reason the Protectors sent these two here.

As if hearing her thought, Aksata smiled, inclining his head to Sunandi and Anzi.

"Greetings, Speaker Jeh Kalawe, General Seh Ainunu. The Council sends its regards."

Sunandi got to her feet, though she kept her gaze respectfully lowered. Beside her, Anzi did the same. "And greetings to you, Esteemed and Wise of Kisua. I bid you welcome to Gujaareh. Was your journey difficult? May I offer you refreshment or rest?"

"Yes, shortly," Aksata said. He glanced around at his fellow Protectors. Mama Yao, who was in perhaps her seventh decade, leaned heavily on one of the palanquin-servants but nodded in weary agreement with Aksata. Sasannante stood straight and inscrutable as the elaborately carved cane in his hands, while Moib was carefully performing some soldier's stretch to work out the stiffness of travel. Aksata himself seemed hale, but then he was only in his late fifties by Sunandi's guess. In Gujaareh, where magic lengthened citizens' lives, he would have been too young to qualify for eldership.

While Mama Yao is so old that the journey alone might have killed her. She has no love of Gujaareh, but neither is she unreasonable . . . So do the other Protectors hope for her to die before she can do much?

It was, sadly, quite possible.

"The journey has indeed been difficult," Aksata said, "in no small part because we hurried to get here. We received word along the way of further trouble beyond the plague of desert bandits you've suffered. Something to do with the Hetawa?"

"Yes," Sunandi replied, keeping her tone carefully neutral. Messenger-birds again, or perhaps a message-rider, traveling upriver to meet the Protectors along the way. Either way, she had no idea how much truth—or falsehood—the Protectors had been given by the spies among Sunandi's staff.

"At the start of the solstice," she began, "a pair of our soldiers were Gathered. Apparently they had been molesting women in the city."

"I was told they were whores," Moib said. His voice was rough as road-gravel; there was another puckered scar, long healed, across his throat.

"Gujaareh has few whores as we call them," Sunandi said. "Servants and timbalin-house women, if they choose"—and even those were never to be assaulted under Gujaareh's Law, but this was not the time to explain that to the Protectors—"but the women assaulted by the soldiers were of another caliber. A kind of priestess."

Mama Yao curled her lip. "Holy whores, then. And no doubt easily mistaken for any other kind. So the Gujaareen slaughtered your men over a misunderstanding?" She looked at Anzi.

Anzi set his jaw for a moment, and Sunandi prayed her husband's temper would hold. "*They* do not consider it a misunderstanding, Esteemed."

"Of course not," said Aksata. He sighed. "Well, we expected something like this would happen eventually. You've executed the Gatherer who did the deed?"

Sunandi frowned. "No, Esteemed."

"No?" Something in Aksata's manner—poor acting, perhaps—told her at once that he was nowhere near as surprised as he seemed. "Arrested him, then? A trial seems overly formal, but..."

So that was it. Sunandi almost smiled. Somewhere in the after-life of dreams, her old mentor Kinja was laughing. But she knew now the role they meant her to play.

"Tensions in the city have been high," she said. She looked past Aksata at the other Protectors. Aksata was irrelevant; he had come with his own agenda. Moib too, most likely. It was possible that *all* of them had come for the same purpose, but she had to try. She focused on Mama Yao and Sasannante, hoping that they had not yet prejudged the situation so much as to ignore reason. "There has been unrest lately with the Banbarra raids, and there are rumors of some sort of sickness loose within the city. I also suspect some of the nobles of—"

"That is enough, Speaker," said Mama Yao. She straightened and fixed a stern look on Sunandi. "We did not come for excuses."

Sunandi closed her mouth for a moment. Then she said, "I would welcome any solution that you suggest, Esteemed."

Sasannante glanced at the other Protectors and smiled. "I told you Kinja's protégé would not be foolish."

"Too conciliatory, perhaps," said Mama Yao. She looked annoyed, as though she had expected a better fight from Sunandi.

"Perhaps." Sasannante looked at Sunandi, thoughtful. "This will be a difficult time for you, Speaker. It's not easy to give up the sort of control you've had up to now. But if you would weather this time successfully, remember that you serve the people of Kisua, not those of Gujaareh."

All of them, then. Sunandi lowered her eyes, inwardly quivering with anger that she would never show. *Damn* them! Ten years of sleepless nights and careful diplomacy, and now they were about to undo it all.

But Sasannante was right; she served Kisua above all. Gujaareh had its own protectors, more dangerous than the council back home realized. And if by bowing and smiling at these fools, Sunandi could find some way to shield her homeland from the worst of Gujaareh's brewing wrath? Then so be it.

So she inclined her head to Sasannante, spreading her hands to the sides in a graceful extra measure of submission, and said, "I have never forgotten that I serve Kisua, Esteemed—and its Protectors, of course."

Moib let out a rough chuckle; Aksata shook his head and smiled. "I fear for the day you become an elder, Jeh Kalawe," he said. "I wonder if we dare let you on the council when that happens!"

Sunandi kept her contempt hidden behind the pleasant mask of her face. *Let me on and the first thing I will do is make sure self-serving, shortsighted fools like you are assassinated in your sleep.*

"So." Aksata stretched, joints popping loudly as he did so; he grimaced. "Redeem yourselves today, Speaker and General. Go to the Hetawa and fetch the man who dared to take a Kisuati life. Bring him here for us to make an example of him."

And Anzi, sweet Anzi, who had spent the past few days learning from Sunandi why that was precisely the wrong thing to do, frowned and stepped forward. "Esteemed, if you would but listen to my wife's advice—"

Sunandi put a hand on his shoulder, and he turned to stare at her. She shook her head minutely. They had been together for nearly ten years; he had come to know her better than anyone save Kinja and a certain Gujaareen priest—both of whom were long dead. She still marveled that at times like this he could look at her and decide, based purely on love, to trust her without question. She could not remember what in her life she had done to deserve such devotion. But he showed it now, and stepped back.

"It shall be done at once, Esteemed," she said, and bowed. Anzi bowed as well, though his bow was less graceful; he was not as good at pretending as she.

Aksata nodded. "Well, then. If you please, we will happily accept that offer of rest and refreshment, and await your return."

*   *   *

Now they stood on the steps of the Hetawa, Sunandi and the sixteen soldiers of Anzi's best troop, waiting while a Sentinel went to announce their arrival. Sunandi had requested that the soldiers be unarmed, but she doubted that distinction would matter much to the crowd of Gujaareen that was already gathering in the square, come to see what Kisuati soldiers wanted of Hananja's Servants. She could make out murmurs among the crowd, feel the undercurrent of anger that lurked just below the surface, but she was not afraid. Not yet, anyhow. No Gujaareen would do violence on the Hetawa's doorstep.

The great bronze doors clacked and then groaned open. Belatedly it occurred to Sunandi to wonder why the doors had been closed—and latched, if she had not mistaken the sound—in the first place. It was mid-afternoon; the Hetawa usually stayed open during the daylight hours.

Then the Superior emerged, looking tired but not at all surprised to see them, and Sunandi quickly focused on the here and now.

"Welcome, Voice of the Protectors," the Superior said, inclining his head to her. He glanced at the soldiers and raised one curling white eyebrow. "Welcome, soldiers of the Protectors as well. I'm surprised to see you without weapons."

Dirakha, the troop's captain, offered the Superior a careful bow, then glanced wordlessly at Sunandi. The Superior gave them a faint smile. "I see," he said. "Thank you, Speaker. We appreciate the respect."

Sunandi inclined her head in return, though only just enough to acknowledge an equal. Among Gujaareen, for whom the Superior officially ranked second only to the Prince in power, this held the risk of insult, but the Superior must have known why they had come. He only sighed a little, his smile fading.

"The Gatherers bid you enter, Sunandi Jeh Kalawe," he said. "And since these men are unarmed, they may enter as well. There's something within the Hall of Blessings that you should see."

This Sunandi had not expected. However, she concealed her surprise and nodded, mounting the steps to follow the Superior inside. Behind her she heard Dirakha hesitate for a moment, perhaps waiting for some signal from Sunandi, but she did not look at him. The choice to enter the Hetawa would have to be his. She knew his decision when she heard a muttered Sua curse and the sudden tromp of sixteen pairs of sandals at her heels.

She passed through the doorway into the cooler, dimmer confines of the Hetawa, blinking as her eyes adjusted. Then, when they did, she stopped in shock.

In twin rows along the central aisle lay pallets. There must have been forty or more, spaced neatly apart and lined up halfway to the bronze doors. On each pallet lay a sleeping person.

Sunandi frowned, moving down the aisle as she tried to comprehend what she was seeing. Was this some new ritual? But some of the pallet-bound folk seemed to be sleeping fitfully, groaning and shifting in their sleep as if unable to wake from a nightmare.

Peering into the face of one of the sleepers, Sunandi stiffened as she recognized the man. This was one of the Sharers, whom she'd met ages ago at some state function or other. She looked around at the other sleepers, and shivered as a chill passed through her. Nearly all of them wore Hetawa garb.

"Mostly Sharers, but Teachers and Sentinels as well," the Superior said, watching her. She turned to him; he offered her another thin, pained smile. "No Gatherers or children, thank the Goddess. A small blessing."

"What is this?" Sunandi asked.

"Your spies must have told you of the plague." He moved past her, stopping to gaze down at another of his comrades. "We've been fighting it for a month now. I will admit we've kept the news relatively quiet, in the earnest hope that we would soon find some cure." He sighed. "Now we have no choice. Rumors are rampant in the city that *we* are the source of this horror. We must reveal everything so that people may find peace in the truth."

Dirakha took Sunandi's arm suddenly. "Speaker, if there is a plague—"

"The plague is passed from dream to dream," said a familiar voice, and Sunandi turned from the captain to see a figure clad in pale robes moving toward them. He stopped and bowed over his hands in the Gujaareen fashion; his topknot of red-brown ringlets swung forward as he did so. The Gatherer Rabbaneh. As he straightened, Sunandi realized that he was not smiling for perhaps the first time in all the years she'd known him.

"There's no danger of contagion," he said. He looked at Dirakha, who abruptly looked embarrassed and released Sunandi. "Not now. But if you were to lie down now and sleep among these people, you would never wake."

"Why did you not inform me of this?" In spite of Sunandi's horror, her mind was racing to the implications. The Protectors would seize upon this chance to blame the Hetawa for Gujaareh's ills. At the least they might ban magic; at worst they could close the Hetawa, demand the arrest or execution of all its priests, and do their best to eradicate this branch of the Hananjan faith.

"We concealed it because the problem was contained," Rabbaneh replied. Bleakness, Sunandi realized. That was the look in his eyes as he looked around the chamber at his dying brethren. He had no hope for them. "Or so we thought. Two fourdays ago we collected all the sufferers of the dream, and anyone else who might have been exposed. Fifty or so in all. We kept them isolated, studying them, but aware that there was one hope if we failed to find a cure: they would be the last." He gazed down at one boy, a slim youth near or just beyond the age of adulthood, and closed his eyes as if in pain. "But two nights ago, we were attacked by the wielders of the dream."

All thoughts of the Protectorate gone now, Sunandi stared at him. *"Attacked?"*

"That's what we believe," said a new voice behind her—the voice she had been dreading. She turned, steeling herself, to face Nijiri. But she saw at once from his expression that he knew why she had come and did not hate her for it. That was when she recalled his last words to her: *I'll forgive you, no matter what the Protectors make you do.*

It surprised Sunandi how much that relieved her.

"The source of the dream is a child," Nijiri said. "Sonta-i found out that much for us. I don't know how any child could have such power, but the fact remains that someone is using the child as a weapon. I and my brother Inmu witnessed it ourselves." He gestured at the sleeping figures. "They did this to us."

"Worse," said Rabbaneh, "we've found that some people 'carry' the dream, without actually falling into unending sleep, for several days. They are as doomed as those who fall asleep at once, but in the meantime they spread the dream to others."

Sunandi shivered, folding her arms over her breasts. "A plague of nightmares. Shadows indeed." Then she paused, something in her own words tickling a memory. "Has this ever happened before? Dreams with such power?"

The Superior looked at her oddly. "No. There are many unusual variations on the magic we use, but none are inherently harmful. In spite of what your people say."

"The Wild Dreamer," Rabbaneh said. He'd crouched beside the

slim youth, gazing down at the boy with unmistakable tenderness. "That was what Sonta-i called it, at the end. But we've searched the archives and found no mention of such a thing."

Sonta-i. Announcements of his death had been posted all over the city; several prominent artisans and crafters who specialized in mourning had created tribute works in his honor. The death of a Gatherer in and of itself was not a cause for grief in the city, for most Gatherers chose their time and went gladly. Now, though, seeing the anguish in Rabbaneh and Nijiri, Sunandi understood what else they had hidden from the public.

But Sonta-i's last words stirred Sunandi's memory further still. *Wild Dreamer.*

"You haven't consulted the archives at Yanya-iyan," she murmured, trying to think. Trying to tease out that niggling bit of memory. "All the material Eninket assembled while trying to uncover the secrets of Reapers. It's taken us years to sort it all out, but I recall seeing something there regarding this plague of nightmares. And a Wild Dreamer."

The Superior stiffened. Rabbaneh and Nijiri looked at each other, then at her. Rabbaneh got to his feet.

"You must arrest me," Rabbaneh said. "Yes?"

Sunandi lowered her eyes. "Yes."

He rose and came to stand before her, holding his arms forth. "Take care to wrap my hands; you know what we can do with a touch."

She stared at him. On some level she had expected this. Even so— She waved Dirakha forward, and stepped aside as his men bound Rabbaneh's arms.

Nijiri came forward as well. Beyond him the third Gatherer, a tall, lanky young man, was walking down the aisle toward them. "And I," Nijiri said. "And Inmu."

"And I," said the Superior, stepping forward. He gave Sunandi a faint wry smile. "I'm only a Teacher, but unfortunately with one Gatherer gone, I would be the best substitute."

Sunandi frowned. "I was sent only for Rabbaneh."

"Your rule was that any harm done to a Kisuati would be repaid fourfold, yes?" Nijiri said. He glanced at his brothers and the Superior. "We're only four and not eight, but perhaps the Protectors will forgive our small numbers given who we are."

"I can't take all of you," Sunandi said, wondering. She looked at Nijiri especially; he would know what her next words cost her. "The city needs its Gatherers."

Nijiri raised an eyebrow, a slow smile crossing his face. "This is true, Jeh Kalawe," he said. "But we can do nothing else for Gujaareh right now. You've felt the mood in the city these past few days. The last thing our people want is peace."

And with you and your brethren in our custody, the city's anger will burn that much hotter. Oh, yes. She could see it in Nijiri's eyes. He knew full well how the people of Gujaareh would likely react when word spread that Kisua had arrested the Gatherers. All talk of the Hetawa inflicting nightmares on the populace would end; the people's unease would sharpen to a fine, hot focus. Kisua, not the Hetawa, would be the target of all that anger.

The swiftest and surest path to stability. That was what Nijiri had warned her the Hetawa would choose.

Looking into Nijiri's eyes, she said, "I'll search the archives in the palace, and share any relevant material."

"Anything will help at this point," he said. Then he gave her a faint, fond smile. "We're a bad influence on you, Jeh Kalawe. Your behavior seems suspiciously Gujaareen these days."

She returned the smile, less insulted than she should have been. "You know I use whatever tactics work best. Hopefully my actions will bring peace to *both* our peoples, with a minimum of suffering."

"So we must pray." Then he held his arms out as two of Dirakha's men came to tie him. Dirakha had them wrap the twine over and around the Gatherers' closed fists as well to bind the fingers, and then they tied all four men to one another in a linked chain.

That done, the soldiers herded them into a single file and marched them out of the temple, through the furious crowds, to Yanya-iyan.

30

◖⊙◗

Soulname

Wanahomen came out of Unte's tent and instantly spotted the templewoman, ten paces away and coming on like a storm. Her fists were tight, her eyes black as cabochons, her sashes and sleeves whipping around her.

Under other circumstances Wanahomen would have admired the sight. Hanani was no beauty like Tiaanet, and she had none of Yanassa's bold allure, but there was something appealing about her nevertheless—especially whenever she shed her shyness and allowed this side of herself to appear. In another time and place, had she been anything other than a Servant of Hananja, Wanahomen might have happily courted her; it was expected that a Prince count some common women among his two hundred and fifty-six wives. Now, though, he had to stop her before she did something stupid.

He intercepted her at five paces and caught her arm. "Come with me."

She looked up at him, startled and angry—too angry, he suspected, to react to his grip with terror as she had before. He wasn't certain whether that was a blessing. "What? Let go of me!"

"*Come with me*, damn you, unless you want to touch off a storm of violence like nothing you've ever seen."

That broke the back of her anger. Stumbling in her confusion, she finally let him draw her away from the tent. He kept hold of her arm all the way back to his mother's *an-sherrat*, where he brought her into the fire circle between the tents and sat her down.

"I cannot stand idle while they abuse that woman," Hanani said at once.

"Indeed you cannot," Wanahomen replied, sitting down across from her. "For once, I'm in agreement with the Hetawa's way of thinking on this."

She blinked, having clearly expected an argument. "Then why—"

"If you had walked in there just now and told two Banbarra tribe leaders how to treat their prisoner, they would have thrown you out and given the prisoner the slowest, most painful death they could dream up between them. If you had offended them enough, they would have made you watch."

She flinched, her face actually becoming paler, which Wanahomen had not thought possible. "That's barbaric!"

"They're barbarians." Wanahomen reached up to pull off his veil and headcloth; he ran a hand over his braids, abruptly weary. He had been a-horse all day, and this after sleeping poorly the night before. The templewoman's visit had left his conscience raw and his thoughts restless. "And they're men, and elders, and the leaders of a people who considered Gujaareh the enemy until recently. You're a guest in their home, for peace's sake; how do you *think* they'll react if you disrespect them? Imagine you let a foreigner into the Hall of Blessings, and he first tried to tell you how to pray, then pissed on the statue of Hananja. How inclined would you be to listen to any-thing he had to say, after that?"

She looked affronted by the very idea of his imaginary offender, but then her face tightened again. "But this is not mere rudeness that we speak of, Prince; this is murder and torture. Some things are wrong in the eyes of all peoples—"

"That isn't true." He leaned forward, resting his elbows on his knees. "In Gujaareh, Gatherers kill over what would merely be bad manners here. A Banbarra slave may buy or earn her way free; in Gujaareh, our servants have no hope of escaping their lot. And consider this: to Unte and the others, what has been done to you is cruelty, a lifelong torment."

"That's—" she blurted, but he cut her off with a sharp gesture.

"I know. But this is how they see it. A woman, taken from her family as a child, forced to dress and act as a man, made to be humble where she should be proud, never permitted lovers or children or property or any of the things that constitute *a good life* in their eyes? Anyone who proposed to do such a thing to a girl-child here would be called a monster and thrown out of the tribe."

She looked astounded by this characterization of her life. Seeing that he was at last getting through to her, Wanahomen pressed the advantage. "The Banbarra are the elders between our two races, Sharer-Apprentice, and like all elders, they're proud and set in their ways. We cannot *demand* things of them, we can only *ask*—and if they refuse, accept that. Press the issue, and you'll only make things worse."

She frowned all of a sudden, her eyes roving his face entirely too keenly now that he had removed his veil. "You speak from experience."

Wanahomen considered, then decided on brutal honesty. "Sometimes a new slave objects to his condition and must be broken. They begin with beatings for days. Then they progress to burning, amputations of anything deemed unimportant..." She had gone rigid. He lowered his eyes, looking at his own clasped hands. It was easy, frighteningly easy, to remember a time when there had been manacles around his own wrists. "When I was new here, I too protested such cruelty. But as I said, it *is* possible to make things worse."

She made a little sound, rising and beginning to pace around the fire to vent her frustration. It was an amazingly unpeaceful thing to do, for a Servant of Hananja; physical expression of distress was simply not done among polite Gujaareen. He watched her warily, wondering if he had somehow done her more harm. When she stopped, her hands kept moving, fidgeting, rubbing one another as if to scrub away some contaminant. But her voice was calm when she spoke.

"I will *ask* them to reconsider cruelty," she said. "But what can I do if they refuse? I couldn't bear it. I don't know the way back to Gujaareh, even if it were possible to rescue her—"

Wanahomen groaned. "Are you a complete fool? Leaving aside the fact that Unte himself would hunt you down for abusing his hospitality, that woman is Shadoun. She would kill you the moment you let your guard down, even if you were trying to help her." He let out a harsh laugh. "*Especially* if you were trying to help her. She's of the desert and knows how to travel and survive here. You would slow her down."

Hanani had frozen during his scolding, her back rigid and fists clenched tight. He braced himself for further battle. Instead she suddenly bowed her head, falling silent. With some alarm, he realized she was on the brink of tears.

"I don't know what to do," she said. Her voice was barely above a whisper. "I'm a Servant of Hananja; I should know what to do. I should be able to find some peaceful means of solving problems." She let out a short, bitter laugh. "But this would not be the first time I've failed in that."

Thrown by her sudden shift of mood, Wanahomen rose and went to stand behind her. Though he had no idea of what to say that might comfort her, he reached for her shoulder—and then caught himself, remembering in time. She was probably thinking of Azima even now, he realized belatedly, watching her fists tremble and her shoulders tighten. Her greatest failure. The Hetawa taught that true strength lay in enduring the torments of others, even if that meant pain or debasement. It was permissible to resist, but only after calm and contemplation, so that in striking back, one did not become as corrupt as the tormentor.

But that made no sense. What strength could Hanani have gained by allowing herself to be brutalized when she had the means to stop it? There was fortitude, and then there was folly. Surely she could see the difference?

Sighing, Wanahomen decided that neither women nor temple-folk were anything resembling sane. He almost felt sorry for this one, doomed by sex and vocation at once.

"Hananja does not concern Herself with the waking realm," he said. "Isn't that what Hananja's Wisdom says? She leaves it to us to make our own fate."

"Yes, that's true..."

"Then don't look for answers in Hetawa doctrine. That's made by mortals, not gods." And though he tried to steer his thoughts elsewhere, he could not help it. For a moment, looking at her, he saw only Nijiri, the Gatherer who had sent her into the desert—and Ehiru, the Gatherer who had trained him. And, too, he saw his father, who had died at Ehiru's hands. "And mortals can be corrupt."

She turned to him, frowning at his shift of mood, and as she moved, the beads of her Banbarra hairstyle rattled together. He blinked and she was herself again—not a Gatherer, not the Hetawa. Just a Gujaareen girl in Banbarra clothes, so out of her depth that she had no inkling of what to do next.

But her fists were still clenched tight at her sides, and there was a set to her shoulders that told him she meant to do *something*, if she could. He could not help thinking too: he liked this about her. She was as mad as the rest of the Hetawa's priests, but he could at least admire her courage.

And he'd done enough woolgathering. "I've done what I can," he said. "The circumstances of the Shadoun's capture were suspicious. She was near the rim of the canyon, in the open, making a fire for tea. It was as though she *wanted* to be captured." He shook his head. "I suggested to Unte and Tajedd that we interrogate her to determine whatever secrets she might hold. That gives her some value, for now."

"And what may I do, to help? If you say I must ask and not demand—"

He shook his head. "Not yet." She opened her mouth again, predictable as the moons, and he spoke faster. "Sometimes the most useful choice is *not* to act, Sharer-Apprentice. If it comes to that, I would rather save your... request... as a last resort. Appeal to Unte and Tajedd's mercy; tell them that Azima's attack still troubles you." She flinched, and he nodded grimly. At least there was some lingering use in what he'd done to her. "Since you *are* a guest, they'll hesitate to do anything that would cause you further harm."

She nodded slowly. "I see. I, I will follow your advice, then." She hesitated and added, "Thank you, Prince. For helping that woman. I know she doesn't serve your cause in any way."

He grimaced, not liking her low estimation of his morals. "It doesn't 'serve my cause' to forget myself, either. I *am* Gujaareen, after all." Annoyed, he folded his arms. She turned and gazed at him so long and so steadily that he began to grow uncomfortable.

"You should sit down," she said abruptly. "I need to make you sleep for your next lesson."

He started. "A lesson? *Now?*"

"You said there was nothing more to be done for the woman, at least for now. Have you other duties?"

Unte and Tajedd would summon him if they decided the Shadoun's fate anytime soon. Until then he had been ordered to keep the troop in the canyon rather than resume patrols, in case the Shadoun were planning some assault. Ezack had charge of a group up on the heights, watching for danger; things were as peaceful as they would be for some time.

"Very well," he said, moving to sit on a log beside the fire. "At least I'll get a nap out of it."

The woman came to stand before him, cupping the back of his head with one hand. He was surprised at this, until he felt her fingers probe the base of his skull, checking how tense he was. She had no jungissa stone, which only Gatherers used; he'd heard it could be difficult to impose sleep-spells in the daytime without that. Mindful of this, he took a deep breath to clear his thoughts, and saw her nod approvingly. Once she was satisfied that he was sufficiently relaxed, she leaned down to peer into his face. "Try to stay within yourself this time," she said earnestly, as if that should mean something to him. "I can't teach you if you drag me all over the realms."

Wanahomen sighed again. "You are the strangest woman I've ever met."

She blinked, and her lips twitched in the first smile he'd seen on her face in days. Then she lifted a hand and hummed a low note, and he closed his eyes, and a moment later he was asleep.

When he opened his eyes, the *an-sherrat* was gone. So was the woman, and the fire, and the ground, and the very sky above his head. He could not see himself; his only awareness was the belief that he existed. He floated in dark nothingness, alarmed and alone.

No. Not alone—

"Here."

The templewoman's voice echoed through the darkness, though he could not see her. He stretched out a hand to touch her and found nothing, though she had been right in front of him in the waking realm.

"What is this place?" he asked.

"The realm between Ina-Karekh and Hona-Karekh, stripped of artifice or layer. It has no name."

That was no help. "Where are you?"

The presence was abruptly all around him, so close and enveloping that he could not turn without feeling her presence. Not her flesh; he still could not see or touch her. What he perceived instead was calm and control and a *femaleness* so quintessential to her character that it almost had a texture. Soft, warm, vibrant. And underneath the smell and the taste and the feel of her was something else. Something harder, like bone, or the stone at the core of a fruit. No; that was not her core, merely its outer shell, and its name was—

She drew back at once, and he forced himself not to show fear at the prospect of being left alone in this empty darkness.

"So strong," she said, gently chiding. "So insistent. Do you never wait to be invited into a place, Prince?"

She didn't sound angry. If anything, he thought he heard amusement in her tone. "Generally I can *see* if a place is off-limits to me," he said, irritated.

"In this realm, if something is not already there for you to perceive, you should quest after it with great caution. If you must pry, do so with your own protections in place. Where is your soulname?"

"I don't have one."

Her calm shifted to pity, which he found even more irritating than her amusement. She, perhaps sensing his annoyance, returned almost at once to calm.

"Forgive me," she said. "I thought you had received at least the training given to children in Gujaareh—"

"My father would not permit it."

"…I see. It's no matter; I'll have to give you that training now. Tell me: do you know what a soulname truly is?"

He was ashamed to admit his ignorance, so said what he did know. "I know they are to be guarded carefully," he said. "To possess another's soulname is to have power over him, in dreams."

"Yes. In dreaming, one can lose oneself. A soulname provides an anchor to all that you are; with it, you will always be able to find your way. The syllables themselves have no power, but the *meaning* that you give them, the incorporation of the concept itself, is crucial to the preservation of your identity." She sighed; he felt concern in her before she concealed it. "Were you still a child, this would be easy. You would be...flexible. As a man grown, with such a strong sense of yourself—" A warning note came into her voice. "This won't be pleasant."

"Little in my life has been, woman," he said, drawing himself up—inasmuch as the gesture had any meaning in this formless place. "Do what you must."

"Very well."

The feel of her presence changed completely. She was still all around him, but he could no longer recognize her. The softness that he had interpreted as female, as *her*, shifted to a feel of flint and metal, sharp-edged and cold. Then she pressed inward, against the existence that he had come to understand was himself. It left the taste of metal in his mouth; he drew back, disliking the sensation. But she pressed in again.

"What are you doing?" he asked. But she said nothing, only pressing further still, and to his alarm he realized that she had left him no outlet for escape. Whichever way he turned, she was there.

And when she pressed in again, the hard edges of her presence ground away at him, like a millstone. It *hurt*, in a way that was both less and more than pain; startled by it, he inadvertently cried out into the empty space. Was the woman mad? Gravel scraped his skin, acid seared the raw flesh underneath...She pressed in again and he began to struggle now, understanding at last what she was doing. The cold, ugly edges of her were tearing him apart, digging into the very essence of his being. If she kept doing it, he had no idea what would happen—would he become her, devoured as if by a Reaper? Would his soul cease to exist, leaving his flesh to die? He had no idea, but if he couldn't figure out how to fight her, he feared he would soon find out.

"Stop this, murdering Hetawa monster!" He poured all of himself into trying to break free. It was like fighting sand; every time he carved a space for *himself* to exist, it filled in with more of *her*. And now, to his horror, he realized that he was losing the contest. She—who was she? He could not recall, but more importantly, *he could not recall his own name*. She tore away more bits of himself. "Get away from me!" he screamed, but the darkness and silence swallowed the cry.

She finished tearing away the outer parts of him and then drew back, gathering herself for the final blow. He panted in her grip, raw and vulnerable and exhausted, aware now that she had access to the innermost core of his self. If she even once touched him here, he would be destroyed; he sensed that with instinctive certainty. He had never been so terrified in his life.

Then she reached for him, for the part of him that pulsed like a heart and was just as vital, and he wept and writhed and finally screamed out the only thing that would save him. Two syllables.

There was a sound. For a moment he could not place it, and then he remembered: his childhood in the palace Kite-iyan. In a fit of pique, one of his father's wives had thrown a cup of fine pottery at a wall, shattering it. But this sound was lighter, clearer, like metal or perhaps crystal—

The instant he thought it, it came to be. Crystal formed around him, hard and clear as diamond, its sharp-edged facets lighting the darkness with their brilliance. The flint and metal sparked against it and withdrew, harmless now. And suddenly he understood.

He was Wanahomen. Hunt leader of the Yusir-Banbarra, Prince-to-be of Gujaareh, scion of the Sun and mouthpiece of the Goddess. But more than that, he was—

He opened his eyes, awake, back in his mother's *an-sherrat*. The woman still stood before him. "Niim," he said, looking up at her in wonder. "I am Niim."

She stroked his hair and smiled. "In dreams, yes."

"What—" He could barely remember how to speak with his mouth. How much time had passed? The fire had hardly burned down, yet it felt as if hours had gone by. Or years. "What did you—"

"That was the only method I knew to force out your name. Fortunately, you were imaginative enough to survive it."

He felt too awed to be angry. "This name—" But he fell silent, startled, as she put her finger on his lips.

"You see, now, why the name is to be shared only with a trusted few." She smiled again, with a hint of self-deprecation. "You'll probably regret telling me. But to reciprocate, I give you this: I am Aier, in dreams."

He understood, now, just how much the name meant. The stone beneath the soft ripe flesh of a fruit. He shivered as he contemplated her, torn between awe and a feeling that he could not define. Desire? Yes, there was some of that, and he was man enough to acknowledge it. Not the deluge of lust he'd felt for Tiaanet, or the ebb-and-flow tide he'd had with Yanassa during their relationship, but something nevertheless. A quiet steady stream of wanting, perhaps. But along with that desire came a more profound feeling, both more powerful and more moving than mere lust. Reverence; a sense of comfort. This was what he felt on the rare occasions that he prayed.

"Thank you," he said, meaning it on many levels.

Hanani ducked her eyes, let go of him, and took a step away. Too much intimacy, Wanahomen realized. She had sworn to Share herself only with their Goddess; giving him her soulname came perilously close to a similar kind of sharing. He missed her nearness, craved more of it. Yet she had already broken her oath once because of him. It would be wrong to harm her further.

With a forced briskness he said, "Is that it, then? The technique you meant to teach me?"

"No." Her shyness had returned; she spoke softly and did not meet his eyes. "Since you had no soulname, we had to do that first. But I believe you may be ready for the humor-balancing technique in the next lesson."

She trailed off, frowning. Abruptly Wanahomen became aware of noise beyond the *an-sherrat*—more shouts and excited calls. Wanahomen's good feeling vanished with a chill; he saw Hanani stiffen. But the noise lacked the ugly, vicious edge that Wanahomen would have expected if the Shadoun woman's sentence had been decided.

Charris stepped around one of the tents, looking relieved when he spotted Wanahomen. "Two more tribes have arrived together," he said. "Madobah-Banbarra, the sentries say, and Issayir."

Wanahomen stood at once, his weariness forgotten. "We couldn't have asked for better timing. How far off are they?"

"An hour, perhaps."

"Good." Turning to the woman, he found her frowning at both of them in confusion. "Nothing will be decided about the prisoner until morning, now," he said. "That's guest-custom. And by morning, cooler heads may make the decision." He put a hand on her shoulder, greatly daring. She looked surprised, but did not start or pull away, so he smiled and allowed himself to give her a brief, reassuring squeeze. "I promise nothing, but I'll do everything in my power to give the Shadoun a peaceful death."

Hope filled her face, a welcome improvement on her earlier mood. She nodded, wordless. Inclining his head in farewell, Wanahomen grabbed his headcloth and veil, and went with Charris to welcome their new guests.

31

(⊙)

The Nightmare

For long moments after the Prince left, Hanani stood between two tents of the *an-sherrat*, gazing from that space of relative safety out into the Banbarra encampment. The Prince's lesson had wearied her, though that was not the reason she now craved the shadows. She simply needed time to digest anew the strangeness of the world. The Banbarra had never seemed more frightening to her than today, and the Prince had never seemed more normal.

Surely all the world has rolled upside down. Perhaps the gods have gotten drunk on comet-wine again, like in the tales.

Her shoulder tingled with the lingering warmth of the Prince's hand. What was it about him that his every touch—even that foul, malicious kiss of his, when he'd sought to fool Azima—stayed with her so? She had spent her whole life among men, many of them beautiful enough to put the Prince to shame. Nor was she any stranger to men's desire, for she would have been blind not to notice that some eyes lingered on her in the Hetawa baths, and some hands shook and grew clammy whenever they touched hers. The Prince's interest had flavored the very air between them in the wake of their exchanged soulnames, and yet he was no different from all the other lustful men she had learned to ignore over the years. Why, then, did she find it so difficult to ignore him?

Perhaps because he has no peace in him, came the thought. Her fellow priests' desire was irrelevant; they were men of discipline, long used to containing or redirecting their untoward impulses. The Prince indulged his impulses freely, without control, heedless of the damage this did to his inward peace—or to others, apparently. Was it fear, then, that made her so sensitive to him? He had used her in a scheme to kill a man. He was little better than a barbarian himself. She *should* have feared him. Yet she did not, not quite, not any longer. He clearly regretted what he'd done to her; she had noticed him struggling not to do anything else that would remind her of Azima's attack. He even spoke to her more gently—a kindness that she appreciated, small as it was. And she had seen him struggling, too, to recall his own Gujaareen nature. It was impossible for her, as a Servant of Hananja, to observe this struggle and dismiss him as hopeless.

She would go find Mni-inh, she decided. She would dance the evening prayer with him, and see if that clarified her thoughts and feelings.

"Hanani. You're here."

She looked around, pleasantly surprised at the sound of her mentor's voice. But when Mni-inh stepped into the space between the tents, his expression was unusually grim.

"Brother? What is it?"

"I've been dreaming with Nijiri again," he said. His eyes gazed at the ground; she realized with some alarm that he was trembling. "I had to wait longer than usual. He had to go somewhere outside the Hetawa to do it, and be certain that his dreamer was safe. Something terrible has happened."

"What, Brother?"

"An attack." His jaw tightened. "Someone *attacked* the Hetawa,

296

several nights ago. The Wild Dreamer. Half—" He shuddered again, his face constricting with anguish. "More than half of our Sharer brethren— Most of them were asleep, Hanani."

It took several breaths for the implication of his words to sink in. Nhen-ne-verra. Fierat, her fellow apprentice who continually forgot she was a girl and made lewd jokes in her presence. All her elder brothers—many of them had snubbed her, treated her like something exotic and dangerous, but they did not deserve death for it. No one deserved a death like Dayu's.

Hanani put a hand to her mouth. "Oh Goddess. Oh, no."

Mni-inh leaned against the wall of the tent nearby—his own. "The ones who survived the initial assault are infected with the dream, just as doomed as the ones who died. They'll stay awake as long as they can, but when they finally give in..." He shook his head. "And in the meantime, no one else in the Hetawa dares sleep at all. Nijiri says we're probably better off, out here, than we would be back home." He shook his head. "That is a foul, foul turn of fortune."

Hanani leaned against a tent as well, too shaken to stand. "Who would do such a thing? Why? Sharers offend no one. It makes no sense."

"It does if someone has been deliberately spreading this nightmare. Our pathbrothers were working night and day to find a cure. The culprit must have feared they'd find one." His jaw tightened with bitterness. "In striking this blow, they've crippled our ability to care for the victims *and* to fight back. The Sharers who remain have no hope of stopping this now. The best they can do is succor their fellows until the end."

It was too much. "I wanted to go home," Hanani whispered. Her eyes stung again, as they'd done when the Prince spoke to her of horrors unimaginable—but what good did tears do? She shook her head. "Just a few moments ago, I questioned whether the Banbarra were even human. But the Prince was right; we're no better. Only a Gujaareen would ever use dreams as a weapon. Only we sentence our enemies to torment for all eternity."

"I've had the same thought," Mni-inh said. She had never heard such bleakness in his voice. "Perhaps we can never weed corruption out of ourselves, not completely. But it's important that we continue to try."

As if in response to Mni-inh's words, they both heard a child's voice calling their names, butchered by a heavy Chakti accent.

Drawn out of her melancholy, Hanani went to see who it was. Tassa stood near Mni-inh's tent, looking around; he brightened when he spotted her. "Sharer," he said. "Nu-dari—Unte, tribe leader—say come. Magic...you magic..." He scowled, trying to remember a word. "*Need* you magic. Yes." He beckoned to her and pointed toward Unte's tent.

Mni-inh stepped out of the space between the tents too, frowning. "Is someone hurt?"

"Hurt? No. Is...is..." Tassa screwed up his face, unable to convey his thoughts. "*Shadoun*, need magic."

A chill passed through Hanani's flesh. Had they hurt the woman?

Mni-inh put a hand on Hanani's shoulder, his expression grim and angry; the same suspicion was in his eyes, Hanani saw. "I'll come," he said to Tassa. "If only to tell these fools that we will *not* pervert our magic for them, if they want her healed only so they can do her more harm. Hanani—"

"I will come as well."

Mni-inh opened his mouth to protest, took one look at her, and closed it. He shook his head. "I've learned by now not to argue with you. You always win."

Hanani nodded to Tassa; he led the way through the camp to Unte's tent.

The scene, when they stepped into the tent's smoky confines, was not so terrible as Hanani had feared. Unte stood near the Shadoun woman, who had been made to kneel, still bound, at the center of the tent. Tajedd sat across the table from her, and beside him sat two other men, their indigo robes dusty from travel: the two newly arrived tribe leaders. The Shadoun woman seemed to have taken little additional hurt beyond a bruise over one eye that looked fresh.

"What is this?" the woman asked, looking Hanani and Mni-inh up and down. Her Gujaareen—probably the only common tongue between Shadoun and Banbarra—was touched with a strange lilting accent that Hanani had never heard. Her lip curled in disgust. "Your people breed with northerners now? These two are pale as sand."

Unte, stone-faced, ignored the woman. To Hanani and Mni-inh he said, "Wanahomen has told me often that your people can cure madness."

Hanani blinked; Mni-inh shared with her a look of equal surprise. "Somewhat," Hanani said at last. "Certain kinds of madness react well to our magic, though not all."

Unte nodded, then inclined his head toward the Shadoun woman. "Please tell us if she is mad."

"Gujaareen!" They both started, for the Shadoun woman had snarled the word, like a curse. The hatred in her eyes was like nothing Hanani had ever seen; suddenly she understood why the Banbarra tribe leaders questioned her sanity. The woman actually shook with it. "Gujaareen and *Hetawa*. I knew your people consorted with dogs, Banbarra, but never once had I dreamed—" She abruptly spat, craning her neck with the effort; the spittle landed an inch shy of Mni-inh's sandals.

As calmly as he had spoken to them, Unte backhanded the woman so hard that she fell over onto her side. Then he grabbed the back of her robes and hauled her upright, holding her until she was steady again.

Hanani had put her hands to her mouth at the blow; Mni-inh had taken a step forward, his fists clenched. "*Stop* that, gods damn you!"

Unte merely looked at them, and the emptiness of his face chilled Hanani to her bones. Even Mni-inh drew back from this, his face paling. When he spoke again his tone was more conciliatory.

"Forgive me," he said. "I spoke without thought. But...I'm sure the P— Wanahomen has told you that our faith, our order, considers violence a great evil."

"I know that," Unte said. Hanani thought—hoped—that she saw some softening of his expression in response to Mni-inh's apology. "Which is why all I ask is that you determine whether she's mad. If she is, I don't ask you to heal her." He cast a glance at his fellow tribe leaders, who were all equally grim. "Others would ask, so that she can be given to the women for sport, but *I* do not. If she's mad, we will kill her, lest her madness infect us all. If she's sane..." He closed his mouth.

By now Hanani understood, and a painful knot inside her eased. Indeed, if she could have, she would have hugged Unte. If she and Mni-inh judged the Shadoun insane, she would be granted a swift death. It meant lying if the woman *was* sane, but no action that served peace could be truly wrong, could it? She glanced at Mni-inh, hoping he would agree, though she took care to keep her expression as neutral as Unte's. It was doubtful the other tribe leaders spoke Gujaareen, because they were men. But it was obviously important that Unte show no sign of kindness toward the Shadoun.

"You will not touch me," the woman said abruptly, glaring at Mni-inh. "I know what you are now, though they have dressed you in their gaudy clothes. *Dash ta hinakri en em*—" She lapsed into her own tongue for a moment, trembling with rage. "Demons! Insects! I will not abide your touch!"

"We're Sharers of Hananja," Mni-inh said, inclining his head. "Healers—"

"I do not care! Let these *tteba* have me." She jerked her head toward the flap of Unte's tent. "I would rather lie under a hundred of these than be in the same tent with you!"

Mni-inh stared at the woman, then exchanged a confused look with Hanani. It was improper in the extreme for a Sharer to force unwanted healing upon a petitioner; only Gatherers had the right to impose magic against a person's will. But if they did nothing, there was no telling what the Banbarra would do.

"I'll do it," Mni-inh said at last. He sighed and rolled up his sleeves, stepping forward.

The woman tensed, her eyes bright as those of a cornered animal. Hanani gasped out a warning only an instant before she lunged at Mni-inh. What she meant to do Hanani could not guess—bite him? But Mni-inh had seen her attack coming too, and he side-stepped her lunge, clamping a hand on her shoulder.

The Shadoun gasped, her eyes glazing, and slumped to the floor. Dreamblood. Shaking his head ruefully, Mni-inh knelt, turned her over with Unte's assistance, and put his fingers on her already sagging eyelids.

It was only then that Hanani noticed the deep circles under the woman's eyes, and the exhaustion that her anger had hidden until now. Traveling alone through the desert could not have been easy for her, especially in enemy territory. The poor woman looked as though she had not slept in days...

As though she had not slept in days.

They'll stay awake as long as they can, Mni-inh had said of their pathbrothers, who now carried the nightmare sickness.

In the silence that had fallen, Mni-inh suddenly gasped, his eyes flying open. Unte, helping to hold the woman, frowned sharply at him.

But when they finally give in . . .

"No." Hanani tried to will herself to move, but her limbs would not obey. In her mind she saw Gatherer Sonta-i; she saw Dayuho-tem. "No—"

It was already too late. Mni-inh began to tremble all over, his face contorting. He made a single abortive sound, half scream and half sob.

"*No!*" Something snapped in Hanani. She ran to him, shouldering Unte aside. But before she could grab Mni-inh, he slumped to the ground.

Hanani threw herself on him, hauling with all her strength to get him onto his back. She had to push his eyelids down with her fingers; they were stuck wide, horrified. It took all her discipline to calm herself enough to enter the healing sleep, but she did it, and cast herself into his flesh, searching and searching for his soul.

There was nothing left inside him but silence.

32

(⊙)

Death

For a moment, stepping into Unte's tent, Wanahomen thought he had gone back in time. Once again Hanani sat unmoving; once again the air felt of death and shock. But there were two bodies on the rugs this time: the Shadoun woman, and Sharer Mni-inh.

"What in shadows happened?" he asked.

It was a measure of how disturbing the event had been that Tajedd was the first of the tribe leaders to answer.

"The woman was gibbering," he said, sounding dazed. "We plied her with food and drink, threatened her, and she only cursed us. So we summoned those"—he nodded toward Mni-inh's corpse, and Hanani's back—"to see if she was mad."

"She did not want them to touch her." Another man, one Wanahomen did not know. Judging by the strong resemblance between him and Unte, this was Unte's younger brother and the leader of the Issayir tribe. "So the man-healer did something to calm her. When he put his fingers on her eyes . . ." He shuddered. "I've never seen a look like that on a man's face."

"It was the death nightmare." The templewoman's voice, soft at the best of times, was barely audible now. She sat with her back to them, her mentor's head in her lap. It struck Wanahomen as odd that she had unbound his hair from its usual knot. One of her hands stroked his hair, slowly and steadily. "The dream that kills like a sickness. Some do not die of it at once, but bear it within them, spreading it to all who sleep nearby." She paused for a moment, though her hand never stopped its incessant stroking. "Night is falling."

Wanahomen stiffened. "You're saying—" But he understood at last. There had been rumors of the nightmare in the city when he'd gone to visit Sanfi, though he'd never suspected it was so serious. And now he recalled how they had found the Shadoun—making a fire for tea. Strong black tea, to keep herself awake. *She must have known she carried death inside her. So she came among her enemies, not caring how she died as long as she took us with her.*

The tribe leaders were watching him, waiting; Hanani had spoken in Gujaareen. He swallowed and explained.

Tajedd flinched back. "A plague! Can those corpses spread it now?"

"Dream magic doesn't work that way. There's no danger." Wanahomen glanced at Hanani, troubled by her stillness. "The Shadoun must have been in Gujaareh's capital recently, trading. Since the Kisuati conquest they're the only desert tribe permitted within the city's walls. If they spent the night in the city, near someone who had the sickness... From what I've heard, it would've taken no more than that."

"Animals," snarled the other tribe leader—of the Madobah, Wanahomen guessed by elimination. He glared at the Shadoun's corpse. "Sneaking cowards! They're too weak to face us in combat, so they resort to tricks?"

"Yes," said Unte. He too gazed down at the Shadoun, who had died with a snarl on her face. "Many of the six tribes' best warriors are here. If she had succeeded in her plan, she would have accomplished in a single night what generations of blood feud between our races could not." He sighed heavily and looked at the body of the Sharer. "Tell the woman—when you deem it appropriate—that her friend will be buried with all the honors due a Banbarra warrior. He may have lost his own life, but he saved us in the process."

Wanahomen nodded. Uncomfortable silence fell; in it they all heard the faint whisper of movement as Hanani stroked her mentor's hair again.

Wanahomen went over and crouched beside her, peering into her face. She was not crying. Instead there was a strange blankness in her expression that Wanahomen did not like at all.

"Sharer-Apprentice." He hesitated for a moment, unsure whether the gesture would be rejected, but then put his hand on hers, stilling the constant stroking.

She looked at him and the blank mask cracked. For one terrible breath, such agony distorted her face that he barely recognized her. In that moment he feared her grief was too great to bear; she would go mad with it, or die. But then the moment passed and her face returned to blankness. She took a deep breath and nodded, then carefully moved her mentor's head off her lap.

"You have business to discuss," she said. "Forgive me."

"Hanani," he said, uneasily resorting to her name. "You should—"

"Will you see to the funeral arrangements?" She ran right over his words as if he hadn't spoken. "In spite of . . . circumstances . . . cremation should be fine. His soul is neither lingering here in Hona-Karekh nor dreaming in Ina-Karekh. His flesh is unimportant now."

Wanahomen wondered where the man's soul *was*, though he could not bring himself to ask. "The Banbarra do not cremate, but I'll teach them how to build the pyre properly."

"Thank you, Prince." She got to her feet, moving slowly and clumsily, as if it took all her effort to keep the calm mask in place. She had no strength left over for grace. "Under the circumstances, I must ask again for donations of dream-humors from the tribe, as I am now the only healer here."

"I'll tell Unte." He spoke quickly, before she could cut him off again. "Hanani. You should not be alone."

She looked at him and he saw the shadowlands in her eyes. "Who will give me peace now, Prince? You?"

"There's more than one kind of peace," he said, scowling. "Yanassa. I'll ask her to—"

"Thank you for your concern." She turned to leave, then paused. "This was clearly an unforeseen accident. When I return to the Hetawa, I'll make sure my brethren understand this."

Wanahomen grimaced, shamed by his own selfishness, because in the back of his mind he had worried about that exact thing. But she gave him no chance to muster a response. With an almost palpable effort to straighten her shoulders, she inclined her head respectfully to the tribe leaders, then walked out of the tent.

"Wana." Unte. He was frowning after Hanani. "I don't know the customs of your land, but—"

"In Gujaareh we would send her to the Hetawa," Wanahomen said, heavily. "My people treat wounds of the soul the same as wounds of the flesh; we never leave such things to fester. But there's no one here who can heal her now."

Unte sighed and nodded. "Well. The end-solstice celebration is tomorrow night. The vote will take place the next day or the day after, assuming the remaining two tribes arrive on time. One way or another, you'll be able to take her home soon."

Wanahomen was not certain Hanani would last that long, but he kept that thought to himself.

"She says she'll tell her brethren of the Hetawa that his death was no fault of ours." He looked down at the two corpses and shuddered. "But this *is* my fault. I brought this horror into the tribe." Clenching his fists, he went to Unte, pulled off his veil and headcloth, and knelt. Though they had agreed that Wanahomen would never bow his head to Unte—kings did not submit to other kings—he did so now, pressing both hands to the floor and bending his forehead to them, in a full and formal Gujaareen gesture of contrition. He hated the words he had to speak, hated himself for having to speak them, but there was no denying that they needed to be said.

"I was careless," he said. He spoke Gujaareen; he could not have humbled himself properly in Chakti. "I assumed the woman could do us no harm, and didn't notice what I should have, though the signs were there. You were right to doubt me, Unte; I do not care enough."

There was silence for a moment, during which Wanahomen counted every beat of his heart. But then Unte touched his shoulder. "I think perhaps you care a bit more now," he said, with surprising gentleness.

Then he switched to Chakti so the other leaders could understand their conversation. "Be at ease, Wanahomen. No one could have anticipated this."

"But my neglect—"

Unte shook his head. "Care for your countrywoman, then, if you would serve penance. But I cannot see how I would have done differently in your place." He looked up at the other tribe leaders; two of them nodded agreement. Tajedd did not, but that was to be expected.

Wanahomen closed his eyes for a moment, relieved and grateful and anguished all at once. His throat clenched, but that would not do, not in a room full of men he still hoped to sway to his cause—though after this his chances would likely fade like mist before the sun. Nothing to be done for it now. He swallowed hard, nodded, and got to his feet. "The woman has asked that he be burned," he said, nodding toward the Sharer's body.

Unte rubbed his chin, thoughtful. "There's a cavern where it may be done," he said. "Toward the north of the canyon, well away from the fields, where the river runs underground. There are many vents there into other caverns; that should dissipate the smoke."

Wanahomen nodded. "I know the place. I'll have my men take care of it." He glanced at the Shadoun. "And her?"

Unte smiled sadly. "She, too, should be buried honorably," he said. "As should any warrior who strikes a useful blow for her people."

*   *   *

Night had fallen by the time Wanahomen went in search of Hanani. By this point he was hot and sweaty, smelling of oils and herbs, and too tired to bathe again before morning. Then too, he was worried about the woman. He did not think she was the type to do injury to herself—or at least not here and now. If nothing else, as a good Hananjan, she would want to donate her dreamblood before she died.

He spotted Yanassa among a small knot of other women, listening to a musician not far from Hanani's tent. With several hundred guests in the canyon and disaster averted, it seemed that Unte had given permission for the solstice celebrations to continue. Even so, there was a subdued feel to the revelry. The musician, Neapha Seven-Fingers, played a slow mournful lament. Wanahomen saw no one dancing, and none of the more raucous and cheerful celebrations that were usual for the penultimate night of the solstice. Tomorrow night, perhaps, they would return to their usual gaiety, especially if the vote went in favor of war. For tonight, the tribe's mood was somber.

Yanassa spied Wanahomen and made an apologetic gesture to her companions before rising and coming to meet him. "You're going to see her?"

He nodded. "Did you? How is she?"

"She let me in for a while, but wouldn't speak of her pain." Yanassa lowered her eyes. "We had words before, about the Shadoun woman, and I think she no longer trusts me. Perhaps you'll do better."

Things were dire indeed if that was the case. "I'll go now."

There was an immediate stir within when he tapped Hanani's tent flap. She pushed it open to see who it was. "Prince. Have you come for your next lesson?"

He started; that had been the last thing on his mind. "Tonight seems hardly the time—"

"Yanassa told me the tribe leaders vote in two days. There isn't much time left for me to teach you. Come." She slipped out of the tent and went around it to the back, heading for the fire circle again.

The *an-sherrat* still had four tents, Wanahomen realized. He would have his men remove Mni-inh's in the morning.

The woman carried herself better now than she had that afternoon. There was no outward sign of pain in her movements or demeanor; no sign of any emotion whatsoever. She looked better physically as well, although that was probably Yanassa's doing. Her hair had been redone into curling twists, the weighted ornaments replaced by tiny ornamental gold coins that jingled faintly as she walked. Banbarra used the tinkling of coins to keep away ill fortune in times of mourning.

Sighing, he sat down on one of the stones beside the fire. She sat down opposite him.

"I've tended your mentor's body as best I could," he said. "I didn't remember all the rites, and I had no wrappings, but I've treated him with dignity. My men are gathering wood tonight; in the morning we'll take him to a place to set a pyre. Do you want to come?"

She said nothing for a moment, her body language as unreadable as her face. "No."

Not a tear, not a tremor, not a single sign of grief. If he hadn't already come to know the peculiar combination of strength and uncertainty that was normal for her, he wouldn't have known anything was wrong. "Did you find tithebearers?"

"Yanassa," she said. "And Charris as well, when he came to visit. A few others."

"Do you have enough now?"

"Enough of everything but dreamblood, but that is to be expected without a Gatherer's aid. The living can spare very little of their own."

Wanahomen had hoped to steer the conversation away from death. "This lesson. Will it be as unpleasant as the last one?" He mustered a smile, which she did not return.

"That depends on you," she said. The flatness of her voice was truly unnerving, compared to her usual compassionate tone. "Please go to sleep now."

Easier said than done, he thought sourly, but nevertheless shifted to sit on the ground, propping his back against the rock. Though he was exhausted, sleep was long in coming. He was all too aware of her eyes on him, the crackling of the fire, the discomfort of the ground.

"You cannot sleep."

The sound of her voice. "It will happen eventually," he snapped. "If I'm taking too long for your tastes, we can always finish the lesson tomorrow."

"Imagine something important to you."

He frowned. "Like what?"

"Some object, or a symbol that has meaning to you. A pictoral, perhaps. Imagine it. Contemplate its contours in your mind."

He considered for a moment, then carefully, reverently, drew the image of the Aureole of the Setting Sun in his mind. Not his mother's imitation, but the true thing: the staff, carved from white nhefti, a wood used only for holy objects. The brass frame, crafted by an artisan so long ago that his name had been forgotten. Plates of polished amber, each carved whole from chunks that must have been the size of melons, and each worth the entire treasury of a lesser kingdom, to represent the sun's overlapping rays. Eight red amber, eight clear yellow. He remembered listening as a child, enraptured, while his father explained that the central plate—the semicircle of gold two handspans wide and nearly as red as blood—represented the Sun, who had founded their lineage on a pretty mortal girl who'd caught his ever-roving eye. It had been mined on a mountain where snow lay thick enough to drown in—

"Niim."

The woman's voice did not disturb him this time. Something shifted within him. Suddenly his skin prickled with a chill far deeper than that of the desert night, and the air tasted dry and bitter, like metal gone to rust. He opened his eyes and found the *an-sherrat* in shades of white and gray. Even the fire that smoldered at his feet had gone oddly colorless. More whiteness, glimmering and strange, covered the tent walls and every surface. He touched a mass nearby, and the cold of it stung his fingers. Snow? He had never seen it before, but he had been thinking of it, remembering his father's tales— At once he understood. "I'm dreaming."

"Yes. But not in Ina-Karekh." The templewoman, when he looked around, stood a few feet away. There was something odd about her dreamform, which shimmered now and again as if trying to warp into a different shape, but for the moment she had it under control.

"This is the realm between waking and dreaming," she said. "Your soul has brought me here again and again, rather than into Ina-Karekh. I believe this is a sign that some part of you has gone out of true." She paused. "Do you have visions often?"

Wanahomen flinched, and lied. "No."

She was silent for so long that he knew she saw right through him. But he had no intention of admitting the truth to her.

"It's no matter," she said at length. "I mean to teach you how to heal yourself, anyhow."

He frowned in confusion, wrapping his arms around himself; the cold was going right through his robes. "I don't like this."

"Then change it," she said. "This is your realm."

"I don't understand."

"A Gatherer is one whose mind creates new worlds via the act of dreaming. Doing so is natural to them. Indeed, if not for the balancing power of dreamblood, some would spend *all* their time in the worlds of their mind's creation. You would call that madness."

He shuddered, or shivered. *She* seemed unaffected by the cold for some reason, though she wore less. "I'm not a Gatherer." When she said nothing in reply, he scowled and changed the subject. "How do I leave this place?"

"Create another. As you created this one."

He had remembered his father's tales and imagined a dreamscape draped in snow. He decided to try another memory of his childhood: the gardens of Kite-iyan, palace of his mothers and siblings. In his mind's eye he saw the delicate miniature palms, smelled the fragrance of the vineflowers and the nearby river, felt the soil between his toes—

His toes. He had been wearing sandals, but now his feet were bare. The air was warm. He opened his eyes to Kite-iyan—colorless, shadowed, but unmistakable.

Hanani looked around, nodding in what might have been approval. "Your will is strong. But that has never been in question." She moved through the garden then, incongruous in her barbarian finery and Hetawa discipline, trailing her fingers over plants, boulders, a stone wall. "What do you see here? Is everything in order?"

He frowned, wondering what in the gods' names she was talking about. "It's as I remember it, yes, except for this ugly grayness."

"Nothing out of place? You're certain?"

"Of course I'm not certain, I haven't been here for ten years." Oh, but how he had missed it! He had played in these gardens as a child, hide-and-find with his brothers and building sand castles with his sisters. He had listened to his mother, in the days long before sickness and age had weakened her voice, sing the songs of the homeland in ancient Sua. He had listened—

A sound. Something in the garden sounded wrong.

Pivoting to orient on the sound, he began to move through the palms and ferns. Water. Yes, the old fountain; he had almost forgotten it. Set into the wall, a sculpted leopard's head poured water into the open mouths of three cubs, which then spilled into a pool underneath.

"It's too soft," he murmured, half to himself. "There's not enough water, it's trickling too slowly."

"Set it right." In silence, the woman had come to stand beside him. Had she even walked, or simply manifested there?

Wanahomen looked around the fountain, searching for some mechanism, though the fountain had been built centuries before and he'd never known how the damn thing worked. But Hanani touched his arm.

"This is your world," she said. The odd blurring of her dreamform had stopped; she was wholly focused on him now. He felt obliquely flattered. "Set it right."

Abruptly Wanahomen understood. He had no need of mechanisms and construction lore when he controlled everything he saw by will alone. So he concentrated on remembering how the flow of water had gone, tuning his imagination. When the sound of the fountain matched the sound of his memory, a shiver passed down his spine that had nothing to do with the flecks of ice still melting in his hair. By pure instinct he looked up, his gaze drawn to the sky. That was wrong too. He had given it the seared, cloudless sky of the deserts around Merik-ren-aferu. Instead he willed a deeper blue, and thin wisps of moisture that would vanish by midday, but always return at night.

The shiver passed through him again, stronger now, and with it came a sensation of *rightness* so powerful that he caught his breath.

"What you feel is balance," said Hanani. "Peace. Remember it. When that feeling shifts or fades, come back to this place and do what you just did. Or create a different place; it doesn't matter. When you invoke your soulname, you shed the artifice of your waking self. When you create a realm in this empty place, everything—all that you see—*is you*. Change it, and change yourself."

He took a deep breath, savoring the sensation of rightness. It amazed him that he had not noticed its absence before. Did that mean he had been slowly slipping into madness? A frightening thought. "I don't understand how this works."

"You don't need to. No one else does." When he looked at her in surprise, she smiled, though there was little humor in it. He had the sense that the expression was more of a reflex. "This is dreaming, Prince. These are the realms of the gods. Only the strongest Gatherers have any hope of understanding: they are born to the Goddess's power in a way the rest of us can only struggle to imitate. This is why they lead us—and why we have such hope for you, Avatar of Hananja."

Wanahomen frowned at this—but even as he did, he realized the signs had been there all along, as obvious as the circles under the Shadoun's eyes. He'd thought the Hetawa's interest in him was purely political. They needed a new figurehead, and military help in ridding themselves of the Kisuati. But now he knew: they actually believed he was *one of them*. Cursed with their magic, untrained and uncontrolled—but blessed with the Goddess's favor too. To the Hetawa, that was everything.

Wanahomen had never truly believed in Hananja. Oh, he dreamed, and he had seen the power of the Hetawa's magic, but the notion that a goddess could possibly care about the tiny creatures who crept into Her dreams seemed ludicrous. The avatar business had always been just another title to him, more meaningless than the rest. But if it was the reason the Hetawa had agreed to aid him, then that title indeed had real power. And what if there was truth in it? What if the power these priests kept saying that he had—power that should have made him a Gatherer—had some other, holier purpose? What was it? And why had She given it to him?

Wanahomen shook his head and got to his feet. He would think on all this later. "So that's it, then? Now I'll be able to keep myself from going mad?"

"You can use this method to keep your humors in balance, yes. But stay vigilant, for madness takes many forms, and not all are affected by dreamblood. Your father's corruption was the proof of that."

He stiffened, and a sudden sharp wind blew through the garden. "He wasn't mad."

"Then you believe he was simply evil? Even we don't go so far, Prince."

He turned on her, scowling. "I don't believe that either."

"You know what he tried to do. He tortured a Gatherer, twice over, until that Gatherer became a monster. He unleashed those monsters on his enemies and allies alike, sentencing all to fates far, far worse than death—"

"It wasn't like that! *He* wasn't like that! He was—"

The garden changed, washing over with bright—though still colorless—sunlight. Now he was in the upper levels of Kite-iyan, standing on the balcony of the sumptuous, many-roomed apartment that once had been his. He looked down at himself and saw the clothing of a different life: his once-favorite leopard-skin loinskirt and a loose shirt of imported silk, the latter overlaid with the jasper collar that his mother had given him for his adulthood ceremony.

His hands were softer, his arms less muscled than they had become in ten years as a hard-living warrior—

"Wanahomen," said a voice behind him, and his heart went still. Then he turned.

Eninket, now King on Gujaareh's Throne of Dreams, crossed the room in the broad strides that had been his habit in waking. A smile was on his face, his arms held out to embrace his favorite son. Nearly paralyzed by shock and memory and still-fresh grief, Wanahomen returned the embrace, his eyes welling with tears as the dream supplied so many important details he'd all but forgotten. His father's scent, sweat and frankincense and clove oil. The tinkle of tiny gold cylinders woven into his hair. The strength of his arms, which back then—even as a young man well past the delusions of youth—Wanahomen had believed could never falter.

The day. Yes, he remembered this too. It was the day before the armies of Kisua and Gujaareh were to meet at Soijaro, in northern Kisua. The day before his father's death.

"Father," Wanahomen whispered, holding him tight. "Father."

When he opened his eyes, however, he saw something that jarred him: the templewoman. She watched them, her form still gray and white and colorless, from the far side of the room. As he watched, she blurred again, and this time he could glimpse flickers of her other self: a weeping, wailing figure. A haggard creature with eyes full of bitter compassion.

That was right. She knew what it meant to lose a father too.

Wanahomen pulled back from his father's embrace, gazing into the face of the man who had been god of his world for so long. Had there really been such sorrow lurking behind his father's expansive smile, back then? Or was that merely a trick of memory?

"What's wrong, Wana?" his father asked, half-smiling in bemusement at his expression.

"Nothing," he said. "I'm just glad to see you." So his father smiled and put a companionable arm around his shoulders, guiding him out toward the balcony.

This is your world, Hanani had said. He would see what he wanted to see. Back then, when he was a pampered prince's child, there had been much he hadn't wanted to see about his father. Now—

Hesitating a moment longer, Wanahomen closed his eyes and willed the memory to become *right*.

When he opened his eyes, his father had stepped away, leaning on the balcony railing as they gazed together at the setting sun. Now Wanahomen saw the worry-lines around his father's eyes, read the uncharacteristic tension in his body. Now Wanahomen noticed—at last—that his father would not meet his eyes.

"I want you to know," his father said, "that whatever I do tomorrow is for you."

The Reaping of the armies. His father had done it to achieve immortality, per magical lore so ancient and forbidden that most of the world had forgotten its existence—but though Wanahomen had not known this at the time, Charris had confessed the truth to him in the years since. Had Eninket become immortal, Wanahomen would have been doomed to the fate that awaited most of his siblings—a life of precarious uselessness, wealth and privilege without purpose. As a favored son, he might have been married into some high-ranking lineage in order to cement that family's ties to the throne, but he could never have achieved power or acclaim of his own, not even if he took up some profession or art. Any son of the Prince whose glory rivaled that of his father was a potential threat to the Sunset Throne.

And would his father have summoned assassins for him in that case, as tradition dictated?

His father threw him a glance then. How had Wanahomen never noticed the shame in those eyes that were so like his own?

"I want to keep you safe," Eninket said, softly. "I want your life peaceful. The burdens of rulership—" He sighed. "I would keep those from you, if I could. I would keep you as you are now, untainted."

Keep me as I am, Father? A boy in a man's body? A pet?

Beyond his father, the templewoman looked away.

"Wana? Do you understand?" His father looked up at him, troubled by his silence.

Yes, I understand. What kind of man chooses such a fate for his son? I understand exactly what you meant to do.

And yet Wanahomen sighed, rubbed his eyes, then reached up to grip his father's shoulder with one hand. That hand, not entirely to Wanahomen's surprise, was the hand he possessed now. It was no longer soft. It was lined and weathered from wind, darkened by the sun, nicked all over with scars from learning the knife, practicing the sword, fighting hand to hand. He had become the man his father never wanted to see.

"I love you, Father," he said, and it was true. "I never said that to you enough. But the wrongness here, in this world that is my soul—" He closed his eyes, hating himself for this betrayal, of his own youthful image of his father if nothing else. "It's *you*."

And closing his eyes, he willed it, all of it, to vanish. They floated again in the space between realms, which had shed its guise and showed its true nature as endless, featureless darkness. This suited his mood.

"I'm sorry," came her voice from somewhere.

"How is it that you're able to be here?" he asked. He felt empty inside the crystal wall that protected his innermost self. All his anger had burned out. He could not even hate the Hetawa anymore— for now, at last, he understood they had been right to kill his father. "If this is my place to control."

"Some part of you must want me here. I can go now, however, and leave you to sleep. The lesson is done."

"No." He willed the crystal wall of his soulname to thin and become permeable, an invitation. "Stay. We can comfort each other."

Abruptly he felt the walls of her self manifest, solid yet brittle as bone. "I need no comfort."

He had never heard her lie before.

But before he could confront her about it, she drew away. "Rest well, Prince. In peace." Swift as light, she was gone.

"And Her peace to you as well," he said. But he knew that too would be a lie for a long time.

33

(⊙)

Invitation

In the dark of her tent, Hanani sat contemplating madness.

She could feel it encroaching on her consciousness with each passing moment. She had felt it in Ina-Karekh with Wanahomen, and even in the realm between. She did not know how to escape the madness. Nor was she entirely certain that she wanted to.

Dayu. Merchant Danneh. Mni-inh. *Everyone I care for dies.*

But it hadn't been just those, had it? Azima, Gatherer Sonta-i, even the nameless Shadoun woman. She might not be the direct cause in every case, but contact with her had heralded each tragedy. She was a living, breathing omen of death.

I have feared the Banbarra, but it is they who should fear me, in truth. I should leave the waking realm before I destroy this whole tribe.

So went the madness.

She knew her thoughts were irrational. The Hetawa taught that there were no omens, save those sent directly from the Goddess in the form of true-seeings. Mni-inh, especially, would be furious with her for thinking such heresy. But no matter how fiercely she tried to hold the thoughts at bay, they always returned. And grew steadily stronger.

The only solution was not to feel at all, and not to think of the things that caused her pain. That was difficult with so many people trying to talk to her, touch her, comfort her. They didn't understand. Nothing could comfort her after Mni-inh's loss. Nothing would ever comfort her again.

Curling on her side amid the cushions, Hanani slept.

*   *   *

The tribe was in high spirits when Hanani finally emerged from her tent that morning. She had slept later than usual, her body failing to wake with the dawn for the first time in her memory. She had had no dreams. Looking around as she came outside, she spied the Banbarra who were awake clustering near the lookout point again. By their excitement and pointing, she guessed that another hunt party had arrived.

She went down to the ground level to bathe, this time surprising a few other Banbarra women at the pool. They waved in greeting and made way for her, showing more courtesy than ever before. Though she had no idea what they were saying as they chattered around her, she found just the tone of the women's voices enough to grate; they were so *happy*. When she could no longer bear their occasional bursts of laughter, she straightened, nodded a polite farewell, and left the pool. They fell silent then, though she felt their eyes on her back as she dressed. No doubt they would gossip about her once she was gone, so she obliged them and left as quickly as she could.

Back on the camp ledge, leaders of the final two Banbarra tribes, Vilisyo and Amaddur, had come up to exchange greetings with Unte and the others. The Banbarra slaves practically blurred as they hurried about, trying to prepare for the final night of the solstice and a celebration that was certain to be wilder than any in recent memory. The women of the tribe were frantic, rushing to pretty themselves; the men were more subtle about it but essentially the same. As the day wore on, Hanani witnessed sparring bouts, speed-dancing contests with a coveted bit of jewelry as the prize, and men surreptitiously lifting their veils to each other to discuss the shine of their teeth.

Hanani was hard-pressed not to hate them all.

But hate was an emotion, and she could not let herself feel that any more than she could grief, or it would all fall apart. So at last she retreated to her tent, and stayed there for the rest of the day.

Toward evening someone drummed on the flap of her tent. She did not want visitors, but she rose and untied the flaps anyhow.

Wanahomen stepped into the tent, leaving the flap wide open so that others could see inside. He, unlike everyone else she'd seen that day, looked grim and grimy, and anything but celebratory in mood. Then Hanani spied the earthenware urn he carried under one arm, and understood why.

He offered her the urn. "It's sealed. You should be able to carry it back to the Hetawa like this."

She looked at the urn and felt the first crack in her defenses. Mni-inh, he of the laughing eyes and gentle voice, reduced to this. She looked away from it and closed her eyes. "Thank you, Prince. Could you put it elsewhere for me?"

She heard him move over to the side of the tent; leather and cloth shifted. "In one of your saddlebags. I've wrapped it in a sash, to cushion it."

She nodded and moved back to the cushions to sit down, not trusting herself to speak because a knot was forming in her throat. *No feeling, no feeling.* She repeated the thought until it became real. When the knot had loosened enough that she could speak, she said, "Will the vote take place soon?"

"Tomorrow. The day after at the latest. If it goes in my favor, the troops will assemble and be ready to march within a day. The Banbarra are indeed barbarians, but in military efficiency they put all civilized lands to shame."

"And if the vote does not go in your favor?"

"That's not likely anymore." Yes, here was someone who understood that war was coming. She heard it in the weight of his voice: he did not sound happy for his achievement. "The Shadoun woman has outdone all my scheming; the leaders are united in their anger now. No doubt if we're successful, they'll ask for Gujaareh's help in wiping out the Shadoun."

"The Shadoun have already suffered, if the nightmare plague is among them."

"It doesn't matter." His voice was flat. "Gujaareh will need allies until we're strong again. And I must pay my debts."

Hanani sighed. "You speak as if it's a given that you'll win the city back."

He'd gone to stand near the open tent flap, gazing out at the camp, or perhaps just letting others see that he was doing nothing untoward with her. He had not removed his veil, but she knew him well enough now to sense his bitter smile. "What else is there for me? If I fail, no army or ally will ever follow me again. I'll have to flee north into exile—that's if the Kisuati don't capture me and make a public spectacle of my execution." He shrugged. "Optimism is easier."

Hanani could only agree. But—"The people will rally around you. You are Her Avatar. Perhaps it *is* a given you'll win."

"Nothing is a given. The Banbarra army—" He paused and sighed. "My father would laugh at even calling them an army. If all the tribes' war troops join together, the total will be a little over sixteen hundred. They fight like demons, but the Kisuati are four *thousand*, with another four who can come up from Kisua in an eightday. The nobles' troops will add perhaps two thousand to my side . . . but those are soldiers I dare not trust. Not all of my allies are as honorable as the Hetawa and the Banbarra, I'm afraid."

He *was* afraid. She could see that in the set of his shoulders and his folded arms, and the way his eyes saw but did not see the gathering revelry outside. But she had no words of comfort to offer him. There were Hetawa proverbs she could have recited, wisdom from her Teachers that she could have shared, but all of it felt meaningless now.

He sighed. "Well. I've stayed too long. Don't want tongues to start wagging." Then he glanced back at her, his expression unreadable. "I understand what you're trying to do," he said at last. "I did it too, after . . . after Mother and I left Gujaareh. But don't stay in here tonight, Hanani. The silence. It cuts you to pieces."

He thought he understood, because his father was dead. But his father had been a monster, while Mni-inh had been good and wise and kind. She looked away from Wanahomen lest she hate him too, and made her voice very cold. "I'll be fine, Prince."

"No, you won't be," he said, sounding annoyed. "But you're as stubborn and arrogant as any other woman— Gods. I shouldn't have even tried. Do as you please, then." He left, flicking the flap closed as he did so.

She retied the flaps behind him and then sat still in the darkness and silence of her tent, wishing that she could feel something of Mni-inh in the ashes he had left behind.

*   *   *

By nightfall, Hanani knew she was going to break.

Wanahomen had been right about the silence. She had sat in her tent for another hour, staring at the saddlebag and fighting the urge to fetch the urn, unwrap it, curl herself 'round it and open it to see whether it smelled like her mentor, knowing full well that to do so would leave her gibbering. Finally she had no choice; she might hate the Banbarra for rejoicing when Mni-inh was dead, but hating them was better than missing him. So finally she emerged from the tent and looked around.

All was as it had been on the first night of the eight-day solstice celebration: both ledges of the Banbarra camp—and several other nearby ledges within Merik-ren-aferu, made habitable just for their guests—were teeming with people. The walkways between tents were brighter than usual thanks to dozens of lanterns hanging from rope-lines; the whole canyon was louder than usual, the air filled with voices and music and clapping and laughter. She could even see the slaves celebrating, at a bonfire down on the ground level. High above, the Dreaming Moon was not as fat as usual, its four-banded face truncated on the right side by encroaching shadows said to herald the time of sharpest cold in northern lands. For the first time in several months the bright, winking star called *Myani* in Old Sua, or Beautiful Boy, had become visible just beneath the Moon's darkened curve. A new year had begun.

Wandering through the camp was like wandering through a dream. No one seemed to notice Hanani—not the knots of men and women, not the children who ran past her in their play. She was a river stone, unmoving while the life of the camp coursed around her. She stood among a thousand other souls and felt utterly alone.

"Hanani!" A familiar voice. She turned and saw Yanassa, sitting with Hendet and several other women near one of the fires. Yanassa rose and came over to her, smiling and taking her hands. "You came out—good! I didn't put all that work into your hair for you to hide it indoors. Come, come."

It was easier to give in than to resist, and so she went with Yanassa to sit by the fire.

"Here," said one of the women, thrusting something at her in a hollowed gourd. She took it and drank without looking, and only realized what it was when her throat seemed to catch fire. Choking and coughing, she nearly dropped the gourd, but someone took it from her. Good-natured laughter surrounded her; someone rubbed her back to help her recover. "Sipri," said the same woman who had given her the drink. "From the tea, yes?"

"Wh-what?" Hanani was still trying to breathe.

"It's made from the same plant as the cold tea you like so much," said Yanassa. She was the one rubbing Hanani's back. "You want more?"

Liquor of some sort. Sharers were never supposed to drink, since narcomancy required an unimpaired will. She took the gourd back and drank another few swallows, grimacing while it burned its way down.

Hendet, who had been watching Hanani from across the fire with narrowed eyes, said, "You aren't well, Sharer-Apprentice."

Hanani looked up at her. Yanassa leaned forward to search Hanani's face as well, her own mirth fading.

"No," Hanani said to Gujaareh's queen. "I'm not."

Yanassa gave Hanani a pained smile, and deftly took the gourd of sipri from her hands. "You will be. We'll care for you. Don't worry."

Hanani was not worried. She simply did not care.

"Well, well," said one of the other women. They followed her gaze. Over at another fire, a young woman of perhaps sixteen or seventeen floods sauntered toward one of the Issayir warriors who sat amid a knot of men. His gaze sharpened with interest; he continued his conversation with the other men, but it was obvious as daylight that he was paying no real attention to them. The girl had a bit of jewelry in one hand; it was difficult for Hanani to see exactly what it was. But as the girl passed the warrior, she looked him in the eye and dropped the item as if by accident. With an innocent look that fooled no one, she moved on toward another of the women's fires.

The warrior grinned and snatched up the item. The men around him elbowed and jostled him good-naturedly, trying to make him drop the thing, but he held on tight.

"So Teniant has made her choice at last!" Yanassa sounded pleased. "That one is the Issayir's hunt leader. A good choice."

"I disagree," said another woman, scowling. "A man readying himself for war may be too rough for such a young girl."

"I'm sure he can quiet his warrior nature for a single night," Yanassa said dismissively. "I can't see a man becoming hunt leader under Unte's brother if he has a taste for brutalizing decent women. The Issayir are not the Dzikeh."

Another woman quickly shushed Yanassa, darting a glance about to see whether there were any Dzikeh nearby, but Hanani ignored them, staring at the Issayir warrior. An urge developed in her heart, neither fully formed nor logical. She would have called it instinct if she had bothered to think about it at all. But she had no desire to think.

And so while Yanassa and the other woman continued to bicker, Hanani rose. Yanassa had given her a beautiful, elaborate earring that clipped around the edge of one ear in three places. She reached up to remove it.

"Sharer-Apprentice?" Hendet's voice, full of surprise and a hint of suspicion. Ignoring her, Hanani walked away from the fire.

She found who she wanted at a fire near the edge of camp, talking quietly with some of his men. Charris stood against the rocky wall nearby, subtly at guard. He saw Hanani coming before anyone else, and frowned in puzzlement as she approached. Then someone nudged Wanahomen, who turned to look at her, curious.

The earring felt cold in Hanani's hand. She clutched it so tightly that its sharper parts threatened to draw blood. But she came forward anyhow, meeting Wanahomen's gaze as steadily as she could, and dropped the earring at his feet.

The men fell silent. She did not look at them; she did not want them. Wanahomen stared down at the earring, his eyes widening. He looked up at her in wordless disbelief.

Silent, empty, Hanani went back to her tent to wait.

34

Dirge

The easternese told tales of souls that could not make the journey to Ina-Karekh for whatever reason, and were doomed to walk the waking realm forever as mist and sorrow. The templewoman had looked like one of these.

Wanahomen stared after her as she drifted away, and then looked down at the earring at his feet. "She can't have intended this," he murmured. He picked it up; it was so plainly meant for him that none of the other men were even pretending to claim it. "She can't know what it means."

"Looked to me she knew exactly what it meant," said Ezack. Even he sounded uneasy, despite his smile.

"Stubborn, arrogant woman," he said, closing his hand around the earring. It was cold, though it had just been clutched in her hand; one of the pendants had broken loose when she dropped it. Cold and broken, just like her. "Thoughtless, *stupid* woman—"

He stood and stormed after her, not allowing himself to question his own fury. Reaching her tent, he went inside, yanked away his face-veil, and threw the earring back at her feet. "You are out of your mind," he snarled.

The tent was lit by a single lantern hanging from the central tentpole. Hanani stood away from it, half in shadow with her back to him. Abruptly Wanahomen's anger chilled as he realized she was staring at the saddlebag he'd put Sharer Mni-inh's ashes into.

"I do not dispute that," she said in a near-whisper. Then she uttered a weak, unsteady laugh that unnerved him even further.

He sighed, pulling off his headcloth and rubbing a hand over his braids, out of habit. "This isn't what you need, Hanani. You need— Gods, I don't know what you need. But not this."

"That's for me to decide, isn't it?"

He stared at her, incredulous. "When it involves *my body*?"

Her unadorned ear tilted toward him. "You wanted me yesterday."

"That doesn't mean I want you now!"

To his alarm, she began to tremble all over, so violently that her hair ornaments jingled. The contrast between this and her too-calm, too-flat voice was truly astonishing. "I see. Forgive me, then; I misunderstood. I'll choose someone else."

"You'll *what*?" He went to her and took hold of her shoulders, turning her around to face him. It was like grabbing a wild animal; she went taut, her eyes wide and mindless with panic. She did not scream, but he suspected that was a near thing.

"Hanani—" He shook his head, though he loosened his grip at once. "Dearest Goddess, *look* at you. You don't want a man. Why are you doing this?"

Some of the panic faded from her eyes, replaced by a misery so deep that all of his remaining anger vanished. She looked away from him and made a halfhearted effort to twist out of his grasp. "It doesn't matter. I know what I want."

"No, you—"

"*I know what I want!*" She screamed the words, her fists clenching, her face so distorted by rage that for a moment he didn't recognize her. Then she lunged at him, hands turning to claws, and suddenly he had to keep hold of her to prevent her from tearing his throat out. Or using her magic on him—but he could not let himself fear her, not now. "Get out! You're no use to me, I can't trust you anyway, *you can't help me!*"

He fought her for a moment, then realized he would have to change tactics. Instead of trying to keep her hands away, he pulled them to his chest. "Here," he snapped, flattening her palms over his heart. "You want me gone? You know the way. Do to me what you did to Azima."

She froze, eyes suddenly wide with fear. "No. I won't kill again."

"You don't have to. Your mentor gave me pain once. Drove me to my knees with a touch. Do that now, and I'll know you truly want me to leave so some other fool can come in here and be 'useful' to you. I'll know you can at least protect yourself." He braced himself in case he'd guessed wrong about her, but he did not think he was wrong. And indeed, instead of hurting him, she tried to escape again.

"Let go!"

"You say you know what you want! Who would you rather have besides me? Shall I send Charris in to you? Unte perhaps—he's old, but he fathered another child just last year. Or will you have the first man who comes at you with lust instead of wits? You should have let Azima rape you, in that case!"

She flinched, but then shook her head. "What does it matter, Prince? You hate me anyhow. Just let me go."

He took a deep breath. "I don't hate you. I did once, but that was wrong. In fact—" He almost laughed; this was the last conversation he'd ever expected to have with a Hetawa priest. "You're fine enough, and admirable enough, that I'm actually tempted. But *this is wrong too*, can't you see that? There's something wrong with you, and *this will not fix it*."

She lifted her head slowly; he could have pitied her for the confusion in her expression alone. While she seemed to grope for words, he squeezed her hands and said, "You said I couldn't help you. Help you how, Hanani? What is it you need?"

She said nothing, but she looked at the saddlebag again. Wanahomen found himself heartily wishing he hadn't given her the damned urn until it was time to return to Gujaareh.

"Your mentor is gone." He said it as gently as he could, and yet she still flinched as if he'd lifted a hand to her. An idea came to him. "Tell me what Mni-inh would do, Hanani, if he were here. Tell me how he would help you."

It was completely irrational. If Mni-inh had still been alive, she would have been fine. But those who dealt in dreams learned to think in dream-logic, so it did not surprise him at all that she frowned and blinked and seemed to focus on him, as though the words made perfect sense. "H-he would hold me." She lowered her eyes. "No. He didn't do that often, not anymore. But I, I wanted him to. I always wanted him to."

"All right." Moving carefully—for she was still tensed, ready to bolt or worse—he let go of her hands and took hold of her shoulders again. He pulled her closer, and when she did not fight or panic again, he slid his arms around her completely. "There. Like this?"

She quivered. Leaned her head against him. Pressed her face into his chest. He felt something in her body gather, poise itself—

And then she *howled*. It was the only word he could think of to describe the sound she made, so far beyond a sob or a moan that it sounded as if it had been torn out of her soul. It was worse even than the sound she'd made after Azima's death. This was agony, torment, and she screamed it out again and again as she clung to him, pulling his robes and shaking with the effort until he thought she would break of that alone.

There seemed no way to deal with such pain other than to let it run its course, so he held her and let her scream.

The flap of Hanani's tent opened, and someone peered in. Hendet. As mistress of the *an-sherrat*, only she had the right to invade Hanani's privacy. She looked them over for a moment, then inclined her head to Wanahomen before withdrawing again and flicking the flap shut. Doubtless she would reassure those outside, who might hear and misconstrue, of what was actually happening.

Hanani's voice gave out sometime after the twentieth or thirtieth cry. She sobbed then, helpless and anguished—and angry too, for now and again she made a fist of one hand and pounded him with it. Resigning himself to bruises and a damp tunic, he finally lifted her and moved them both to the cushions, lying down and arranging her so that she could spend the rest of the night crying on him if she needed to. He'd realized after the first unleashing that there was more to this than grief over Mni-inh's death. Perhaps she cried for other losses, or perhaps she simply sought to vent feelings suppressed for all her Hetawa-bound life. Regardless, he found himself rubbing her back and murmuring vague reassurances—"Shh, shh, you're not alone, don't worry"—which seemed to soothe her.

And perhaps, given his new understanding of his father, and his fears of the coming battle, he soothed himself a little as well.

Gradually she quieted. Wanahomen dozed at one point, waking when instinct prompted him. Hours had passed, though the sounds of the celebration outside hadn't dimmed at all. The Banbarra could and would revel all night when sufficiently motivated. The lantern had gone out, but there was plenty of the Dreamer's light coming through the tent's smokehole. He guessed it was midnight or thereabouts.

Turning his head, he saw that Hanani was awake, her head pillowed on his chest, her eyes open and dry but lost in thought. One hand was still fisted on the cloth of his tunic. It made her look very young.

"Feeling any better?" he asked.

She drew in a deep breath, her eyes still gazing into the distance. "Tired," she whispered. Her voice was hoarse.

"You should rest, then."

Her brow furrowed; she lifted her head and looked up at him. He suppressed a grimace as the movement of her head exposed a wide wet area on his tunic. "Do you have to leave?"

"No." He smiled ruefully. "In fact, after accepting your invitation I'm *supposed* to stay all night, or until you tire of me. Are you tired of me?"

She ducked her eyes and smiled. It was a weak, barely noticeable thing as smiles went, but he was relieved almost to tears to see it. It was the first normal thing she'd done in days. "No. But then, we've done nothing that would tire either of us." Her shoulders tensed again, the beginning of unease.

She should have been exhausted after that storm of grief, but he decided not to point this out to her. He did address the unease, however. "The Banbarra will think all sorts of things, but we know the truth." He shrugged. "As long as word of tonight doesn't get back to the Hetawa, there's no problem. Let me up for a moment."

She seemed surprised that she still had tight hold of his tunic, but she let him go. He sat up and pulled off his tunic and the under-shirt, and laid them on the rug to dry. Then, spying an uneaten meal at the side of the tent, he got up and checked the flask: cold tea. There was only one cup, but he brought that over and filled it, offering it to her. She gave him a weary nod of thanks and drained it. After she'd drunk a second cup, she gave it back and he poured the last of the tea for himself. Then he lay back down, holding his arm out so that she could curl against his side again.

She hesitated, apparently shy of his bare chest. "Skin dries faster than cloth," he explained. "That way you can weep on me to your heart's content."

That earned him another tired smile. The tiredness won out; she lay back down, her hair tickling his shoulder, her hand resting lightly on his belly. He sighed, pulling a nearby blanket over them both against the night's cool, and enjoying the contact. He'd always preferred it when women took pleasure in him for more than just the one thing.

The silence stretched out, punctuated by the distant beat of a drum and a dozen voices singing a raucous song. Wanahomen had begun to drift again when Hanani's voice pulled him back. The tea had done her good: she was not so hoarse now.

"I don't care," she said. "Whether word gets back to the Hetawa."

He closed his eyes and rubbed her back, wishing she would sleep. "It would make things awkward for you when you return. Me as well."

"I'll tell them that I made you come to me. They can't fault you for that. And I'm the one they would blame anyhow. You never made an oath to Hananja." Her hand on his belly tightened; he hoped she didn't hit him again. "But I don't care what they think anymore."

She would, of course, when her grief over Mni-inh's death had faded and she had the wherewithal to consider her future again. He would ask Yanassa to help control the rumors that constantly ran rampant through the tribe, to lessen the chance that word might reach the ears of Hanani's superiors.

"Sleep," he said firmly. "No lessons this time, and no magic. We both need rest."

She nodded and fell silent, and eventually Wanahomen slept.

* * *

The city again, in color this time. This was Ina-Karekh, true dreaming, and not the mirror of his soul that was the realm between. Yet for some reason he seemed to have been drawn to the shadowlands. The sky was a charnel pit of tumbling, scattered clouds flecked with lightning. Wanahomen stood on the steps of the Hetawa, and in its doorway stood a shadowed, swaying form.

"Father," Wanahomen said. He inclined his head in greeting.

The shadowed form said nothing, and did not move beyond its unsteady shift from side to side. Wanahomen looked down at himself, but saw none of the creeping foulness of before. The damage had been repaired.

"My son, my heir," said the shadowed figure in its clotted voice. "My reborn soul."

"No," Wanahomen said, frowning. "Your son, your heir if Hananja wills it, but my soul is my own, Father. As is my future."

There was silence for a moment. He thought he sensed surprise from the thing in the doorway. Then teeth gleamed from the dimness, whether in a snarl or a smile he could not tell.

"Niim." The voice had changed. It was less sibilant all of a sudden, more human and real. "Strength devours strength in the realms of dream, Niim. Hate and fear grow ever stronger. But compassion...She has had so little of that. And trust? Love? Against these she has no power."

"Who?" Startled by the dream's change, Wanahomen climbed one step, another. "Who, Father? Hanani? Yanassa?" Those names did not feel right. "Tiaanet?" Closer, though more troubling. "Do you warn me against the woman I want as my queen?"

Another gleam of teeth; definitely a smile now, and a real one. *This was his father.* He felt it with every instinct he possessed: not a phantasm, not a distorted memory, but truly the soul of Eninket, damned to the shadowlands for his cruelty and greed. The Hetawa had declared Eninket mad, and he had been, in waking. But somehow, in this realm, it seemed he had found some measure of peace.

And it was as a whole, healed man that Eninket said, "Be well, my son. Be a better man than I."

"Father!" Wanahomen lunged up the steps, no longer caring what horror waited for him in the shadows. "Father, no, wait—"

But the city faded, and the silence between dreams was his only reply.

35

(·⊙·)

Comfort

Hanani waited in a dream of the Hetawa's Hall of Blessings. After a long while—the time meant nothing, it was a dream, but she marked it anyhow out of waking habit—the shimmering shadows near the donation alcoves stirred, and Gatherer Nijiri stepped forth.

"Hanani?" He frowned. "Where is Mni-inh?"

She got to her feet, came down from the dais, and bowed low over both hands. "Dead, Gatherer."

She heard rather than saw Nijiri's soft intake of breath. He said nothing, but the Hall reverberated, just a little, with his shock. Since she'd expected this—he had loved Mni-inh too—it was an easy matter for her to hold the dream steady, balancing its structure against his surge of anguish.

"The nightmare plague," she explained. "A woman of the Shadoun brought it into the Banbarra camp. We didn't know. Mni-inh-brother tried to heal her."

Nijiri let out a sigh that was half moan, and turned away to rest his hands against the nightstone statue of the Goddess. In waking this was never permitted, but in dreams there were no rules. When

Hanani looked up, she saw him leaning against the statue as if he needed the support to stand; his head hung out of sight. She sat down on the edge of the dais to wait.

"Even in the desert!" he breathed, then let loose another great sigh. "Mni-inh was all I had left for friends in the Hetawa beyond my pathbrothers. This plague is an abomination worse than the Reaper. *Indethe etun'a Hananja*, let him walk in Your peace until dreaming ends."

Hanani remained silent, allowing him time for grief, as was proper. When he finally turned, however, his expression was stricken; he came to her and crouched, taking her hands at once. "Forgive me, Hanani. I think first of my own pain and forget yours. Let me give you peace—"

She got to her feet and stepped back from his touch as politely as she could. "I will find my own, Gatherer. Thank you. The P— The Banbarra, they are very kind. They're helping me."

He looked surprised, but nodded. "Was the plague spread to others before..."

"No. Mni-inh-brother's death ended it."

"Such a terrible thing to be thankful for." He fell silent for a moment, and the air felt heavy with his sorrow. Then he shook his head. "But I have little time. Share this with the Prince: the city is as ready as we could make it. If he attacks soon, the people will fight at his side. They're angry enough to fight without him, really, but we hope they'll hold 'til the right time."

She nodded. "I shall pass the message, Gatherer. I believe the Prince's plans culminate in the next few days."

"Good. The Sentinels have made agreements with some of the military caste—those few of the Sunset Guard who managed to escape the purges, officers of the former army, a few mercenary companies persuaded to return and fight for free. They have a series of sabotages to implement as soon as the Prince's force begins its assault. This should disrupt the Kisuati's defenses and prevent them from regrouping as effectively. Beyond that, it's up to him."

"Yes, Gatherer."

He paused, then, and looked hard at her. She had chosen to appear in the Banbarra clothes that Yanassa had given her, rather than her red drapes. His Gatherer eyes no doubt recognized other, more subtle changes. "Are you truly well, Hanani?"

She had expected this too, but that made it no easier to endure. "I'm better than I was, Gatherer, and I believe I'll be better still with time. But—" She hesitated, then spoke what was in her heart, since he had already sensed it. "But I don't know if I can ever again be *well*. Mni-inh, he and Dayuhotem—" She bowed her head. "I know we're to love all our brothers, but there was no one in the Hetawa who meant more to me than the two of them. Without them I am a river barge set adrift with no steering pole, headed for the yawning sea."

His expression was more compassionate than she had ever seen it. "I understand," he said, very softly. She believed that he truly did. "I have no comfort to offer, unfortunately. Dreamblood is only cautery; it can ease pain for a time, when the wound is fresh and most in danger of festering. Beyond that, it's best if the soul heals itself—" He caught himself. "But you are the healer here."

"Only of the flesh," she said. "You Gatherers have always taken care of the soul."

He gave her a smile so gentle and kind that she wondered how she had ever thought him cold. "There's more overlap than you think, Apprentice. Your mentor taught me that."

Before she could speak again, he paused and abruptly looked away, frowning. "I must go. My dreamer is waking." Like all Gatherers, he could not dream on his own. He must have come to her through the dreams of some acolyte or apprentice at the Hetawa, or perhaps a fellow Servant of some other path. It was odd, however, that he had not simply put his jungissa on the dreamer to hold that person asleep.

"Be well, Hanani," he said, stepping back. "Dayu and Mni-inh were not your only friends in the Hetawa, no matter how you might feel. You aren't alone." Then, holding up a hand in farewell, he vanished.

*   *   *

Hanani opened her eyes in the dimness of the tent. She couldn't tell the hour, but the sounds of the celebration outside had faded. There was still plenty of activity in the camp, but the music was softer and slower now. She could hear no children running or shouting, which meant that it was at least past their bedtimes.

Beside her—her head still rested on his shoulder—Wanahomen slept, his eyes flickering beneath their lids. She wondered what Gatherer Nijiri would have made of her decision to train him. Had Mni-inh told him about that? Knowing Mni-inh, she doubted it. For that matter, she wondered what Nijiri would have made of Wanahomen in her bed, however innocently. She would not be the first in the Hetawa to endure embarrassing rumors. There was Gatherer Nijiri himself, and Sentinel Renamhut was said to have a woman and daughter in the artisans' district, and Teacher Ide was known to have a taste for shunha-dark apprentices. In fact, to judge by the rumors, quite a few of the Hetawa's acolytes and priests carried on secret affairs, though much of that was probably exaggeration. Hanani had never understood why Mni-inh took such care to keep his distance from her when half the Hetawa suspected them anyhow, and the rest had their own secrets to hide.

She sighed, contemplating the weight of Wanahomen's arm against her back. Gatherer Nijiri would have understood, she decided. Wanahomen was not a Gatherer himself, and he had no dreamblood to give her, but he had a Gatherer's gift for sensing when comfort was needed. She would have broken if not for him. Mni-inh: she closed her eyes, allowing the pain to wash over her for a moment. It was as if someone had reached inside her and hollowed out her soul. The edges of the empty place were raw, shaped to fit him; nothing would ever fill it. Still, Wanahomen's presence eased the ache.

Restless from her own thoughts, she shifted to get more comfortable. Her hand, on his belly, caught on a line of roughness; a scar. Puzzled—the belly-wound she'd healed should have left no scar—she traced the roughness and realized it was a different injury. This one was not as long, but the thickness and shape of the scar was troubling, as was its location just under his rib cage. It had been deep, this wound, and it had healed badly, reopening at least once.

"It was a serrated knife," Wanahomen said.

He'd spoken softly, but Hanani still started in surprise. She felt his hand rub her back, soothing, which almost made her jump again. She had noticed that the Banbarra constantly touched one another in ways that Gujaareen did not: casual linking of the arms, nudges, affectionate caresses for children or even animals. Wanahomen had been among them long enough that he must have picked up some of their habits. She found his easy, careless touches exotic and disturbing.

Then she focused on his words. "A *serrated* knife? Why would anyone use such a thing on a man?"

"To cause pain, I assume. Probably encourages festering, too. I almost died from the fever alone." His voice was heavy with sleep; in the Moonlight she could see that he had not opened his eyes. "It's a foolish sort of thing to use in battle—too likely to catch on something at the wrong moment. But the man who used it on me was no warrior. Just a coward, corrupt as any other slaver."

Hanani shook her head, privately amazed that he had survived at all without a Sharer's aid. "You were a slave?"

He nodded and yawned, coming more awake. "For a brief time, I and my mother and Charris. We were captured fleeing the city by Damlushi traders, who had camped out along the northgoing trails like vultures to take any Gujaareen they could because they knew our army was busy elsewhere. Apparently Gujaareen are known to make good slaves—healthy, educated, nonviolent." Wanahomen's lip curled. "And though we'd taken the last of the Sunset Guard with us, we were overwhelmed. They'd hoped to get riches from us too."

Hanani frowned and looked down at his wrists. She had noticed marks there before, though they were faint. The remnants of scars. "They chained you."

He nodded again, opening his eyes at last. "They were taking us south, afraid to sell Gujaareen so close to home. In the south we might have been separated, and it would have been much harder to escape or buy our way free. So I challenged the head of the caravan to some game. I don't remember what. If I won, he had to sell us hereabouts. I won, but he was a poor loser. As they made us ready for the sale, he knifed me and bound the wound so that it wouldn't show. I had to pretend I felt nothing, and look healthy, or no one would buy me."

Hanani caught her breath. Such an act was indeed corrupt—but then, out here beyond the Gatherers' reach, corrupt souls seemed plentiful as ants. "And the Banbarra bought you?"

"Mmm-hmm. Unte's firstwife, Widanu. She was furious when she found out about my wound. My mother saved us then, because I was already coming down sick with wound-fever and Widanu would have killed me to put me out of my misery. Mother bargained with Widanu for my life, offering all the jewels she'd brought out of Gujaareh; we had hidden them in a cave in the foothills before the Damlushi took us. That established her as a woman of value in the eyes of the Banbarra, and gave me value too as her son, so we were set free. Charris...Well. Widanu had to bring back *something*. But as soon as Mother had built our wealth enough—she's always been shrewd—we bought him back. He won't let us free him because having a slave adds to our clan's prestige. Stubborn old man."

Hanani absorbed this, tracing the scar again with her fingers for the simple novelty of the thing; she had not seen many scars. Magic left no marks. Then her eyes picked out another blemish on his skin—a little divot the size of a glass coin, carved from the flesh just beneath his collarbone. She sat up, curious, and then noticed two other marks: one just above his hipbone, and another perilously near his heart. If all of them had stories like the first, she understood better why there was so little peace in him.

His skin was soft as chamois leather around the scars. Such fragile stuff to have withstood so much violence. She traced along his collarbone to his shoulder, then drew her fingers down one arm, over the rise and fall of the muscles there. She had studied the bodies of the Gathered as part of her training, knew the names of every tendon and bone, had searched within parts that had no name to find the soul's ever-moving seat—but that was a different matter, somehow, from contemplating the warm, breathing whole of a living being. It took so little to reduce all this solid *aliveness* into ash. Someday Wanahomen would be like Mni-inh, a little jar of nothing. All that mattered of him would have gone on to Ina-Karekh.

So important to treasure life, protect it, understand it in fullness, while it yet lived.

"Prince," she said. His eyes were still on her, faintly puzzled now. It was the Banbarra way to touch casually; it was not the Gujaareen way. She had confused him with her explorations. "Are you Gujaareen?"

He stiffened, angry all of a sudden. "You know damn well that I am—"

"You act more Banbarra than you realize, I think," she said, still

342

studying his body, tracking his breathing. "I understand why—out here, it's safer to be Banbarra than Gujaareen. Safer to be *anything* than Gujaareen." She stopped then, her hand on his belly. Beneath her fingers, his abdominal muscles were more tense than they should have been. "But is it an act? Something you've pulled over your true self like a cloak? Or have you *become* the cloak? I ask because you have been kind to me, and you have also been cruel, and I don't know which is the real you."

His belly rose slightly with his inhalation, though he was silent for a moment. "Both, I suppose," he said at last. "It isn't a thing I think about. I've lived among the Banbarra for nearly half my life; when I'm with them I think as they do. I even think in Chakti. But when I'm around you, and your mentor—" He sighed. "I suppose I must become a bit more Gujaareen. A strange feeling, being two men." He hesitated a moment more, then reached down and caught her hand. She felt him searching her face. "But the cruelty is not a *Banbarra* thing, Hanani, if that's what you want to know. That part of me is all Gujaareen, and it comes from my father. You've helped me understand that, these past few days."

She nodded. "Does it please you? To be as cruel as your father?"

He did not answer for several breaths; when he spoke, the word was very soft, and tinged with shame. "No. I need that cruelty. I would not have survived this long without it. But I do not *like* it."

Hanani nodded. She got to her feet, then, and stepped out of her shoes, beginning the laborious process of removing all the dangling bangles and tinkling jewels Yanassa had made her wear. She dropped them into the decorative bag they were meant to be stored in. "Then you aren't corrupt."

Wanahomen sat up on one elbow, frowning at her. "Good to know. But what are you doing?"

"Undressing." She was surprised at her own calm.

There was sudden, startled stillness behind her. She tugged off her overshirt and hung it from a tent-peg; when she turned back to him, he was staring at her. "That isn't a good idea, Hanani."

She was heartily sick of people speaking to her as though she could not understand the implications of her own actions.

"I do not demand. I ask." She stepped out of her skirts; his eyes followed them down her legs, as if he could not quite believe what he was seeing. "I ask your Banbarra self, or your kinder self, however you prefer to think of it. I would like sex. Will you do this with me?"

When she turned back from hanging the skirts, Wanahomen's expression showed something close to fright. He had grabbed his own shirt, clutching it in his hands as if he meant to ward her off with it. "Have you gone mad again?"

"I was never mad." He had helped her back from that edge, and she was glad for it. It was unfair of her to ask him for more, perhaps, but there was no one else who would understand. She had to hope that the part of him that was a Gatherer, however unrefined it might be, would want to help again.

"You're serious. This is—" He froze as she untied her loincloth and dropped it in a basket. "You really mean it."

Hanani tugged off the shift that had been beneath her shirt. She wore only her breast-wrappings beneath, and when she finished laying the shift aside, she was amused to see that his eyes had gone straight to this part of her, as though he had never seen her in Sharers' garb. Perhaps her breasts had been unattractive to him then, framed by men's clothing? She began the laborious process of unwinding the wrappings as he gazed at her like a thirsty man in the desert. "Obviously I do, Prince."

He dragged his eyes upward, and there was a clear wariness in his expression. "You don't love me."

At this she paused, surprised. "No, I don't. Must I?"

A half-smile, half-grimace rippled across his face. "I suppose not.

No one can fault you for honesty, templewoman, I'll give you that."
He got to his feet and turned to face her at last, still holding his
shirt, though he made no move to put it on. "But you must *trust* me
for this, at least, and—" He looked away. "And as you said: I have
been cruel to you."

Hanani sighed and began to wonder whether she'd made a mistake. He felt so deeply, so quickly, this man. She had hoped he
would simply act on his desire, not talk things to death. Yet she
should have expected this too: a man so ruled by his emotions must
of course serve them before making any decision. Mni-inh had
taught her that long ago, when she'd asked him why he'd volunteered to serve as her mentor. *It wasn't something I thought about,* he'd
told her. *I just saw you needing a mentor, and the other Sharers balking
as though your femaleness were a plague that would taint them. That
sort of foolishness— I suppose it made me angry. I acted because of that.*

The thought that Wanahomen had something of Mni-inh in
him, however unwelcome he would find the comparison, made
Hanani feel better about her decision.

"I've let you into my dreams," she said. "I have seen the secrets of
your soul, and shown you a few of my own. The body—" She
shrugged. "It can be healed, changed, ended. It's an easy thing to
manipulate. But the soul has meaning and permanence..." His
frown deepened, and she faltered silent. It was too hard to explain.
She was no Teacher.

"This is nothing to you, then." He sounded bitter, and she didn't
know why. She stepped closer, touching his arm to try and understand, but he would not meet her eyes. Was he offended that she
wanted to use him in this way? Perhaps. But perhaps she could still
persuade him with the truth.

"No, Prince." Up close, he smelled of sweat and sand—but also
herbs, like those used by most Gujaareen for bathing and medicine.
Anise and calendula, which she had seen growing around the

canyon, and something finer that he must have bought in Gujaareh: aged ambergris. It was a scent that reminded her of the Hetawa, where it was burned as incense. Another luxury she'd failed to question, like her red Sharer-drapes; she'd seen ambergris in the market, and it was fantastically expensive. But it did not surprise her at all that Wanahomen, despite his exile and spare barbaric existence, would still find some small way to treat himself like a prince.

She smiled and touched the scar beneath his collarbone again. He straightened, perhaps in surprise. Barbarian skin, Gujaareen blood and bone. He thought of himself as two men, but she saw only one.

"This is life to me." She met his eyes, trying to speak to the wariness there. "This is flesh. It is...pain and weakness and things that frighten me. But flesh is something I can control, Prince. I can make it stronger. I can heal it when it goes wrong. I need that, that certainty, right now. Does that make sense to you?"

His face twitched through several expressions, all too quick and complex for her to interpret. "I...Yes. Strange as it sounds, it does. But what of your Servant's Oath, Sharer-Apprentice? I've taken so much from you already. I would not add more to the pile."

"The oath is mine to discard, not yours to take." Hanani set her jaw. "Tomorrow, maybe, I'll be able to give all of myself to Hananja again without qualm. Tonight—" She sighed, feeling both ancient and young, and incomparably lonely. "Hananja has also taken enough from me, Prince."

More than She has had any right to take. But Hanani did not say this aloud, because he was just Gujaareen enough that it would disturb him.

Wanahomen looked at her hand on his arm, then at her face, searching. Hanani had no idea what he sought, but after a moment he sighed. Very deliberately, he let his shirt drop back to the floor.

"Flesh is not just pain," he said softly. "You shouldn't think of it that way."

She shrugged and resumed unwinding her breast-wrappings. "It's all I know."

"I can show you more." He looked almost shy as he said it.

In spite of herself, she smiled. "I would be grateful."

When she let the last of her breast-wrappings fall to the floor, he looked at her for a long while, studying her with his eyes as she had done him with her hands. When he stepped out of his pants, very ready for her, she turned back to the cushions to lie down. He stopped her with a hand on her shoulder, then—to her great surprise—knelt at her feet. His breath had gone harder, but there was reverence as well as need in his gaze.

"Women are goddesses," he said. "Pleasure is your due tithe. That *is* the Gujaareen way, after all—I remember that much. And it is my duty as Prince to see the tithe delivered properly." He said this with no hint of irony or mockery; Hanani stared at him in wonder. And when he spread his arms, lifting his chin and making an offering of himself, something within her that had been held tight, despite her words, relaxed.

She stepped closer, and his arms folded around her in the most careful of embraces.

This, then, was the manifestation of peace: silence. They were Gujaareen. They had no need of shouts, moans, names gasped as declarations of pride or devotion. He pressed nothing she did not want, held back nothing she desired. While he moved against her, she studied the steady flex of his muscles, the pace and pitch of his breath, the way her every sigh and touch redirected the humors within the miracle of his flesh. This was real magic, not dreamstuff, written in solid, aware blood and bile and ichor and seed. At the height of the matter Hanani channeled this new magic into a prayer for Mni-inh, so that the Goddess might bring his soul back home. And in that held breath, as Hanani hovered almost outside herself, the Avatar of Hananja gripped her tight and shuddered within her and breathed hot into her ear: "*Yes.*"

She closed her eyes, grateful, and at peace.

36

(⊙)

Legacy

It had not been difficult for Sunandi to arrange certain matters within Yanya-iyan once the Gatherers and Superior were interned. The Protectors had not cared where the prisoners were kept so long as they were secure, and so Sunandi installed them in a set of guest-rooms that had apparently been made to fit northerner tastes: with sturdy lockable doors, and only the narrowest of windows. The rooms would have been unpleasantly hot during the growing-season months—there was a reason Gujaareen left doors off rooms—but in these not-quite-floodseason days they were comfortable enough. In addition, she had selected rooms that were spaced widely, and posted a guard outside each door, so that no one would think her lax. However, she had asked Anzi's aid in selecting guards with certain useful characteristics. One, whom she placed in charge of the Superior, was the secret-son of a Teacher from the Hananjan temple in Kisua. Two more were Hananjans themselves; perhaps a fifth of all Kisuati had devoted themselves to the faith. The fourth was a Gujaareen man, one of the few military-castes who'd managed to find employment with the Kisuati army. He was a lowly foot soldier now; in Gujaareh's army he had been an officer.

Such guards, she would tell the Protectors if they asked—she doubted they would ask, but it was always wise to have explanations ready—would ensure that the Gatherers and Superior were not mistreated during their confinement. Already there had been incidents in the two days since the Gatherers had been taken into custody: a spate of arrests as artisans refused to hand over work commissioned by Kisuati citizens, and merchants turned away Kisuati buyers or stopped accepting Kisuati coins. After several pairs of soldiers were attacked and beaten by gangs of angry Gujaareen, Anzi had ordered that soldiers patrol only in troops of sixteen, and he had stationed a troop in every neighborhood of the city. Despite this, a curfew and ban on assemblages had not prevented a riot—the first that had occurred in centuries—in the Unbelievers' District. Only later had they learned that an armory was looted during the chaos. The district was being searched, but none of the weapons had yet been found. Sunandi suspected they had already made their way through the wall into the rest of the city.

The only thing that surprised her was that the violence had not yet become widespread. It felt to her as if the city was holding its breath, waiting, though for what she could not say.

The corridor where the priests were being kept was quiet when Sunandi arrived—a far cry from the busy, hectic upper floors where the Protectors had been living and working since their arrival. Indeed, the silence reminded Sunandi of the Stone Garden, a prayer space within the Gatherers' Hall at the Hetawa: the corridor had that same pervasive calm. Three of the guards nodded solemnly to her as she approached; she returned their nods. The fourth guard, the one who should have been at Nijiri's door, was missing.

Sunandi paused and glanced at the other guards. They had not yet raised the alarm, nor did they even look concerned.

A moment later, the door of the room opened and the guard—

the Gujaareen military-caste—stepped out. Spotting Sunandi, he inclined his head to her respectfully. "Dinner, Speaker," he said in accented Sua.

"Ah." She gazed at him for a moment longer, until he began to look uncomfortable. It was after midnight—late for dinner, even for a nocturnal Gatherer. But finally she came forward, and he opened the door to let her inside.

Within, the room was quiet, lit only by a single lamp and the Dreamer's light coming in through the window. She saw a meal laid out on the table: so the guard had at least had the wit to be truthful about that. Nijiri sat on the bed nearby, his back propped against the wall, watching her with as much of a look of innocence as he could muster. That, for him, wasn't much.

She folded her arms. "Good evening, little killer. Or should it be little schemer instead?"

He smiled, almost to himself. "I asked the guard to help me send a message to a friend, nothing more," he said. Then he sobered. "But the friend was…not there."

She frowned in confusion. "The guard already delivered it for you?"

"Through his dreams, yes. It's something skilled narcomancers can do." He folded his hands, his eyes lighting on the trio of scrolls she carried under one arm. "Have you brought me a gift, Jeh Kalawe?"

She ignored his question. "How long before you run out of dream-blood?"

He didn't bat an eyelash, long used to her rudeness. "Three or four eightdays, for all of us. We had time to prepare, remember."

That was a relief. "And when does the storm you summoned strike?"

He raised his eyebrows, innocence again. "Storm?"

"I know the nobles are up to something. And it's becoming more and more obvious by the day that this city is gathering itself for a fight. Are you influencing them all in their dreams?"

That elicited a genuine smile. "No Gatherer has *that* much power, Jeh Kalawe."

"Ehiru did."

A pause. "Ehiru was not a Gatherer at that time." His voice had gone cold, his smile vanishing. Instantly Sunandi regretted her words, but there was no way to rectify her error. He was Gujaareen, anyway; he would let it pass for the sake of peace between them. Forgiveness would take longer, but so be it.

She let out a sigh and forged on. "Earlier you implied that one of Eninket's sons was still alive, and with the Banbarra. My sources say there are rumors of this floating about the city as well—that a new Prince is coming who will free Gujaareh. Is this true?"

He lowered his eyes. "I told you I would forgive you, Jeh Kalawe. That promise stands even if I don't answer your questions and you have me punished for my silence."

"I'm not going to have you punished, you fool! I'm trying to help us both!" She stepped closer, lowering her voice. "The Protectors brought a thousand additional troops with them, Nijiri. They're being deployed in the city now, to help keep the peace, and they've been given orders to respond to any problems *very* harshly—death to anyone who resists. And something else is being planned, in case there's some sort of attack or citywide revolt. Something meant to break the people's spirit." She set her jaw. "I don't know what. I'm not in favor right now; nor is Anzi."

Nijiri got up and went over to the window, glancing up as if to check the Dreamer's position. It was the closest she had ever seen a Gatherer come to restlessness. "You won't regain favor by helping us, Jeh Kalawe. So why are you?"

Sunandi rolled her eyes. "I'm helping *Kisua*. This land has become too dangerous for us to hold. A few of the greedier members of our populace—some of whom are here now, in charge—will become wealthy as tensions grow, but the rest of Kisua is who will suffer as Gujaareh devours our resources and soldiers and gives back nothing but headaches. And I'm terrified of this nightmare plague getting into our populace. You know we have no defense against magic."

"We would help you, if that happened, once we learn how to fight it ourselves. Though it may require your people to attempt magic again."

"It won't require magic. Just a miracle."

He turned to her slowly, studying her face, and then his eyes flicked to the scrolls under her arm. "You found something."

She nodded, stifling excitement, then went over to the table, moving the tray of food to the floor. "In his search for the secret of immortality, Eninket had assembled quite a collection of lore on all sorts of magical curiosities."

Nijiri grimaced, helping her lay out the scrolls. "Like the Reaper."

"And more interesting things. This, for example." She pointed to one scroll, covered in archaic pictorals drawn with heavy black lines. She had not been able to read half of them, but the scholar who had given her the translation had been so excited to see the words of his ancestors that he'd charged a quarter less than his usual fee just for the privilege. "This speaks of a plague that nearly consumed the city—a plague no healer could combat, spread through dreams. It mentions hundreds of victims, despair throughout the land... *This has happened before*, Nijiri."

He stiffened. "We have no record of such a plague in the Hetawa."

"You have no lore regarding immortality either, yet Eninket found a way. Someone, probably many someones down the centuries, has kept your Hetawa records very neat and clean. The filth, and the truth, are all here." She patted the scrolls again.

He sighed, though he did not protest her characterization of the matter. "They must have found some way to combat the dream back then, or Gujaareh would be abandoned ruins by now. Is there any mention of the cure?"

"Yes." Sunandi shuffled the scrolls and laid out another, this one tattered and stained, written in crabbed hieratics. This one she could read herself—and had, late into the night, with a placard on her door warning Anzi and even the servants not to enter. Her eyes still ached. "This one says, here, 'A child housed the dream, drawing and trapping all others within it. When the child dreamed horrors, all suffered them, and many died. Others died sleeping, unable to eat or drink. Only when the child was slain were his victims freed.'" She straightened, looking hard at him. "It goes on to say that only a few knew of this, and that the solution was discovered by the Superior of the time. He *killed* the child, Nijiri—and then ordered the deaths of anyone who knew about it."

Nijiri's frown deepened. "Why?"

"Unknown. This was written by a former acolyte of the Hetawa—he witnessed the child's death, but no one noticed him. If they had, he would have been killed as well." She put her hand on the scroll, splaying it over the hieratics to get his attention. "This Superior was not corrupt, Nijiri. He went on to found the Sharer path, wrote some of your faith's most beautiful prayers, and enacted laws that made the city better. He was a good man. Good people kill only to keep the most dangerous secrets."

He raised his gaze to her, slowly. "What is your point, Jeh Kalawe?"

"That you must be open to solutions you wouldn't otherwise consider. That corruption is a matter of intent, not action, as your mentor told me long ago."

He was silent for a moment. "The scholar who helped you with these documents. What have you done to him?"

She had already decided to answer, if he asked—though she had

354

hoped he would not ask. "He'll be given a proper funeral with the other victims of the plague. Because that is *why* he died, if not how." When Nijiri's lips tightened, Sunandi leaned forward, bracing her hands on the table and deliberately putting her face in reach of his long, deadly Gatherer's hands. "And how many people have you murdered to keep Eninket's secrets, over the years?"

He did not reach for her, or flinch, to his credit. And she kept herself from flinching at the cold death in his eyes, which was a salve to her own pride.

"Gatherers do not murder," he said softly, with a hint of irony in his voice that chilled her even further. "All that we do is a blessing, given by Hananja unto Her people."

In the wake of that, Sunandi could do nothing but allow a moment of proper Gujaareen silence. There was something to the custom, she had decided some years ago, of letting a brief passage of time cleanse the air, after dangerous words and thoughts had tainted it.

"I make no claim to holiness, but I too do what I must for peace," she said at length. She tapped the tattered scroll. "The man who wrote this should never have committed it to paper. He did it to salve his conscience, and his weakness may save us... But when we find the ones using this pestilence as a weapon now, we must be more vigilant than our ancestors were. We must make sure this evil magic *dies here*. Will you agree to that?"

He nodded. "This is corruption of the highest order. The Hetawa must do whatever is necessary to see it cleansed."

"Even if the cleansing means killing a child?"

"That may not be the only way."

It was a relief that he hesitated, Sunandi decided, even though she could not permit him to remain stubborn on this. She would know to fear him only when his conscience died—or if she ever did anything harmful without purpose. Then he would come for her. She had always known and accepted that.

"It's the only *certain* way. Will you do it, if it comes to that? Gather an innocent?"

Another necessary moment passed.

"I'm not my mentor," he said softly. She was surprised to read shame in his face. "I've never had his honor."

She hesitated, but then reached out and put a hand on his shoulder. "You're different from Ehiru, true, but that isn't a bad thing. He thought only of Hananja, while you think first of Hananja's people."

He gave her a thin smile whose sadness surprised her. "Don't be fooled, Jeh Kalawe. I think only of myself. I must be able to look him in the eye when I see him again, in Ina-Karekh."

She would never get used to the way Gatherers constantly looked forward to their own deaths.

"There's more in the records." An awkward transition this time, but unavoidable. She pulled the third scroll from the bottom of the stack, and spread it atop the other two. "Do you recognize this?"

Nijiri frowned at the document, which was covered in some sort of chart. Name-pictorals sprawled across the page, linked by neat, precise lines. "Should I? I'm no Teacher." He paused then, spotting the small creator's stamp at one bottom corner of the sheet, and stiffened.

"Inunru." Sunandi watched him. "The name was more common back then, but there's reason to believe this was indeed the same Inunru who founded your faith, and narcomancy, and the Gatherer path." And the man who had created the first Reapers, she did not add—because he knew it anyway, and because avoiding painful subjects was custom in Kisua and Gujaareh alike.

Nijiri's jaw flexed anyhow, but he said nothing about it, his eyes roving the scroll's lines. "What is this? Mothers, fathers, uncles..." He scowled in impatience. "I was born servant-caste, Jeh Kalawe; we bred as we pleased and never obsessed over lineages as you high-castes do. What does this mean?"

"From what I can tell, your founder was researching certain lineages. The dreaming gift runs in families, does it not?"

He nodded absently. "More through fatherlines than motherlines, yes. Whenever a fatherline produces a child suitable for the narcomantic paths, we watch it thereafter."

She pointed to a tiny pictoral of a bird in flight beside some of the names. "This is the first character of your word for *dream*. That may mean Inunru suspected those people of bearing the gift."

Nijiri touched a descent-line, one of several that had been drawn in red rather than black. "But this is a motherline," he said. "A sister of a Sentinel who was a strong dreamer..." He traced the line. "Produced three children, all daughters..." His finger stopped in an empty space below the line. "He lost track here. But that's no surprise; we've never watched women."

"Because women more rarely inherit the gift?" Sunandi asked, folding her arms. "Or because your faith shuns women?"

He looked annoyed. "We *revere* women."

"If you overlook women who carry the gift, it amounts to the same thing. That girl you took in as a Sharer— What was her name?"

"Hanani."

"Is Hanani's gift strong?"

Nijiri considered for a moment. "Strong enough," he said at last. "Mni-inh—" He faltered for a breath, inexplicably. "Mni-inh never complained about her ability, only her confidence."

"Could she have become a Gatherer, instead of a Sharer?"

His face twitched, though he mastered his reaction beyond that. "She lacks the temperament. But Gathering and Sharing are two faces of the same coin, in the end." He sighed. "So, yes."

Sunandi tapped the scroll near the names of the three Sentinel-nieces. "So any one of these women may have possessed a gift of Gatherer or Sharer strength. Do women often go mad, here in Gujaareh?"

Nijiri looked away, troubled. "Not often, but it isn't unheard of, either." A bit defensively he added, "We give them dreamblood to control it, the same as we would any man."

"But men with the gift are found early and taken into the Hetawa, before they can suffer much. They're valued, nurtured. Isolated, though..." A new thought occurred to her then, and it was an ugly one. She grimaced as she turned it over in her mind. "Your Hetawa's restriction against female Servants may have been purposeful. Men with the gift become celibate in the Hetawa, but women with the gift are under no such restriction; most make sons and daughters. It's no different from leaving useful mares in a herd, while culling the more troublesome stallions who have the same traits! These women"—she pointed at the red motherlines—"*keep the dreaming gift in Gujaareh*. Otherwise the Hetawa would take them all, and soon there would be no more Sharers, no more Gatherers."

Nijiri said nothing for several breaths. Sunandi noticed that his eyes were on the lineage-chart, fixed on the creator pictoral in the bottom corner.

"It was Inunru who decreed that women were not to serve," he said at last. "So I was taught in the House of Children. He said it was because women are goddesses, and their magic is like the dreaming realm—powerful, but unpredictable. Too unstable for use in narcomancy. That's why so many blamed Hanani, when..." He trailed off, frowning to himself.

"Hanani is proof that women with the dreaming gift are no different from men," Sunandi said firmly. "How many others like her are out there now, I wonder? Perhaps some have married men whose own lineages carry the gift. Their sons might become Gatherers, and their daughters lunatics."

He winced at that, but then shook his head; Sunandi wanted to strike him for his resistance. "Not all with the gift go mad, Jeh Kalawe."

"No, but those who do *did not have to.* I suppose your faith considers that a small price to pay." She uttered a bitter sigh; he said nothing. "And every so often, a child is born whose gift is so strong as to be a danger to everyone near." She tapped the scroll. "I would wager my fortune that your founder was looking for a child like this."

"*Looking* for one? Why would—"

"For the same reason he kept notes on the potential of Reapers! Immortality, magic, dreams that can kill armies—or nations. *Power.* Your founder was fascinated by it."

And privately, Sunandi was glad Inunru was long dead. She would not have wanted to square off against a man so brilliant, and so utterly ruthless. Just as well his fellow Servants of Hananja had killed him for his many crimes—but he had seen nearly three hundred floods of the river before that day, using his own magical lore to extend his life. He had spent most of that time shaping the Hetawa, and Gujaareh, to suit his designs. A long time in which to sow evil.

If only the poisoned fruit did not keep ripening in my time.

Nijiri let out a heavy sigh. "This knowledge hurt Ehiru, when he learned it," he said. "He thought so highly of our faith. It troubles me less because I've always known the evil we can do, but even so…" He sighed. "*Indethe ne etun'a Hananja.* Clearly You do not watch us closely enough, my Goddess."

Sunandi glanced back at the door, trying to gauge how much time had passed. She could not stay missing from the Protectors' floors or her apartments for long, not without raising suspicion. "Can you send this information to your brethren at the Hetawa? By dreams or whatever?"

"Yes. We have acolytes scattered about the city, away from the

Hetawa, where they may dream safely. I'll contact one of them." He sat down on the bed again, solemn. "You want the Teachers to search the city's birth-records for the lineages that have produced strong narcomancers, but this time follow the women."

"Just the strongest lines, or the ones that most recently begat Gatherers or Sharers. There's no time to search them all. You may find nothing, but the alternative is to search every household in the city to see if you can find a nightmare-dreaming child hidden in a closet."

"Very well, Jeh Kalawe. We shall do as you suggest."

Sunandi nodded and quickly began collecting the scrolls, watching him surreptitiously as she did so. He seemed low in spirits, but that could have been just confinement and uncertainty. Still, she could not help asking, "Is there anything I can do for you? Anything you need?"

He shook his head. "You've risked yourself enough." But the frown did not leave his face, so she was not surprised when he spoke again. "There is one other thing that troubles me."

"Which is?"

"Inunru made many decrees in the time that he guided our faith. The more I come to know of him, the more I realize every one of those decrees had some ulterior purpose." Sunandi nodded, glad that she was not the only one who had considered this. He rubbed his hands together as if cold, though the room was not. "There's one father-line in the city that the Hetawa never claims—not completely. By tradition and Inunru's decree, every Prince of the Sunset must have the dreaming gift in some measure. Only the Hetawa's Council of Paths knows of the decree—but as Inunru's inheritors, we have worked to carry out his will all these centuries. In fact, that was one of several reasons we decided to endorse Wanahomen; his father tried to hide it from us, but the boy is a powerful dreamer." He sighed. "Some of us even took that as a sign from the Goddess."

Sunandi frowned. "Why would Inunru command such a thing?"

"I don't know, Jeh Kalawe. But I have suspicions, and they frighten me."

She guessed, from his hesitation. It was obvious, really. If Inunru could not *find* a Wild Dreamer, he had meant to *create* one. Princes of the Sunset took many wives and sired many children; that alone must have made the lineage perfect for Inunru's purposes. Such a child in the wrong hands, even untrained, was a formidable living weapon. In Inunru's hands... Sunandi shuddered to think of it.

And now the Hetawa was helping Wanahomen—descendant of madmen and magicians, heir of another monster who'd slipped their control. Another of Inunru's dangerous secrets.

Sunandi tucked the scrolls under her arm and sighed. "Save that one for the next war, you fool," she said. "Don't we have enough troubles?"

He stared at her, then chuckled. It was the first real laugh she could ever remember hearing from him. "Rest well, Sunandi. I'll pray for you tonight."

And he had never, in Sunandi's memory, called her by her given name. She hadn't been offended by that extra layer of formality between them despite their years of friendship; he was Gujaareen. Still—

"In peace, Nijiri," she said, and stifled her smile until she'd left the room.

37

☾ ⊙ ☽

War Leader

The morning was half over by the time Wanahomen finally left Hanani's tent. She was still asleep, tangled in a thin blanket and the scattered pile of cushions. He paused to kiss her neck and one artlessly bared breast before leaving; she did not stir.

Outside, the camp was only half awake, as most of the tribe and its guests had kept up the celebration until the setting of the Waking Moon. He glimpsed a few bleary-eyed slaves cleaning up, and a few even more bleary-eyed warriors drinking strong tea around the cookfires; aside from this the camp was still asleep. Returning to his own tent, he took a quick basin bath and put on fresh clothing before reporting to Unte.

"Well, well," Unte said as a slave let him into the tent. Unte was sprawled across a long flat cushion with his feet up, nursing a large cup. By the bitter scent, Wanahomen knew it held a tea for hangovers. "Do you never go at things the easy way, Wana? Half the camp is in awe of you, and the other half thinks you may be the death of us all."

Wanahomen settled on the cushion across from him, smiling

ruefully. "Good. Not so long ago, only a quarter were in awe of me. Which are you, by the way?"

"I'll judge when I see the lady's face. I trust she was satisfied?"

It was practically law among the Banbarra to brag about one's sexual exploits. Men spun tales of unattainable women attained and impossible positions achieved, while he'd heard rumors that the women kept a chart somewhere for betting purposes, complete with skill rankings for each of the tribe's men. But while Wanahomen had done his share of tale-spinning—some true, most not, as was the way of such things—he had no great desire to talk about his time with Hanani. The whole matter was too fragile and powerful, almost holy, like the templewoman herself. He did not know how to feel about it yet.

"I would say so," he said to Unte, trying to sound nonchalant. "Though of course it's always difficult to tell with women. I think her sorrow has been eased as well. At least, enough that she will not go mad or kill herself."

Unte stifled a yawn and frowned. "Was that really a danger?"

"Last night? Gods, yes. And she'll bear careful watching for some while longer." He reached for the tea to pour himself a cup. "My people don't deal well with pain."

"Then just as well you gave her pleasure. Though now I worry that her priest friends, those cold-faced fellows who kill in the night, will be annoyed with us."

"They'll be annoyed with *me*, yes." The tea was foul, but it contained a strong stimulant; he grimaced and forced it down. "But it's her they'll blame, not me."

"They might claim you seduced her."

"Templefolk are many things, but not liars. If they question her, she'll tell them she asked me for my favors." He sighed and drained the cup. "I don't know what they'll do to her at that point."

"Well." Unte sat up, grimacing and touching his temple as if the movement pained him. "Either way, it will happen after the battle."

Reaching for the tea decanter again, Wanahomen froze and stared at him. "The vote? But I thought—"

"Asnif of Madobah was the only other possible dissenter, and he was most impressed with you after the healer's death the other day. He said last night that he means to support you, and the others admitted that they planned the same. Even Tajedd—though he has no choice." Unte smiled thinly. "So rather than stand on ceremony, we called that the vote. The others will inform their hunt—no, *war* leaders this morning. They have granted you the title of war chieftain." Unte smiled. "Our first in generations."

Wanahomen closed his eyes and murmured a brief prayer of thanks to Hananja, then drew in a deep breath, feeling the first stirrings of battle-readiness in his blood.

"Then we leave tomorrow," he said. "Please have the tribe prepare rations for all the warriors, and packhorses to carry fodder. I'll organize a meeting of the war leaders for this afternoon, to prepare. And send a message-rider; it will take us three days' hard ride to reach the rendezvous point with the Gujaareen soldiers."

Unte raised his eyebrows, amused, though he nodded to each item on Wanahomen's list of requests. "The rations are prepared already, of course, since we half-expected this. And the fodder, and the horses; the rest can be done at speed. But you will be careful, Wana, won't you? I don't want to see ten years wasted."

Wanahomen grinned and shifted to kneel at Unte's feet. "I told you I would make you a king among kings, didn't I? Gujaareh will be mine again, and all shall know the strength of the Banbarra before we're done. I'll make you proud."

Unte chuckled, reached out and gripped Wanahomen's shoulder, then sat up and—much to Wanahomen's surprise—kissed his forehead. "You already have," he said.

*   *   *

The sun was well set by the time Wanahomen returned, tired but satisfied, to the Yusir camp's ledge. He had spent the afternoon discussing strategies with the other war leaders—now his lieutenants—while the men of the troops made the final preparations for war. He had little thought of anything more than a meal and his bed, but of course that changed when Yanassa appeared and attached herself to his arm.

"Yanassa," he said in wary greeting. "The wind blows fresher for your presence."

She smiled sweetly, though he was not at all fooled. She wanted something. "What gift have you brought for Hanani?"

Hanani. He had thought of the templewoman, of course, but with so many other concerns to occupy his mind, that one had slipped away. It was Banbarra custom for a man to compensate a woman for her virginity. And while Hanani was not Banbarra and likely did not care, it was clear Yanassa meant to see that he did right by her.

"Shadows," he muttered.

She patted his arm. "I think that amber anklet of yours will do nicely."

He started, frowning at her. He had given Yanassa the anklet years ago, when they'd first become lovers. She had given it back when they'd fallen out, but he had always hoped—"I don't know," he said.

"So you care nothing for her? She was just a night's release to you?"

"No, I just . . ." He faltered, troubled. He had grown to like Hanani in spite of himself, but what good did that do? She did not love him. She had used him, really, though he'd allowed it. Only fair after what he'd done to her— But when all was said and done, she would return to her Hetawa and eventually forget him, and he her. "I had intended that anklet for one of my wives," he finished.

Yanassa stopped walking, scowling at him. "Always the same with you. One night in a woman's arms and you want to lock her away in a palace somewhere. And if for some reason you can't have that, she's nothing to you. Why can you never simply accept what's offered, Wana, without demanding so much more?"

He stopped as well, putting his hands on his hips, not caring that they stood in the middle of a walkway and half the tribe was probably watching. "Because I'm not Banbarra, flinging my seed at any willing woman and bragging of my aim!"

"She isn't Banbarra either!" Yanassa snapped. "Gods, no Banbarra woman is stupid enough to put up with you after watching what I've gone through! But Hanani is like you, angry and hurt and lonely under all her airs, and she needs someone to care for her even if it must be *you* of all people. So if you break her heart I will scorn you forever!" With that she stormed off in a swirl of sashes and dangling jewels, leaving him gaping after her.

Charris stepped out from between the tents, coming to stand at his side.

"My father never had this much trouble with women, did he?" Wanahomen asked through clenched teeth.

"No, my lord. Though that may be because he kept all of his locked away in a palace somewhere."

Wanahomen threw a sharp look at him, but Charris kept his face politely neutral.

He sighed and rubbed his eyes over the face-veil. "Fetch the amber anklet for me, would you?" When Charris did not move, Wanahomen glanced down and saw that a small wrapped parcel lay in the palm of Charris's hand.

With a final sour look, Wanahomen snatched the parcel and headed for Hanani's tent.

She wasn't there. A few questions about the camp revealed that she'd appeared around the midday rest, gone to bathe, then come back and asked several of the Banbarra to share dream-humors with her. "How did she seem?" he asked one elder from whom she had collected dreamblood.

"Well enough," the old man said, then grinned. "Not displeased, if you have hopes of another busy night." Biting back an impolite retort, Wanahomen bid the man a good afternoon.

Finally he spoke with someone who had seen her heading for the heights. He found her halfway up the ledges, where she'd given him that first lesson in narcomancy only a fourday before. She sat on the same stone slab, in fact, with her knees drawn up and arms wrapped around them, gazing out over the canyon as the last colors of sunset faded from the darkening horizon.

Wanahomen went over and sat down beside her; she jumped when he did so, coming back from a million miles away. "Oh," she said. "Good evening, Prince."

He stifled the urge to brush a lock of her thick, sand-colored hair away from her face. Despite the previous night, it felt somehow odd to take liberties touching her. He kept his hands awkwardly in his lap. "How are you?"

"Well, thank you," she said. Her tone was nothing but politeness. He wondered suddenly whether she was displeased with him. Then he recalled Yanassa's words, and realized that she might not be thinking of the previous night at all.

"The vote went your way," she said softly, confirming his guess. "Everyone is talking about it."

He nodded. "It'll be over soon, one way or another." Glancing at her, he added, "You'll be able to go back to the Hetawa then."

Watching her face, Wanahomen just caught the fleeting dip of her eyes. "Yes."

He braced himself and then asked, "Regrets after all?"

Her lips tightened. "Concerns."

"Concerns that...?"

She shook her head slowly, as if unsure of her own words. "The peace I once felt as a Servant of Hananja is gone. It was fading before, but Mni-inh's death has shattered it for good. Death follows me like a shadow. I'm a healer: I should bring life. Shouldn't I? What does it mean that I don't?"

Wanahomen was taken aback for a moment. Had she been sitting up here brooding on such questions all day? And how was he—not a priest by any measure—supposed to answer?

He sighed and removed his veil, gazing out over the canyon himself. "You didn't cause Mni-inh's death," he said. "And Azima brought about his own by attacking you."

"If I had healed the Shadoun myself, Mni-inh would not have died."

He stared at her. "Because *you* would have died instead! Hanani—" He shook his head, sighed, and reached for her. She stiffened, and he stopped, leaving his hand hovering in midair until she relaxed. Then he pulled her to sit across his lap. He had the sense she permitted this only because he'd surprised her into it.

"Prince, what—"

"*Wanahomen.*"

"What?"

"I've been in your tent and in your body. You can at least call me by my shadows-damned name."

That certainly startled her out of the melancholy. A flush deep enough to see even in the dimness spread across her face. Her shy smile followed; he counted this a minor victory. "Very well, Wanahomen."

"Good." He settled his arms around her, loosely. "Now, you're being foolish. And the last time you were foolish, holding you seemed to bring your wits back. It's all I know to try."

He was relieved to see her smile widen. "Yes, P— Wanahomen. It is oddly helpful."

Mollified, he shifted to get comfortable on the hard stone, so that his legs wouldn't fall asleep. "The war has begun," he said, more seriously. "None of us can afford to be foolish now. Only getting through this will bring the return of peace."

She nodded, sobering as well. "I've made arrangements to ride at the rear of your army, with the slaves and smiths and others who won't fight."

It had not occurred to Wanahomen that she would come along when he rode out. But then, that was why the Hetawa had given the Sharers to him in the first place, wasn't it? Troubled, he dared to rest a hand on the small of her back, considering the dangers. "Keep wearing this clothing," he said. "No one will bother a Banbarra woman, not with hundreds of Banbarra warriors about. But a lone Gujaareen would be seen as vulnerable."

She frowned. "A Sharer is supposed to be easy to find," she said. "The red drapes—every Gujaareen knows what those mean. In the midst of battle that could help me reach the wounded—"

"I don't *want* you easy to find," he said, scowling; she drew back in surprise. "I don't trust my allies from the city, Hanani. They may hope to damage my alliance with the Hetawa by harming you."

"No one would—" But she stopped, not finishing the sentence. She had seen enough now to know better.

He reached up to massage her neck and shoulders, not liking that she had grown tense. "During the battle, I'll have the wounded brought to wherever we set up field camp. You may heal them there. Once we've breached the city walls, I'll take you back to the Hetawa. Until then you are *my* healer, and you serve only my men. Is that understood?"

Hanani looked at him for a long moment, and belatedly he wondered what he could do if she said no.

"I'll wait until you deem it safe before I assist any beyond the Banbarra," she said at last. "But only because doing otherwise might cause more harm."

Wanahomen exhaled and nodded. They sat that way for a long while, until the blood-red uppermost curve of the Dreaming Moon began to fill the sky above the canyon. "Are you hurt?" he asked, when sufficient time had passed that they could discuss something more intimate.

"Some soreness. Not enough to bother healing." She shrugged. "You were very careful. Thank you."

It bothered him that she seemed surprised by his care. It bothered him more that she seemed completely unaffected by what had happened between them; it might have been just another dreaming lesson, for all the warming of her manner. Because of this, he blurted, "*Do* you have regrets, Hanani? Now that the light of day has cleared your thoughts?"

She sighed, but to his relief shook her head. "Do you?"

He felt the slight tension in her body and was surprised by how much it pleased him. She liked him enough to care what he thought of her, at least. "Only that you must return to your Hetawa."

That seemed to bring back some of her sadness, and it sobered him as well.

"What will happen to you?" he asked. "At the Hetawa?"

She sighed. "I'll tell the Superior all I've done. He will decide my penance, though the elders of my path will have a say as well—and the Gatherers, given that I've taken a life. Word will spread, either way, and my reputation will suffer more. There are those who have always said that a woman lacks the discipline to serve Her properly, and now I've proven them right in so many ways."

He did not like that the Gatherers would be involved in deciding her fate. Not one bit.

"More foolishness," he said, with a dismissiveness that he did not truly feel. "You couldn't have become a Sharer in the first place without discipline."

"But I'm not a Sharer, not yet. And now, I may never become

one. Mni-inh…He was my champion in the Hetawa. He—" She shuddered and faltered silent; he felt her tremble.

"Your mentor and I, we were not friends," Wanahomen said, awkwardly. But he felt her listening. "Perhaps he saw my father in me. I certainly saw the Hetawa in him—and in you, at first. But he was strong and fierce in his convictions; even I must admit that I admired him for that. I cannot imagine such a man endorsing you if he did not believe you worthy to serve Hananja."

"What good does that do if no one else believes it?" There was no strength in Hanani's voice, only resignation, and finally Wanahomen realized that what she had been suppressing was *not* regret, but a despair so heavy that it was like stones on her soul. She was still a woman in mourning, however unorthodox a method she had chosen to take her mind off the pain. It took so little to aggravate her wounds.

"Then they don't deserve to have you among them," he snapped, angry on her behalf. "But think now: the Gatherers tapped you to carry out a mission of great importance, isn't that true? Your mentor deemed you worthy of your red drapes; that much was obvious to me. Unte and the Banbarra respect you; even my mother does— and *that's* no easy thing to earn, believe me."

Hanani said nothing, but he felt some of the tension ease in her back. Pleased, Wanahomen shifted position and laid a hand on her belly. "And—the Banbarra don't understand this, but I won't lie with just any woman. You may become mother to Gujaareh's next king, after all."

Wanahomen could not see the nuances of her face in the dark, but he thought she looked away. "There won't be a child," she said. "It isn't the right time."

He blinked in surprise, but of course she was a healer; she would know. For a breath he was disappointed, before sense reasserted itself. "Nevertheless," he said. He stroked her thigh through her skirts, then reached up to cup her cheek. "Lovely as you are, delicious as you were last night, I would never have consented to your request had I not seen your strength and wit, and desired them for my heirs."

She gave him an odd smile, but there was genuine amusement in it. "I'm not certain what to say to that."

"Say, 'Thank you,'" he said, with mock hauteur. "And I would also appreciate praise for my skill, impeccable taste, and good judgment."

He was gratified to see her utter a soft laugh, but even more pleased when she put her arms around his neck.

"Thank you for being kind, for me," she whispered in his ear. And then she pulled back and kissed him.

Surprised, Wanahomen held her and returned the kiss, marveling yet again at the way she put her whole self into the moment. Perhaps that was because it was a betrayal of her oath for her to be with him: if he had been in her shoes, he would've wanted to savor every moment too. To make the betrayal worthwhile.

So he sighed and pushed her back gently, and pulled Charris's parcel from his robes. "The thanks is mine," he said, opening the folded cloth. She caught her breath as he took out the anklet; even in the faint Dreamer's light she could see the gleam of its dangling pendants. He fastened it 'round her ankle, and had to admit that it looked finer than he'd expected against her pale skin.

"But why?" she asked, finally sounding moved by something he'd done. That satisfied his pride, at last.

"You gave me pleasure," he said. He caressed her calf; it was the only part of her he dared touch, lest he be tempted further. One night was all he could expect from her, and that was done. He found himself wishing there could be more. "And you gave me the honor of being your first lover. Even aside from your oath to the Hetawa, that's a powerful and special thing."

She shook her head. "That was a mutual gift, Prince. Wanahomen. You gave me pleasure as well."

"True. But among the Banbarra, nothing is free—" She put her fingers to his mouth, much to his surprise.

"You're not Banbarra," she said. She got to her feet and stood over him, looking wild and barbarian, though her calm determination was all Gujaareen. "The Sisters say pleasure honors Hananja because it brings peace. Tonight I mean to pray for a quick end to this war. If you wish—" She ducked her head, her shyness returning for just a moment, but then she looked up at him through her lashes in a way that made all his regrets vanish. "P-perhaps we can pray together."

She whirled and headed down the path at a not-quite-peaceful pace, and was halfway to camp before Wanahomen's mind registered that he had just been seduced.

Then, as quickly as he could without endangering his life, he scrambled down the steep slope after her.

38

(⊙)

Secrets

Tiaanet and her father had not been back at their greenlands estate for half a day when servants came to inform her that visitors were approaching the house. "An eight of soldiers, lady, and a man with a spear," said the wide-eyed girl. "All Kisuati."

Tiaanet's father had been preparing to travel to the foothills, where the nobles' armies were assembling for their bid to retake Gujaareh. There was no time to hide the saddlebags or stacked supplies in the house's courtyard; she would have to think of a suitable excuse to explain them. "Invite them in when they arrive," she told the girl. "Treat them as guests, but if they ask questions, simply tell them you know nothing." The girl nodded and ran off; another servant hovered nearby, looking equally anxious. "Inform my father," she told him, and he hastened away at once.

It was improper for a woman of the shunha to greet guests when servants were available to manage that menial task. Arranging herself opposite the entrance of the greeting room, Tiaanet composed herself to wait and wondered what she would do if the Kisuati had discovered her father's schemes. They would kill him in that event—probably in public, and slowly, in typically brutal Kisuati justice. The lineage would be hers to rule, then, and her mother and Tantufi would fall into her care. But that would happen only if the Kisuati did not judge her guilty along with her father, which they would do unless she pleaded ignorance well enough to convince them. If they had caught any other conspirators, such as the other lords and ladies who had discussed the plot in front of her, they would surely name Tiaanet along with her father. She would not plead ignorance then, but her father's control. And if they pressed, she would show them Tantufi, and all the secrets would come out.

If Tiaanet had still been able to feel, she might have felt something very like anticipation.

But there was a commotion at the front of the house as the soldiers entered. She heard a servant's voice rise in protest, followed by the sound of flesh striking flesh—she knew that sound well—and a surprised grunt of pain. Then the soldiers appeared in the greeting room, flanking their leader, and suddenly Tiaanet began to suspect that they had not come for her father after all.

The leader indeed carried a short-handled spear strapped across his back, as the servant girl had reported, in addition to the traditional curved sword at his hip. But the girl was servant-caste and ignorant; of course the spear was all she had noticed. Tiaanet noted entirely different things: like the fact that the man was shorter than most Kisuati, though lean and well-muscled, and there was more than a hint of westerner in his rounded features. He wore his hair loose, unlike most people of either Gujaareh or Kisua—slicked down into a neat oiled cap and cut blunt to the length of his ears. And in place of the loose cloth drape that most Kisuati captains wore about their shoulders, this man wore a thick black-furred pelt, held in place with an elaborate ivory clasp. The originator of that pelt had perhaps also been the former owner of the teeth that adorned the man's necklace.

A hunter: a member of one of Kisua's oldest and most honored castes, though their glory and numbers had dwindled in the past few centuries.

"You are the Lady Insurret, of shunha caste, out of the lineage of Insawe?" the man asked, then checked himself. His Sua accent was strong; even knowing the tongue herself, it took Tiaanet a breath to adjust to his choppy, oddly-inflected Gujaareen. "No, you are too young. You would be Lady Tiaanet, her daughter."

"I am," Tiaanet said, with a careful bow that acknowledged the man's rank, and nothing more. "And you are?"

"Bibiki Seh Jofur," he said. "A captain of Kisua, lately attached to the Protectorate in Gujaareh. Where is Insurret?"

"She is indisposed," Tiaanet said. She had told that lie so often that it came easily to her lips, and it seemed safer than asking what had happened to her door-servant. "I've managed her affairs for some while now, with her and my father's permission. May I convey a message to her on your behalf?"

"You may escort my men to her quarters," he replied, "and then you may come along with us yourself."

For a moment, Tiaanet was certain she had misheard him. "My mother is—"

"Now, please." Bibiki smiled, all politeness. "We have far to go, and I would like to be back in the city by nightfall."

"What is this?" Sanfi came into the room, indoor-shirted and still dabbing at his forehead with a cloth to wipe away the moisture from his bath. He looked frightened to Tiaanet's experienced eyes, which meant that he acted belligerent and angry as he spoke to Bibiki. "Who are you? The servants tell me—"

"Ah, Lord Sanfi," said Bibiki. "I'm pleased to meet you at last. I have heard a great deal about you." With a flick of one hand he signaled the two soldiers on his right. They immediately crossed the room and passed Sanfi, heading into the house. Sanfi caught his breath and turned to protest, but they ignored him.

"*What is this?*" Sanfi demanded.

"A service requested of all the Gujaareen noble families by your Protectors." Bibiki assumed a relaxed stance, his hands folded behind his back, a congenial look on his face that fooled no one. "It would appear that some of the Gujaareen nobility—we're not certain which, alas—have begun to plot against our governance. I find that hard to believe, particularly in the case of families like yours that have striven so honorably to keep the ideals of our homeland. But until we're able to single out the villains, I regret that your women must enjoy the hospitality of the Protectors for an indeterminate length of time."

At an unseen signal from Bibiki, one of the remaining soldiers came to stand near Tiaanet.

"This is ridiculous." Sanfi looked at the soldier near Tiaanet, then down the corridor where the other two had gone, then at Bibiki again. He was trembling with anger, barely in control of himself. "You're taking them *hostage*? We've served Kisua faithfully—"

"Yes, yes," said Bibiki, and now his voice held an edge that made Tiaanet tense, though he maintained his polite smile. "Faithfully, without a doubt. By the way, we won't have any trouble from your household soldiers, will we? I didn't notice any, coming in across your fields. How do you defend yourselves against the Banbarra and other raiders?"

Sanfi fell silent, his expression swiftly turning to calculation. The estate's hired soldiers had left the day before, to join the army gathering in the foothills. Bibiki had already known this, Tiaanet realized; otherwise he wouldn't have come with only an eight of soldiers. Sanfi knew it now too.

"Captain," called one of the soldiers in Sua, from the back of the house. Then and only then did Tiaanet realize the true danger. Since their return from the city the night before, Tantufi had been ensconced temporarily in a storage room until they could move her to the field house, which Tiaanet had planned to have the servants do after nightfall. But if the soldiers were searching the house—

"No," Tiaanet whispered. Bibiki glanced at her speculatively, and then glided around them and headed into the house to see what his men had found. Tiaanet heard murmured voices, and then a few moments later the men emerged. One of the soldiers guided Insurret by the arm. The other soldier carried Tantufi.

Tantufi could not walk. Years of being chained to the floor had done their work on her body: her legs were spindly, the muscles atrophied to uselessness. Despite the sleep she had been permitted in Gujaareh, the toll of years without proper rest still showed in her slack, prematurely aged face; in her gaunt limbs, thin hair, and dull skin; and most of all in her huge, mad eyes. The soldier had her in his arms, resting her against one hip; her head lolled back. "Mama Mama Mama Mama," she whispered. The chain that the soldiers must have broken to get her free—Sanfi kept the key hidden from Tiaanet—dangled from one ankle.

Tiaanet immediately stepped toward Tantufi, but the soldier who'd taken up position near her caught Tiaanet's arm and pulled her back. Insurret, who had been shuffling docilely along in the soldier's grip, flinched at the sound of Tantufi's voice. "What is *that* doing here?"

Sanfi stepped toward Bibiki. "You cannot—" Another soldier pointed a sword at Sanfi before he could get close; Sanfi stopped at once.

"Lord Sanfi," Bibiki said reproachfully. He stared at Tantufi in frank curiosity. "I was told you had only the daughter, and your wife."

"Please," Sanfi said. "My wife is ill. And that child—" He looked at Tantufi and away. "You can see she's ill too. Please, let them go, and my Tiaanet."

In another life, under other circumstances, Tiaanet might have smiled. Her father would never have pleaded for either Insurret or Tantufi by herself.

"What's wrong with them?" Bibiki cupped and lifted Tantufi's head with surprising gentleness, peering into her rolling eyes. Tiaanet's belly unknotted a little as he took such obvious care not to hurt the girl.

"A longtime complaint," Sanfi said. "It afflicts some women of the lineage. They need constant care."

Bibiki gave him a mild look. "They can have constant care in the city."

Tiaanet stepped forward again, though not so far that her soldier jerked her back. "Respectfully, sir, my father and I, and our servants, know best how to care for them. In the city—"

"I won't take them to the Hetawa for healing, if that's what you fear. Naturally we hunters, like you of the shunha, could never condone such a thing." Bibiki nodded to the soldier, indicating that he should cup Tantufi's head himself, which the man did. Then Bibiki gestured for both men to leave with Tantufi and Insurret.

In a flash, Insurret went wild, lunging at Tantufi with hands like claws. *"Get that monster out of my sight!* Drown it—burn it—beat it—kill it, get it away, get it out of my head, get it out of this world!"

The soldier who held her was so startled that he almost lost his grip. That was enough for Insurret to get her hands on Tantufi's sparse curls. She gave the girl's head a savage yank, plainly trying to break her neck. Her face was a rictus of glee, her voice a screech. *"Drown it burn it beat it—"*

"No!" Tiaanet grabbed her mother's arm before she could give Tantufi another yank. "Mother, no!"

The soldier got hold of Insurret again and hauled her back, but Insurret clung to Tantufi's hair like a leech, snarling incoherent violence now. Of them all, only Tantufi was silent—and calm, even as Insurret managed to give her head another tug. Sanfi stepped forward, scowling; Bibiki reached for his short spear; but Tiaanet had had enough.

She put her face right in front of Insurret's manic one, forcing her mother to look at her. "This is why he hates you," she said.

Insurret flinched back from her. She stopped struggling; her arm went slack. "Wh-what?"

"Look at you." Tiaanet filled her voice with contempt. It was not difficult. "A selfish, hate-filled beast, blind to the pain of your own flesh and blood, so spiteful you would even kill a child. Why would any man want you?"

Insurret's eyes filled with tears. "But, but—" Her face twisted. She let go of Tantufi's hair and covered her face with that hand. "You don't understand what it was like. Carrying you, your dreams always whispering at me, pushing and pulling at my soul—" But then her mood changed again, dream-swift, and she glared at Tiaanet from between her fingers. "Ah, but I forget. You *do* know what it's like, don't you? Betraying whore."

She drew back her head and would have spat on Tiaanet, but Tiaanet slapped her so hard that her head turned aside. Insurret blinked, looking startled. Tiaanet turned to Bibiki.

"As you can see, sir, my father was correct." She tried to keep her tone flat and could not; she was too angry, actually angry, at what Insurret had done to Tantufi. Her voice reverberated with the force of her fury. "Only he and I can care for these family members properly."

But Bibiki was staring at her. He looked at Tantufi, then at Tiaanet again, and narrowed his hunter's eyes. "I see," he said softly. "The child is your daughter, not your sister."

Tiaanet said nothing, though inwardly a great knot of tension unraveled. Was that relief? She thought perhaps it was. It took everything she had not to smile at Bibiki. *Go on*, she thought—

hungered, pleaded. *You see so much so well, hunter. See the rest, will you? Say it aloud.*

Sanfi went stiff beside her, though he put on a smile.

"You guess correctly, sir," Sanfi said. He put just the right touch of embarrassment into his voice: the respectable nobleman, forced to admit a shameful but minor family secret. Tiaanet wondered if he had been practicing those words in his mind for the past six years. "We sent her to live with relatives in Kisua for a year when we learned of her condition. Some local boy, not at all suitable; we had to keep her marriage prospects clear. Surely you understand, if you're a family man yourself."

"I am not, as yet," Bibiki said, and threw him a look of cool contempt. "But if I were, I doubt I would be so depraved as to impregnate my own daughter."

Tiaanet closed her eyes for a moment, savoring the feeling of being without secrets. She could love this Bibiki, if she were still capable of love for anyone but Tantufi.

Sanfi flinched at that, truly thrown for the first time in Tiaanet's memory. "I—" he said. He opened his mouth once or twice more, but in the end fell silent. Perhaps he had not practiced that particular response.

Bibiki nodded to himself. "Well. It seems you have many things to contemplate, Lord Sanfi." He turned then, gesturing for the soldiers to fall in behind him. The one who had come to stand near Tiaanet reached for her arm to pull her along. Tiaanet walked forward before he could touch her.

"Tiaanet—" Sanfi's voice was anguished. Tiaanet turned back to gaze at him; he stepped forward. "Tiaanet, I never meant— It wasn't— You *understand*, don't you?"

She had never understood. In all the years since he had first climbed into her bed, and all the cruelties since, she had never understood what drove him to do the things he did. After a time she had ceased to care, for what did it matter why he did them? Yet the habit of obeying her father, pleasing him, was too ingrained for Tiaanet to ignore, even now.

"I do, Father," she said. His face lit at once with relief and joy.

"Don't worry," he said, his expression fierce. "I'll go to the Protectors themselves, if I must, to get you free. Don't worry."

She was not worried. She did not care what happened to her, or to him or Insurret for that matter. She did not care what the Kisuati, who had never done her harm, thought of her bearing a child by her father. They had already shown more kindness and attention to Tantufi than her own family had. Nothing they did to her could be worse than what she'd already been through.

But Tiaanet inclined her head to her father. He could still be useful to her, after all. Then she stepped closer to Tantufi.

Bibiki regarded her contemplatively throughout this exchange, as if he had guessed her chain of thought. Perhaps he had; she had never made much of an effort to conceal such things. (She'd never needed to. Sanfi saw what he wanted to see.) When Bibiki inclined his head to her in a gesture that might have been one of respect, or simple courtesy, she nodded back. He could be useful to her too. That was the most important lesson her father had taught her, long ago: anyone could be used. No one could be trusted.

The Kisuati marched out, leading Tiaanet, her mother, and her daughter away.

39

C ⊙)

The War Begins

Hanani woke to the sound of a hand slapping at the walls of her tent. "Wake, little mouse," said Yanassa's voice through the camel hide. "I know that fool gave you no time to sleep, but you have much to do."

Blinking away grogginess, Hanani sat up, finding herself covered by a light cloth. The space among the cushions where Wanahomen had lain was empty, and he had left the tent-flaps untied on his way out.

"Enter," she said absently in Chakti. Yanassa poked her head in, then slipped inside.

"He would have left before dawn," Yanassa said gently, reading Hanani's confusion. She came over and knelt beside Hanani, peremptorily reaching up to begin untwisting Hanani's hair. "Many preparations to be made before the army rides out. Ah, he gave it to you!" Hanani's leg had slipped free of the blanket; Yanassa pointed at the amber anklet.

Hanani felt her cheeks heat, though she resisted the urge to hide her ankle; there was no point now that Yanassa had already seen it. "Yes."

Yanassa patted Hanani on the shoulder. "He should have given it to you at once, of course, but don't think less of him. He was never taught proper male behavior. Now, you understand how things must go between you?" She got Hanani's hair loose and rose to fetch new hair ornaments from the nearby jewelry box.

"Go?" Puzzled, Hanani reached for her breast-wrappings and began searching for the knotted end. After Mni-inh's death, Yanassa had come to offer comfort—and apologies, for her harsh words in the matter of the Shadoun woman. In Gujaareh Yanassa would have been required to offer apologies to the Goddess as well, for her unpeaceful willingness to see another person murdered in such a horrific fashion. The Gatherers might have gotten involved, evaluating her soul for signs of corruption; she would almost certainly have had to pay an extra tithe, and undergo ritual purification at the Hetawa or a satellite temple, at the very least. But here in the desert, the matter was settled by the apology alone, and Yanassa had resumed their friendship as if the incident had never occurred. Hanani was still struggling to catch up.

"You may not lie with another man for one full month, or until your blood next comes, whichever happens first," Yanassa said, finger-combing Hanani's hair. The twists had left it in tangled curls, which fortunately Yanassa seemed to know how to handle. "A man deserves at least that much of a chance to prove his value before you discard him. Now, obviously you've seen that you need not make your invitation in public again. You may also visit *his* tent, if the mood takes you and the mistress of his *an-sherrat* is agreeable—" Abruptly she sighed. "Though with this war business, knowing Wana, he may refuse you. He never allows himself a luxury when his men do without."

Abandoning the effort to dress with dignity, Hanani drew up her knees and wrapped her arms around them while Yanassa tended her hair. Wanahomen had spent hours on her the night before, massaging and caressing her long after their first passion was spent. *I want you to miss me when you return to the Hetawa,* he had told her, while doing things that had left her breathless and needful again. *If you must face punishment for lying with me, then I should at least give you pleasure worth the price, shouldn't I?* Then he had given her more, and more still, until she'd at last fallen into an exhausted, dreamless sleep.

It would do, she had already decided, as a farewell.

"There won't be another time," she said. It was nearly a whisper. Yanassa's hands paused in her hair.

"I'd planned to caution you against loving him," Yanassa said, her voice full of compassion. "He holds too tight; it's unseemly in a man. But was love never a danger for you?"

Hanani's hands tightened in her lap. She couldn't find the words to voice what churned within her. Wanahomen had committed a full four of wrongs against her. Yet since then he had been considerate of her in his rough way, even kind. The consideration had confused her; the kindness had turned her anger into something entirely different. It bothered her to realize that she would lose him too when this was all over, as surely as she had already lost Mni-inh and Dayuhotem.

But Wanahomen would not be like them in one crucial way. She might never see him again if he survived his war, but at least she would have the comfort of knowing he was alive.

Yanassa sighed, taking her silence as an answer of its own. "I'm glad my people don't follow your goddess in earnest," she said at last. "She demands too much of you."

"She grants us great power. It's only fair She demand a high price for it."

Yanassa made a disparaging sound. "There's no fairness in this." She fastened something on Hanani's head and then moved around in front of her. "Can you not leave your Hetawa? We would take you in."

385

Hanani stared at Yanassa, too surprised to be offended. "The Hetawa raised me from the year of my sixth flood. It's my home. The Servants of Hananja are all the family I know."

"Family does what's best for you! What proper family censures a woman for following her nature? You've learned your value, found some pride in yourself. If you live among us you could nurture sons and daughters, build a wealthy clan on your skills as a healer, live surrounded by those who honor you as you deserve. Will your Hetawa ever give you that?"

"Not sons and daughters, and any wealth I earn would go to the Hetawa, but..." She frowned, considering Yanassa's words. When she returned to the Hetawa—if she was allowed to continue serving at all—she would be assigned penance for her misdeeds. If she atoned fully, she might someday be allowed to attain Sharer status. Then she could build a reputation based on her skill, gain acolytes and apprentices to guide, learn the deeper lore of her craft, perhaps even ascend to the Council of Paths—

But she frowned, troubled. That might be the natural path of any male who served the Goddess, but would it be so for her? What acolyte would serve her, after Dayu? What apprentice would want the Hetawa's lone, maligned woman as a mentor? Could she ever earn enough respect from her pathbrothers that they would allow her to represent them in important Hetawa matters? Even Mni-inh had been unable to do that, and he had not been hampered by controversy.

But it was the thought of Mni-inh that silenced her doubts.

"They're my family," she said again, more firmly. "My mentor spent half my life training me, believing in me. He wanted me to wear the ruby collar and become a full Sharer at last. I can't just put that aside, Yanassa."

Yanassa sighed, settling back on her heels. "That I understand. Sometimes honoring our families means looking beyond our own needs." She gathered the leftover hair ornaments and rose to put them away. Hanani looked in the mirror and saw that the curls had been pulled back from her face and held in place by a ring of overlapping bronze plates. A good style for traveling. But she paused, puzzled, as she spied a thin red cord among the curls. She picked it out and found that it had been clipped into her hair, and a second one lay beside it.

"One for your blood cycles," Yanassa said, noticing her confusion. "The other for your virgin blood. The third won't come unless you bear a child, and the fourth would be for the end of your cycles. They're your mark cords."

"Mark...?"

"Mmm-hmm. Men have a great fancy ritual in their twelfth year. They do something with their penises, dance around with their uncles and brothers, grunt and fart and tell themselves they're men. We women need only look to our own bodies." Yanassa finished putting away the ornaments and came over to rest her hands on Hanani's shoulders, smiling at her in the mirror. "Forgive me if you have your own Gujaareen ways for such things. I mean no disrespect. Among us, the cords are a badge of womanhood." She turned so that Hanani could see the three cords woven into a braided lock of her own hair.

Hanani had no idea whether there were Gujaareen ways for such things. She stared at Yanassa's cords, then at her own, and her sight blurred. "O-one of the priests in the Hetawa," she began. She faltered, her throat tightening, and then took a deep breath. "He said that I would never be a true woman."

Yanassa's mouth fell open. "What in shadows would *he* know of womanhood? You didn't actually listen to that stupidity, did you?"

"I—"

Yanassa groaned and turned Hanani to face her. "Listen to me. Earning honor for your clan—or your Hetawa, whichever—*that* makes you a woman. Glorying in your own beauty, mastering the power of your body, taking care of the world or at least the part of it close by... The cords simply mark the most obvious stages." She gave Hanani a rueful smile. "I've always said there should be more cords—one for putting up with fools, one for every sassy child—but alas, then our heads would be weighed down with red."

Hanani couldn't help smiling at that, though very quickly her throat tightened again. She swallowed and let the cords fall back into her hair, and decided to let go of something else as well. "Yanassa, thank you. There's much that I still don't understand about you, but you have been kind to me, and that is what matters most." An idea occurred to her; she gestured around at her tent. "All these things I have. I can't take them back with me. May I give them to you?"

Yanassa started, her eyes going wide. "You would give me so much wealth? But I'm not even of your clan!"

"Where I come from, family is a matter of heart, not blood ties. You're my friend—the only woman-friend I've ever had. That has great value to me, worth more than wealth."

Yanassa shook her head and leaned forward to embrace her. "That was only proper," she said in Hanani's ear. "Any woman can face the world alone, but why should we have to?"

Hanani held her tightly, trying not to wish for what could not be, and finding herself only partially successful.

Finally Yanassa let her go, sniffing and dabbing at her eyes with a scented sleeve. "Well. Any more of that and the army will leave you behind."

Hanani nodded, not trusting herself to speak, and turned away to finish packing. The bags were only partially filled by the time she was done, though she'd put in her Hetawa clothing, her small toiletries and healing ornaments, and the packets of rations that Yanassa had brought from the tribe's quartermaster for the journey.

"What of these?" Yanassa asked, lifting the box she had given Hanani for her jewelry.

"They're yours as well."

"What? No, you need them—" Yanassa made a face. "Oh, Hananja, they're going to make you wear that stupid red outfit again, aren't they?"

Hanani grimaced in consternation, but reminded herself that this was the hazard of befriending a barbarian. "My role in the Hetawa is a man's role. In Gujaareh, when a man takes a woman's path, or a woman a man's, that person must take on an appearance to suit."

Yanassa rolled her eyes. "Do they plan to give you a clay penis too, and big bronze balls? Mind you, Wanahomen will be very cross if yours are bigger. And he *will* compare, trust me."

This idea was so ludicrous, the image it brought to mind so ridiculous—and Yanassa's characterization of Wanahomen so spot-on—that Hanani could not help bursting into giggles. "No, of course not!"

"Well, then." Yanassa went to one of the bags, opened it, and dumped Hanani's jewelry in. "I've seen the men in your land: they like finery just as much as the women. And here— Men wear eye paint, don't they? That means you can wear it too." She tossed in cosmetics after the jewelry.

Hanani didn't know whether to laugh or groan. "Men do *not* wear lip tint, Yanassa."

"Then let them start!"

Closing the saddlebag, Yanassa came over to Hanani and took her hands. It took a moment for Hanani to stop fighting laughter enough to see the seriousness in the Banbarra woman's face.

"Don't forget yourself, when you go back to that place," Yanassa said, her eyes intent. "If you must go back to them, go back on your own terms. Serve your Goddess *your* way."

Hanani sobered and looked away. "That's well and good for lay-folk," she said. "But I'm a Servant of Hananja. How can I break tradition, disrupt the Hetawa's order, and still claim to follow the path of peace?"

"You will never be a man, Hanani, no matter how tightly you bind your breasts. You don't *want* to be a man. And they may never accept you, no matter how well you follow their rules and ape their behavior. So why shouldn't you embrace what you are? And serve in whatever damned way you want!"

Hanani faltered, thrown by the very idea. Only then did it occur to her: what she did would be regarded as precedent, if ever another woman sought to join the Hetawa. Everything she did, all that she achieved, would set the pattern.

And Yanassa was right about something else. She had tried, again and again, to do things the way her fellow Sharers had done them. She had worked harder, trained longer, humbled and stifled herself in an effort to be perfect—and still Yehamwy had been afraid of her. Still some of her fellows saw her, not as a Servant of Hananja, but as a woman pretending to be one.

There was no peace in continuing to do what had already proven unworkable. Sometimes tradition itself disrupted peace, and only newness could smooth the way.

There was a drumming at the tent flap, and a man's voice called Yanassa's name. "Here," called Yanassa, and a young man, not much older than Hanani and with the most beautiful long-lashed eyes over his veil, thrust his head in. He said something in Chakti, and Yanassa nodded. The young man inclined his head to Hanani as well, then withdrew.

"Pretty, isn't he?" Yanassa grinned at Hanani, who had been staring. She blushed.

"H-he has pretty eyes."

"Ha! Look away from that one, mouse; he's mine. The tribe's potter, so he *won't* be going off to war, thank the gods. Wana was the last warrior I dealt with, and he quite soured me on the idea years ago." She turned away from Hanani and picked up one of the saddlebags, indicating that Hanani should take the other. "And a potter can use his hands well indeed when it comes to certain other arts—"

Hanani gasped, covering her mouth to stifle a laugh. "Yanassa!"

"Well, it's true." With a smug smile, Yanassa held the tent-flap for Hanani. "Now. Come with me and I'll show you a marvel."

Hanani followed Yanassa through the camp, nodding to those Banbarra she had spoken with, or healed. Some still did not return her greeting, and several young women in particular had been snubbing her since her first night with Wanahomen. But more people nodded to her than turned away, and Hanani was surprised to realize how many of them she had come to know, if only a little. She had been among them less than a month; it seemed far longer.

They reached the ledge overlooking the long view of the canyon, where Hanani stopped in awe.

The canyon was filled, from one wall to the other and on either side of the river, with row upon row of men. What she was seeing must have been only a portion of the whole, for they were moving slowly forward as they filed out of the canyon to begin their journey. Hanani could almost taste their eagerness to fight, wafting on the air like the dust stirred by their horses' hooves. It was a profoundly unpeaceful feeling—and yet Hanani could not bring herself to disapprove. Instead, to her own great surprise, she felt excited, hopeful. Surely Gujaareh would be freed, with these warriors' help. Surely they could restore the land to peace for another thousand years.

Yanassa startled her badly then by reaching into some unnoticed fold of her garments and drawing a knife. She raised this over her head and let out an ear-piercing, singsong cry: "*Bi-yu-eh!*" Before Hanani could fathom what she was doing, other cries went up

391

around her, and she looked about to see that most of the tribe's women had come to stand at the ledge along with them, seeing the army off. They too raised weapons where they had them, and let out that unearthly cry.

Someone touched Hanani's arm, and she turned to see Hendet beside her. "Sing," Hendet said, in her low, aristocratic Gujaareen. "For the warriors' victory. For peace and few casualties, if that pleases you more, and a quick end to this whole mess. Think of it as a prayer—but sing." And to Hanani's shock, Hendet too raised her voice in a deeper, though no less barbaric-sounding cry. Something in Sua.

It seemed a strange custom, but Hanani saw the meaning in it. She had no weapon, having refused to carry one even after the Azima incident. Such things had no purpose other than to cause pain, to her mind. But she had killed Azima with her bare hand, hadn't she? Magic was both a useful tool and a deadly weapon, no different from any knife, for all that it was a gift of the Goddess.

And so, hesitantly, she raised her hand. She closed her eyes, drew in a breath, thrust aside propriety, and joined in the women's farewell. She called Hananja's name and made the word a prayer, thinking, *Let there be peace again soon, for me and for all these people, and when You have done that, take no more from me.*

When she ran out of breath and the other women's songs began to fade, Yanassa clapped her on the shoulder. Bowing over her hands in farewell to Hendet, who returned the bow with regal grace, Hanani and Yanassa ran to the ladders and clambered down to ground level. Tassa waited by the corral, holding the bridle of Hanani's saddled horse and looking anxious. He and two other boys quickly helped Hanani strap on the saddlebags. Then Hanani mounted Dakha, who stamped her feet, impatient to be off with her fellows. The last of the warriors were beginning to pass, followed by the farriers and trappers and others who had chosen to travel with the army in support.

Ready at last, Hanani looked down at Yanassa and Tassa, her throat tightening. "Yanassa—"

Yanassa shook her head. "No farewells. It's unlucky."

Hanani nodded, but could not resist at least a blessing, if not a farewell. "Walk in Her peace dreaming and waking, Yanassa. Know that I will see you again in one or the other."

Yanassa smiled. "You'll see me in waking, foolish girl. Once Wana has his city back, I mean to come there to trade and grow rich, and I promise you, I *will* seek you in your Hetawa. You had better be wearing at least earrings! Now go."

Swallowing, and straightening her posture as befitted both a woman of worth and a Servant of Hananja, Hanani turned and rode off to join the army's train.

40

(•⊙•)

Alliance

With the wind at their backs and the smell of greenlands to guide them, the Banbarra army made good time reaching Sabesst, among the western foothills of Gujaareh. Sabesst was a forbidding, boulder-strewn pit of a valley, with steep sides and only the most narrow of passages in or out. Gujaareen myth said that Sabesst was where Merik, the god who had shaped the mountains, had once set down his tools while he took a nap. It was one of the few places in the foothills where an army could form in secret.

Riding at the head of the Banbarra column, Wanahomen led them through the middle of his allies' camp, trying not to curl his lip at the makeshift corrals, the haphazard tent-rows, the tiny smithy that looked ill prepared to handle even a horseshoeing. The men, at least, were the one positive Wanahomen saw: there were perhaps thrice as many of these soldiers as there were of his Banbarra. But the ones Wanahomen first noticed were a sorry lot. None of the nobles' men were in formation or drilling as they rode in. Most just came to stare at the foreigners in undisciplined curiosity. All wore varying colors and emblems, showing their allegiance to this or that noble family; there had been not even an attempt to unify them with a single sash or color. Worse, Wanahomen noted a troubling number of soldiers who were elderly, or little more than boys. Some were too scrawny to lift a sword, or too fat to sit any but the largest horse.

"*This* is what you mean to take against the Kisuati?" Ezack spoke in Chakti, but he wisely kept his voice low in any case, perhaps so that their new allies would not hear the disdain in his tone. "A good number of these should be sent into the desert to die and ease the burden on the rest."

Wanahomen shared his disdain, but dared not let himself dwell on it. These soldiers, poor as they were, were all he had. "Many are hired men," he said, and then amended himself when Ezack looked confused. The concept of fighting for pay was unknown to the Banbarra. "Not true warriors. More like slaves: they obey anyone who can feed them."

Ezack made a sound of disgust. "They have slaves fight for them? And you call *us* barbarians."

Looking farther, Wanahomen spied a few signs of hope. Not all of the soldiers had come forward as the Banbarra arrived. A good number remained back among the tents, watching. These men were fitter, and there was something more than bored curiosity in their eyes. They watched Wanahomen in particular, as he was the only one in indigo at the head of the column; the other war leaders were back with their own men. They knew who he was supposed to be.

"There," Wanahomen said to Ezack, taking care not to look toward the men of whom he spoke. "*Those* are the warriors—men of the military caste, and others who were once of Gujaareh's army. I'd hoped we would see at least a few. They'll make up for the rest."

Falling silent, Ezack assessed these men more thoughtfully, and straightened a little as if self-conscious.

Up ahead was a cluster of large field-tents, each in the elaborate Gujaareen style—woven of yellow cloth, tasseled in leather and gold thread, three times the size of even the finest Banbarra tent.

With eyes trained by ten years in the desert, Wanahomen could not help feeling contemptuous of such excess. The field-tents took hours to set up and break down, and probably had had to be transported on multiple pack animals. The thin, shining cloth was pretty, but it would let in cold air at night and heat by day.

Still, he schooled his expression as the tent-drapes stirred and his allies emerged to greet him. There were more of them than he'd expected to see—nearly twenty people in all, of varying ages and castes, though most were richly dressed and dignified in bearing.

"So these are war-leaders among your folk?" asked another of his men.

"More like tribe-leaders."

"Your people don't smile enough," Ezack said. "I can't tell what they're thinking on those stone faces. Some of this lot look like they want to kill you."

Wanahomen smiled. "Some of them probably do."

"Oh, so they have sense, then."

Ignoring this, Wanahomen raised one fist to signal the column halt. Instantly his seconds raised their fists as well, and the war-leaders of their respective regiments, and their seconds, until within a span of breaths the entire mass of a thousand men had halted to a one. Pleased by this display of discipline—it would go over well with the military-castes—Wanahomen dismounted and went forward.

He knew many of their faces from his days as his father's chosen heir, though he recalled only a handful of names. The rest, as far as he could tell, were minor or impoverished nobility, wealthy merchants, even a handful of well-known crafters and artisans. The sight of such a mix of folk both pleased and troubled him; each had probably brought additional resources for the army, but what did their presence really mean? How many were spies for Kisua—or worse yet, for other lands, keeping an eye on the affairs of what had once been the world's most powerful kingdom? He worried too that the hardships of the occupation had become more dire for his people than he'd thought. Only great suffering, or righteous anger, could prompt so many Gujaareen to cast aside Hananja's Law.

But that's a blessing for me. Come, then: follow me and I'll put your pain to good use.

"Greetings," Wanahomen said. He reached up to remove his headcloth and veil and was gratified to see the instant recognition in several pairs of eyes. He had always looked like his father, save for the height and deeper coloring of his shunha heritage. Given that his father had been a dancer's son and lowcaste-pale because of it, he was always glad for that small advantage.

"My Prince," said one of them, an older man who immediately knelt in manuflection. Most of the others followed suit—though not all, Wanahomen noted. He smiled at each of the ones who had not knelt and saw challenge on some of those faces, outright hostility in others.

"My friends," he said, speaking directly to those. "There's no need to call me *Prince*—not yet. Not until I sit before the Aureole and have received the blessing of our Goddess. Until then I am simply Wanahomen, a fellow citizen who shares your dream of a free Gujaareh." To those who had knelt, he nodded. "Please rise."

There was a shuffle among the group as they rose, murmuring among themselves, and finally a man Wanahomen had never met stepped forward. "I am Deti-arah, shunha, of Mun-arah's lineage," said the man. "You are most welcome, Pr— Lord Wanahomen. If you'll join us in the tent, we have much to discuss."

Wanahomen nodded and turned to Ezack. "Have the men make camp," he said in Chakti. "Choose someplace more suitable; I don't like the layout of this valley." Not least because it was full of people he did not trust.

Ezack frowned. "Beyond it, our fires and tents might be seen. If you mean to keep this army secret—"

"It doesn't matter anymore." Wanahomen looked around the valley. So many thousands of folk, all willing to fight for him. He could not help smiling, and repeating the words in Gujaareen so that all of them would understand. "At this point the Kisuati have no hope of stopping us, even if they know exactly where we are."

"Ah." Ezack, who'd frowned in concentration as he parsed the Gujaareen, looked pleased at that. "Well, then." He straightened, giving the signal to turn about. The column did so and began heading back the way it had come. There had been a likely-looking hill just before they'd entered Sabesst: Wanahomen suspected that was where Ezack meant to go.

But before they left, four of the warriors from the front-most rank reined their horses and leaped down, taking up guard positions at Wanahomen's back. One was Yusir-Banbarra and one was Charris, which did not surprise Wanahomen; the other two were Banbarra from other tribes, which did. He glanced at them in surprise, then looked up to see Ezack watching him. Ezack's eyes crinkled in a smile before he turned his own horse and rode away.

"Your allies seem quite imposing," Deti-arah said. He glanced nervously at the men flanking Wanahomen. Charris could still cut a striking figure when he wanted, but even he looked small compared to the other three, whom Ezack seemed to have chosen for their size alone.

Wanahomen stifled the urge to laugh. He would have to commend Ezack later. "They can be."

Deti-arah nodded. "Well, then." He stood aside and gestured for Wanahomen to precede him. Wanahomen did so—and the Banbarra bodyguards immediately moved to follow. As he had suspected, this unnerved Deti-arah even further.

"My lord—" Deti-arah glanced meaningfully at the Banbarra.

Wanahomen affected an innocent look. "Surely you have guards of your own, Lord Deti-arah?"

"I do, my lord, but—"

"Well, then." Smiling genially, Wanahomen gestured for the Banbarra to follow him, and went into the tent. A moment later, looking irritated, Deti-arah followed, along with several of the other nobles. The tent quickly became crowded with Charris and the three Banbarra in attendance, but Wanahomen walked to the central table easily; people in the tent made way for him.

A tall, slim young woman stood at the table within the tent, glaring down at what appeared to be a map-scroll. Wanahomen managed to keep his own eyebrows from rising at the sight of her, for she had pulled her hair back into a severe braid and wore a martial costume—leather half-armor loosened to accommodate her small breasts, a man's loinskirt, boots, and archery gloves, with a sheathed dagger on one hip. She raked Wanahomen with a wary, assessing glance as he came in; after a moment she gave him a vaguely respectful nod.

"Iezanem," said Deti-arah, gesturing to the woman. "Of zhinha caste and the lineage of Zanem."

"Zhinha *and* military caste, my lord," she corrected Deti-arah. "In principle my mother's caste takes precedence, but I've chosen to embrace both insofar as I can. My father passed on to me what skills he could. You are Wanahomen."

Deti-arah looked more annoyed still, though it was hard to say what had offended him most: Iezanem's claim of two castes, her forwardness in not waiting to be introduced, or just her presence. She was the palest Gujaareen woman Wanahomen had ever seen, with hair the color of rusted iron-clay and a dusting of freckles—and sunburn patches—across the bridge of her nose. She wasn't pretty, either, with narrow hips, lips so thin that they vanished when she spoke, and a nose too broadly Gujaareen for the northerner rest of her. Small wonder she was so belligerent, then: even among the zhinha she would have endured scorn for her looks. But there was something about the combination of strength and defensiveness in her manner that obliquely reminded Wanahomen of Hanani and predisposed him to smile at her—which caused her to blink in wary surprise.

"I am Wanahomen." He nodded toward the map, which seemed to be of Gujaareh's streets, and stepped over to the table. "Since you've studied the situation, would you brief me?"

She eyed him sidelong before she tapped the map. "Our current plan. We thought to approach the city by the western gate, at sunset with the light at our backs and then darkness in our favor to foil their archers. Our agents in the city will attack the gate-guards from within, which will at least distract them so that we encounter a light defense and can raise ladders to breach the gates. At best, of course, there will be *no* resistance, and the gates will open for us to simply walk in." She smiled thinly. "That's when the true battle will begin."

"For the palace." She nodded.

"The Kisuati troops will fall back to Yanya-iyan," said another man. Ghefir, Wanahomen's memory supplied—a distant cousin of his mother's lineage. He nodded to the man in silent acknowledgement, and Ghefir returned the nod. "An eightday ago, four Protectors arrived from Kisua to oversee the city. The Kisuati will fight to a man to protect them. That's sure to be a hard battle, but it's one we must win. Kisua will pay heavy ransom to get its elders back unharmed, since otherwise its own citizens will be up in arms. Taking them hostage may win this war."

Wanahomen shook his head, examining the map. "No. Yanya-iyan is a bad target."

Iezanem's expression turned instantly derisive. "Is it? Should we aim here, instead?" She tapped the artisans' district. "Or rescue the servant-castes first?"

"Servants, yes," Wanahomen said. He ignored Iezanem's sarcasm, knowing it for what it was now. She was no different from the youngest men in his war troop, all of them terrified and desperate to prove themselves. Some covered their fear with belligerence; there was no harm in it, so long as they learned not to cross the line of his patience.

"Our goal should be the Hetawa," he said. "Yanya-iyan is built to defend against attack. It has metal gates that cannot be climbed easily, doors we cannot batter quickly. Archers would pick us off as we came down any avenue toward it—the avenues are straight for that purpose—and in the narrower streets, chariots would ride out to finish off any survivors. Even if we laid siege, Yanya-iyan's store-rooms hold a village's worth of grain and provisions. They could last long enough for reinforcements to arrive from Kisua."

Ghefir frowned. "But the Protectors—"

"Must be taken, yes—that I agree with. But there are other ways to take them. Yanya-iyan's great weakness is its size, and its many entrances. To defend a gate against an army is easy, but to defend every garden door, every servant-entrance, every inch of every wall, against solitary infiltrators? Much harder."

Ghefir's eyes widened. "Assassins? You want to *kill* them?" He sounded horrified, and rightly so. Wanahomen himself was still Gujaareen enough to balk at killing elders—though he meant to do it, and worse, if that was the way to victory.

"No." Wanahomen tapped the Hetawa district again, his finger stopping on the Hetawa itself. "I was thinking of a different sort of infiltrator."

But Deti-arah was shaking his head. "You haven't heard, then. The Kisuati took the Gatherers hostage almost an eightday ago. They're being kept in Yanya-iyan."

"They're—" Wanahomen stared at him, then began to grin. He could not help it. "Damn, what an opportunity."

"Opportunity?"

"Yes!" Wanahomen leaned across the table to make his point; Iezanem drew back, as if repelled by his excitement. "One distraction, one slip in the Kisuati's guard, and the Gatherers will be free. *Inside* Yanya-iyan. We should do everything we can to facilitate that—and we will definitely need the other priests' aid, in that case. They can speak to one another through dreams." He frowned, contemplative. "That alone would be valuable, if they can help us coordinate our efforts. But most importantly, the people will rally around the Hetawa. The Kisuati can fight an army, but not a whole city."

Iezanem's expression worked from surprise through consternation toward grudging acknowledgement. "The Hetawa does have symbolic value," she said at last. "It would also make a good base of operations, if the Servants allow." She glanced at Wanahomen, her expression turning cool. "Would they?"

"I believe so." He met her gaze, understanding then that they knew of his alliance with the Hetawa. Good; let them reckon with that too, if they planned to betray him. "They've pledged to do whatever is necessary to swiftly return Gujaareh to peace. If that means burning Yanya-iyan to the ground along with every Kisuati inside, then I believe they would do it."

Silence fell for a moment as they absorbed that.

"Yes," said another man, who had not been introduced and had the look of a merchant; he was looking at Wanahomen, nodding, his eyes alight. "Yes."

"Dreamer-on-high," said Ghefir at last. "I begin to think this may actually work." The words broke the tension of the moment; several of the assembled nobles laughed nervously.

"Then there's one more greater matter to be settled, before we tackle the endless smaller ones." Wanahomen looked at Deti-arah, Ghefir, and Iezanem. Sanfi was not present; Wanahomen did not allow himself to speculate about that. "No army can be run by council, however esteemed. And the Banbarra will follow no Gujaa-reen but me."

There was silence for a moment longer, and then Deti-arah gave him a slow nod.

"None of us, save Iezanem, are warriors," he said. "We've always known there would be power in having you at our head." He looked then at Iezanem.

Iezanem looked as though she wanted to dispute this, but when Wanahomen turned a hard gaze on her, she sighed. "We will follow your command," she said. Ghefir nodded vigorously in agreement.

A deep sense of readiness settled over Wanahomen. This was what he had awaited for ten years. This was what his Goddess intended. He surprised himself abruptly by wishing that Hanani were present. She too knew the power of Hananja's blessings. It would have been nice to share this moment of peace with her.

And then it would have been dangerously, temptingly easy to seek out her tent later that night in the followers' area. Not for love-making, not on the eve of battle—but he also enjoyed the simple comfort of talking to a woman, and perhaps sharing his dreams with her. Still, he had made his farewells three nights before in Merik-ren-aferu, and speaking to Hanani again would only be awk-ward for them both. She knew it too, he understood, for she had not tried to see him since that night.

"So be it, then," he said to the assembled nobles. "We march in the morning. Moons willing and dreams sweet, Gujaareh will be ours again soon."

With that said, they gathered 'round the table and spent the next few hours in planning.

41

ᗕ☉ᗒ

Broken Peace

On the fourth day of the new year, the sunset brought great change to Gujaareh.

The battle began with a late-afternoon rumor, which quickly grew to an alarm. A dust trail had been spotted against the horizon, diminishing rather than growing with nearness, and it eventually became an army passing from the dusty foothills into the wetter greenlands, then coming along the irrigation roads toward the city. It would arrive in hours. Kisuati units that had been dispersed throughout the city to keep the peace quickly responded as runners brought new orders from Yanya-iyan. Some went to the walls in defense; others prepared to defend the defenders, aware that the city presented a greater danger than the army outside. Still others went to Yanya-iyan, there to marshal their forces for the biggest battle of all.

As the rumors became confirmed reports, the citizens of Gujaareh came into the streets, gathering in markets and parks and dancing squares. Many had brought weapons or tools that could serve as weapons; most had brought nothing other than their anger. This proved formidable enough as the Kisuati soldiers retreated.

Those soldiers who were unlucky or too slow found themselves surrounded by crowds of citizens who only a month before would have been easily cowed. Now those same crowds beat men to death, or tore them to pieces and carried the bloody bits through the streets as trophies. The same fate awaited any Kisuati civilians who had not seen the warning signs and fled ahead of time. Merchant-shops were looted. Several traders' homes burned with women, children, and slaves still inside. Gujaareen citizens fell as well, mostly to the swords and knives and arrows of the soldiers, but there were many, many more of them than there were of the Kisuati, and for every Gujaareen who died, another four came to fight in his or her place.

And among the angry crowds moved those who had been waiting for exactly this circumstance. On the steps of the Hetawa, Teachers preached to cheering crowds and exhorted them to be as swift and decisive as Gatherers in their violence, and to not prolong their enemies' suffering more than necessary. At the western gate, military-caste warriors in the garb of ordinary citizens attacked the Kisuati, encouraging screaming mobs to overrun defensive positions. Lending quiet but decisive support, the Sisters of Hananja shot Kisuati archers from shop entryways and timbalin cupolas. Their Hetawa brethren of the Sentinel path ambushed and disarmed reinforcements from within alley shadows, preventing the Kisuati from forming any effective defense. They also saved the now-helpless survivors of these ambushes from the mobs when they could, though that was not always possible. The people of Gujaareh were too angry, and there was not much peace in their hearts.

As darkness came and the streets smoldered, the last of the gate defenders fell to a cluster of barely pubescent boys armed with bricks and shards of broken pottery. The gates were immediately opened, and less than an hour later the first of three thousand saviors began riding into the city. The vanguard was comprised of fierce barbarians in pale desert robes, who brandished shining swords and let loose arcing victory cries as they spread throughout the streets. These cries were swiftly drowned out by cheers from the Gujaareen themselves, as the barbarians' leader rode through and the word spread that here, at last, was Hananja's Avatar. Gujaareh's long-lost Prince: a handsome, noble-looking young man carrying the sword of the Morning Sun.

He stopped his horse in the center of a packed market, gazed around at the crowd that watched him with pent breath, and said four words that traveled through every street and neighborhood with the speed of dreams.

"I have come home."

* * *

In the same moment, on the eastern side of the city, Teacher Yehamwy stood on one of the Hetawa's wall walkways with Sentinel Anarim and two other members of the Council of Paths, watching the smoke and firelight from the west draw closer.

"This is getting out of hand," Anarim said.

"As chaos does," said Ni-imeh of the Sisters. She and others of her order—those not fighting—had come into the Hetawa for shelter at the first word of trouble. "You believe the Prince will come here first?"

"That was the suggestion sent into his dreams," said Yehamwy. "Nothing can be certain, of course, without the control of dreamblood." He glanced at Sharer Anakhemat, who nodded wearily.

"We can't say until he arrives on our doorstep, and even then we may never know if the decision was the result of our influence or his own wishes," said the Sharer. "His dreaming has become sharper lately; we had to be subtle. Distance-narcomancy is always difficult. And no one has had time to travel to the borders to reinforce it, not in several days."

Ni-imeh nodded. "We must be content with that, then. If he's not seen to seek our blessing in restoring his rule, the rift between Hetawa and Yanya-iyan may never heal."

"Is there any word from the searchers?" asked Yehamwy.

Anarim answered. "They tracked down five motherlines before this whole business began." He nodded toward the glowing horizon. "Several women and girls have been found with considerable untrained dreaming gifts; only one had seen visions or showed signs of losing control. But even her power was nothing that could explain the plague." He grimaced. "Unfortunately, with so much chaos in the city, the remaining searches will be delayed."

"Would it help if we aided your efforts?" Ni-imeh asked. "The House of the Sisters has been relatively unscathed by these nightmares. Those of our members and apprentices who have the necessary narcomantic skill can travel in disguise, for the sake of safety."

Yehamwy and Anarim looked at each other in surprise. Ni-imeh's lips thinned in faint irritation. "Just because *you* have only now realized the potential of women does not mean that *we* have been fools all this time."

Anarim's expression softened into as much of a smile as the Sentinel would ever allow himself. "We would appreciate any assistance, of course. But it may require travel out of the city. Several of the motherlines are noble or farmer families, with residences in the greenlands or upriver towns."

"That's no difficulty—" Ni-imeh broke off, startled, as a sound broke the relative stillness of the Hetawa's courtyard. They turned to see a boy, too young yet to serve as an acolyte, running across the flagstones as fast as his small legs could carry him. Even from the wall-height, they could hear the child weeping as he ran.

"What in nightmares?" Yehamwy stepped forward and drew breath to call out to the boy. He was forestalled by Sentinel Anarim, who reached out and clapped a hand over his mouth unceremoniously.

"The House of Children," said Anarim. They could see the House from their vantage—at the far end of the long Hetawa court-yard, opposite the Hall of Blessings. Though most of the House's windows should have been dark—the children were sent to bed shortly after the evening prayer-dance and bath—they could see lanterns moving throughout the building, and as the wind shifted they could hear children's cries of fear from within. A moment later, another figure ran out through one of the House's gates. This one was taller; one of the House's adults.

"'Ware, Kisuati!" he shouted as he ran. His volume was a shock against the Hetawa's stillness; they stared at him, even Anarim frozen in a kind of horrified disbelief. "In the House of Children, Kisuati soldiers—"

More figures ran out after him. They all heard the sharp hiss of an arrow as it flew; an instant later the Teacher went silent and fell to the ground.

"Oh, Goddess," whispered Ni-imeh.

Yehamwy put a shaking hand to his mouth. "Bahal, that was young Bahal, he was Deshephemun's apprentice—"

"Get inside," said Anarim. "Go to the Hall of Blessings; tell everyone you see to gather there. It may be only the children they want."

"Only the children?" Anakuhemet looked horrified. "What are you saying?"

"They're taking the children hostage. I and my brothers will deal with this. Go, now!"

"But—" Yehamwy took a step away but then stopped, hovering. "Anarim, most of your brethren are—" He looked out toward the western city, where Yanya-iyan rose above the rooftops.

"There are eight of us left," Anarim said, with a tight, ready smile. "An eight of Hananja's Sentinels is an army." And he ran into the shadows before they could protest again.

*   *   *

There was something about Lord Sanfi as he prostrated himself in Yanya-iyan's throne room—lately redubbed the Protectors' Hall— that made Sunandi think of crocodiles.

"—A misunderstanding, or perhaps even foul slander," the lord was saying. He had been on his knees nearly from the time he entered. It was that, among remembered observations from their dinner evening, that gave him a reptilian manner in Sunandi's eyes. The ease with which he humbled himself, as if his pride was only another tool in a vast arsenal used to manipulate those around him. The way he studied the faces of his audience, reading them for weaknesses. The quick slide of his eyes over Sunandi, assessing and dismissing her all at once. She was no longer useful to him; he sought richer prey.

"So you say, Lord Sanfi," said Protector Yao. It did not sound as though she liked him either. "But we've heard testimony from the foreign merchants from whom you purchased weapons and other goods of war. What excuse can you offer for that?"

"Only that I am innocent, Esteemed," he said. He spoke in fluent Sua, but there was an awkwardness in the way that he used the supplicative forms. He was clearly unused to them. "If it will satisfy you as to my innocence, I know of others among my peers who may have transgressed—"

Sunandi had heard enough, revolted by the man's bald-faced betrayal. Tiaanet, she decided, would do well to kill her father off and take over the lineage before he embarrassed them any further.

"Respectfully, Esteemed," she said, interrupting Sanfi, "we have no time for this. The last report from the western gate was that it might fall at any moment. Let us imprison this man—with his wife and daughters, if that would please him—and devote our efforts to defense."

Mama Yao nodded at this, as did Sasannante, but Aksata rubbed his eyes, looking bored and weary. They were all weary. Aksata had been the one to insist that the Protectors take over the throne chamber, putting their own chairs where the Sunset Prince's oxbow seat had once stood alone. The palace servants had been serving cold food and misplacing laundry—and "accidentally" making loud noises in the small hours of the night—ever since.

"There's no need for worry, Speaker," Aksata said, mastering his mood enough to smile at Sunandi. "The western gate is no great loss. Indeed, we have already sent orders to your husband to withdraw, and bring his remaining forces here."

"I see." Sunandi frowned, trying and failing to make sense of whatever strategy Aksata might be planning. "Then, Esteemed, this Gujaareen prince and his fighters will enter the city. They'll be able to attack Yanya-iyan itself at that point."

"Yes, they will," said Aksata, and he exchanged a brief smile with Moib, who chuckled softly. "That suits our purposes for the moment."

Sanfi was listening closely at the foot of the dais; Sunandi noted a slight frown on his forehead, though he did not rise from his knees. It almost amused her to see his concern, given that he had just offered to turn on his own allies, but that did not trouble her half so much as the idea of enduring a siege.

But before she could formulate a question that might not annoy Protector Aksata further, there were loud voices at the door of the chamber. A moment later the door opened, and one of the palace guards came in at a brisk pace, stopping beside Sanfi and kneeling to report.

"Esteemed and Wise, forgive my intrusion, but my commander has sent me to inform you we are under attack," he said. His Sua was flavored with the rough accent of the forest-country: a lowcaste. "They're already inside the palace. All the archers of the first tier are dead...We believe they came in with the retreating troops, wearing the uniforms of our men..."

"Wait," said Mama Yao, frowning. "How can they be inside the palace? The Prince and his army of traitors were only just at the city gates at last report—"

"These aren't the Prince's people!" the soldier interrupted, plainly forgetting his manners. "I don't know who they are. They came among us in disguise, as I said— We found thirty members of the shield-guard dead, with no wounds that bled but plenty of broken necks and crushed throats. No one even heard them cry alarm! And now the men in their clothes are..." He trailed off, shaking his head. "Some say they climb walls like scarabs." He glanced up at the throne room ceiling, as if to be certain there was no one there.

Sunandi shivered, a chill prickling the nape of her neck as understanding came. "Sentinels," she murmured. "Hetawa priests."

Moib frowned. "The ones who guard? I was told only the Gatherers—"

"The Sentinels *train* the Gatherers, Esteemed," Sunandi said. It was unspeakably rude to interrupt an elder, but she had to find some way to convey to them how dire a development this was. It was a possibility she herself had never anticipated; she too had thought of the Sentinels as defenders rather than attackers. But that had been folly on her part, for Nijiri had warned her. The whole city was the storm he'd summoned, and his brethren were the lightning poised to strike.

Sunandi walked forward to stand beside Sanfi. "I have seen a Gatherer, unarmed, break a mounted soldier's sword-arm with what seemed a glancing blow—and they are the lesser fighters. The Sentinels are the ones trusted to hunt down Gatherers when they go mad and turn into Reapers. They have no magic, but they have armament, and their sole purpose is to fight."

Sasannante said, "But we have nearly the whole of the force we brought from Kisua—" He sat up, scowling. "Wait, how many of these warrior-priests are there?"

"Dozens or hundreds. No one but the Hetawa knows for certain," Sunandi said, shaking her head. "Esteemed, you should come: there are safer places to hide than this."

Mama Yao bristled. "*Hide?*"

"Yes," Sunandi said. She wanted to scream the word. "We can hide, or we can wait here and fight an unknown enemy, of unknown strength, and hope we're lucky enough to win. Which do you choose?"

Mama Yao pursed her half-toothless mouth, but finally looked at her fellows. Aksata looked as though he would have liked to object, but Sasannante and Moib stood at once. As they came down from the dais, soldiers moved to surround them, and Sunandi gave the order to take them to the garden of Yanya-iyan—the palace's most defensible point.

And as they moved, Sunandi vowed to herself that when she was an elder, she would *listen* to the younger people around her. Youth did not make one stupid, and true wisdom was clearly something even elders had to work to achieve.

Behind them, as they left, the shunha lord Sanfi slipped out unnoticed.

*　　*　　*

From the depths of contemplation, Gatherer Rabbaneh felt the presence of new dreamers beyond his door. Four where there had been one—and another four for Nijiri, and a four for Inmu, and even a four for the Superior. And four more beyond that, lurking in the hall beyond the guest suite. All just to subdue three Gatherers? Rabbaneh almost chuckled out loud.

The door opened. Rabbaneh opened his eyes, listening as three of the soldiers quietly spread themselves around the small room, flanking him. The fourth— Rabbaneh smelled fresh-forged metal and leather, and heard the rattle of some sort of hinge or lock mechanism. So that was what they were up to.

Ah, Ehiru my friend, you frightened these people too badly ten years ago. They think us all little better than Reapers. For that alone I should teach them a lesson—

"Gatherer Rabbaneh?" That was the young soldier who had guarded him this past fourday. Rabbaneh had developed a fondness for the youth, who turned out to have been artisan-born as Rabbaneh himself was, from a distinguished family of chanters in Kisua. He had been kind enough to share some of his chants with Rabbaneh at mealtimes. Rabbaneh would take care not to hurt him as much as the others.

He got to his feet and turned to face the boy, who held a nightmarish leather-and-iron contraption designed to clamp Rabbaneh's hands into closed fists. A rogue's yoke, of some sort of Kisuati design. There were all sorts of flanges and latches on the thing; Rabbaneh curled his lip at its sheer ugliness. "I suppose that is for me."

The young soldier nodded, swallowing audibly. He darted a look at his companions, who all stood ready with swords drawn, and finally faced Rabbaneh again. "I'm sorry, Gatherer, but the Protectors have ordered this. With all that's going on—"

One of the other men, an older soldier and likely the boy's superior, barked something at him in Sua. Rabbaneh, whose Sua was ceremonial at best, guessed the man was telling him to get on with it.

That one first, then.

The soldier had not finished berating the boy when Rabbaneh darted a hand at the soldier's eyes. Instead of laying his fingers lightly on the man's eyelids, he jabbed hard. While that one screamed and clapped his hands over his eyes, Rabbaneh crouched low to get beneath the sword of the soldier to his left—not that swords were any great threat in such a confined space, especially not when the men had spread themselves out so conveniently for him. Mildly affronted that they had come at a Gatherer so ill prepared, Rabbaneh struck the soldier's kneecap rather harder than strictly necessary. The sound of the breaking joint was unpeacefully loud, like a tree limb cracking in the wind. The soldier's shout was even louder, and mingled most cacophonously with that of his eye-gouged comrade.

Should have silenced them, Rabbaneh thought with belated guilt. *Sonta-i would scold me so if he were here—*

The third soldier was coming at him now, sword already raised and face contorted with rage. That made him the easiest target, for he was no different from the hundreds of violent men Rabbaneh had Gathered over the course of his twenty-two years of service. Three quick punches to the face and the man sagged to the ground, dazed and half-blind. There was no real need to put him to sleep after that, but Rabbaneh did it anyway just to be thorough.

When that one fell—the whole affair had taken perhaps three deep breaths—Rabbaneh turned to face the young soldier. The boy had not moved throughout the attack, except to take a step backward and begin trembling like a river-reed.

"I'm sorry," Rabbaneh said, making his voice soothing. "This was necessary—" He stopped, startled, as a curved sword-blade appeared from the middle of the boy's chest.

"Gatherer," the boy blurted, then looked down at himself in equal surprise before sagging forward, dead. As he fell, Rabbaneh saw that two more Kisuati soldiers were coming through the doorway, jostling each other and shouting to their comrades in their panic.

Whether they had mistaken the boy for Rabbaneh from behind, or whether the boy had simply been in their way, Rabbaneh would never know. He was on them before they had fully gotten through the doorway, covering each of their faces with his hands and driving pure fury into their waking minds. Such was the force of his rage that they screamed as their souls tore loose; Rabbaneh did not care where those souls went. He dropped the bodies and lunged through the doorway to kill the rest, kill them all, peace be damned—

The blow that rang through his body jarred him out of the rage. He tried to turn, batting aside a sword that slashed toward his face as an afterthought, but found his movements hampered in an odd way. Then came another of those curious jarring sensations, and he was free to move again.

The soldier who had been behind him—just to one side of the doorway; Rabbaneh had not seen him—stepped back, raising his sword to swing again. It was already coated with red.

Rabbaneh raised a fist to strike at the soldier, but his arm moved sluggishly, as in a dream. That was foolishness, because in a dream he had total control, and movement was a simple matter of focused will—

Another jarring blow. Rabbaneh turned his head, still marveling at his slowness, to see another soldier completing a lunge. His hand was around the hilt of another sword, the tip of which was thrust between Rabbaneh's ribs just to one side of his breastbone.

"Rabbaneh!" Nijiri's voice, unpeacefully alarmed. The head of the soldier who had just struck Rabbaneh suddenly twisted at an ugly angle. He flew off to the side, dislodging the sword in the process. Rabbaneh felt a completely inappropriate and disrespectful urge to laugh at the look of surprise on the corpse's face, but for the moment he was more concerned by his sudden inability to stand. He managed to sag to his knees with some semblance of grace, but then could not help falling sideways in a clumsy, mortifying sprawl.

Then Nijiri was there, and Inmu too, both of them looking frightened and anxious. So too the Superior, behind them, all of them gazing at him in alarm. But why? The soldiers had been dealt with. They were free.

"The Protectors..." Rabbaneh started to say, and then realized he had forgotten the end of the sentence. What about the Protectors?

"Rabbaneh-brother." Inmu, still so young even after seven years of Gathering, looked on the verge of tears. "Nijiri, can you not—"

"I'm no Sharer," Nijiri said, his face grimmer than usual. "Small cuts, perhaps, I could heal. Not this, not before his life bleeds away."

Inmu choked back a sob. Rabbaneh opened his mouth to remind Inmu that such histrionics were unbecoming of a Gatherer. And they had more important matters to concern them, such as...such as...what? He could not remember. It was so difficult to breathe.

"Then there is only one thing to be done," Inmu said. When Nijiri looked away, Inmu's expression shifted from pain to resignation, and Rabbaneh was amazed to witness the transformation of his shy, hapless youngest pathbrother into a Gatherer of Hananja.

"My brother," Inmu murmured, reaching down to stroke Rabbaneh's cheek. "You've served Hananja well. I'm sure She waits to welcome you." He swallowed hard. "Give my love to Sonta-i-brother, will you?"

He laid his fingertips on Rabbaneh's eyelids, and Rabbaneh knew no more in waking.

42

Return

Riding with the other supporters at the rear of the army, Hanani entered Gujaareh for the first time in a month. It did not seem at all the same Gujaareh she had left behind.

She could not see for smoke. A Kisuati armory near the western gate had been gutted by fire, its timbers collapsing inward, only black-streaked mud-plastered walls still standing. In the distance she could hear shouting, screams, the occasional cheer of a crowd. Dakha shied abruptly, tossing her head at the smoke and sidestepping to avoid something on the ground. Hanani reined in the horse and caught her breath as she looked down into the sightless eyes of a Kisuati soldier. It was only one of several hundred bodies splayed all around the gate-square.

The Banbarra beside her, a man of Unte's age, put a calloused hand on Hanani's arm and spoke something reassuring in Chakti. He was one of the craftsmen who had come to lend aid to the soldiers; some sort of weaponsmith. He and several other of the Banbarra men had kept protectively close to Hanani throughout the journey, though none of them were warriors or armed beyond the standard knife that all of them seemed to carry. She nodded to him, grateful for the comfort, though it did little good as she looked around at the lurid nightmare that had once been called the City of Dreams.

But as they progressed beyond the gate into the avenues that would take them to the eastern half of the city, Hanani saw with relief that the destruction was not so great as she had feared. There were no other buildings on fire, though she saw several shops that appeared to have been vandalized. Most of the houses' windows were dark, yet Hanani glimpsed people at the windows, peering through the hangings at the riders. The markets were not as peaceful—there were more bodies here, and as they passed under an archway still festooned with colorful solstice ribbons, Hanani saw a Kisuati soldier run by on a parallel street. He was followed a moment later by ten or fifteen shouting Gujaareen youths.

The riverfront district was silent as they passed over one of the bridges, the familiar reek of fish almost lost beneath the smells of smoke and horses. As they passed into the artisans' district, the column ahead abruptly slowed, and Hanani's group found itself standing still periodically as the army's progress crept along. Only then did Hanani realize that the army must be gathering in the Hetawa Square, the only open area in this part of the city large enough to hold them as a unified group. Sure enough, as they entered the square Hanani saw that the soldiers were arranging themselves in ordered clusters, with shieldmen on the outermost fringes and archers on the roofs of the nearest houses and buildings. A handful of war chariots, nimble and gleaming, rattled up and down the nearby streets on patrol.

There were common folk here too: men and a few women, of all ages and castes, lurking at the edges of the gathering. Hanani glimpsed more beyond the square, and clustering on street corners and in open doorways. A gaggle of boys, barely at the age of choice if that, ran up to one of the Gujaareen horsemen and began begging, loudly, to join up. The adults that Hanani could see were more reticent, some craning their necks for a glimpse of Wanahomen, some pointing at the Banbarra. Others whispered to one another behind hands, their eyes alight with a kind of excitement and anticipation that Hanani would have found frightening only a short time before. Now, though it still disturbed her, she understood what she saw in her people's eyes. It was no different from Mni-inh's righteous fury whenever he'd felt Hanani wronged, or the determination that had kept Wanahomen going through slavery and treachery. There was no peace in such passion, and she knew now just how dangerous it could be if unchecked—but neither were unpeaceful feelings corrupt in and of themselves. It was all a matter of when, and how, they were expressed.

But as Hanani gazed at the Hetawa's sandstone walls again, she found her heart full of both joy and unease. Here was her home. Here were her brothers, her only family. Would they welcome her back, tainted as she was by broken oaths and barbarian ways? Could they somehow heal her of the pain of Mni-inh's death and the life she had taken? Or would they take one look at what she had become, throw up their hands, and ask the Gatherers to put her out of her misery?

She was distracted from her brooding by a stir among the ranks of soldiers before her. A moment later they parted, and a man in tan Banbarra robes walked his horse into view. Something familiar in the set of his shoulders told her who he was even before he spied her and stopped. "Sharer-Apprentice," Charris said. "Our Prince bids you come, that he may escort you home."

Startled, Hanani froze for a breath or two. It had never occurred to her that Wanahomen might do this now. There had been no fighting thus far; her skills as a healer had not been needed. Was that it, then? She was of no further use, and now Wanahomen meant to rid himself of an unwanted responsibility?

But no, she was being foolish. Wanahomen had come here, to the Hetawa rather than Yanya-iyan; there must be some strategic reason for his visit. And it was only prudent for him to return her while he could. Swallowing her anxiety, Hanani nodded and urged her horse forward to walk with Charris's.

In silence, Charris led her through the column of warriors until they reached the front, at the foot of the Hetawa steps. She spotted Wanahomen at once, for he had discarded his headcloth and veil and dismounted from his horse. He turned from his perusal of the bronze doors as Hanani and Charris approached; his nod of greeting was informal but impersonal. "Thank you, Charris. Please bring her bags."

His eyes shifted to Hanani and stayed there for a long moment. She saw a muscle in his jaw flex; there was a weight of words in his eyes. But instead of speaking them aloud, he extended a hand up to her and said only, "Sharer-Apprentice?"

She was inexplicably clumsy in dismounting, taking two tries to finally get out of the saddle. When she went to him she stumbled, though there were no obstacles on the ground. Wanahomen stepped forward and caught her arm, holding her until she steadied herself. When she looked up he was watching her.

"Prince—" Her throat was tight; she could barely get the word out. What was wrong with her? She did not love him. He had been what she needed, a friend in a time of loss, but nothing more. Why did she feel worse, now, than she had on leaving Yanassa?

Wanahomen sighed at the confusion on her face, and put a finger on her lips.

"Say nothing," he murmured, only for her ears. "Or I may keep you, and we'll have a whole new war on our hands." He spoke lightly and smiled as he said it, but for the briefest of breaths Hanani felt the tension in his grip. Abruptly she understood: if she asked it, he would make good on his words and keep her with him, no matter what that might mean for his newly won kingdom.

This was what Yanassa had tried to tell her about Wanahomen, and it was no more than Hanani had seen for herself. There was no middle ground with him. He hated and loved with equal ferocity, and could be dangerous at either extreme. It was not madness in the usual sense, but it *was* a lesser version of the same folly that had destroyed his father.

Knowing that made it no easier to smile back, as though he really had only made a joke. The slow, resigned fade of his own smile left an aftertaste of guilt on her lips.

"Take me home, Wanahomen," she said. After a long moment he inclined his head, let go of her, and turned to walk with her up the steps. Charris fell in behind them, carrying Hanani's saddlebags over his shoulder.

The great bronze doors of the Hetawa unlocked with a sound that echoed through the square, swinging open to reveal darkness beyond. Hanani kept her eyes forward, her head high, though her heart was pounding and her mind empty of thought. They stopped halfway, Wanahomen pausing so that he could untie the heavy bronze sword from his hip. He set the sword down on the step in front of him, then untied the belt and sheath of his Banbarra knife and laid that beside it. Lifting his empty hands so that all would see that he came to the Hetawa with proper reverence, he stepped forward.

Two arrows sang out of the darkness of the Hetawa's mouth. One thumped into Wanahomen's chest, the other his right thigh.

The shock in Wanahomen's face was complete. It matched Hanani's horror as he stumbled back a step, then slowly sagged to his knees. But it was the massed scream from the warriors and citizens around them that filled the silence, and their fury that instantly consumed the Hetawa Square.

*   *   *

The Kisuati soldiers had taken the Hetawa of Hananja with surprising ease. The only resistance came from a handful of Sentinels who struck while Bibiki's forces were herding the Hetawa's hundred or so children from the House into the courtyard, from there to be marched to the Hall of Blessings. The priests had been swift, silent, and utterly deadly, charging the soldiers and slaughtering them by the four despite the fact that the soldiers outnumbered them ten to one. The children had cheered; for a time it had seemed as though they might win. Bibiki had stopped them with a simple gesture—ordering his archers to take aim instead at the children huddled together on the courtyard flagstones. The Sentinels froze. Bibiki's next order turned the arrows on them.

Tiaanet, carrying Tantufi, and Insurret had been among the Kisuati at that point, along with perhaps thirty other "guests of the Protectorate." Tiaanet recognized several of her fellow hostages, but only two were of families involved in the conspiracy: Orenajah, a zhinha elder and aunt to Iezanem; and Uayad, the eight-year-old son of Deti-arah. Orenajah stood straight-backed and angry, walking only when the soldiers forced her along. Uayad was trying hard to be brave, but when the Sentinels fell, Tiaanet saw him quickly wipe his eyes with one fist.

Once the Sentinels were dead, Bibiki's men herded the hostages forward through the complex of buildings, with small detachments of soldiers breaking off to search each building and capture or kill any templefolk they found. Upon reaching the Hall of Blessings, they discovered that most of the Servants had gathered there, already aware of the invasion.

There were no fighters left among the templefolk at that point, only a few hundred brown-robed Teachers and red-draped Sharers, along with acolytes and apprentices. They stood silent and watchful, unnaturally calm in the manner of their kind, flanking the door in two ragged lines as Bibiki's soldiers entered. One line blocked the steps leading to the dais, so that Hananja's altar would not be defiled by men with unpeaceful intentions. The other line blocked rows of prone, silent figures on pallets, fours of them arranged on one side of the Hall. The victims of the nightmare plague.

Being herded along by the soldiers, Tiaanet stopped to stare at the sleepers, then stumbled and nearly fell as people behind her pressed forward. An old Sharer, as pale as Tiaanet was dark, stepped forward from the nearest line to steady her. "Are you all right?" he asked.

"Yes," Tiaanet said. "Thank you." When he said nothing else she looked up at him, and realized that he was staring at Tantufi.

"Shall I—" he began.

"No," Tiaanet said, pulling Tantufi closer against herself, and quickly moved on.

Bibiki commanded his men to secure the Hall, which they did in short order, the bulk of the foot soldiers and archers clustering around the main entrance to prepare against an assault. A few archers entered the Hall's back corridors and moved up to the balconies. He then ordered the hostages into the donation alcoves, along the side of the Hall of Blessings. The rooms were small, and very quickly the children filled them, leaving Tiaanet and the other adult hostages to find resting places along the walls and at the foot of the Hall's vine- and flower-bedecked columns. After a long, contemplative look at the templefolk, then at the sleepers, Bibiki moved to the center of the room.

"You will not be harmed if you cooperate." He spoke loudly, as the Hall tended to swallow sound. Tiaanet saw several of the Servants grimace at the volume of his voice. "Unless the people of this city decide that you are not worth saving, but that is a matter for your concern and not mine."

Some of the Servants relaxed at this, but most remained stiffly silent, more affronted than afraid. After a moment one elder in Teachers' robes stepped forward.

"We will cooperate," he said. Perhaps to rebuke Bibiki for his loudness, he spoke so softly that Tiaanet could barely hear him. "If you allow, we can provide your men with food and drink, and care for any injuries they might have. Not with magic." He glanced around, at the sleepers, and uttered a soft sigh. "Our magic depends on sleep, and sleep is dangerous around these poor souls—take heed. But we still have herb-craft, surgery, and some small alchemy. All we ask is that you commit no further acts of violence in this hall. We stand before the likeness of Hananja, and Hananja treasures peace."

Bibiki stared at him, plainly incredulous. "You foment open rebellion in the streets, then offer us hospitality?" He shook his head and sighed. "I may never understand you people. My men will eat and drink nothing from your hands, and we need none of your healing. However, if any of the hostages have need, you may see to them."

The Teacher inclined his head and started to turn away. "As for violence," Bibiki said, forestalling him, "on that I make no promises. We are soldiers and this is war. We do what is necessary."

There were murmurs of approval from the edges of the room: Bibiki's soldiers, most of whom watched the templefolk sullenly. The Teacher regarded Bibiki and them for a long moment, disgust curling his lip. Then, wordlessly, he turned away and began speaking to his brethren.

Weary, for she had not rested well in the past fourday, Tiaanet settled down in the shadow of one of the pillars, shifting Tantufi into her lap to ease the strain on her arms and shoulders. She had snatched naps when she dared with Tantufi so near, in between being bundled onto horses or shoved into makeshift corrals with the other hostages. It helped that she had long ago cultivated the knack of sensing when Tantufi was moving into dreaming sleep, and waking before her own soul could be ensnared.

But although the usual drugs must have worn off days before, Tantufi had kept herself awake the whole while, employing all the little habits she had cultivated over the years: constantly moving some part of her body, rolling her eyes, biting her tongue and hands, and whispering to herself in an unending monotone babble. She could not keep it up forever, and indeed Tiaanet had already noticed the signs that she would soon sleep whether she wished it or not. Her manic movements were slowing. Whenever her moon-round eyes blinked shut, it took her longer and longer to reopen them. With the brutal aid of their father's guards, Tantufi might have gone longer, but amid the strain of the past few days, with the lulling peace of the Hetawa all around them now, Tiaanet suspected it would not be long before Tantufi gave in.

Insurret settled against the wall across from Tiaanet, watching her with glittering eyes. The trip had made Tiaanet's mother more lucid than she had been in years, as if the hardships of traveling had forced her mind out of its endless loops of insensibility. That had done nothing to ease her hatred. But to Tiaanet's relief, she had not spoken a word since the soldiers had taken them from their green-lands estate.

"Will you have water, lady?" A Hetawa youth, probably set to the task by his superiors, paused beside her with an urn and dipper in his hands.

"Thank you," Tiaanet said. The boy gave her the dipper, which Tiaanet held for Tantufi, then drank herself before handing it back. "And my mother," she said, nodding across the aisle at Insurret.

The boy nodded absently, and Tiaanet saw that he too was star- ing at Tantufi. Giving the boy a cold look, Tiaanet shifted so that Tantufi's face was hidden from casual view. The boy flinched at the silent rebuke, bobbed over the dipper in apology, and turned away to offer water to Insurret.

"This is pointless," Orenajah murmured at Tiaanet's side. Like the other hostages, she had peered curiously at Tantufi the first day, but by now the child's appearance did not trouble her. "The city has gone mad. No one will care that we are being held here."

Tiaanet knew that her father would care, and very much. He would certainly care enough to offer ransom; he might even care enough to betray his comrades and the resistance, though Tiaanet suspected he would stop at incriminating himself. And others of the conspirators would care that the Hetawa had been breached—so many that they might withdraw their support from Wanahomen, now when it was essential that he have unity among his allies.

"The Kisuati are still strong," Tiaanet said. "I heard Bibiki telling his men that the bulk of the Kisuati forces had retreated to Yanya-iyan. If the Prince's alliance falls apart, then the Kisuati need only exert themselves a little to regain control. Kill the Prince, destroy the Hetawa, and the people's spirit will be broken. Gujaareh will be theirs again."

Orenajah frowned, contemplating that. "I don't care so much if I die," she said at last. "I would have commissioned a Gatherer soon anyhow. But—" She looked across the aisle at the alcoves, where weeping children could be heard within.

Tiaanet could not help turning to gaze at the pallets of sleepers. Sharers and acolytes moved among them now, tending them as they must have done for the past month; she saw one woman, older than herself, being diapered.

"It doesn't matter," she murmured, turning away. She had seen victims of Tantufi's power before. Nothing could be done for them; best to regard them as already dead. "We must consider ourselves now."

Behind her she heard Orenajah's faint sniff of disapproval at this, but the old woman said nothing more.

"Mama," whispered Tantufi. Tiaanet looked down at her; the huge, bloodshot eyes were on her face, lucid for the moment. "The people."

The sleepers. "Shh," Tiaanet said. "Are you hungry?"

Tantufi shook her head fiercely. "No no no." She turned, looking over Tiaanet's shoulder at the pallets; her face tightened in palpable distress. "So many, Mama."

"It doesn't matter," Tiaanet said again. "Nothing matters for you but me, and for me but you. Hasn't it always been thus? Be still now."

Tantufi fell silent at last, resuming her manic movements, but her eyes lingered on the sleepers, and now and again she made a low, fluting sound of despair. Across the aisle, Insurret uttered a faint contemptuous snort, but otherwise kept her silence, and so Tiaanet ignored her.

A relative silence fell in the Hall as they waited—for what, Tiaanet did not know. Another acolyte passed, this one carrying slabs of flat bread; apparently Bibiki was allowing some templefolk to visit their storerooms under guard. Tiaanet took a piece of bread, more to keep herself awake than out of any real hunger, and pressed Tantufi to eat for the same reason. The girl had begun to grow still for brief periods of time, another warning of impending sleep.

But before Tiaanet could get Tantufi to eat, she jumped as one of the soldiers near the Hetawa's main doors called sharply, "Captain!"

Bibiki, conferring in a corner with some of his soldiers, immediately went to the doors to see what was the matter. There was nothing else for a long while; Tiaanet ate and fed Tantufi, chewing some of the bread for her, as the child's teeth were loose. But eventually it became clear that something was happening outside. The soldiers had become more alert, clustering at the front door and windows with weapons held ready. Their tension jarred the Hall's air of peace.

Abruptly Tiaanet heard Bibiki murmur, "I do *not* believe this," and laugh. "Well, well. Perhaps this mess will end sooner than I first thought. Let us see if we can take him alive."

The men shuffled themselves quickly, though Tiaanet could not see what they were doing or why. Then she heard the deep bronze groan of the Hetawa's doors being opened.

The Servants, all around the Hall, tensed at once. "They are drawing weapons," said one Sharer in an audible, incensed whisper. He clenched his fists. "Weapons!"

"Peace," said the Teacher near him, but he looked no happier about it.

Then Bibiki's voice called, "Now!" and Tiaanet heard the twang-hiss of arrows. A great roar echoed into the Hall, a thousand angry men's voices, and the voices of women and elders and children as well. Over this she heard Bibiki shout, "Fire into the front line! Drive them back! You four, go and fetch him. Hurry. The rest of you, cover them!"

There was a great flurry of activity at the Hetawa entrance before a moment later the doors groaned shut. And then a cluster of Bibiki's men came running into the center of the hall, one of them pulling along a woman in barbarian garb who struggled wildly in his hands. One Kisuati soldier dragged another Banbarra, but even from her vantage Tiaanet could see that this man was dead; a single arrow had stuck through his throat. Blood began to pool around him as soon as they dropped him to the floor.

The third figure that they dragged with them bled as well, but cursed and struggled as they dropped him to the floor. Wanahomen.

"Mind your snakeling, daughter." Insurret's voice pulled Tiaanet back to her own concerns. Insurret was smiling; she nodded toward Tiaanet's arms. With a sharp stab of alarm Tiaanet realized that

Tantufi's body had gone slack, her eyes shut and mouth hanging open.

"No—" Immediately Tiaanet shook her, as hard as she dared short of injury. Tantufi's eyes, glazed and unseeing, opened a crack but drifted shut again almost at once. "'Tufi, wake. You *must* not sleep, not now."

Not in a room full of sleepers, their souls already weakened by long captivity. Not in the heart of the Hetawa, surrounded by narcomancers who would know Tantufi at once for what she was.

But it was too late. Tiaanet shook her again, slapped her, even lifted one limp hand and clamped her own teeth over one of the recent scars there, but Tantufi did not stir. It was always so whenever she finally fell asleep; if not woken at once, her body demanded recompense for the days of abuse. Nothing short of a beating would wake her at that point.

Leaving Tiaanet helpless and terrified as her daughter sighed, snuggled closer to her breast, and quietly began to dream.

43

☾⊙☽

The Battle of Flesh

Wanahomen would not stop struggling beneath Hanani's hands. "Shadow-spawned belly-crawling shit-eating sons of jackals!" He pushed her hands away when she tried to examine the arrow in his chest, glaring fury at the Kisuati soldiers clustered around them and trying to sit up. "Have you no honor at all? For defiling the Hetawa you should suffer the wrath of every god—"

The cluster parted and a Kisuati man, wearing a black leopard-skin mantle and an air of command, came to peer down at them. "Very likely we shall, Prince," he said in heavily accented Gujaareen. "But as I suffer, I shall content myself with the fact that for a time, at least, I was accorded a hero by my people for capturing you. You," and he looked sharply at Hanani. "Are you some sort of healer, or just his woman?"

The wound in Wanahomen's thigh was bleeding too much. The arrow in his chest might have gone deep enough to pierce his lung, but the thigh was more dangerous in the short term. "I'm a Sharer-Apprentice of this Hetawa," she said to the Kisuati, getting a good grip on Wanahomen's robes and tearing them open so she could see the wound. "Loaned to the Prince in token of our alliance."

She heard rather than saw the Kisuati commander's surprise. "I see. Well, then—since that is your purpose, please keep him alive. I'll send someone out to let his troops know he'll die if they try to batter down the door."

"Keep me alive so you can execute me." Wanahomen laughed bitterly, then winced as this pained his chest.

"Yes, yes, as you like," Hanani snapped, impatient with both men. Unnecessary threats and pointless resistance; she had no time for their barbaric posturing. Beyond the soldiers, she could see some of the templefolk gathering, and among them a familiar face. "Nhen-ne-verra-brother!"

Nhen-ne-verra started, then came forward. "Yes...?" His eyes widened in belated recognition. "*Hanani?*"

"I think this arrow has nicked the great artery of his leg," she said. She sat up and unbuckled one of the girdles Yanassa had given her—the one meant to carry the affection-tokens of her lovers. She pulled it off and looped it around Wanahomen's thigh above the arrow. "I can work the healing, but I dare not pull the arrow yet. That may be the only thing stopping the flood..."

She trailed off as one of the soldiers moved aside and she saw Charris, still carrying her saddlebags, facedown in a pool of blood. Someone had pulled the arrow from him, but he did not stir.

"*Charris!*" Wanahomen tried to get up; one of the soldiers pointed a sword at his throat and he swore a string of Banbarra invective. "Hanani—" He turned to her, his eyes wide with fear. "Help him. Please."

There was too much blood around Charris's body. Hanani concentrated on tightening the tourniquet around Wanahomen's thigh to delay telling him the truth a moment longer. But Nhen-ne-verra crouched beside her. "One of our acolytes is seeing to him, Prince."

A boy nearly old enough for apprenticeship had knelt beside Charris. His examination took only a moment; the look on his face was confirmation enough. "No," Wanahomen whispered, and then made a sound that was half moan and half sob. "Gods, no."

Hanani forced herself to concentrate on the wound. There would be time to comfort him later. "I think we have a piece of luck," she said to Nhen-ne-verra. "The arrow in the chest may not have pierced the lung. I can't hear air, and his breathing doesn't seem impaired."

Nhen-ne-verra moved to rip the clothing around the chest-arrow for a closer look. "Ah, yes—it lodged between the ribs, just a flesh wound. One moment." He yanked the arrow out of Wanahomen's chest. Wanahomen screamed, then glared at Nhen-ne-verra in pure affront. Hanani almost smiled; if anger and pride alone could sustain a man, Wanahomen would be recovered within a day.

"If you tend the leg, Brother, and pull the arrow when the time seems appropriate—" She reached for Wanahomen's eyes. But Nhen-ne-verra caught her wrist sharply.

"You can't heal him," he said. "Not with magic, not here." He gestured around the Hall, where Hanani at last noticed the rows of sleeping figures.

"And more than this dead," Nhen-ne-verra said, when she caught her breath in horror. "Every few days, something sweeps through them like a flood. These are just the new ones brought since the last culling. We can do nothing to save them—or to save anyone else, since healing sleep is enough like true sleep that— Well." He lowered his eyes.

Completely thrown by this turn of events, Hanani looked at Wanahomen, who had faded somewhat; he lay panting in the aftermath of the arrow's withdrawal. The beads of sweat on his brow pulled her out of her daze. "In my saddlebags, the ones that man was carrying," she said to the acolyte who had seen to Charris, and who now hovered nearby. "My ornaments are there. Please make preparations for a surgery ritual." The youth looked startled for a breath, but then he immediately went to Charris's body to rummage for her tools.

"Hanani—" Nhen-ne-verra shook his head. "Do you have dream-blood to ease his pain? With the Gatherers imprisoned, we have almost none left, among us. If he passes out, the nightmares will take him."

"If I do nothing, he'll bleed to death," she said, struggling to remain respectful. Of course she understood the danger. Did he think she was a fool? But he did, she now realized—and so did many of the full Sharers, who had often spoken to her as if she were still an acolyte, or especially stupid, long after she'd proven herself the equal of the other apprentices. She'd thought she had grown used to their casual disregard. What had changed so in the past month that she no longer had the patience for it?

"And you can't use magic to cleanse his body," Nhen-ne-verra continued. Lecturing. "When the wound takes poison—"

"I would welcome any alternate suggestions, Brother." She looked him in the eye, knowing he had none. Finally Nhen-ne-verra looked away and shook his head.

Hanani looked at Wanahomen's face. He had subsided after the arrow, and now watched her. She was reminded suddenly of the night he had held her while she mourned Mni-inh, and a fierce, painful fear took hold of her. She was tired of losing people. It was one thing to lose Wanahomen to his throne, and her duty; another altogether to lose him to death.

"You're strong, Prince," she said, reaching up to touch his lips. Some of his blood was on her fingers. It left a smear like Banbarra lip paint. "You've survived too much to falter here, now."

Wanahomen lifted his eyebrows in surprise at her gesture. Belatedly it occurred to her that she had never done anything affectionate toward him before. Perhaps it pleased him. "Of course I won't die," he said, and she was heartened by the scorn in his tone. "Hurry up and make me well."

Hanani nodded, then got to her feet.

Her Banbarra robes—loose, filthy with travel dust and horse sweat—were completely unsuitable for surgery. She removed her outer tunic and tossed that aside, then the loose shift underneath. She had stopped wearing breast-wrappings since Wanahomen's first visit, because they were an annoyance when she wanted sex. The Banbarra leather breast-bands chafed her, however, and having found no suitable substitute, she had finally opted to wear nothing underneath her shift. Nhen-ne-verra turned bright red in the way of pale men, but after a single shocked glance at her breasts he looked away and said nothing, knowing as she did that now was not the time to quibble about propriety.

The acolyte returned, carrying Hanani's ornaments and a water jar, followed closely by another youth who carried the wide basin of heated red wax kept in one of the prayer chambers for the surgery ritual. If either of the boys was thrown by Hanani's breasts, neither was foolish enough to show it. "May we assist, Sharer-Apprentice?" asked the first boy.

Hanani blinked in surprise. She had never expected another acolyte to serve her after Dayu, much less two. Ah, but of course: surgeries were rare, and they might never have another chance to witness one. "You may assist," she said. "Hold the bowl." Bracing herself, for the wax was still hot enough to sting, she thrust her hands into the bowl. The wax was beeswax—said, like honey, to prevent festering—mixed with hekeh fiber and herbs known to aid healing. She dipped her hands four times, whispering an invocation to the Goddess after each, and after the fourth dip lifted her hands; the wax coated them to the mid-forearm in thin, flexible gloves.

While Nhen-ne-verra came over to dip his hands, the other acolyte held forward her ornaments on a leather pad, and she saw that he had polished them with stinging-acacia ointment and laid them out in the proper order. When Hanani nodded approval, the boy's delighted smile reminded her, for a jarring instant, of Dayuhotem.

But she pushed that memory aside, picked up the long, wafer-thin white-opal knife, and crouched beside Wanahomen. "Do you want something to bite down on, Prince?"

He was gazing at the ceiling, taking deep breaths. "What good will that do? Just get on with it."

Hanani nodded, then bent forward and made a quick, bone-deep slice with the opal knife on either side of the arrow. The knife's thinness made it pass through skin and muscle as easily as butter. Unfortunately butter felt no pain, while Wanahomen caught his breath and went rigid in pure agony. He managed not to make a sound as Hanani put the opal back on the pad and prized the wound open with her fingers, though his breath came very hard and his hands tightened into trembling fists.

It was difficult to see around the seeping blood, but the damage to the great artery was plain enough; the arrow crushed and cut into its outer side. That too was luck, for the arrowhead blocked most of the hole it had created. Otherwise he would have bled out already.

"Jade," she said, and the acolyte quickly offered her a thin, curved needle, already threaded with fibers of dried horse sinew. "Nhen-ne-verra-brother." Nhen-ne-verra took hold of the arrow. When Hanani nodded, he pulled it free. Blood gushed at once, a small fountain that would have been far worse if not for the tourniquet. As quickly as she could Hanani slid the needle through the artery several times and pulled the sinew tight. That stopped the flood, though not the smaller leaks—

"Hanani." The urgency in Nhen-ne-verra's tone warned her. She looked up to see Wanahomen's eyelids fluttering, his eyes rolling back.

"Prince," she said, making her voice sharp. "*Wanahomen*." He blinked several times, finally managing to focus on her, though it clearly took an effort. "Do you want to know what Yanassa told me about you?"

That woke him, though he groaned softly. "Sh-she told you . . . ?"

Switching to the tiny nightstone needle, Hanani worked quickly to seal the leaks, nodding for one of the acolytes to dribble salted water into the wound so she could see. Wanahomen uttered a strangled scream at that, stiffening again and panting through his teeth. "Oh, many secrets," she said, to distract him. "She said you called for your mother, once, at the height, and your mother yelled back through the tent-wall for you to cry some other name and not embarrass her."

Nhen-ne-verra was waiting, his hand on the tourniquet. As soon as she pulled the last suture tight, Hanani nodded. Nhen-ne-verra loosened the belt. The wound welled with blood almost immediately—but most of it was from the wound-widening Hanani had done, not from the great vein. Hopefully that meant he would take no gangrene in the limb. Hanani exhaled in relief; Nhen-ne-verra nodded approval. Taking up the jade again, Hanani quickly began to sew the muscle back together.

"Sh-she . . . told you . . . nothing of the sort," Wanahomen gritted through his teeth. One of his hands opened and closed convulsively with each dip of the needle. "You are—ah, gods, gods!—the most incompetent liar I have ever seen."

The skin was the easiest to stitch, and the worst for pain. Hanani worked as quickly as she could, but Wanahomen shuddered with every dip of the needle, tossing his head from side to side and panting like a bellows. By the time she was finally done, his body ran with sweat and the pool of blood under his leg had soaked Hanani's skirts from knees to ankles.

"It needs wrapping," Hanani said at last, sitting back with a sigh, "but it's done." Nhen-ne-verra looked relieved as well, and belatedly Hanani realized he had been nearly as tense as Wanahomen. It was a Sharer's instinct to attack pain, not inflict it.

Wanahomen made no sound, though, and Hanani looked at him

quickly, fearing that he had fainted. He was awake, though staring off through the pillars at something else, a frown of confusion on his face. Hanani followed his gaze to see a young woman, tall and slim in the way of a shunha or Kisuati, sitting against the far wall with a spindly-limbed child in her arms. She was shaking the child, murmuring endearments to wake her, but the child flopped about bonelessly.

"Fetch bandages," Hanani said absently, and one of the acolytes immediately ran off to obey, going to the compartments between the alcoves where healing supplies were kept. "Nhen-ne-verra-brother, that woman..."

Nhen-ne-verra looked. "Yes, I saw them as they came in. The child has some sort of wasting sickness. I offered to examine her, but the woman— Well, they're shunha."

"Tiaanet?" Wanahomen said suddenly. His speech was slurred; whatever strength had sustained him through the surgery was fading. "T-Tiaanet?"

Beyond the pillars, the woman looked up. Hanani saw that she was incredibly beautiful, though there was a deep anxiety marring her features now. She gazed at Wanahomen for a moment, but then looked away, and resumed shaking the child in her arms.

"I can wrap this, if you want to see to her," Nhen-ne-verra said.

Hanani nodded and rose. She looked a sight with her skirts drenched in blood from the knees down; her own red drapes, she thought bleakly. But she peeled the wax from her hands and gave it to the waiting acolyte, then went to the woman.

"Pardon me," she said. The woman looked up, her eyes wide with a taut, flaring protectiveness that made Hanani stop in her tracks. Standing over them, Hanani could see then what Nhen-ne-verra meant: the child was obviously ill, though with no sickness Hanani could recognize. She was nearly bald, and although Hanani guessed by her size that she had seen five or six floods of the river, her skin was as thin and papery in texture as an old woman's. Her bones showed so starkly that Hanani could see where some of them had been broken in the past, then had healed crookedly, or in knots. It was equally obvious that the child had never been well nourished.

All troubling enough on its own. But even worse, the child was asleep.

Forcing her eyes away from the child's appearance, Hanani focused on the—mother? Sister? Mother, she decided on instinct. "If you like, we can tend her for you," she said to the woman.

"She's fine," the woman snapped.

Hanani shook her head slowly. "This sickness is a thing of magic," she said. "Your child will not wake on her own. But we can at least make her comfortable." She gestured toward the other sleepers.

The little girl moaned then, her face tightening in sleep so that she looked even older. Her whole body tensed, frail as it was, and she tossed her head as Wanahomen had done, reacting to some inner torment. A nightmare. Hanani looked away. This was how Mni-inh had died.

But a sound, soughing through the Hetawa like a wind, startled her out of melancholy. She turned, confused, and realized: the sleepers. Some of them were shifting in their sleep, moaning just as the little girl had. The sound was the massed voice of their suffering.

"Oh Goddess, protect us." Nhen-ne-verra got to his feet, his wax-coated fists clenching. "Please, not again."

The Kisuati soldiers were equally unnerved, some of them lifting weapons. Hanani saw their commander come into the center of the room, frowning around at the suddenly stirring sleepers. "What?" Hanani began, but suddenly she understood. Nhen-ne-verra had spoken of something that swept through the sleepers from time to time. Now she saw that it was a nightmare: *the same* nightmare, attacking all of them at once.

But—

"Nononono," whimpered the child in her sleep. "Nono, Papa."

An instant later:

"No!" cried a woman nearby, her words blurry with sleep but intelligible. "No, Father, please!"

An old man uttered a weak, shaken moan. "My father, I beg you...no, no..."

"Don't," wept another man, a heavyset fellow who had the look of a soldier or guard. "No, gods please—no!" The last was wrenched out of him, a startled, agonized cry. His eyes flew open as he arched upward, seeing nothing. One of the Sharers who had been tending the sleepers ran over to him, but before he could get there, the warrior gasped and clutched his chest. A great shudder passed through him and a moment later he sagged, his eyes rolling back. The Sharer crouched and examined him, then groaned in an echo of the sleeper's own anguish.

The skin along the back of Hanani's neck prickled. She turned, slowly, back to the woman and the strange child.

The woman—Tiaanet, Wanahomen had called her—was watching Hanani, crouched and tense as a wild animal. In the interminable breath that passed, Hanani suddenly understood what was happening, and what the child had to do with it. In that same instant, the woman saw that Hanani knew.

The child stiffened in her arms, choking back a cry. A breath later all the sleepers cried out, some screaming at the tops of their lungs. As if this had been a trigger, the woman bolted, leaping to her feet and deliberately slamming into Hanani with the child in her arms. Hanani fell to the floor, and the woman ran past her toward the back of the Hall of Blessings.

The Kisuati soldiers, distracted by the screaming sleepers, did not react to the fleeing woman at first. Hanani scrambled to her feet and cried a warning, but it was lost amid so many raised voices. Only when the screams began to fade—some of them stopping with ominous abruptness—did Hanani manage to make herself heard. "My brothers, that child!" She pointed after the woman. "*That child is the source of the dream!*"

The soldiers finally noticed, but none of them were near Tiaanet. The templefolk reacted more quickly, some of them gasping and starting after the woman at once. The woman ran through the heavy-curtained door that led to the inner Hetawa.

The Kisuati commander gave a round curse and shouted something over the din of the sleepers. Four soldiers immediately jumped and went after the woman. There was a scuffle at the door as the soldiers shouted at three Sharers who were also running to follow the woman. Hanani wanted to follow as well, but duty stopped her; until Wanahomen was healthy, she had no business leaving him. So she went back to Wanahomen's side and knelt, taking his hand.

"Tiaanet," he murmured. "That was Tiaanet. I'm certain of it." He frowned, looking troubled. "She saw me. Why did she not . . . ?"

"She was afraid for her child, I think, whoever she was," Hanani said. One of the acolytes had cleaned up the spilled blood and was bandaging Wanahomen's leg. The other was placing a pad of leather and herbs over the chest wound. Hanani nodded approval at the boys, who returned her nod with great seriousness. "Though if that child is indeed the source of the nightmare that's killed so many, it explains much. Do you know her?"

Wanahomen nodded slowly. Hanani was troubled by the fact that he was still sweating, and now shivering faintly. She touched the boy applying the poultice and signaled for him to fetch water and a blanket. "Shunha. Her father—one of my allies. I had hoped—" His frown deepened. "Her *child*, you said?"

"I believe so." She paused then, startled, as someone pushed quickly through the crowd around Wanahomen: Teacher Yehamwy.

"Apprentice, what did you see? Are you certain about that child?"

Hanani blinked, as thrown by the councilor's appearance as the questions. Yehamwy looked drawn and deeply weary, as if he had not slept well in days—as perhaps he had not. But there was a feverish intensity in his expression now that unnerved her.

"I'm not certain, no," she said. "But it seemed to me the sleepers were reacting to the child's dreams." Hesitantly she added, "The Prince says the woman is Tiaanet, of shunha caste. The child is her daughter."

Yehamwy caught his breath and turned to another Teacher whom Hanani did not know. The Teacher nodded grimly and said, "Insurret's lineage. That was one of the motherlines we meant to investigate."

"She's a snake," said a voice from amid the pillars, and they all turned to see a woman of middle years crouching against the far wall. The resemblance between her and Tiaanet was immediately discernible, as was the glitter of madness in her eyes. "Always hissing, hissing in my mind, worse when I slept. I knew she was poison even in the womb. Couldn't wait to get away from her. Now she has birthed her own viper-child, and may it kill her. May it kill her!"

Yehamwy threw a look at the other Teacher. "Insurret?"

"So it would seem."

Yehamwy took a deep breath and went to the woman, crouching before her. "I give you greeting, Lady Insurret," he said. "Tell me: what did you mean about your daughter 'hissing in your mind'?"

Insurret abruptly grew sullen. "Why do you ask about her? Everyone asks about her. Everyone *wants* her, not me."

Yehamwy looked uneasy, doubtless wishing he could call a Sharer to heal the woman's madness. But he leaned forward, speaking urgently. "We need to find her, lady. If what we believe is true, she and the W— She and her child may hold the key to saving many lives."

"So you want her too." The pure vitriol in Insurret's voice sent a shiver down Hanani's spine. If she had not seen madness in the woman's eyes before that, she would have known it by that tone. "Take her then, if you like; I don't care. Comes weeping to me, she does, comes weeping and tells me that her father— Her father has—" Insurret began to rock back and forth, her face tightening. After a moment she fell silent, rubbing her hands on her knees. Abruptly she shook her head. "Lying, spiteful whore! If he did, it was her fault. *Her* fault!"

Yehamwy drew back, his face reflecting the same shock and revulsion Hanani felt. Then he visibly steeled himself and tried again. "Be that as it may, lady, we need to understand the sickness that plagues her child. Will you tell us? Can the child release the people she captures with her dreams?"

"Why are you asking about *her*?" Insurret glared up at him. "That abomination should have been strangled at birth. But always, always, *he* does as she pleases. 'Let me keep it,' she says, and *he* indulges her, always, such a pretty girl, so much prettier than me, the child is her burden to bear so *why should I care about that whoregotten demon child?*"

And before Yehamwy could react, Insurret surged up from her crouch and shoved him. With a startled cry, Yehamwy tried to rise and stumbled back, and although Hanani saw what was coming, she could not react fast enough to prevent it. Flailing his arms, Yehamwy fell across Wanahomen's legs.

Wanahomen screamed, stiffening in agony, and before the last breath had left his lungs, his eyes rolled back, the lids fluttering shut.

"*No!*" With no regard for propriety Hanani shoved Yehamwy off him, but it was already too late. All around them were sleepers, the survivors still moaning and thrashing. Wanahomen would fall right into the worst of the horror.

And Hanani would lose one more person she cared about to that Goddess-damned dream.

No, I will not.

Without another thought, Hanani put her fingers on Wanahomen's eyelids and flung herself into nightmare.

44

☾⊙☽

The Battle of Soul

The world was made of red and bones. Tumbling as he fell, screaming, the man who had been Wanahomen found himself reduced to a cipher. The memory of waking was still in him, though distant and faded, as with childhood. He was no longer a prince. The red world had remade him. Here he was a weak thing, lowest of an unfathomable hierarchy, and he knew without question that there was no hope for his survival. For this was not the imperfect mirror of the realm between, or even the necessary shadow of Hananja's brilliant soul. This was another place altogether, someone else's place, and within it *hope* was a word with no meaning.

He did not so much land as mire himself. The red was thick and clotted in places, not solid enough to stand on but sufficient for crawling. So he crawled, up to his chin in warm, redolent filth, his arms and legs straining to make their way past bones that made no sense: human skulls with extra jaws, hands with ten fingers, unidentifiable jointed masses. And he wept, for his heart was filled with despair such as he had never known in the waking realm. He was alone. He was afraid. He felt so weak. And soon—the taste of imminence was like bitter apples on his tongue, or perhaps that was the muck—he would meet this realm's master.

For endless seasons, the man struggled. When light and heat blazed toward him from on high, he thought it was death come at last, and part of him rejoiced. But the fire that seared through the red had a cleanliness to it that he knew instinctively was not of this place. Where had it come from? He did not know, but he felt only dull envy—until it enveloped him and lifted him free of the muck.

"This place rapes the soul," said a familiar, female voice. Who was she? He did not know, but he clung to her bright, shapeless presence, pathetically grateful to no longer be alone. "I've never seen a construct so foul! Protect yourself, Prince."

He did not understand what—or who—she meant at first. Was he "Prince"? And what was a construct?

But then there came a great pulsing stir in the red, and the bones underneath them heaved as a great mass crawled from within the landscape. He beheld a long, sinuous shape, like a snake, if snakes grew to the thickness of rivers. Down its length sprouted marching, matching limbs—like those of a scorpion or centipede, though each ended in massive hands the size of buildings. Most were balled into fists, and as they lifted and fell with the creature's movements, the man spied rings on some of the fingers. These left blood-filled imprints in the spongy flesh of the ground as the hands walked.

But it was the creature's head, which rose from the muck on a long, thick shaft of a neck, that made the man begin to scream—for it was *his father*.

The face was the same, though distorted with a kind of gleeful, sadistic hunger. In that face the man saw all his father's madness made manifest. *This* was the monster who had nearly destroyed his own nation to feed his ambition—and who had devoured his son's future with the same ruthless greed. A more terrible monster than ever the Reaper had been, for both ate lives, but only one did so knowingly. *Lovingly.*

But as the man screamed, the woman blazed bright with sudden fury. "*You,*" she snarled.

Startled out of terror, the man flinched silent as the woman beside him took shape—but it was not a shape that matched his memories of her. When he sought those memories, what came to mind was softer, somehow: gentle fingers, a flood of coiled hair the color of wet sand, a stammering voice, ripe brown-nippled breasts that tasted of sea salt and sweetness—though how he knew all this he could not recall. But the woman who appeared was different from his imaginings. She had dressed herself as a man, in loindrapes too starkly straight for her curving hips, a collar too broad for her narrow shoulders, with her flood of hair dammed away behind bindings and bun. And some things about her actively bothered him, for they felt wrong somehow. The loindrapes she wore were red, but there were darker wet spots all over them. Thick redness coated her gentle hands— blood? The thicker, bitter stuff of this place? He could not tell, but it flexed like fine gloves when her hands became fists.

"*Take that face off,*" she said. Her voice was a whisper—but so filled with rage that it made the whole of the red world ripple. A wind, sudden and cold, swirled out of nothingness and whipped across the bone plain. The woman's face blurred with it, doubling. Beneath her angry face: a weeping, wailing figure. When she shrieked the next words, there was a scraping edge of madness in her voice. "How dare you pretend to be Mni-inh-brother when you killed him? *Take that face off, you abomination!*"

She is forgetting herself, the man thought. He knew it was true, even if he did not know how.

And the woman was gone, running across the red muck as if it were packed earth, *toward* the monster. Which reared up—it was a hundred times her size—and raised its many fists, roaring challenge in a bull elephant's trumpeting voice.

Leaving behind the man, who stared after her from the muck, distracted from his own misery. But as his earlier despair faded, he began to understand.

Not just his father. The beast wore the faces of *all* fathers, any father, the void left by a father's absence, for whoever dared to look upon it. It used those faces, and the memories they elicited, to strike silent blows and leave unfading bruises. But beneath this nightmare face—

—nightmare, nightmare, gods, wait, this is a dream—

—What face did it truly wear?

The beast's fists struck the earth. The red substance quaked and heaved beneath the man, throwing him onto his back into the muck. When he struggled upright, he was shocked to see that the beast had gone down. Several of its dozen arms on one side had crumpled beneath it, shriveling even as the man watched. And there—moving among the monster's flailing limbs, screaming like a beast herself, was the woman. She touched another arm and it went dead, the muscles knotting and snapping with a sound like cut rope. When she set her feet and shouted at the thing's face—*"TAKE IT OFF! TAKE IT OFF!"*—something rippled forth from her mouth, and her very voice made the thing's neck twist and turn black with gangrene. Its head sagged to the ground, its face—

—my father, no, no, not him—

—Contorting in agony. She was killing it with every touch, making its flesh sicken and die by will alone.

And that was *wrong*. The man felt it down to the core of his being. She was not the soft thing he had considered her, that had been a mistake—but neither was she this wild, avenging death-bringer. He knew as well as anyone how grief could flense the soul, leaving wounds that festered until nothing eased the pain but anger and violence. But this was *not her*. She was—

—*the stone within a ripe fruit. Flint and metal, blood and tears. A prayer at the height of lovemaking*—

—Aier. She was Aier.

And he, he was not some nameless coward; he had not been lost in this realm for seasons, centuries, eternities. In waking he was a warrior. He lifted a hand, made a fist, remembered the feel of a sword-hilt within it. As he did so, the sword appeared. Yes. His father's sword, Mwet-zu-anyan. The sword of the Prince of the Sunset Throne.

His sword. Because in waking he was Wanahomen, leader of the Yusir-Banbarra hunt. And in dreaming—

(Hanani. Her name was Hanani, and she was his lover and his healer.)

—In dreaming he was Niim.

And Niim was a dreamer of portents and omens, nephew of Gujaareh's greatest Gatherer, scion of brilliantly mad and madly brilliant kings. He was the Avatar of Hananja. He would be Prince someday, and when that ended he was destined to sit at the right hand of the Goddess of Dreams Herself.

The Prince of Gujaareh got to his feet, sword in hand, and headed across the red world to bring Hananja's Servant back to herself.

*　　*　　*

Yanya-iyan's garden was the secret stronghold of the palace. It was accessible only by a single glass door—an actual door rather than the useless open entryways Gujaareen thought of as doors—that could be locked shut. It contained a small shed full of gardening implements: sharp-bladed hoes, wicked-tined pitchforks, axes, long knives. Its walls were lined with thick plates of obsidian, meant to hold the garden's warmth at night—but also too hard for any battering ram to easily break. The plates allowed the growth of exotic plants from far-away lands, including poisonous herbs that could be used against an enemy or for a final escape, should all other defenses fail.

The Gatherers and Sentinels had taken it in half a breath. Anzi had lined his men up to defend the Protectors, directing his archers to fire at the door in waves as the Sentinels began their assault. They had not expected the glass door to hold of course, and it had not; a stone was thrown through from the corridors beyond the garden, and Anzi's soldiers braced themselves as the glass shattered and fell apart. But instead of a battle cry, Sunandi had heard then a familiar, chilling sound: the high-pitched whine of a jungissa stone.

When Sunandi woke, she lay sprawled in a bed of liti flowers and moontear vines, and Nijiri stood over her.

"I am told," Nijiri said quietly, "that a force of soldiers has invaded the Hetawa, taking my brethren, our children, and other Gujaareen citizens as hostages."

That brought her fully out of sleep with a gasp. Sitting up, she looked around and saw Anzi and all the Kisuati soldiers kneeling bound in a corner, surrounded by hard-eyed warrior-priests. Sunandi, the Protectors, and the other Kisuati courtiers had been left free in the bed of vines, but the Gatherers were their guards—and, apparently, interrogators.

But if the Protectors had been stupid enough to attack the Hetawa, they would all be lucky if *interrogator* was the only role the Gatherers played tonight.

Nijiri stepped closer to her, and despite their long association Sunandi found herself shivering under his regard. There was no compassion in his face, no friendliness in his eyes at all.

"You didn't know of this, Speaker?" he asked.

"I did not, Gatherer," Sunandi said. He knew full well that she would have tried to stop it if she had. Bad enough the Hetawa was involved at all. The new Gujaareen Prince—for he had won, wherever he was—had a vested interest in keeping the Protectors alive. The Hetawa had no such motivation, and now they would be furious beneath their cool, peaceful facades.

Nijiri nodded to himself. Beside him, the other Gatherer—the youngest, she thought his name was Inmu—looked angry as well, though Sunandi was less unnerved by his anger. The anger in Inmu's face was hot and human. The anger radiating from Nijiri was something different.

"Which of you orchestrated this offense against our Goddess?" he asked, looking down the line. "Speak, and present yourselves for judgment."

Aksata scowled at this. "You have no right to judge us," he said. "We've committed no wrong, and—"

Nijiri's hand darted forward, and an instant later Aksata sagged to the ground unconscious, a humming, dragonfly-shaped jungissa stone attached to his forehead. Nijiri jerked his head peremptorily at Inmu, who crouched and laid his fingers on Aksata's eyes.

"Oh, gods." Sasannante, his voice rising in pitch as he understood. "You can't kill him, you can't!"

But after several breaths Inmu stood and handed Nijiri's dragonfly-jungissa back to him. As an added gesture of contempt, Inmu left Aksata's corpse in an undignified sprawl. Sasannante let out a little moan of horror and fell silent.

"Stop this!" Anzi shouted from across the garden. Sunandi glared at him, willing him to be silent, but he ignored her. "How dare you? The Protectors of Kisua are—"

"Hananja's City obeys Hananja's Law," Nijiri said. He actually raised his voice; even Anzi subsided at the edged fury in his tone. "If you had no wish to be judged by that Law, you had no business coming here."

Mama Yao, with a bravery that Sunandi might have admired under saner circumstances, straightened at that. "This is war, Gatherer," she said. "There is no law in war. Your own people have committed atrocities; will you judge them too?"

"Yes. And those whose souls have been corrupted by this violence must die. Their peace can be used to soothe and heal the rest, and thus shall the Law be upheld." Nijiri's eyes narrowed at Mama Yao. "Did you order the attack on the Hetawa?"

"I did not," she said, frowning and blinking. Nijiri's statement that he intended to kill Gujaareen citizens had unnerved Yao; this was the first time Sunandi had ever seen the old woman nonplussed. "But I support the right of my fellow Protectors to do as they think is best for the good of Kisua."

Nijiri did not nod, but Sunandi thought she read a lessening of the anger in his face. He focused on Sasannante. "And you?"

"I knew nothing of the planned attack," he said, his voice low and miserable. Nijiri narrowed his eyes at him.

"You suspected, though."

"Yes, but I never thought they would go through with it! Taking children as hostages...I would never have condoned such a thing. But Aksata didn't bring this idea to us, Gatherer, before he decided to go through with it! He acted on his own—probably because he knew we'd say no. Or perhaps to protect us from the repercussions." Sasannante shook his head bitterly, gazing at Aksata's body.

After a moment, Nijiri nodded and moved on to Moib.

"I had nothing to do with it," said Moib, and again Nijiri set his jungissa on the man's forehead, dropping him like a stone. As he crouched beside Moib's body to do the Gathering himself this time, Anzi shouted again.

"He said he wasn't involved, gods damn you!"

"He was lying," Nijiri said flatly. He closed his eyes, and ten breaths later Moib was dead too.

Rising, Nijiri turned to Anzi. "Will you go to the Hetawa and call off your comrades?"

Anzi ground his teeth, trembling in rage. "I do not answer to you!"

To Sunandi's surprise—and intense relief—Nijiri only nodded. He turned back to Mama Yao. "Please order General Anzi to do as I've asked," he said. "You have lost. It is your choice whether to stay and face our Prince and his barbarian allies, or begin the journey back to Kisua. If you choose the latter, we will escort your people to the gates and give you supplies for the desert journey."

Mama Yao looked deeply shaken. They had all known Moib was lying; he and Aksata had been two of a kind in their plotting. That the Gatherer had sensed the lie was a more devastating display of his magic than any sleep-spell.

Yao looked at Sasannante, who nodded; with a heavy sigh Mama Yao nodded as well. "General," she said, "please convey our orders to Captain Bibiki at the Hetawa. The hostages are to be released, and he and his men are to return here, along with any remaining Kisuati in the city. We shall leave at once for home."

* * *

Tiaanet stumbled as she ran across the flagstones of the Hetawa courtyard, nearly spilling both Tantufi and herself amid the bodies there. She righted herself and saw that a Kisuati soldier lay at her feet, his neck broken and face frozen in an expression of surprise. Bibiki's forces had not yet returned to gather the bodies from their battle with the Sentinels, and she had tripped over this one's out-flung arm. Like Bibiki, the man wore an animal's pelt as a cloak: tawny gold short fur patterned with faint white rosettes. Another hunter. She had no idea what animal had made the pelt, but a wickedly long bone-handled dagger lay across the man's palm. Without thinking, Tiaanet shifted Tantufi over one shoulder and crouched to claim the weapon for herself.

The pause reawakened her wits. She had headed toward the House of Children in the vague hope of escaping through there into the city, exploiting the same means the Kisuati had used to enter the Hetawa complex. Now there were shouts behind her, and answering shouts ahead—Kisuati soldiers, raising the alarm. Of course they would have guards in the House of Children, and every other way in or out of the Hetawa. There was no way for her to escape. She needed to hide.

So she veered out of the courtyard, darting instead into one of the many other buildings in the Hetawa complex. A corridor; some stairs; a curtained entrance. She found herself in a tiny room, with an unmade pallet on one side and a few shelves and chests holding personal effects. Some templeman's private quarters.

Laying Tantufi on the pallet, she went to crouch beside the curtain, turning and turning the knife in her hands.

With her mother standing guard, Tantufi dreamed on.

*　　*　　*

She had not hated Azima.

She knew this now, as she walked toward the fallen monstrosity that was the Wild Dreamer, her red-coated hands held out from her sides. Azima had been a stranger to her; she had killed him out of fear and anger and the simple desire to survive. But she had not *known* him. He had done nothing to earn her wrath but be a hate-twisted fool.

The Wild Dreamer swung a vast fist at her, snarling in its inhuman voice, but she did not fear this. She had walked the nightmares of a goddess; why would a mere mortal trouble her? So it was a simple matter to raise a wall of blood around herself, which caught the swinging fist and held it fast. Yes, that was always the trick with working a healing in the shadowlands, though once she'd had trouble understanding this. The soul of a petitioner did not want *healing* in such a circumstance; it wanted more pain and ugliness. It wanted someone to acknowledge the filth of life, its foulness and bile. To enter a soul trapped in nightmare, one had to *become* a nightmare.

That was why Sonta-i had failed to kill it; he'd had no emotions, no way to understand. And Mni-inh, for all his skill and quick temper, did not have much of what this dreamer needed: slow-burning, long-simmered, helpless fruitless rage. Knowledge of what it meant to be betrayed (*given away disrespected exploited*) by those who should have nurtured and protected. Familiarity with being weak among the strong, with receiving not even the basic respect due another living being. Knowing how it felt to be a low and unworthy *thing* in the eyes of others.

(Sonta-i? Mni-inh? Azima? For a moment the memory of who they were slipped away, but then it edged back, hesitant.)

But even if Mni-inh had understood how to get through the beast's defenses, he would not have had enough hate in his soul to outmatch it.

"You took him from me," she said. She touched its straining fist, and it crumpled beneath her touch, flesh crisping and bones turning to ash. It screamed, and she began walking down its length, killing it as she went. (Did the beast cringe further, at her words? Hard to tell. Harder to care.) "Mni-inh. And you took my—" She faltered for an instant, trying to remember the name. It came sluggishly through the red and bones in her mind. "My Dayuhotem, him too. You've destroyed so many people, corrupted so many souls. *You will take no one else.*"

"Hanani."

She ignored the word. It did not matter who she was in this place. All that mattered was hate. She slapped a broad patch of the creature's flank and watched its skin turn gray and mottled like a swiftly spreading infection. It writhed, trying to escape, but she kept her hand there, baring her teeth and pressing down until its dead flesh puckered between her fingers. Hard to control, so much dreambile. There was too much of it in her, churning up from the grieving currents of her soul. It needed to suffer; she would have to be careful not to kill the thing too quickly.

"You should never have been born!" she cried. The creature twitched again, unmistakably this time, shivering and moaning in its sudden helplessness. Good.

The voice again, behind her. "There's no peace in this, Hanani. This cruelty, it doesn't suit you."

She did not care what suited her. "Go away."

"Will you kill me, if I don't?"

She shook her head to shake off the voice's distraction. Kill? Yes. It would feel good to kill anyone who got in her way. No. There was only one soul here who had earned her hate.

"It killed Mni-inh!" she snapped, trying to focus. "It has to die."

"Not like this." There was a pause. "Remember who you are, Aier."

A jolt.

She stopped pouring dreambile into the beast of hands, blinking. "Aier? Who is—"

Dancing red drapes red wax red carnelians st-st-stammering a nightstone statue closed eyes Mni-inh's smile Wanahomen's mouth her hair unloosed incense beeswax the sound of bells the taste of sipri jungissa Dayu a rippling grain field her parents' half-forgotten voices. *I vow in Hananja's name to cause no harm.*

Hanani gasped, and looked down at the beast.

Which suddenly curled at her feet, no longer a beast at all but a tiny, spindly figure whimpering in the wake of torment. When the Wild Dreamer looked up at her, Hanani looked into the face of Mni-inh's killer and saw:

A child.

Just a child. One who might have become a bright, cheerful little girl, if someone hadn't broken her soul and ground the shards to powder. One who moaned and cringed from Hanani, raising hands that had been broken too many times already, as if to ward off a blow.

What had she done?

"To hurt another, one must teach the soul to crave its own torment," the voice—Wanahomen, he was Wanahomen—said behind her. Some quality of his words reminded Hanani of Mni-inh, and she flinched anew, staring down at the child. Wanahomen continued, his tone sad now. "I think perhaps this one has had enough, Hanani."

"Oh, Goddess," she whispered, dropping to her knees. The girl was trying now to crawl away—and failing, her weak limbs useless in the soft muck that her own soul had conjured. And suddenly Hanani knew there had been other times, other tormentors whom the girl *hadn't* escaped. Other cruel words and beatings and the endless, aching, desperate yearning to rest, just rest for a little while—

"Mama," the girl whispered. A plea for someone to *save her from Hanani.* Hanani reached for the child, but the child made a high fluting sound of distress, and she dropped her hand.

"I'm sorry," she said at last, when she could think through her horror. "I'm sorry, I didn't think, I'm so sorry, please, I didn't mean to hurt you." That was a lie. She had meant every destroyed limb. "I didn't mean to hurt *you.*" That much was true. The beast of hands—a manifestation of the child's fears, born from all the violence inflicted on her; Hanani had rightly hated that. But she had forgotten the most important rule of Sharing: a person was not her dreams. And no narcomancer could face the dreaming conjurations of the soul without a calm heart—or else she would become lost in the dream and forget herself. Those had been the first lessons Mni-inh had taught her.

Wanahomen drew near. "Hanani?"

"I don't know what to do," she whispered. "There's no peace left in me. I don't know how to be—to be what she needs." She could not bring herself to say *a Sharer*. She was not that, not anymore. "I can't think how to help her."

Wanahomen sighed and crouched beside her, putting an arm around her and drawing her close. "It's all right. You can find a way."

From the corner of Hanani's eye, she saw the child stop crawling and turn to stare at them with great round eyes.

"I, I have never felt such anger, Wanahomen—" She still trembled with it. She had enjoyed it: stalking the beast, inflicting pain, thinking to herself *I need no weapon* because her hands were deadly enough. They were still coated in red wax— No. Was that wax at all? Her gorge rose; frantically, she scraped at her arms and wrists to get the stuff off, using her nails and not caring about the bloody streaks this left behind. Wanahomen scowled and caught her hands to stop her.

"No touch," said the child. Startled, Hanani saw that the Wild Dreamer had risen to her feet. Here in dreaming the girl was not crippled, not if she willed herself otherwise. Now she stood, though waveringly, watching them. Watching *Wanahomen*, her small face filling with lethal hatred. "No touch no sleep *you do not touch you do not hurt*."

Wanahomen opened his mouth to say, "I'm not hurting her, you fool—"

But in the next instant his mouth was gone.

He inhaled, eyes widening, reaching up to touch where it had been. But his hands vanished then, shriveling until only the stumps of his wrists remained. There was no blood; the stumps were smooth, sealed flesh, as if there had never been hands to begin with. Then the forearms split apart and disappeared, to the elbow. Wanahomen made a sound, quick, panicked—

"No!" Hanani leaped to her feet, moving in front of him. The Wild Dreamer twitched, glaring at her, and Hanani felt her awareness blur, her sense of herself shivering and retreating again. She was not Hanani, she was Mother, full of rage—

No! I am Aier! She clenched her fists and fought to remain herself. This was the Dreamer's power, here in this world she had created in the realms between. In Ina-Karekh, dreams reflected the self, as the Goddess Hananja had decreed. But in the Wild Dreamer's construct, the self reflected *her*—what the Dreamer saw in her victims, or wanted them to become. Did the child even realize she was killing people, total strangers who'd done nothing to merit her wrath? Hanani did not know—but as Wanahomen fell to the ground behind her, uttering an animal howl as his legs twisted into nothingness, all her fear disappeared as well.

"Hush," Hanani said, stepping forward. The Dreamer's will pushed at her again, and this time she let it change her, at least on the surface. Within, she was still Aier. Without, her appearance shifted, becoming taller, darker, willowy, more beautiful than she could ever be in waking. "There, now," she said, and her voice had become low and soft. A mother's croon. "Don't be afraid."

And the Wild Dreamer's anger faded. She twitched back a step, then forward again, and a look of desperate anxiety came over her pinched face. "Mamamama?"

Hanani reached her and folded both arms around the child, holding her close. The child shivered and then buried her face in Hanani's breast. "Mama," she said again—and smiled.

"Yes," said Hanani. She stroked the bony shoulders, her fingers trailing delicate red threads. So much pain in this one, more than any mere magic could ease. The Wild Dreamer's soul soaked up dreamblood as the desert swallowed water—and then Hanani had nothing left, save her own dreamblood, which would cost her life. It did not trouble her to pay that price, but it would not solve the problem. The Dreamer needed too much. Hanani could pour her whole life into the child and never make a difference.

Her soul was damaged beyond the ability of magic to repair, Yanassa had told her once, speaking of grief and loss—and mercy. Her brother Sharers had killed that woman, Yanassa's great-aunt. And what Yanassa had not said, what she had perhaps not even known, was that those Sharers had likely also obliterated her soul rather than letting it travel to Ina-Karekh. A soul so corrupted could never find peace, not even with a woman's innate magic, not even with a Gatherer's help. It would only drift to the pain and darkness within the Goddess's mind, like calling to like, there to suffer nightmares for all eternity. Kinder to end the soul than leave it like that.

Yanassa would probably have understood, if she'd known. *We were glad for it.*

So when the red threads ran out, Hanani closed her eyes and sent forth black instead.

But not to cause pain this time. "Stillness," she whispered in the child's ear. "Silence."

In a muzzy voice, so weary that Hanani's eyes stung with tears, the Wild Dreamer asked, "Sleep?"

"Sleep," she replied. "Yes. You may sleep now. As much as you like."

And the Wild Dreamer sagged against her with a deep, contented sigh. It was a simple matter for Hanani to weave dreambile into that sigh, spinning it into a longer one, drawing the child's breath out of her until it stopped. Simple, too, to then unravel the soul itself.

The ugly world of blood and bones vanished. They floated, Hanani and Wanahomen, in the cleaner darkness of the realms between. Of the Wild Dreamer's soul there was nothing. She had ceased to be.

"Prince," Hanani said softly, into the darkness. "Go back to waking now. Tell my brothers, if they don't already know, that the nightmare plague is done."

After a moment's pause—probably counting all his parts to make sure they were still there—Wanahomen exhaled. "Thank the Goddess for that." A pause; in that bodiless space, she felt his sudden suspicion. "But surely you can tell them yourself."

She sighed. "No, Prince. I can't."

Silence and shock—and sudden fear. He did not want her to die. He wanted *her*, but that was not surprising. As Yanassa had warned her, Wanahomen held too tight.

You shared your strength with me, Niim, when I needed it after Mni- inh's death. But this you cannot share.

"My soul is corrupt too," Hanani said. In the soft darkness her voice echoed, hollow. "Twice now I've killed with hands that were meant to heal, and even enjoyed another's suffering. Again and again, I have broken my oaths. But I still love Hananja; I know my duty."

His anger made the darkness ripple, trying to become some other place—but his will was too scattered and frantic to shape anything specific. He did not have a Gatherer's control, just the power. "No, no, you will not do this, Hanani, I forbid—"

"You have no right to forbid me." She cut him off, no longer caring about rudeness. She was tired, so tired. Everyone she loved was dead, and her dreams were gone. Perhaps she would not bother traveling to Ina-Karekh. Perhaps she would simply remain here and let her soul fade as the Wild Dreamer's had done. "There's nothing left for me in Gujaareh."

"Then go back to Merik-ren-aferu," he blurted. "Stay with the Banbarra. I'll tell them you died."

"Don't be foolish, Prince. Will you corrupt yourself for my sake? And destroy everything you've worked for?" He lapsed into silent consternation, and she shook her head. "A Servant of Hananja does not fear death. And I—"

She faltered, then. Everything inside her hurt. Damn him for making this harder for her. Did he think of no one but himself? She would miss him. She did not want to, but she would—and that was just one more hurt, one more burden, on top of so many others that she had already crumpled beneath.

"I *want* to die," Hanani said at last. "Please."

That should have settled it. If he had been a proper man, a civilized man, it would have. No Gujaareen would disrespect another's wish for peace.

But Wanahomen was half barbarian and half mad—and a prince used to getting his way, and a warrior used to *making* his way, and atop all that a Gatherer. So he came at her, and when she resisted in surprise he spoke her soulname. Not to harm her, though he could have—as she could have harmed him, knowing his name in return. He simply held her, and pressed close so that she could know his hopes, his will, as clearly as her own.

"I won't let you," he breathed.

"I told you, you have no—"

"I am Her Avatar, nightmares damn you, that gives me some right! And if you do this, you will do to me what Mni-inh's loss has done to you."

"That's selfish."

"Yes! It is! But that doesn't mean I'm wrong!"

Enmeshed with Wanahomen, she felt the thread of his fear. Out of habit she followed it and found its root in his soul, just behind his heart, where removing it would leave a gaping and perhaps fatal wound. *Losing her* would make this wound in him.

So surprised was Hanani by this that she listened to him, instead of rejecting him entirely. She felt him sense this, and knew when he decided on a new tactic, pressing his advantage.

"Let the Gatherers decide," Wanahomen said quickly.

"What?"

Hands that she could not see held her close and tight. "How can

461

you presume to judge yourself corrupt? You're only a Sharer, Hanani, and an apprentice at that. Go back to waking and present yourself to them. Tell them the truth." A flicker of fear from him, swiftly suppressed. "They will see, as I do, that your choices had no corrupt intent."

It made surprising sense. Some part of her wanted to listen, or perhaps she was just so tired that it was easier to let him win, for now.

"Very well," she said at last. But before he could exult, she added, "But I *will* present myself to the Gatherers, Prince. And I'll abide by their judgment, whatever that might be."

His fear faded only a little, because he knew as well as she did that she had committed great crimes. Gatherers were not known for their leniency, and Hananja's Law had little room for nuance.

"So be it," he said at last. She was surprised to feel solemn resignation in him. "You're a Sharer of Hananja; I've known what that means since I met you. I shall abide by whatever you choose."

Then he took them back to the waking realm, to face all its threat and promise.

45

(⊙)

The Battle of Blood

Tiaanet walked alone through the city with the hunter's knife in her hand. The streets, peopled only by lingering smoke and capering shadows, echoed faintly with the sound of her sandaled feet. Several times she heard other footsteps or voices on adjoining streets, but none came near. The city was still angry, but not at her, so she was left in peace.

She had left Tantufi's body behind in the little room for the templefolk to find. They would see the child's scarred, neglected flesh and show kindness, perhaps even hiring mourners to weep the tears that no one else would. Perhaps they would use their magic to somehow see how her final hours had gone; Tiaanet had heard they could do that. Then they might see that Tantufi had cried out for her mother once, from the depths of sleep. They might see that Tiaanet had lifted Tantufi in her arms upon finding her face wet with tears; they would see Tantufi nestle herself closer, burying her face in her mother's breast and uttering a sigh of deep contentment. And they might experience the terrible, magnificent moment when some inexplicable force had rippled through Tantufi, and through Tantufi into Tiaanet. That force had touched the old, deep scars within

Tiaanet and softened them a little, perhaps whittling away one or two of the oldest and thickest. But when the moment passed there was a fresh, raw wound to replace them, for Tantufi was dead in Tiaanet's arms.

She turned a corner, entering the highcaste district.

The Kisuati soldiers had been gone from the Hetawa by the time she left. It would have been easy for Tiaanet to remain where she was and wait for the Servants of Hananja to find her; she had no more reason to fear them with Tantufi gone. But instead, as Dreaming Moon began the latter half of her nightly trek across the sky, Tiaanet left the Hetawa by way of the empty House of Children. Her path had meandered since then, mostly to avoid areas of fire and noise, but she had known all along where she meant to go.

Their city house was dark when she arrived. She had been prepared to use the key hidden in the guest area—most Gujaareen did not lock their doors, but Sanfi had always demanded it—but the main door came open at her try. She pushed it shut and stood listening in the entryway for a moment. There were furtive sounds from the back corridors, and down one hallway she could see a faint light. A single lantern, probably, its wick kept low by someone who hoped to avoid the notice of neighbors.

Tiaanet walked toward the light.

Her fear had returned. That had been the unfortunate side effect of the power that killed Tantufi—or perhaps it had been 'Tufi's doing, somehow. The child's muddled notion of a gift. And perhaps someday Tiaanet would be grateful for the return of the emotions she had lost so long ago, but not now. Not with her heart pounding in her ears, and ugly memories behind her eyes.

But was that not fitting? She stood in the doorway of the study, watching in silence as her father sorted through reedleaf papers and muttered to himself. Down all the years of their father's torments, Tiaanet had retreated into emotionlessness, but Tantufi had had no such refuge. If Tiaanet had retained her self-loathing, she might have overcome the inertia that kept her obedient to her father's will. Would not a good mother have somehow found the key that Sanfi used to keep her child chained? Would not a good mother have hired her own assassins?

Would not a good mother have killed Tantufi herself, if there was no other way to escape so much suffering?

Tiaanet made certain the knife was out of sight behind the door frame. "Father," she said.

Sanfi started badly, dropping a scroll with a loud clatter and almost knocking over the lantern. When he saw her, however, the fear in his face was replaced by delight. "Tiaanet! Goddess-eyes-upon-me! What— How— Did you escape from the soldiers? I went to Yanya-iyan, I pleaded with the Protectors, but they would not hear me—"

Tiaanet looked around as she came into the room. Three of the flower troughs had been shifted aside or knocked over, exposing compartments she had not known were there. One of the compartments was open; within it she could see a small empty chest. An open satchel—she could see in it money, jewels, and scrolls bearing a property seal-knot—sat on the floor beside Sanfi. So did a familiar key on a long twine cord.

"Tantufi is dead," she said, turning her eyes from this key to his face.

A flash of elation crossed his face before he cleared his throat and pretended discomfort. "Yes, well, your sister's health was—"

"Daughter, Father. There's no one else here; we need not lie to each other." Angling her body just so, she stepped around a wooden stool, closer to him. "My daughter, and yours."

He scowled, as he always did when reminded of his perversions. "What of your mother?"

"Still at the Hetawa. They'll heal her, I imagine, as much as she can be healed." She watched his frown deepen at that, watched him calculate the chance that a rational Insurret would tell the priests of her husband's many, many crimes.

"We must leave the city," he said finally, turning to pick up the fallen scrolls. "I have acquaintances in the upriver towns, and in Kisua, who can assist us. There may be a way to salvage our plans, if—"

Tiaanet thrust the Kisuati hunter's knife into his back. She used both hands and an overhand swing, although the knife was sharp, because she needed to be sure of getting through his ribs.

He spun to face her, looking more puzzled than anything else. "Tiaanet?" He reached back and fumbled for the knife, then brought his hand forward, his eyes widening at the sight of his own blood. "What— You—"

She had missed the heart. Quickly, before he could recover himself, she shoved him backward with both hands. He stumbled backward, tripped over the open satchel, and fell clumsily among the chests and scrolls. While he struggled to rise, she picked up one of the metal flower troughs. It was too heavy for her to raise high, but she could carry it over to him, which she did.

"Tiaanet!" His confusion had given way to fear. He kicked back from her in a panic, forgetting all his efforts to be discreet. "*Tiaanet!*"

She dropped the trough. He put up an arm at the last instant, which caused it to land across his throat and chest rather than his head. He made a thick, inarticulate bubbling sound, probably as the knife was pushed deeper into his lung or some other organ, but he was still struggling to get free, albeit feebly now. Tiaanet watched for a moment, considering, and then moved to sit on the trough.

The lantern ran out of oil in the time that it took her father to die. The Dreamer's light through the high window was a sufficient substitute, but Tiaanet found that she did not enjoy watching. She did it anyhow, because otherwise she would never be certain that he was dead. But however much she forced herself to remember the things he had done, however much her heart rang with the hate she had never dared to feel before, her vision blurred as she watched him gargle and gasp for breath. Her hands shook when she finally touched his throat to see if his heart had stopped. She stayed on the trough for an extra measure just to be sure, but finally had to get up when nausea struck.

Dead. He was dead. Dead. Dead.

After the nausea, she wept for a while.

Once she had recovered, she took the satchel and packed the remaining space with travel clothing and food. She took the key to Tantufi's chains too, tying it 'round her neck and tucking it into the brocade of her gown. There was no thought to this gesture. She did not hope to remember her daughter by the tool used to enslave her. It simply felt right—and for Tiaanet, who had survived as long as she had by relying on reason and not emotion, by outthinking her father if not overpowering him, letting *feeling* guide her actions was new and somehow a relief.

On the doorstep she stopped, abruptly at a loss, for she'd thought no further than her father's death. But as the last sliver of the Dreaming Moon vanished amid the rooftops of the city, she looked up and noticed the topmost star of the constellation called the Griever. It appeared only during the first season of a new year; already Waking Moon was creeping out of hiding to cover it. For now, however, the star shone brighter than any other, low in the western sky.

Turning to follow it, Tiaanet began to walk.

46

Prince of the Sunset

The world had changed again by the time Wanahomen opened his eyes.

"Greetings, Prince." A familiar voice—though not an entirely welcome one. Wanahomen looked over to see the Gatherer Nijiri crouched beside him.

"Wana!" Wanahomen blinked. Ezack sat on his other side, scrambling to his feet now that he saw Wanahomen awake.

Pushing himself upright, Wanahomen found himself painfully stiff, and as weary as if he hadn't slept at all. He rubbed his face, and only belatedly recalled that he was supposed to be injured. But there was no pain in his chest or thigh, and when he examined himself he found that the wounds had closed, leaving only bloody holes in his Banbarra robes.

"Hanani," Nijiri said. "She healed you, even while saving you from the Wild Dreamer. How do you feel?"

"Tired," Wanahomen replied. He could have slept for a week. "Hungry."

"We feed you," Ezack said in wretched Gujaareen, grinning wickedly. "Or you feed us, now you rich king."

Wanahomen looked about. Sunlight and rainbows shone into the Hall of Blessings through the prism windows, and through the wide-open bronze doors. He lay on one of several healing benches that had been set up on the dais, at the Goddess-statue's feet. Beyond the Gatherer and Ezack he could see many others, his own men mingling with his Gujaareen allies, and the Servants and Sisters. Iezanem was deep in conversation with a Teacher; Deti-arah had crouched to speak to his son. There were no Kisuati soldiers present. The pallets where the sleepers had lain were gone as well.

"You sleep all night, into day," Ezack said, sobering. "We think the *fuh atat* Kisuati, they poison, but priest say no. Say you busy with magic."

"I was," Wanahomen said, frowning. The memories were hazy, thick. If he had ever been trained to remember his dreams, perhaps he might have pulled clarity from them, but all he remembered was redness, and revulsion. And . . . a frightened child? Something about the Gatherers?

He looked at Gatherer Nijiri, noticing only then that the man looked as weary as he felt. And there was an odd sort of weight to the Gatherer's mannerisms that puzzled Wanahomen for a moment—until he remembered how many people had died. Including Charris. Then he understood the Gatherer's mood.

"You may never remember," Nijiri said. "Even for those of us raised in the Hetawa, not all that happens in dreams can be explained by the light of day. Suffice it that the nightmare plague has ended, and Gujaareh is—at least in dreams—safe."

The memories were like morning mist in Wanahomen's mind, burning off as he came fully awake. He shook his head to clear it and carefully got to his feet. For a moment he was dizzy, but the sensation passed quickly.

"The sleepers went still while you and Hanani battled the Wild Dreamer," Nijiri continued, rising with him. "They did not wake, but they stopped dying. That was how we knew something had changed. A few moments later, they began to wake. That was how we knew you had won."

A few moments. He felt as though years had passed.

"What of the Kisuati?" he asked to distract himself, stretching to ease his stiffness.

"Gone from the city with the dawn. Those were the terms of the surrender we demanded."

That woke Wanahomen up. "*Surrender?*"

One of the templefolk nearby, an elder who had been talking with one of the black-clad warrior-priests, turned and smiled at Wanahomen. "It was unconditional," he said. "I'm told they abandoned Yanya-iyan in a rather unpeaceful hurry, in fact, which I suspect may have been motivated by the large crowd of angry citizens who had begun to gather at the palace gates."

Wanahomen looked to Ezack for confirmation of this. Ezack, who had managed to follow the conversation, shrugged. "Not an arrow fired from our bows," he said in Chakti. "Some dead, mostly when you were ambushed, but far fewer than we'd expected, in all. The wounded have already been healed, too. If you'd told us it would be this easy, we would have come to get your city back for you a long time ago."

There was nothing easy about it, Wanahomen almost said, but of course Ezack was not Gujaareen. He would not understand.

So Wanahomen turned to the Gatherer. "This was not the war I had in mind," he said. "Chariots and spears I was prepared to face, but dream-demons and magic?" He shook his head.

"The Goddess gives us the burdens we are each best suited to bear," said the Gatherer. "They're not always the burdens we expect."

"You should have plenty of perfectly ordinary burdens now, Prince," said the elder, who came around the bench to clap Wanahomen on the shoulder companionably, though Wanahomen had never met him before. "This may help—"

He beckoned forward two of the Hetawa's children, each of whom carried a cloth-wrapped object. One of the objects was a long pole, by the shape of the wrapping. The other— Wanahomen caught his breath, intuiting before he saw it. The boy stopped before him and with the assistance of his fellow unwrapped the object, revealing the red- and gold-amber plates of the Aureole of the Setting Sun.

"We took it to our vaults for safekeeping when the Kisuati claimed the city," said the elder, speaking softly as Wanahomen took reverent hold of the Aureole. He lifted it to the light, marveling at how much brighter it looked than he'd remembered. "If you like, you may borrow one of these young ones, to bear it for you as you ride to Yanya-iyan."

To ride through the streets of the city with the Aureole behind him... Wanahomen swallowed hard past the knot in his throat and nodded mutely to the boy, who grinned and immediately began working with his companion to unwrap the staff.

"There's much work to be done, putting Gujaareh to rights," Wanahomen said when he could speak again. "I would appreciate the Hetawa's aid in this. And that of the shunha and zhinha, and my Banbarra allies."

He turned to face the people assembled on the dais, and suffered a momentary pang of nerves as he saw that their eyes were all on him, expectant. But his nerves settled very, very quickly.

"You shall of course have the Hetawa's aid," said the elder, whom Wanahomen finally realized must be the current Superior.

"And that of the shunha," said Deti-arah, lifting his son in his arms so the boy could see. "I cannot speak for the zhinha, but..."

"I can," said Iezanem, looking affronted that Deti-arah would even consider doing so. "We have already pledged our support to the Sunset Lineage. Though some details of that support must be discussed."

She threw a meaningful glance at Wanahomen, and he inclined his head to show that he understood. He would have to share more power with the nobles than his father had done, and likely with the merchants and military too. That he did not necessarily mind—but if she thought he would tolerate becoming a mere figurehead, Wanahomen hoped she was prepared to fight another war.

Perhaps I'd better marry her; that might shut her up.

"Does this mean I'm hunt leader now?" asked Ezack in Chakti. He stretched, nonchalant.

Wanahomen stared at him, torn between amusement and amazement at his audacity. "That would be up to Unte."

"Damn. He doesn't like me."

"I'll send him a recommendation on your behalf," Wanahomen said, "if you'll keep the Yusir troop here and serve as my palace guard for an eightday or two. I need warriors I can trust, in case of assassins."

Ezack brightened at once. "I've never killed an assassin! Will there be many?"

"Hopefully they'll all be frightened off by so many fierce barbarian warriors."

Ezack sighed. "I suppose we can stay for that long. Unte shouldn't mind, since the women will be coming into the city soon to start dickering with our new trading partners. They might like having some of us nearby in case of foolishness—though frankly, your people seem so glad to see us that I can't imagine there being much of that." He paused, watching another zhinha pass by with a barebreasted servant girl walking a step behind him. All the hunt men were staring at her; Wanahomen made a mental note to educate them, quickly, about Gujaareen customs. "Speaking of gladness, will there be a party?"

"Later," said Wanahomen. He turned to the Superior, but could not help meeting the Gatherer's eyes as he spoke. "First we mourn the dead and see to the living. All things in their proper time. That is the way of peace, is it not?"

The Gatherer nodded, silently. "So it is," said the Superior.

"Then let us begin," Wanahomen said.

And although no one cheered, there was a palpable shift in the mood of the Hall. Wanahomen saw elation on many faces as they turned away to resume their duties, or left to begin the long, arduous process of repairing a damaged nation. Ezack gave Wanahomen a jaunty salute and then headed down from the dais, probably to speak to the other hunt leaders. The Gatherer vanished into the crowd, as his kind did. But as the Superior turned to leave, Wanahomen put a hand on the man's arm to forestall him.

"All things in their proper time, Superior," he said, speaking low and stepping near. "Sharer-Apprentice Hanani; what of her?"

The Superior sobered at once. "She's well," he said. "She woke a few hours before you, and told us of what had transpired in the realms of dream. If you like, I can convey your farewells—"

"I'll convey them myself, thank you."

The Superior hesitated, looking distinctly uncomfortable. "She has spoken freely to us of Mni-inh's death," he said, slowly, "and of— and of other events that occurred while she was in the desert. I realize that you may have developed some, er, attachment— That your feelings—" He took a deep breath, then finally just shook his head. "We are her family, Prince. It's best that you not see her again."

Only his mother's training kept Wanahomen from snapping an immediate retort at that. He would have to relearn tact, he realized regretfully; the sharp tongue that had served him so well among the Banbarra would no longer do in Gujaareh.

"If that is her decision, then of course I shall agree," he said instead, keeping his tone respectful despite the intractability of the words. "So I'll just see her now, to hear it from her own lips."

The Superior looked sour, but finally sighed. "Come with me," he said, and Wanahomen went with him into the inner Hetawa.

* * *

Several hundred bodies had been laid out on the courtyard flagstones. Nightmare victims, Kisuati and Gujaareen who had died in the uprising, Sentinels fallen in the battle for the Hetawa...and Charris. The Superior paused at a tactful distance while Wanahomen went to see his old friend, nodding a greeting to the Sister of Hananja who was wrapping the body for cremation. But the Charris he had known was long gone from that flesh, and after a moment Wanahomen moved on.

Hanani knelt amid the bodies. She had obviously been awake for some while, having taken the time to wash and change into the Hetawa garb she had worn at their first meeting—though with changes, Wanahomen noted. She had kept her hair in the loose, ornamented Banbarra style, the thick sandy curls held back from her face by a band of beaded leather. To the kohl on her eyes, which nearly every Gujaareen wore as a ward against sun-blindness, she had added a soft brown lip tint that suited her coloring; and she still wore the amber anklet above her plain, functional sandals.

But the collar that draped her neck and shoulders now bore several dozen small polished rubies, rather than the carnelians she'd worn before.

Swallowing against sudden unease, Wanahomen stopped behind her and cleared his throat. For a moment he thought she had not heard him, but then she said, "The Gatherers have judged me not corrupt."

And then, at last, he remembered. The bargain he'd made, in his desperation to coax her back to Hona-Karekh, and life. It had never occurred to him that she might seek judgment before he even woke up. Damned stubborn woman—but he was glad, more glad than he could say, that they had let her live.

"Good," he said. "Because you weren't."

"So they say." She sighed, stroking the face of the body before her. "But I have killed a full four now."

The words confused Wanahomen utterly until he looked at the small, emaciated body she tended, and recognized its now-peaceful face.

"Mercy is not murder," he said. "You were a blessing for that child, Hanani. Look at her; her suffering is done now. Surely that was the Goddess's will."

"And what does that mean?" Hanani looked up at him. She was not weeping, but the lost look in her eyes was painfully familiar, joined now by a weariness even deeper than that in his own heart. Wanahomen scowled; the Superior had said they would take care of her. Why were they leaving her here, then, to sit amid the dead—and envy them?

"Dayu's death was an accident, but I can't forgive myself for it," she said. "Mni-inh, the same. Azima—that was pure corruption, no matter what the Gatherers say. So was what I did to this child, in dreaming. But what does it mean that I committed such sins and have been named a full Sharer anyhow? What does it mean that I prayed for guidance, and *this* was my answer?" She gestured at the Wild Dreamer's body.

Wanahomen sighed. Here was the proof that he was no Gatherer, regardless of his so-mighty dreaming gift: no words of comfort came to his mind. And here, in the middle of the Hetawa, he could not take her into his arms and hold her as he might have done elsewhere. Not with the Hetawa's collar 'round her neck like a leash of blood.

"I don't feel like a Sharer anymore, Prince." She turned back to look at the body. "I don't know what I am, now."

He could not bear her anguish. He was also furious with her superiors or pathbrothers, or whoever had arranged this little display, because he understood now that it had been done for him. To warn him that he lacked the skill to ease her pain. They were hurting her to drive him away.

So he squatted beside her and took her hand. "Come away from this place."

She blinked in surprise. "What?"

"The girl is dead and it had to be done. That's what peace requires, sometimes. Accept that or not as you please, but don't sit here and wallow in it. Come."

He pulled her hand until she got up, then took her with him as he headed for the Hall of Blessings. But the Superior moved neatly to intersect them, frowning at their joined hands. "My Prince, Sharer Hanani has duties—"

"Yes," Wanahomen said, "tending the *living*, not the dead. I'm taking her where she's actually needed."

The Superior was so surprised by this that he actually fell silent for a moment. "Where?" asked Hanani.

"Every man, woman, and child in this city has just been through a battle."

"Then let them come here," said the Superior in a stern tone. "The acolytes and Sisters are out now, collecting those who can't travel, and the Sentinels are dealing with those who resist returning to the ways of peace. We'll heal those we can, and for that we need Hanani here—"

"But *she* does not need *you*." Wanahomen heard the anger in his own voice and realized he was doing a poor job of being tactful, but he no longer cared. "What will you do? Stuff her full of dreamblood and lock her in a cell until she stops crying? That's not what she needs!"

"You presume to know best what she needs," said the Superior just as hotly, though he kept his voice down. "We would—"

"Enough." Hanani spoke more softly than either of them, but the bleak disgust in her voice cut across their anger like a reprimand. "There's no sense in this. Superior, I ask a few days' leave. I know every Sharer is needed, but..." She shook her head. "Right now I'm no good to anyone."

The Superior looked taken aback. "Well, that's—improper, but—I, I suppose it's a reasonable request, and yet—"

"Thank you," Hanani said, cutting him off with breathtaking rudeness. Pulling her hand from Wanahomen's, she walked away from them toward the Hall of Blessings. Just as taken aback, Wanahomen found himself exchanging a confused look with the Superior.

But at the door to the Hall, Hanani stopped and looked back at them. "Prince?"

Unable to resist a smirk of triumph, Wanahomen gave the Superior a barely civil nod and hurried after her.

* * *

He rode to Yanya-iyan with the Aureole carried on a horse behind him, and Hanani seated before him on his own mount. Had Charris and Hendet been present, no doubt they would have disapproved of the latter. Not only had he made it blindingly obvious to all the city that Hanani was his lover—gods knew how the Hetawa would react when they heard of it—but in showing favor to her, he damaged himself. Every noble and wealthy family in the city would be angling for political alliances now that he had returned. His choice of firstwife in particular could strengthen his still-fragile rule. He had no more illusions about Tiaanet. But what other high-ranking, well-connected woman would willingly become firstwife to a man who so plainly already had a favorite?

As they traveled the avenues of the city with his army and allies in tow—Wanahomen nodding to the crowds that formed to cheer and weep at his passing—Hanani seemed not to care about propriety for once. She rested against him as they rode, her head on his shoulder, her eyes open but lost in some inner turmoil. He could not have said whether she took any actual comfort from his nearness.

At Yanya-iyan, the faces of the servants and staff bore welcome—and a surprising amount of familiarity from the days of his youth. It seemed the Kisuati had not been foolish enough to interfere with such competent and efficient function. Thus Wanahomen felt safe in turning Hanani over to their care, ordering them to treat her as they would one of his wives. It troubled him, though, that she did not look back as she went away with them.

He spent the next hours holding meetings to secure the city and set in place the nascent structures of his rule. It was necessary but trying work, and Dreaming Moon had shown her full four-banded face by the time he finally retired to the apartments that he would think of as his father's for many months more. There the servants bathed and perfumed him, took apart his ragged braids and rewove them rope-fashion, took away his Banbarra clothes and dressed him in a golden torque and a loinskirt of such soft cloth that he barely felt it on his skin.

It was in this state—feeling naked and alien to himself, weary and incomprehensibly lonely—that he went to Hanani.

She lay curled amid the pillows of his great round bed. The servants had tended her as well, replacing her Banbarra headband with a diadem of gold and tigereye, and dressing her in a pleated linen gown that clung to her curves and was far, far too sheer for a woman of her pale coloring. The sight of a fully dressed woman had never aroused him so powerfully.

But he restrained his desires as he came to the bed, for he knew with a warrior's instinct that to move too clumsily now would mean losing her. And suddenly *keeping* her was powerfully, desperately important to him.

So he lay down beside her and waited. As he had hoped, Hanani turned to face him. He noticed only then that she still wore the ruby Sharer's collar.

"Congratulations," he said, jerking his chin toward the thing. It was a more graceless and stiff gesture than he should have made, but he thought it foolish to pretend what he did not feel.

She nodded slowly. "Mni-inh-brother would be proud." She reached up to touch his fresh-woven hair. "As your father would be, of you."

He could not resist; he caught her hand and kissed the open palm, then rubbed her arm to assuage some of his longing. To his great pleasure, some of the melancholy left her eyes. It returned quickly, however.

"I don't know what to do," she said. "The Hetawa...I sat today in the Sharers' Hall, in the Hall of Blessings, and felt like an interloper. I've spent most of my life there, but it's no longer home to me."

He forced himself to say, "That feeling might pass with time."

"No. I don't think it will." She swallowed hard, clearly struggling for words. "I still love the Goddess. I think I could love healing again, in time. But to go back to that life...I no longer have the strength, Prince. Not after all I've lost. Not—not knowing what else I might have instead."

And Wanahomen privately rejoiced when her eyes met his, for just a breath, before she looked away.

But oh, softly, softly. He wanted so much from her, and things between them were fragile still.

"Stay here and decide," he said. "A fourday, an eightday, a season, a year. However long you need. Spend every day praying in the garden, if it pleases you." *And every night with me.* "You'll have no troubles here."

She frowned. "I won't presume upon your hospitality—"

He touched her lips to silence her, as she had once done him. "As

479

you have reminded me, we aren't Banbarra," he said. "And Gujaareh is Kisuati-free. Now we may behave again like civilized people, and be kind to each other *without* compensation or cause."

She smiled back, shyly, though again the smile faded. It troubled him that her happiness was so fragile. She nuzzled his hand and pressed closer to him, seeking greater comfort. He pulled her into his arms, savoring the warm scent of her, and would have been content to lie that way all night. But she lifted her face and sought his mouth, and her tongue tasted sweet with desire.

Softly, he reminded himself, though his body forgot its weariness all at once. But before he could begin the slow seduction that was in his mind, she abruptly pulled back.

"I don't love you, Prince," she said, looking troubled. "Do you understand that? I want to, but there is a part of me that withdraws. I've lost everyone I loved, lately. It's easier—safer—not to love you."

Taken aback, Wanahomen sat up on one elbow, and considered this. In a way, it was only to be expected. She had coupled with him in the midst of mourning, to ease her heart. Would she have wanted him at all if not for that? Impossible to say. The waking realm was not like dreams; one could not will it to change as one wished. He could only accept, or reject, what was given to him.

And he did not want to reject her. That much, if nothing else, was clear.

"I won't pretend I like that," he said. But as he said it, he put a hand on her belly. "I'm vain enough to want every woman I lie with to love me. But I'm a prince: love is not a necessity." He hesitated. "I suppose I owe you honesty too, though: I *had* thought to marry you. But I've learned from Yanassa that it's a poor idea to propose to a woman too quickly, and without settling certain matters first." He pretended lofty consideration. "I can wait a fourday, perhaps."

He was glad to see her smile return. "You asked once if you were nothing to me. I want you to know...that isn't true. You are my friend, Wanahomen. One of the only people I have ever called that." She sighed. "That's part of it, I suppose. I, I don't know how to have friends, Prince. I don't know how to be a lover, let alone a wife. I don't know what I want."

He leaned down and kissed her broad forehead. "Then stay until you do."

She said nothing at first, and that troubled him.

"You want children too." Hanani's face was solemn. "If you want me as a wife."

"Of course. You'll make a fine mother . . ." But he trailed off at the look on her face.

"We can never make children together, Prince," she said. "The dreaming gift is a chancy thing; the Goddess's will can never be predicted. But I've told you before that you could be a Gatherer—and there has never been a child made between Gatherer and Sharer. There never *should* be such a child. At best we might only strengthen the dreaming gift that runs in your lineage—and that alone would be a dangerous thing. At worst . . . we could make another Wild Dreamer, between us."

That shocked Wanahomen into silence for a full minute. He sat up, troubled on so many levels that he could not put his feelings to words.

With a heavy sigh, Hanani sat up, leaning against his back. Her breath tickled the nape of his neck. "I'm sorry. But I will never lie, Prince. Perhaps that's something proper lovers do, but— I am who I am."

Was he glad of that? She could easily have kept silent, lain with him for years and pretended to simply be barren. She was a healer: she could prevent anything she didn't want. It was better, wasn't it, to know why?

Still, she did not love him. She did not want his seed for children. She did not need his wealth, for she could return to the Hetawa; she did not need his strength, for she had plenty of her own. What, then, could he offer her? He was not used to feeling so at a loss.

"If you want me to leave," she began.

"No."

"Prince—"

He turned and lay down with her again, stroking the curls back from her farm-girl face, wondering what was wrong with him. Was it Yanassa's rejection that had made him want this woman so much? Tiaanet's falsehood? The looming fact that he was unlikely to love or even like his other wives, whom he would marry for duty? He yearned to have one woman who would love him back. It was not so impossible a dream; his father had had that much in his mother. But apparently Wanahomen's heart had chosen *this* woman.

So he said, "I am certain of nothing else between us, Hanani, than that I do *not* want you to leave."

The unease faded from her expression, and she relaxed. "Thank you." She shifted closer then, and put a hand on his. She seemed to like his hands more than any other part of him. He let her open his left, parting the fingers, stroking the palm with her thumb. When she lifted his hand to her lips for a kiss, however, her collar shifted, the stones clacking together, and he realized there was something else he felt sure about.

He took a deep breath. "Well. Whether we make a child or not is a matter for your healer's judgment," he said, reaching up to finger the collar's stones. They were beautiful, high-quality rubies, easily the rival of jewels he'd seen in the palace collection. The Hetawa had accorded her proper value at last. "I'll have servants fetch the necessary sheaths and unguents, if you'd rather not waste magic, or there are other ways we can please each other. But it is you I want, Hanani, not the Hetawa. Choose me or not; I will live with either. At least choose *something* regarding them."

She touched the collar for a moment, thinking, for longer than his held breath. It was not a fair thing he had asked of her, and he knew it. The Hetawa was more than a power of Gujaareh, to her; it was her family. But her eyes were clear as she gazed at him. Whatever her decision, she'd already made it.

When she sat up to unfasten the collar, he stifled triumph. He knew better. Still, it was difficult not to smile when she folded the collar neatly, laid it aside, and lay back down with him.

"I've given Her enough," she said, lifting her chin. There was a resolute, hard-edged note in her voice. "I've given *everyone* enough. It's time I had something for myself."

So Wanahomen tried to give her what she wanted. He moved slowly when he touched her, allowing her time to think, ready to stop if she changed her mind. But she only sighed while he caressed her and tasted her soft flesh, and when he moved between her legs to make her ready, she made a sound of delight that he would hear in his best dreams ever after.

So he joined himself to her, carefully, reverently—for were not women goddesses? He lavished effort on her pleasure even as he gratified himself, aware that this might be his one chance to win her. She seemed satisfied when the fires had cooled, so he wrapped his arms around her—loosely, bearing Yanassa's scold in mind—and finally allowed himself to rest.

But in the morning when he awoke, Hanani was gone.

47

A Servant of Peace

When the Hetawa of Ina-Karekh formed around Hanani, she was unsurprised to find Nijiri waiting for her. "Greetings, Gatherer."

He stood and turned to face her on the dais, where he had been praying, and examined her face for a moment. "You've made your decision, then."

She nodded and came to stand before him. In the dream she wore a Sharer's garb; now she reached up to remove the ruby collar. She held it forward, and after a long silent moment he took it.

"I can return it in waking as well—" she began.

"No. Dreaming matters more." The collar vanished from his hands. "I'm sorry, Hanani. I never meant for this trial to do you such harm."

The lines in Nijiri's face were deeper, his eyes older than the last time she had shared a dream with him. They had told her of Gatherer Rabbaneh's death. In waking she would have kept her thoughts to herself, but in dreaming there was no point. "You've been harmed just as much, Gatherer."

He did not bother to deny it. "Will you find peace with him?"

"Peace? With Wanahomen?" In a lighter moment she might have laughed. "No. I don't know. Perhaps. There's an emptiness in me,

Gatherer, that nothing will ever fill. I don't know what to do about it. Dreamblood—" She shook her head. She could not find the words to explain, but she felt with an instinctive certainty that dreamblood would do her no good.

Nijiri sighed in agreement. "Time and friends will fill the void, Hanani. But..." He looked away. "The loss will never go away, not completely. At least, it hasn't for me."

There was comfort in his words, to her very great surprise. It helped, somehow, to know that she would not stop missing the people she loved. It felt—not good, but right, that the loss of her faith should leave a lasting scar.

Hanani turned to face the bronze doors at the far end of the Hall. He stepped away from the statue; they began to walk together down the pathway between the pillars.

"Inmu and I have begun to find souls adrift in the realms between waking and dreaming," he said. "Many do not remember themselves fully; sharing the Wild Dreamer's pain was too much for them. But they are intact enough to be sent to Ina-Karekh, and left there in peace."

She caught her breath, stopping in her tracks. "Mni-inh? Dayuhotem?"

"Not yet. But it's only a matter of time."

She closed her eyes, feeling tears prick the lids—and, too, feeling the great emptiness inside her ease, just a little. It was as though someone had lit a lantern within her. Just a small warmth, useless in true darkness, but even that was better than nothing. "I wish I could see them again."

He said nothing. It was custom to reassure a grieving person that she would see her loved ones again someday. But Ina-Karekh was infinite. Hanani might search lifetimes and never find the single soul she sought, much less two. Nijiri's silence was honesty, and she was grateful for it.

But hope was honest too. As long as she was alive, she could dream—and because she was a woman, she could continue searching after death as well. So she decided: she *would* see them again, someday.

"Thank you, Gatherer," she said.

He inclined his head. "Do you mean to keep healing?"

"I would like to. I like helping people. But the Superior was right; no one has need of my skills here in Gujaareh. The Hetawa provides all the people need."

"There's more to the world than Gujaareh," he said cryptically, and then stopped. They had reached the bronze doors, which here in Ina-Karekh opened onto not the steps and square, but a solid, featureless expanse of brightness. The way back to the waking realm.

"Mni-inh trained you well," he said, "so we'll trust your judgment in this and all other matters. Only take care to teach your Prince no more magic, if you decide to keep him. You were wise to teach him balance, but he lacks the discipline to attempt the higher narcomantic arts. After all the effort we invested in him, it would be a shame to lose him too quickly."

Hanani lowered her eyes in agreement. "Yes, Gatherer."

Nijiri nodded, then took her hands. "You will always be of the Hetawa, Hanani. Whether you serve in our way or yours, we're still your brothers. Don't forget us, please?"

Hanani smiled, and then on an impulse stepped forward and put her arms around him. He seemed badly startled, for one did not hug Gatherers. But finally he shook his head, relaxed, and folded his arms around her as well.

"Clearly," he said into her hair, amused, "we must consult the Sisters on proper handling of women before we ever attempt it again."

"Clearly," Hanani said, and closed her eyes. "Farewell, Gatherer."

Opening her eyes in Hona-Karekh, she lay awake in Wanaho-men's arms for many hours.

*   *   *

One of the Banbarra warriors agreed to guide Hanani to Merik-ren-aferu. She had expected Unte to be reluctant, but to her surprise he agreed to nearly all her requests. Later she commented on this to Hendet, who had also chosen to remain with the Banbarra for the time being. "They're barbarians," Hendet said, with a shrug. "We have mostly forgotten what it means to make hard choices; they have not."

"And... you?" Hanani asked this with some unease; she had abandoned Hendet's son, after all, and she did not know how the other woman felt about it.

"I have made harder choices than you will ever know," Hendet said, and walked away.

Per her requests, they built Hanani a solitary camp at the far end of the canyon, on a stable ledge that was low enough not to frighten her. With Gujaareh's rich markets open to them at last—and Wana-homen paying the hunt warriors for their guard duty besides—the tribe had chosen to forego its usual springtime journey to the western lands. This meant Hanani could rely on their protection and assistance for at least another year.

For the price of her ruby collar she had a fine tent and ample supplies, with fresh goods and messages brought once a week by a hunt rider. Yanassa and the tribe's women came often too, sometimes bringing other guests: a child with a twisted spine, a woman whose hair was falling out, a man with an embarrassing genital injury. Hanani sent them away healed and more came. Banbarra from other tribes began making journeys to visit her, and per Hanani's agreement with Unte, they were welcome in Merik-ren-aferu regardless of how matters stood politically between the tribes. Her little ledge was sovereign territory within the Yusir's, even more than any other woman's *an-sherrat*, and no one who approached under flag of truce for the purpose of seeing her could be harmed—not even those from tribes at feud with the Yusir. She had not yet persuaded Unte to permit the Shadoun to come too, but she would keep pressing for that.

In exchange for the tribe's aid and protection, Hanani did not charge individual Yusir for her services. So even the poorest members of the tribe came, and Hanani healed them. Before long she had visitors nearly every day. Even Unte came once—to see how his tribe's exotic prize was doing, he said, but she repaired his bad knees before he left.

Yanassa eventually coaxed her into closer contact with the Yusir, though Hanani worried this would damage her efforts to establish herself as a neutral ally rather than a member of the tribe. She could not help it, though, for the desert nights were cold and long, and Nijiri had been right: the presence of others helped keep the grief at bay. So she attended the tribe's celebrations and rituals, and she even took a little girl—the one she'd cured of fever some while back—as a sort of apprentice. The child was a poor dreamer and would never be able to use more than basic sleep-spells to aid her herbal and surgical skills. Still, it was good to have someone to teach again.

At Yanassa's urging, Hanani even tried the young man who'd volunteered several times to bring her supplies. He was younger than she, shy and with a worse stammer than she'd ever had, artlessly obvious in his liking for her. She liked him too, especially given how delighted he'd been by her invitation to stay the night. This turned out to be a mistake, however. His lovemaking was pleasurable enough—he had a great deal of enthusiasm—but she had no great desire to see him again afterward. Which made his disappointment all the more painful for both of them, when he realized it. She almost took up with him again for pity, until it occurred to her that this was disrespectful. He deserved a lover who genuinely wanted him.

And this reasoning, when Hanani finally applied it to herself, prompted her to at last send a scroll to Gujaareh via the next message-rider. A few fourdays later—nearly a year after she'd left him—Wanahomen arrived in Merik-ren-aferu.

*   *   *

He did not shout. He did not demand explanations. Later Hanani would learn that Yanassa, Hendet, Ezack, and Unte were behind this. They had refused to lead Wanahomen to her camp until he promised to stay calm. He was not sufficiently angry to declare war on the six tribes, though it was a narrow thing.

Instead he sat beside Hanani on her ledge, both of them letting legs dangle over a drop of thirty feet or so. He was resplendent in a headdress of lapis beads, fingerloop gauntlets, and a floor-length brocade waistcloak. She wore only plain beige robes; this made her feel quite the drab peahen given his bright plumage.

Still, he kept looking at her. She didn't know what that meant.

"I'm sorry," she said, at length.

He sighed. "I pressed you too hard and too fast. The apology is mine to make."

This startled Hanani, because she had not expected him to apologize for anything, let alone that. At the look of open-mouthed shock on her face, Wanahomen scowled, and Hanani quickly turned away to hide her smile. She had missed his scowls, amazingly.

"I suspected you might be here," he said, when she had recovered. "Where else could you have gone easily? But I did not come, because I was angry."

"Understandable," Hanani said.

"And because I hoped you would change your mind, someday, and come back to me."

She looked down at her sandals, which dangled over the valley, and kicked them a little. "As I have done, at least partially."

"What, then, would you have of me?" And he turned to look at her, his expression guarded and haughty—but he still hadn't fully shed his Banbarra self. His tension was obvious in the way his eyes never left her face, and the strength with which his hand gripped the ledge, the knuckles going pale.

"I, I would like to be your lover again," she said, feeling her cheeks heat. "And your friend, and perhaps more. If you'll have me."

The wariness that crossed his face hurt to see. "That depends," he said in a too-neutral tone. "Do you love me?"

She nodded, and saw him relax. "You were part of the empty space within me," she said. "I didn't realize it at first because the emptiness was so great. But Gatherer Nijiri was right: time and friends have eased it, and now I see that I am happier with you than without."

A muscle flexed in his jaw. "If that's so, then I require that you marry me." When Hanani looked at him in surprise, his jaw tightened further. She'd forgotten his stubbornness. "I feel the need of ties with you, Hanani, for some unfathomable reason."

She almost smiled, but the moment was too weighty for that. "I'm willing, though I know nothing of how marriage goes. Should I not meet your other wives first? To be certain of peace between us, if nothing else."

"I have no other wives."

Hanani frowned. It had been a year since Gujaareh's liberation, and any prince had enemies. "Isn't it . . . well, irresponsible, for the Prince of the Sunset to have no wives? No heirs?"

"I have a son of my flesh already, and I have a woman who loves me and wants me, but they're both half-wild. They flee into the desert whenever I try to love them back. If I were a less confident man, I might become concerned."

Hanani ducked her head to cover her smile. Wanahomen at last unfolded somewhat. He touched her hand where it rested on her thigh, then ran his fingers down her leg, tugging up her skirts. She blushed when she realized what he was looking for: the amber anklet, which she still wore. At the sight of it he looked pleased, then closed his eyes in a heavy sigh.

"Don't run from me again, Hanani," he said, his voice almost a whisper.

She put her hand over his. "I won't."

"And you'll be my firstwife?"

"I—" That made her start; the implications of his having no other wives had bypassed her. "*First*wife? But I'm not highcaste. I have no important connections, my wealth among the Banbarra is a pittance by Gujaareen reckoning—"

"I don't care."

"But—"

"Woman, I *do not care*. But if it will satisfy you, the common folk should be pleased that I've taken a lowcaste firstwife. That will make it clear I haven't forgotten who helped me back to power. And our marriage can symbolize reconciliation between the Hetawa and the Sunset, or something." He made an impatient gesture. "Now: your answer?"

She could not make herself speak. There was a tightness in her throat, but this was not caused by sorrow, so instead she nodded. He let out a long, heavy sigh, the last tension easing visibly from his body.

"I'll arrange a ceremony, then. Something quick, lest you change your mind, and with plenty of wine, since I know the Banbarra will make a madhouse of it. Perhaps two ceremonies: one in the city so that the templefolk can attend, and one here…" He trailed off, thinking. "Would you rather live in Yanya-iyan or Kite-iyan, after?"

It surprised Hanani how easy that decision was. Or perhaps it was only easy by comparison. "Put your other wives in your palaces. I'll stay here and be healer for the Banbarra."

"Stay and be—" He stared at her, incredulous. "A Prince's first-wife should not sully her hands with labor."

"A Prince's firstwife who was born farmcaste, and has been reared by the Hetawa, and is an ally to the Banbarra, would naturally find fulfillment in labor that serves the Goddess and others. Will that not please the common folk too?"

"But what if I want to *see* you, for nightmares' sake?"

She shrugged. "Then come here. It's no longer a journey than to Kite-iyan, is it? Though here, you may have to forego servants: this ledge isn't wide enough for another tent—"

He groaned loud enough for his voice to echo off the far canyon wall. "Demons and shadows, you truly are the strangest woman I've ever met! It makes no sense at all that I want you."

"I'm glad that you do," she said, very softly. He looked at her, and the anger faded from his face. Then he took her hand again, and she did not pull away.

They watched the shadows lengthen down the red walls of Merik-ren-aferu, in silence. A suitably peaceful transition for the start of a new life. Then Hanani got to her feet, offering Wanaho-men a hand up. He glowered at it in mild annoyance at first, then finally took it and let her help him.

As the last light faded from the sky, she led him into her tent, where he pulled her close and there was more silence. This was pleasing to Hananja, for even the smallest act of peace is a blessing upon the world.

Glossary

Acolytes: Boys of between twelve and sixteen floods who have elected to pursue the service of Hananja, but who have not yet sworn themselves to one of the four paths.

Age of adulthood: In Gujaareh and Kisua, four times four, or sixteen floods of age. The age at which young citizens are granted legal and all other rights of majority, and may be confirmed in their choice of vocation.

Age of choice: In Gujaareh and Kisua, three times four, or twelve floods of age. The age at which young citizens are counted old enough to pursue a chosen vocation, court a spouse, or undertake many other significant decisions.

Age of eldership: In Gujaareh, four times four times four, or sixty-four floods of age. The age at which citizens are counted old enough to hold positions of leadership or esteem. In Kisua, citizens are deemed elders at fifty-two years of age.

Anzi Seh Ainunu: A general of Kisua, assigned to oversee the occupation of Gujaareh.

Apprentices: Youths who have passed the age of adulthood and begun higher training in one of the four paths.

Aureole of the Setting Sun: Symbol of the authority and divinity of the Sunset Lineage. An emblem consisting of alternating plates of red and gold amber arranged in a sunburst pattern around a central gold semicircle, which sits atop a staff carved from white nhefti.

Banbarra: A desert race, longtime enemies of Gujaareh. Consists of six autonomous tribes that dominate trade in the Empty Thousand. At feud with the Shadoun.

Body wrap: A garment worn by men and women in Kisua. A woman's wrap is usually ankle-length; a man's wrap may be knee-length or shorter and accented by a shoulder-drape.

Caste: The social/vocational classes of Gujaareh and Kisua, assigned at birth. An individual may transcend his or her assigned caste only by entering public service (such as in the Hetawa or the military).

City of Dreams: Colloquial name for the capital of Gujaareh. Also known as Hananja's City. Officially, the city's name is simply "Gujaareh."

Collar: Decorative item worn in Gujaareh and occasionally in Kisua. Consists of a band around the neck and dangling ornaments that drape about the chest and shoulders.

Council of Paths: With the Superior, the governing body of the Hetawa. Includes senior members of the Sentinels, Teachers, and Sharers, as well as one (non-voting) liaison from the Sisters. Out of courtesy, Gatherers operate under the authority of this body, although they are officially autonomous.

Donation: The monthly offering of dreams required of all citizens of Gujaareh. Donors are referred to as *tithebearers*.

Dreambile: One of the four dream-humors that form the basis of Gujaareen magic. Culled from unpleasant dreams, it is useful for discouraging harmful growth and destroying unnecessary tissue in the body.

Dreamblood: One of the four dream-humors that form the basis of Gujaareen magic. Culled from the final dream that occurs at the moment of death, it is useful for bringing peace.

Dream-humors: The magical energies culled from dreams, used by Sharers for healing.

Dreamichor: One of the four dream-humors that form the basis of Gujaareen magic. Culled from ordinary "nonsense" dreams, it is useful for repairing damage in the body.

Dreaming Moon: The mother of all gods and goddesses save Sun and Waking Moon, and mistress of the sky. Also called *the Dreamer*.

Dreamseed: One of the four dream-humors that form the basis of Gujaareen magic. Culled from erotic dreams, essential for stimulating growth that ordinarily occurs only in the womb (e.g., new limbs).

Easternese: Collective term for people from lands to the east of the Sea of Glory.

Empty Thousand: The desert that stretches from the southernmost edge of the Gujaareen Territories to the northernmost reaches of the Kisuati Protectorate.

Endless, The: The great ocean to the west of the Sea of Glory.

False-seeing: A dream that appears to be a vision of the future or past, but is too distorted for interpretation or is simply inaccurate.

Flood: An annual event in which the Goddess's Blood river overflows its banks and fills the Blood river valley, renewing the fertility of the soil. Also: the marker by which valley-dwellers count perennial changes, such as age.

Founding Sages: The founders of Gujaareh, foremost among them Inunru.

Four: The number of bands on the face of Dreaming Moon. A holy number, as are its multiples.

Four-of-four: Four by four by four by four, or two hundred and fifty-six. A holy number.

Gatherers: Those in one of the four paths to the Service of Hananja, responsible for enforcing Hananja's Law.

Goddess, The: In Gujaareh, an alternative term for Hananja. In Kisua, may refer to any female deity.

Goddess's Blood: A river whose source is in the mountains of Kisua. Its mouth is along the Sea of Glory in northern Gujaareh.

Gujaareh: A city-state whose capital (also called Gujaareh, or the City of Dreams, or Hananja's City) lies at the mouth of the Goddess's Blood along the Sea of Glory.

Hamyan Night: The shortest night of the year, when dreams become so sparse that the Goddess Hananja starves.

Hanani: A Sharer-Apprentice of the Hetawa.

Hananja: One of the divine children of Dreaming Moon and Sun. The goddess of dreams, also associated with death and the afterlife.

Hananja's City: Alternate name for Gujaareh's capital.

Hananja's Law: The body of law that governs Gujaareh. Its principal tenet is peace.

Hananja's Wisdom: A collection of proverbs, prophecies, and other lore that faithful Hananjans must learn.

Healing: Any non-magical healing art, including herbalism and surgery. In Gujaareh, these arts are practiced primarily by Sharers of Hananja.

Hekeh: A fibrous plant native to the Blood river valley, cultivated in Gujaareh and other river nations. Useful in making cloth, rope, and many other products.

Hetawa, The: The central temple, and physical center of spiritual life in Gujaareh. The Hetawa oversees education, law, and public health.

Hieratics: A shorthand or "cursive" form of the Gujaareen written language.

Highcaste: The Gujaareen royal family, shunha, and zhinha. In Kisua, highcastes include the sonha and hunters.

Hipstraps: Straps used to hold loindrapes in place.

Hona-Karekh: The realm of wakefulness.

Ina-Karekh: The land of dreams. The living may visit this land for short periods during sleep. The dead dwell here in perpetuity.

Indethe: Sua word for attention/honor/love.

Inunru: A great and honored figure in the history of the Hananjan faith.

Jungissa: A rare stone that resonates in response to stimuli. Skilled narcomancers use it to induce and control sleep. All jungissa are fragments of the Sun's seed, fallen to earth from the stars.

King: In Gujaareh, the most recently deceased Prince (may he dwell in Her peace forever).

Kisua: A city-state in the mideastern region of the continent, motherland of Gujaareh.

Kite-iyan: The Prince's alternate palace, home of his wives and children.

Loindrapes: A garment worn primarily by men in Gujaareh, consisting of two long panels of cloth (knee-length or ankle-length) linked about the hips by straps of leather or metal chain.

Loinskirt: A garment worn primarily by men in Gujaareh, consisting of a knee-length wrap of hekeh or a pleated drape of linen.

Lowcaste: A member of any of the castes at the bottom of the Gujaareen social hierarchy. Includes farmers and servants.

Magic: The power of healing and dreams, used by Gatherers, Sharers, and Sisters of Hananja.

Manuflection: A gesture of respect offered only to those who bear the gods' favor. The supplicant drops to one knee, crossing forearms (palms outward) before the face. A lesser version of this (arms held parallel before the chest, palms down, with an included bow depending on the depth of respect shown) is offered as a routine greeting or gesture of apology in Gujaareh.

Mark-cords: For Banbarra women, a decorative set of cords worn to mark the stages of life: menarche, loss of virginity, childbirth, menopause.

Merik: One of the divine children of Dreaming Moon and Sun. Grinds down mountains and fills valleys.

Merik-ren-aferu: A valley to the west and north of Gujaareh's capital, on the edge of the Empty Thousand. Home to the Yusir-Banbarra tribe.

Midcaste: A member of any of the castes in the middle of the Gujaareen social hierarchy. Includes merchants and artisans.

Military: Like the Servants of Hananja, a branch of public service in Gujaareh, and a caste into which one may be born or inducted.

Mnedza: One of the divine children of Dreaming Moon and Sun. Brings pleasure to women.

Mni-inh: A Sharer of the Hetawa.

Moontear: A flower found along the Goddess's Blood that blooms only by the light of the Dreaming Moon. Sacred to the Hananjan faith.

Narcomancy: The Gujaareen skills of sleepcasting, dream control, and the use of dream-humors. Colloquially called *dream magic*.

Nhefti: A hardy, thick-trunked tree that grows near the mountains of the Blood river valley. Its wood is amber-white and pale when polished. Used only for holy objects.

Nijiri: A Gatherer of Hananja. The blue lotus.

Northerners: Collective term for members of the various tribes north of the Sea of Glory. Polite term for barbarians.

Numeratics: Graphical/symbolic depictions used in mathematics, said to have their own magic.

Physical humors: Blood, bile, ichor (plasma), and seed.

Pictorals: The glyphic/symbolic written form of the Gujaareen language, based on written Kisuati. Used for formal requests, poetry, historical annotations, and religious writings.

Prince/Lord of the Sunset/Avatar of Hananja: The ruler of Gujaareh in the waking realm. Upon death he is elevated to the throne of Ina-Karekh, where he rules at Hananja's side until a new King comes (may he dwell in Her peace forever).

Protectors: The council of elders that rules Kisua.

Rabbaneh: A Gatherer of Hananja; the red poppy.

Reaper: A narcomancer whose soul has been devoured by the lust for dreamblood. Possessed of great power, and great corruption. Abomination.

Sanfi: A man of the shunha, father of Tiaanet.

Sentinels: Those in one of the four paths to the Service of Hananja. They guard the Hetawa and all works of the Goddess.

Servant: In Gujaareh, a member of the lowest social/vocational caste. Servants are not permitted to accumulate wealth and may select their own masters.

Servants of Hananja: Priests sworn to the service of the Goddess.

Shadoun: A desert tribe, once enemies of Gujaareh, now allied to the Kisuati.

Shadowlands: The place in Ina-Karekh that is created by the nightmares of all dreamers. Those who die in distress are drawn here to dwell for eternity.

Sharers: Those in one of the four paths to the Service of Hananja, responsible for the health of the city. They use narcomancy and occasionally surgery and herbalism.

Shunha: One of the two branches of Gujaareen nobility, whose members claim to be descended from liaisons between mortals and Dreaming Moon's children. Shunha maintain the customs and traditions of the motherland (Kisua).

Sisters of Hananja: An order (independent of the Hetawa) consisting predominantly of women, who serve Hananja by collecting dreamseed in the city.

Skyrer: Nocturnal birds of prey who hunt the Empty Thousand. It is an ill omen to see skyrers by day, or away from the desert outside of the rainy season.

Slave: In Kisua, captive enemies, debtors, the indigent, undesirable foreigners, and criminals sentenced to involuntary servitude. Slavery is illegal in Gujaareh.

Sonha: Kisuati nobility, who claim to be descended from liaisons between mortals and Dreaming Moon's children.

Sonta-i: A Gatherer of Hananja; the indigo nightshade.

Soulname: Names given to Gujaareen children for protection in Ina-Karekh.

Southlands: Collective name for the various tribes beyond the source of the Goddess's Blood river, many of which are vassal-states of Kisua.

Sunandi Jeh Kalawe: A woman of the Kisuati sonha, assigned to Gujaareh as governess and Voice of the Protectorate.

Sunset Lineage: The royal family of Gujaareh, said to be descendants of the Sun.

Superior: The administrative head of the Hetawa, whose decisions are made in conjunction with the Council of Paths and the Gatherers.

Surgery: A dangerous but periodically necessary healing ritual, which only the most advanced apprentices and full Sharers of the path may invoke.

Teachers: Those in one of the four paths to the Service of Hananja, responsible for education and the pursuit of knowledge.

Territories: Collective name for the towns and tribes that have pledged allegiance to Gujaareh.

Tiaanet: A maiden of the shunha, of Insurret's lineage.

Timbalin: A popular narcotic in Gujaareh. Allows uncontrolled dreaming.

Tithe: A Gujaareen citizen's due offering to Hananja.

Tithebearer: One designated by the Hetawa to receive Hananja's highest blessing, in return for a tithe of dream-humors.

True-seeing: A dream-vision of the future or past.

Umblikeh: The tether that binds soul to flesh and permits travel out of the body into other realms. When severed, death follows instantaneously.

Una-une: A Gatherer of Hananja, recently deceased. Ehiru's mentor.

Voice of Kisua: An ambassador of Kisua. The proper title for a Voice is "Speaker."

Waking Moon: Younger sister of the Dreaming Moon. Visible only shortly before sunrise, and after sunset (until the Dreaming Moon appears).

Wanahomen: A son of Eninket, heir to the Sunset Lineage.

Yanya-iyan: The Prince's main palace in the capital city, seat of Gujaareh's government.

Zhinha: One of the two branches of nobility in Gujaareh, whose members claim to be descended from liaisons between mortals and Dreaming Moon's children. Zhinha believe Gujaareh's strength lies in its ability to adapt and change.

Acknowledgments

As with *The Killing Moon*, my thanks here are more for resources than people—but in this case people provided the resources, so they deserve a special shout-out.

In 2004 I won the Gulliver's Travel Research Grant, offered by the Speculative Literature Foundation (SLF). The grant was small, only six hundred dollars at the time, but it allowed me to travel to Canyon de Chelly in Chinle, Arizona, within the Navajo Nation. I'd done some research that suggested that the civilization of the Anasazi, the ancient pueblo people who were the first to dwell within the canyon (the Navajo occupy it now, but pay respects to its previous tenants), may have collapsed due to a sudden and drastic religious upheaval—either a foreign religion migrating up from the south, or some internally developed new revelation, striking at the same time as a terrible long drought. At the time I'd had a vague idea of writing a fantasy set in a culture wrestling with such an upheaval. Those ideas sort of dissolved and distributed themselves among many novels and short stories in my head, but the part that stuck to this book was the canyon itself, to which I've attempted to pay homage in the form of Merik-ren-aferu. The Yusir-Banbarra's

Acknowledgments

cliff-village is based on the Anasazi villages I saw, which were routinely positioned a thousand feet or more above the canyon floor. So thanks, SLF, for giving me the chance to see that.

(For more on the Anasazi, the Navajo, and the other American nations that did cool stuff back in the day, I highly recommend Charles C. Mann's *1491: New Revelations of the Americas Before Columbus.* Blew my mind. Also, Robert Lister and Florence Lister's *Those Who Came Before*; lovely photographs of the ruins themselves.)

Please note that the SLF is a nonprofit organization to whom donations are tax-deductible. If you want to help other writers see cool stuff, you should donate at www.speculativeliterature.org!

Also thanks to the folks at the Totsonii Ranch in Chinle, from whom I *almost* got a fantastic horseback tour—but alas, the canyon was flooded with spring melt, so it was too dangerous to go. They told me lots about the canyon, though, free of charge. And bigger thanks to Tim of Canyon de Chelly Jeep Tours, who took me on a truly harrowing high-speed ride through the (yes, flooded) canyon, and who informed me when I openly worried about, well, violent watery death, that at least I would die doing something interesting.

extras

www.orbitbooks.net

about the author

N. K. Jemisin is a career counselor, political blogger, and would-be gourmand living in New York City. She's been writing since the age of ten, although her early works will never see the light of day. Visit nkjemisin.com

Find out more about N. K. Jemisin and other Orbit authors by registering for the free monthly newsletter at www.orbitbooks.net

if you enjoyed
THE SHADOWED SUN

look out for

THE DROWNING CITY

by

Amanda Downum

1229 Sal Emperaturi

CHAPTER 1

Symir. The Drowning City.

An exile, perhaps, but at least it was an interesting one.

Isyllt's gloved hands tightened on the railing as the *Black Mariah* cleared the last of the Dragon Stones and turned toward the docks, dark estuarine water slopping against her hull. Fishing boats dotted Ka Liang Bay, glass buoys flashing in the sun. Cormorants dove around them, scattering ripples as they snatched fish from hooks and nets.

The west wind died, broken on the Dragons' sharp peaks, and the jungle's hot breath wafted from the shore. Rank with brine and bilge, sewers draining into the sea, but under the port-reek the air smelled of spices and the green tang of Sivahra's forests rising beyond the marshy delta of the Mir. Mountains flanked the capital city Symir, uneven green sentinels on either side of the river. So unlike the harsh and rocky shores of Selafai they had left behind two and a half decads ago.

Only twenty-five days at sea—a short voyage, though it didn't feel that way to Isyllt. The ship had made good time, laden only with olive oil and wheat flour from the north.

And northern spies. But those weren't recorded on the cargo manifest.

Isyllt shook her head, collected herself. This might be an exile, but it was a working one. She had a revolution to foment, a country to throw into chaos, and an emperor to undermine with it. Sivahra's jungles and mines—and Symir's bustling port—provided great wealth to the Assari Empire. Enough to fund a war of conquest, and the eyes of the expansionist Emperor roved slowly north. Isyllt and her master meant to prevent that.

If their intelligence was good, Sivahra was crawling with insurgent groups, natives desperate to overthrow their Imperial conquerors. Selafai's backing might help them succeed. Or at least distract the Empire. Trade one war for another. After that, maybe she could have a real vacation.

The *Mariah* dropped anchor before they docked and the crew bustled to prepare for the port authority's inspection; already a skiff rowed to meet them. The clang of harbor bells carried across the water.

Adam, her coconspirator and ostensible bodyguard, leaned against the rail beside her while his partner finished checking over their bags. Isyllt's bags, mostly; the mercenaries traveled light, but she had a pretense of pampered nobility to maintain. Maybe not such a pretense—she might have murdered for a hot bath and proper bed. Sweat stuck her shirt to her arms and back, itched behind her knees. She envied the sailors their vests and short trousers, but her skin was too pale to offer to the summer sun.

"Do we go straight to the Kurun Tam tonight?" Adam asked. The westering sun flashed on gold and silver earrings, mercenary gaud. He wore his sword again for the first time since they'd boarded the *Mariah*. He'd taken to sailor fashions—his vest hung open over his scarred chest, revealing charm bags around his neck and the pistol tucked into his belt. His skin was three shades darker than it had been when they sailed, bronze now instead of olive.

Isyllt's mouth twisted. "No," she said after a moment. "Let's find an extravagantly expensive hotel tonight. I feel like spending the Crown's money. We can work tomorrow." One night of vacation, at least, she could give herself.

He grinned and looked to his partner. "Do you know someplace decadent?"

Xinai's lips curled as she turned away from the luggage. "The Silver Phoenix. It's Selafaïn—it'll be decadent enough for you." Her head barely cleared her partner's shoulder, though the black plumage-crest of her hair added the illusion of more height. She wore her wealth too—rings in her ears, a gold cuff on one wiry wrist, a silver hoop in her nostril. The blades at her hips and the scars on her wiry arms said she knew how to keep it.

Isyllt turned back to the city, scanning the ships at dock. She was surprised not to see more Imperial colors flying. After rumors of rebellion and worries of war, she'd expected Imperial warships, but there was no sign of the Emperor's army—although that didn't mean it wasn't there.

Something was happening, though; a crowd gathered on the docks, and Isyllt caught flashes of red and green uniforms amid the blur of bodies. Shouts and angry voices carried over the water, but she couldn't make out the words.

The customs skiff drew alongside the *Mariah*, lion crest gleaming on the red-and-green-striped banners—the flag of an Imperial territory, granted limited home-rule. The sailors threw down a rope ladder and three harbor officials climbed aboard, nimble against the rocking hull. The senior inspector was a short, neat woman, wearing a red sash over her sleek-lined coat. Isyllt fought the urge to fidget with her own travel-grimed clothes. Her hair was a salt-stiff tangle, barely contained by pins, and while she'd cleaned her face with oil before landfall, it was no substitute for a proper bath.

Isyllt waited, Adam and Xinai flanking her, while the inspector spoke to the captain. Whatever the customs woman told the captain, he didn't like. He spat over the rail and made an angry gesture toward the shore. The *Mariah* wasn't the only ship waiting to dock; Isyllt wondered if the gathering on the pier had something to do with the delay.

Finally the ship's mate led two of the inspectors below, and the woman in the red sash turned to Isyllt, a wax tablet and stylus in her hand. A Sivahri, darker skinned than Xinai but with the same creaseless black eyes; elaborate henna designs covered her hands. Isyllt was relieved to be greeted in Assari—Xinai had tutored her in the native language during the voyage, but she was still far from fluent.

"Roshani." The woman inclined her head politely. "You're the only passengers?" She raised her stylus as Isyllt nodded. "Your names?"

"Isyllt Iskaldur, of Erisín." She offered the oiled leather tube that held her travel papers. "This is Adam and Xinai, sayifarim hired in Erisín."

The woman glanced curiously at Xinai; the mercenary gave no more response than a statue. The official opened the tube and unrolled the parchment, recorded something on her tablet. "And your business in Symir?"

Isyllt tugged off her left glove and held out her hand. "I'm here to visit the Kurun Tam." The breeze chilled her sweaty palm. Since it was impossible to pass herself off as anything but a foreign mage, the local thaumaturgical facility was the best cover.

The woman's eyes widened as she stared at the cabochon black diamond on Isyllt's finger, but she didn't ward herself or step out of reach. Ghostlight gleamed iridescent in the stone's depths and a cold draft suffused the air. She nodded again, deeper this time. "Yes, meliket. Do you know where you'll be staying?"

"Tonight we take rooms at the Silver Phoenix."

"Very good." She recorded the information, then glanced up. "I'm sorry, meliket, but we're behind schedule. It will be a while yet before you can dock."

"What's going on?" Isyllt gestured toward the wharf. More soldiers had appeared around the crowd.

The woman's expression grew pained. "A protest. They've been there an hour and we're going to lose a day's work."

Isyllt raised her eyebrows. "What are they protesting?"

"New tariffs." Her tone became one of rote response. "The Empire considers it expedient to raise revenues and has imposed taxes on foreign goods. Some of the local merchants"—she waved a hennaed hand at the quay—"are unhappy with the situation. But don't worry, it's nothing to bother the Kurun Tam."

Of course not—Imperial mages would hardly be burdened with problems like taxes. It was much the same in the Arcanost in Erisín.

"Are these tariffs only in Sivahra?" she asked.

"Oh, no. All Imperial territories and colonies are subject."

Not just sanctions against a rebellious population, then, but real money-raising. That left an unpleasant taste in the back of her mouth. Twenty-five days with no news was chancy where politics were concerned.

The other officials emerged from the cargo hold a few moments later and the captain grudgingly paid their fees. The woman turned back to Isyllt, her expression brightening. "If you like, meliket, I can take you to the Silver Phoenix myself. It will be a much shorter route than getting there from the docks."

Isyllt smiled. "That would be lovely. Shakera."

Adam cocked an eyebrow as he hoisted bags. Isyllt's lips curled. "It never pays to annoy foreign guests," she murmured in Selafaïn. "Especially ones who can steal your soul."

She tried to watch the commotion on the docks, but the skiff moved swiftly and they were soon out of sight. A cloud of midges trailed behind the craft; the drone of wings carried unpleasant memories of the plague, but the natives seemed unconcerned. Isyllt waved the biting insects away, though she was immune to whatever exotic diseases they might carry. As they rowed beneath a raised water gate, a sharp, minty smell filled the air and the midges thinned.

The inspector—who introduced herself as Anhai Xian-Mar—talked as they went, her voice counterpoint to the rhythmic splash of oars as she explained the myriad delta islands on which the city was built, the web of canals that took the place of stone streets. Xinai's mask slipped for an instant and Isyllt saw the cold disdain in her eyes. The mercenary had little love for countrymen who served their Assari conquerors.

Sunlight spilled like honey over their shoulders, gilding the water and gleaming on domes and tilting spires. Buildings crowded together, walls of cream and ocher stone, pale blues and dusty pinks, balconies nearly touching over narrow alleys and waterways. Bronze chimes flashed from eaves and lintels. Vines trailed from rooftop gardens, dripping leaves and orange blossoms onto the water. Birds perched in potted trees and on steep green- and gray-tiled roofs.

Invaders the Assari might be, but they had built a beautiful city. Isyllt tried to imagine the sky dark with smoke, the water running red. The city would be less lovely if her mission succeeded.

She'd heard stories from other agents of how the job crept into everything, reduced buildings and cities to exits and escape routes, defenses and weaknesses to be exploited. Till you couldn't look at anything—or anyone—without imagining how to infiltrate or corrupt or overthrow. She wondered how long it would take to happen to her. If she would even notice when it did.

Anhai followed Isyllt's gaze to the water level—slime crusted the stone several feet above the surface of the canal. "The rains will come soon and the river will rise. You're in time for the Dance of Masks."

The skiff drew up against a set of stairs and the oarsmen secured the boat and helped Adam and Xinai unload the luggage. A tall building rose above them, decorated with Selafaïn pillars. A carven phoenix spread its wings over the doors and polished horn panes gleamed ruddy in the dying light.

Anhai bowed farewell. "If you need anything at all, meliket, you can find me at the port authority office."

"Shakera." Isyllt offered her hand, and the silver griffin she held. She never saw where Anhai tucked the coin.

The she stepped from the skiff to the slime-slick stairs and set foot in the Drowning City.

The Phoenix was as decadent as Xinai had promised. Isyllt floated in the wide tub, her hair drifting around her in a black cloud. Oils shimmered on the water, filled the room with poppy and myrrh. Lamplight gleamed on blue and green tiles and rippled over the cool marble arch of the ceiling. She was nearly dozing when someone knocked lightly on the chamber door.

"Don't drown," Adam said, his voice muffled by wood.

"Not yet. What is it?"

"Dinner."

Her stomach growled in response and she shivered in

water grown uncomfortably cold. She stood, hair clinging to her arms and back like sea wrack, and reached for a towel and robe.

The bedroom smelled of wine and curry and her stomach rumbled louder. The *Mariah*'s mess had been good enough, as sea rations went, but she was happy to reacquaint herself with real food.

Adam lit one of the scented-oil lamps and sneezed as the smell of eucalyptus filled the room. The city stank of it at night—like mint, but harsher, rawer. Linen mesh curtained the windows and tented the bed. The furniture and colorful rugs were Assari, but black silk covered the mirror, true Selafaïn fashion.

Adam sat, keeping the windows and doors in sight as he helped himself to food from the platter on the table. He'd traded his ship's clothes for sleek black, and the shadows in the corner swallowed him.

"Where's Xinai?" Isyllt asked, glancing at the door that led to the adjoining room.

"Scouting. Seeing how things have changed. The curry's good."

She tightened the towel around her hair and sat across from him. The bowls smelled of garlic and ginger and other spices she couldn't name. Curries and yogurt, served with rice instead of flat bread, and a bowl of sliced fruit.

"We should find our captain tonight." She stirred rice into a green sauce. "The Kurun Tam may take all day tomorrow."

The *Black Mariah*'s legitimate business would keep her in port at least half a decad, but Isyllt wanted to make sure their alternate transportation was resolved before anything unexpected arose. She scooped up a mouthful of curry and nearly gasped at the sweet green fire. A pepper burst between her teeth, igniting her nose and throat.

The sounds of the city drifted through the window, lapping water and distant harbor bells. Night birds sang and cats called to one another from nearby roofs. Footsteps and voices, but no hooves or rattling carriage wheels—the city's narrow streets left no room for horses or oxen.

"You don't want to be here, do you?" Adam asked after a moment. Shadows hid his face, but she felt the weight of his regard, those eerie green eyes.

She sipped iced-and-honeyed lassi. "It isn't that, exactly."

"You're angry with the old man."

She kept her face still. She hadn't cried since the first night at sea, but emotions still threatened to surface when she wasn't careful. "I know the job. My problems with Kiril won't interfere." Her voice didn't catch on his name, to her great relief.

"I hope not. He'll skin me if I don't keep you safe."

Isyllt paused, cup half raised. "He said that?"

Adam chuckled. "He left little room for doubt."

Wood clacked as she set the drink down. "If he's so bloody concerned, he could have sent someone else." She bit her tongue, cursed the petulant tone that crept into the words. The side door opened with a squeak, saving her from embarrassing herself further.

Xinai slipped in, feet silent on marble. "I found Teoma. He frequents a tavern on the wharf called the Storm God's Bride." Izachar Teoma had made most of his wealth and notoriety smuggling along Imperial shores, but sailed north often enough to have encountered Kiril's web of agents before. A ship quick and clever enough to escape harbor patrols would be useful if they had to flee the city.

Xinai tossed a stack of cheap pulp paper onto the table. "News-scrawls, from the past decad or so. The criers will have stopped spreading those stories by now."

"Thanks." Isyllt flipped through the stack—wrinkled and

water-spotted, and the ink left gray smears on her fingers, but the looping Assari script was legible. The latest was three days old. She took a moment to adjust to the Assari calendar; today was Sekhmet seventh, not the twelfth of Janus; 1229 Sal Emperaturi, not 497 Ab Urbe Condita.

She often found the pride of nations silly. Trade and treaties between Assar and Selafai had to be twice dated, because the founders of Selafai had abandoned all things Imperial when they fled north across the sea five hundred years ago. But if not for the pride of nations, she'd be out of a job.

She sipped her drink again, watery now as the ice melted. Moisture slicked the curve of the cup. "Did you hear anything about the protest we saw?"

"Not much. The guards ran them off not long after we arrived, it sounds like. There were arrests, but no real violence." From Xinai's tone, Isyllt couldn't tell if she was disappointed in that or not.

Adam rose, taking a slice of mango with him. "Finish your dinner, Lady Iskaldur." The title dripped mockingly off his tongue. "We'll leave when you're ready."